THE BANSHEE BRIDE

MARK L'ESTRANGE

For Emily Ivy. This one is for you, beautiful girl.

Chapter One

MICHELLE CALVERT WALKED ALONG THE COASTAL path, her woollen shawl barely keeping out the biting wind which whipped across the beach from the North Atlantic Ocean.

But the cold was the least of her worries. Michelle was a woman on the edge of a nervous breakdown. Five years ago, she had her life all planned out. She would marry Emmet Calvert and inherit his fortune when he died.

Back then, his old doctor had diagnosed an inoperable brain tumour which the medic claimed would take his life in a matter of a few short years.

At the time, Michelle had been Emmett's housekeeper. It was not a position she relished or even took seriously. She managed to get away with doing the bare minimum for the old man, winning him over with her charm and cheek.

She flirted with him shamelessly, all the time hinting that if he wanted to take things further, he would have to make an honest woman of her first.

Michelle made sure she gave Emmet just enough encouragement to convince him that she would be worth the effort and that, if she became his wife, she would ensure that his last few years left on this earth would be spent in pure sexual bliss.

Eventually, he gave in and took her for his wife.

All those who knew Michelle were rightly suspicious of her ulterior motive, but they kept their opinions between themselves.

Then, the doctor himself passed away, and the new man from the mainland who took over insisted on some further tests on Emmett before condemning him as his predecessor had.

The results showed that an operation was possible. One with a high success rate. So, Emmett jumped at it and within a few short weeks, post-op, his condition was no longer life-threatening.

Naturally, Emmett was over the moon, and Michelle – as his devoted wife – should have been likewise. But the truth was that now she had to face the prospect of spending her formative years shackled to a man she did not love, and whose touch had begun to repulse her.

She hid the truth from everyone as best as she could, especially from Emmett.

Michelle still harboured dreams of one day inheriting his vast fortune and enjoying a quality of life that most people could only dream of.

The question was, could she endure the years ahead with a man she despised?

She was still relatively young. Certainly, young enough to find love and start again.

She considered divorce but she had foolishly signed a pre-nuptial agreement at the insistence of Emmett's solicitor which would leave her with very little after the event.

Michelle knew that she had dug herself a deep hole and the fact that she saw no easy way out of it became more apparent with each passing day.

Since his operation, Emmett had grown far more adventurous in his sexual appetite.

Beforehand, his needs had been placid and simple, and Michelle had dealt with them as best she could without making too much of an effort. She had complained to the doctor that she had been having trouble sleeping, so he prescribed her some strong sleeping tablets which she casually popped into her husband's nightly after-dinner cognac.

By the time they were ready for bed, regardless of how frisky he was feeling, Michelle knew that all she had to do to avoid sexual contact with him was to take her time in 'preparing' herself for him, which usually concluded with Emmett snoring before she even emerged from the bathroom.

His general lethargy, as a result of his condition, ensured that Michelle did not have to perform her wifely duties on too many occasions.

This all changed post-op.

The success of his operation had given Emmett a new lease of life, which included a ramped-up libido. The new doctor had refused to renew Michelle's prescription, expressing concern that they were not designed as a long-term fix, and as such he was afraid that she might be becoming addicted to them.

The end result was a constant tirade of sexual advances from Emmett, which Michelle was obliged to entertain unless she could think of a valid excuse without making him suspicious.

His new-found exuberance for sex was becoming more than just an irritation for Michelle. In fact, his constant groping and fondling – whenever no one was looking – had manifested itself into a nauseating condition which made her skin crawl at the very thought.

She had hoped that, like several wealthy men in his position, Emmett might seek out a mistress to satisfy his cravings. Michelle had even considered advertising for such a girl online, even if she had to pay the woman out of her own pocket to keep up the illusion it would be worth the effort. So long as the creature kept her mouth shut about their arrangement.

There was of course the risk that her husband might actually fall in love with the woman, but at least then the pre-nuptial allowed her a much larger slice of the pie if Emmett divorced her, rather than the other way around.

The problem with that idea was that Emmett genuinely seemed to be in love with her to the point of obsession. Whenever they travelled to the mainland to attend one of his many corporate functions, Michelle would purposely drift away so that she could spy on him from a safe distance, and not once did he even appear to glance at another woman for more than a second or two.

Even the ones who made a very obvious and drunken play for him were quickly, although politely, rebuffed. After which, he would make a beeline for Michelle looking extremely guilty, as if it had somehow been his fault that another woman had come onto him.

No, she had to admit it, Michelle was well and truly stuck with him until death 'do them' part, and she had reached the end of her tether.

This evening was just another example of how much she despised her husband.

Before dinner, Emmett had suddenly decided that he needed to make passionate love to her the moment he saw her emerge from the shower. Michelle could have cried off with a headache, but she had already used that excuse the night before, and as her husband had already mastered her monthly chart, she knew that such an excuse would not wash.

He had always been a gentleman, and never once complained when she was not in the mood, but if he suspected that her reason was false, she could always tell by that 'oh so familiar' look of hurt in his eyes, so sometimes it was better just to concede and allow him to have his way.

Fortunately, over time, Michelle had managed to figure out how to bring him to climax quickly. It was a trick she often employed when she had run out of plausible excuses.

So, tonight, she gave in without too much fuss.

Michelle faked her orgasm, as usual, and managed to finish Emmett off in less than ten minutes. He even apologised for being so quick, but she assured him that he had already satisfied her.

The touch of his hands caressing her naked body made Michelle feel physically sick, so she immediately took another shower.

As was often her custom, Michelle informed Emmett that she would take a stroll along the beach after dinner. Even after his operation, Emmett had little taste for the night air after his last meal of the day, so Michelle had been confident that her husband would not offer to join her on her nightly jaunt.

But tonight, her reason for leaving had another, darker, purpose.

Every resident of the island passed the age of ten knew the legend of Molly McShane, and how she had thrown herself from the westside cliff into the sea, having first pledged her soul in return for becoming a Banshee.

Despair and sorrow had turned to anger and revenge, and it was said that at the moment of her passing her heart was as black as any demon. Therefore, her wish to become a Banshee was granted, and from that day forth, her spirit would appear whenever an untimely death was about to occur.

Furthermore, it was rumoured that her deathly spirit could be conjured up by anyone who recited an ancient script. But following such a procedure came with a warning all of its own.

For it was written that once summoned, the Banshee could not return back to its deadly slumber without capturing the soul it was promised, and if that soul was no longer available, it would take the one who had summoned it as payment, instead.

There were several other myths and legends attached to the tale of the Banshee, and although the original text was kept under lock and key in the vaults of the local church, several academics had been allowed over the years to study it, and from their research had come the many variations of translation which now were available in their own volumes.

The library attached to Emmett's study housed several such volumes, and since formulating her plan, Michelle had spent many hours engrossed in those learned texts, desperately evaluating the most prevalent translation in order to secure her bidding.

Finally, confident in her endeavours, Michelle made a copy of the relevant text and held onto it for as long as she could before reaching the end of her tether.

Even though the legend of Molly McShane was widely known and believed throughout the island, no law in the land could possibly be held against Michelle for conjuring up the Banshee to fulfil her deadly request.

Following the guidance which she had prepared, Michele lit a small fire on the beach.

Sitting on the sand and gazing out to sea, she closed her eyes and began to recite the ancient incantations which she had copied from the books in Emmett's library.

The sound of the waves crashing against the rocks and the wind echoing through the caves nearby filled her ears, but Michelle kept her eyes tightly shut as she continued with her spell fearful that, according to legend, to even see the Banshee could result in sudden death.

Like the call of a lonely siren, the sound of a faraway inhuman cry began to fill her ears. Michelle placed an index finger into each ear, as she had even heard that just to hear the Banshee cry was enough to send a person insane.

Her heart trembled as a palpitation of guilt and fear rumbled in her chest.

For a moment she began to regret her decision. But then she quickly reminded herself that she had not come to this lightly or without deep consideration. The thought of spending another minute with her aged husband with his icy hands creeping over her body, made her cringe inside.

This was the only way out for her.

A few short moments and it would all be over.

Then she could play the grieving widow to her heart's content and to hell with what others may, or may not, think.

She would claim that the memories were too painful for her to remain in their house. Therefore, she would sell up and move abroad, somewhere hot and sunny where no one knew her, and she could start a new life just for her.

Michelle pressed her fingers in harder as the screeching sound drew closer.

Despite an obtuse eagerness she felt to open her eyes and witness the spirit which she had summoned to do her bidding, Michelle kept her eyelids tightly shut. After all, there was no point in tempting fate.

Even with her fingers rammed tightly inside her ears, the awful wailing sound seemed intent on piercing her defences.

She could feel the Banshee hovering over her as if daring her to open her eyes and gaze upon the wretched creature

The wind around her picked up, cutting through her flimsy attire and almost extinguishing her fire. Michelle could feel the ashes brush against her bare skin as they flew through the air.

The noise in her ears grew louder with each passing second.

It was almost as if invisible hands were pulling at her elbows in a desperate attempt to force her to hear what she had brought forth.

Finally, it became too much for her.

Michelle opened her eyes and witnessed the gruesome form of the Banshee floating above her.

Her heart began to race as she looked into the black pits that had once been eyes.

The figure had no structure but instead resembled a white sheet billowing in the wind.

The gaping maw beneath the eye sockets opened wider as the shrieking cry grew louder and higher in pitch until Michelle feared that her ears would explode.

She could not understand.

She had followed the text implicitly this was not meant for her.

Michelle scuttled backwards along the ground as if mere distance could save her.

Her mind reeled.

Surely the Banshee craved the soul it had been summoned to take and thus would not punish her for merely daring to gaze upon it. She had followed the instructions implicitly, so why was she being punished?

Michelle screamed as the ghastly apparition lowered itself over her.

Chapter Two

DOCTOR EDMUND CLEARY PULLED THE SHEET OVER the body of Emmet Calvert.

Behind him, the man's housekeeper Mrs Sandra O'Leary sobbed uncontrollably. It was she who had called the doctor out when she discovered the body of her employer at the bottom of the stairs. Dutifully, she had tried calling her mistress, only to discover that her mobile was still in the dining room.

Police Constable Clark had already given the grief-stricken woman his only hankie to wipe her eyes, so he moved in closer and placed a comforting arm around her shoulder.

"Come now, Mrs O'Leary," he began, "you've had a terrible shock. Why don't you allow me to pour you a shot of something warming to settle your nerves?"

The woman tried in between sobs to speak, holding the hankie away from her face, but each time a fresh batch of tears intervened, making coherent speech impossible.

The constable looked over at the doctor and raised his eyebrows.

The housekeeper was a well-known fixture on the island and had been all her life. Since her own husband passed away twenty years earlier, she had devoted her life to looking after others, first as a teacher's help at the local primary school, then as a nursing assistant for old Doctor Michaels and for the last five years as housekeeper for Emmet Calvert.

Over time she had obviously grown extremely fond of her employer, and both the doctor and the constable appreciated that his sudden loss would take a great deal of time for her to come to terms with.

Just then the doorbell sounded.

Mrs O'Leary instinctively made a move to answer it, but the doctor held up his hand as he was closer to the door.

Father Boyle, looking suitably sombre for the occasion, nodded to Doctor Cleary as he crossed the threshold. Although it was summer and it had been a warm day, the old priest had his overcoat buttoned to the top to keep out the wind.

As a man of strict habits, the priest rarely left the presbytery without his overcoat on.

Even in summer, he found the Wind which whipped in off the sea too severe for his old bones to handle.

He wiped his feet on the mat as the doctor closed the door behind him.

The priest removed his hat and made the sign of the cross when he saw the dead body on the floor. But before reciting the last rites, he decided that the old housekeeper needed his attention more.

Mrs O'Leary was a devout Catholic and had always been a regular attendee at church, so they were on very close terms.

"Oh, Sandra, my sincerest condolences for your loss." Father Boyle walked over to her and held out his hand, which the housekeeper took and held tightly in both of hers.

Feeling a little like an odd wheel, Constable Clark removed his arm from around her shoulders and took a step away.

"He'd been doing so well since his operation, Father," the housekeeper blubbed. "Only today he was telling me that he intended to take Mrs Calvert on a surprise holiday to Paris next month. He was so looking forward to it, his eyes lit up with child-like wonder while he was discussing it with me." She glanced past the priest and stared down at the covered corpse at the bottom of the stairs. "And to think, he never had reason to believe he would not live long enough to go."

A fresh batch of tears erupted from her while the priest patted her hand.

"There, there, you know he wouldn't want you to be upset about his passing. He is with our Lord now and all his worries are over."

"But he was too young to die," the housekeeper protested. "He should have had years before him yet. Why should God decide to take him now?"

Father Boyle looked into her tear-stained eyes. "None of us can foretell the true depth of God's plans," he reminded her comfortingly. "He is our shepherd and only he knows when to call us home."

Mrs O'Leary seemed to take comfort in his words. She nodded her head while wiping her eyes.

"How on earth did it happen?" asked the priest, glancing over towards the doctor. "Was it his heart?"

The doctor shook his head. "No, Mrs O'Leary says that he was as right as rain this evening. He finished dinner with his wife, sat in the lounge for a while listening to music and enjoying a small after-dinner cigar. Then just as Mrs O'Leary was about to pour him another drink, he told her needed to fetch something from upstairs."

"I told him I was happy to bring whatever it was for him," the housekeeper informed the priest. "But he insisted on fetching whatever it was himself. He asked me to refill his glass and told me he would be back in a minute. He left the room. And then…" She tapered off as more tears began to form.

"The next thing she heard was the sound of Mr Calvert

crying out as he fell down the stairs," Constable Clark continued. "By the time Mrs O'Leary reached him, it was all over."

"I see," replied the priest. "A tragic accident then?"

Doctor Cleary nodded his agreement.

"And Mrs Calvert?" Father Boyle asked, looking around the hallway as if half-expecting the woman to suddenly appear as if by magic.

"Mrs O'Leary said she went out for her customary after-dinner walk," replied the officer. "We're expecting her back any minute now."

"The poor woman," the housekeeper sobbed. "Not gone a full hour and looking forward to returning to the warm embrace of her husband. What will I say to her?" She looked up, turning towards each of the men as if desperate for an answer.

"Now don't you go worrying yourself over all that," Father Boyle assured her. "Between us, I'm sure we can break the bad news to her."

"I thought perhaps the lady could do with a drink to help steady her nerves," offered Constable Clark.

"Now I think that's a splendid idea," agreed the priest. "Under the circumstances that'll be just the ticket. As a medical man, I'm sure you'll agree doctor."

Doctor Cleary smiled. "Of course, I was just about to suggest it myself."

"Excellent," agreed the priest. "Now if you gentlemen will take the dear lady through, I'll start administering the last rites before joining you."

"No, please, Father," Mrs O'Leary objected, "I want to be here to pray for him with you."

The priest thought for a moment. Generally, his calling required that last rites be given at the first possible opportunity, preferably while the victim was still alive.

But under the present circumstances, he felt sure that a few moments' delay would not impact too deeply on the deceased.

"Tell you what," he said, "perhaps it would be better for us to wait for Michelle to return, I'm sure she'll want to be present as well."

"Good idea," agreed the doctor. "In the meantime, I need to phone the mainland to organise removing the body. It'll take them a while to reach us at this time of night."

They all moved into the study where Constable Clark poured them a generous measure of single malt, which they raised in honour of Emmet Calvert.

Sandra, not being much of a drinker, took a sip and started choking as the burning liquid slipped down her throat. Fortunately, the doctor was close enough to relieve her of her glass before she dropped it. Placing it on the table, he gently rubbed her back to help soothe her coughing fit.

Although on duty, Constable Clark was never one to refuse a single malt. Certainly not one as fine as that held in Emmet's cabinet. Besides, as far as he was concerned, technically he was always on duty, being the only member of the force on the island. Many was the time he had been called from his bed in the wee small hours to attend an incident –usually involving a couple of locals too drunk to remember why they were fighting.

He and Father Boyle both enjoyed a second measure before the constable suggested that he wait outside for Michelle Calvert to arrive, not wanting her to open her front door to be confronted by the dead body of her husband lying on the cold linoleum.

They waited another half an hour, but when there was still no sign of Mrs Calvert Father Boyle decided to go ahead with the last rites with Mrs O'Leary standing behind him, clutching her bible to her chest as fresh tears began to flow down her cheeks.

Another half hour passed before Constable Clark let himself back in.

"Mrs O'Leary," he asked, "how long does Mrs Calvert usually take on her walks?"

"An hour at most," the old housekeeper glanced at her watch. "She should have been back ages ago. You don't think she's had an accident, do you? Holy God no!"

"I'm sure she's just fine," the officer assured her. "It's a lovely clear night, She probably just decided to stay out a bit longer."

He glanced over at the doctor and the priest, neither of whom believed his version of events, but realised he was merely attempting to relieve the housekeeper's anguish.

"Is there any particular route she used?" continued the constable.

"Well, she often said that she liked to follow the coastal path and gaze out at the sea," Mrs O'Leary stated. "Perhaps she's fallen asleep on the beach," she added. "She sometimes took one of the garden chairs with her, but I'm not sure if she did so tonight."

Constable Clark smiled. "I'm willing to bet that's what's happened," he said, confidently. "I'll take a little stroll down there meself and see if I can find her. The sooner she knows about this tragedy the better."

The housekeeper suddenly appeared concerned. "But what if you miss her, or she comes back another way?"

"Then the doctor and I will wait with you until she arrives," Father Boyle assured her. "Don't you worry yourself over that."

Chapter Three

Declan Higgins squeezed Sarah Byrne closer to him, his left arm engulfing her tiny shoulders allowing his hand to hang loosely on top of her breast. Every now and then he afforded himself a little fondle, doing his best to make it seem as if it were by accident.

Sarah knew exactly what he was up to, but she allowed him the odd liberty just to keep him interested.

She knew that if her mother ever found out that they were an item again she would raise merry hell and probably ground Sarah for the rest of her life.

It was not that Patricia Byrne was by any means a prude. After all, she had had a reputation all her own when she was younger and still blushed when she passed certain people in the street.

But the Higgins clan were beneath contempt so far as she was concerned, and she knew that many on the island shared her opinion.

But they were islanders and had been so for as long as anyone could remember.

Their names appeared in the parish records dating back to the twelfth century, so there was nothing anyone could do or say to have them removed, regardless of their reputation.

It was not because they were Travellers either. There were many quite respectable groups on the mainland who took pride in their heritage and worked hard to prove their worth to society.

But on Manus, the Higginses believed that only mugs made an honest living, and that the trusting souls in the world were only put on this earth for people like them to take advantage of.

The majority of the male members of the group had all spent time behind bars on the mainland, including Declan who at the ripe age of twenty-two already had three terms under his belt for breaking and entering, car theft and fraud.

Those who were willing to still give him the benefit of the doubt often referred to him as a product of his environment. But Patricia Byrne knew a wrong-un when she met one, and he was one of the first order so far as she was concerned.

Quite what her daughter ever saw in him she had no idea.

Sarah was no fool, not by any length. But she somehow seemed to lose all her senses whenever Declan was around. Patricia had hoped that his last sentence on the mainland would have been longer, thus keeping him away from her daughter and allowing her to concentrate on her studies.

But the defence barrister he had been assigned managed to somehow convince the judge that Declan had a good heart and merely needed a fresh start in order for him to become a responsible member of society.

As a result, he had only been sentenced to twelve months, which meant with good behaviour he was out in less than six, with Sarah waiting for him to rekindle their relationship.

Naturally, Patricia's greatest fear was that Sarah would fall pregnant. The Higgins men were renowned for their eagerness to spread their seed. There had been countless incidents over the years of court orders from the mainland for paternity suits. But as the clan claimed to 'live off the land' without any discernible income to speak of, there was very little the courts could do.

As a nurse, Patricia had ensured that she and Sarah had 'the talk' as soon as she was old enough to understand the changes her young body was about to undergo. Up until Declan started hanging around her, Patricia had complete faith in her daughter that she would not do anything stupid. But as soon as she realised the hold Declan had over her, Patricia's maternal instincts went into overdrive.

Regardless of how many times Sarah promised her mother that she would not do anything stupid, Patricia insisted that Sarah always carry a packet of condoms with her, just in case. She had not forgotten what it was like to be seventeen and feeling peer pressure to lose your virginity.

Patricia had even threatened to drag Sarah down to Doctor Cleary's office to have her put on the pill. But when she saw the pure horror on her daughter's face at the prospect of such an embarrassing appointment, she relented.

"Come on," enticed Declan, "there's a nice warm spot over here. The rocks form a barrier against the wind."

He tugged Sarah gently, guiding her towards his intended location.

Sarah gave in without too much objection. She knew what Declan wanted. It was what he always wanted, but she had warned him on several previous occasions that she would not relinquish her virginity to him until she was good and ready.

The truth of the matter was that she was besotted with him with his shaved head, multiple tattoos and tongue stud, which he assured her that he had only inserted for her pleasure.

In truth, Sarah had no specific qualms concerning the loss of her virtue. But the sound of her mother's voice echoing in her ears, warning her of the potential consequences of either falling pregnant or, worse still, being labelled a *whore* when word spread throughout the community that she was sleeping with Declan, kept her hesitation in check.

Sarah knew that she was not the only girl on the island who had caught Declan's eye. Rumour had it that he was more than happy to spread his seed far and wide, although to date there was no evidence of him managing to get any of the local girls pregnant.

He of course denied such gossip to Sarah, but he was so full of himself that she suspected that the gossips were telling the truth.

Eve Higgins, a distant cousin of Declan's, had also been heard to say that she had been selected by the clan to marry him when she was sixteen, and would beat up any girl who dared to interfere with her intended in the meantime.

But, once again, Declan had assured Sarah that Eve was nothing more than a jumped-up little squirt whom he would not touch with a bargepole.

Regardless of the truth, all Sarah knew was that her heart skipped a beat whenever she was in his presence, and for now, that was all that mattered.

Declan guided Sarah around the jagged outcrop of rocks, using the torch on his phone to illuminate the puddles which had formed in the dips in the sand.

Eventually, they reached a spot which afforded them protection from the wind as well as a modicum of privacy from anyone else passing by.

Declan lay down on the sand and pulled Sarah down on top of him.

She squealed as his efforts caused her to lose her balance and her knee took the full force of her weight as she landed. Even with the relative softness of the sandy floor, Sarah still felt a jolt as her knee made contact with it.

"Ow," she cried, "that hurt."

"What?" replied Declan, as if astonished by her reaction.

"My knee, stupid. You're being too rough."

"Oh, you poor baby. Come here and I'll kiss it better for you."

Declan leaned over and placed his hand on Sarah's sore knee, rubbing it gently. He moved down her body until his mouth was in line with it, then began to cover it in little kisses, like a parent comforting a child.

His touch felt good, so Sarah did not object, even when his mouth surreptitiously began to move further up her thigh.

She lay back on the sand and closed her eyes as Declan swept the hem of her dress out of the way of his probing mouth. He switched thighs and started to work on her other one, switching back and forth at will as he made his way closer towards the point where her thighs came together.

The distant sound of the tide lapping lazily against the shore had always had a calming effect on Sarah. She could almost feel herself drifting off as Declan hooked both index fingers over the rim of her knickers.

Sarah manoeuvred her hips to allow Declan to guide her knickers down her legs. She could hear him growing frustrated as he attempted to pull them off, managing instead to ensnare them in her heels. Eventually, he gave up and left them dangling around her ankles.

Sarah bent her legs, rising slightly off the ground, anticipating the moist wetness of Declan's tongue as he delved inside her.

It was odd that he seemed to find pleasuring her that way so unpleasant, especially when he had insisted that was the main purpose for him having his tongue pierced.

Declan claimed that he had read an article online where cunnilingus had been linked to throat cancer. Whereas, according to the alleged same article, fellatio was actually beneficial to a woman's health.

Either way, he knew that for now at least, oral was the only form of sex she allowed, so he had to either like it or lump it.

As Declan leaned forward Sarah placed her hand on the back of his neck to guide his head towards her opening.

She moaned in anticipation, unaware that Declan had managed to unbuckle his jeans and slide them down his legs, taking his shorts with them.

Suddenly, instead of feeling his tongue lapping at her vulva, Sarah could feel Declan's hands pushing her thighs apart as he desperately attempted to guide the head of his erect penis into her.

She opened her eyes, seeing his head in front of her, a cruel knowing smile stretching across his face.

"What the hell are you doing?" Sarah screamed. "Get off me!"

"It's alright, baby," Declan assured her. "I'll pull out in good time, don't you worry."

Instinctively, Sarah attempted to close her legs, blocking him entry. But Declan's hands were too strong for her to compete. She reached up and tried to grab at the back of his head, but with no hair to grant her purchase her fingers merely closed on thin air.

Out of desperation, Sarah swept her right arm out in an arc, her hand gliding over the sand until she finally felt the solid surface of a large stone. Gripping it tightly, she swung it at Declan's head.

She managed to catch him on the side of his jaw, the full force of the blow sending him reeling to his right. Declan was knocked off balance but still managed to keep his legs wrapped around Sarah's lower half.

Sarah dropped her weapon without realising it. Perhaps as the result of an automatic feeling of guilt, she might have done more damage than she anticipated.

Sarah reminded herself that Declan was the aggressor and

she had only done what any self-respecting girl would have to defend herself.

Even so, she could not help but feel bad for her actions.

She needed to check that he was alright. Then she heard him groaning and swearing under his breath, so she decided he would live to tell the tale after all.

Taking full advantage of the situation, Sarah pushed off the ground with all her might managing to topple Declan off her, sending him crashing to the sand on her left.

Before he had a chance to recover, Sarah rolled over and moved to her knees. She stood up and stepped out of her knickers to save herself some time.

As she bent down to pick them up, Declan's hand shot out of the darkness and latched onto her wrist. Sarah screamed in shock, trying to pull away from him. But Declan kept a firm hold of her, not willing to relinquish his prize without a fight.

To her horror, Sarah saw him stumbling to his feet. She knew that the moment he was up she would have no chance of breaking free and making good her escape.

Her mother's warnings about him ran through her subconscious as she tried to figure out her best plan of action.

As he reached his full height, Sarah pulled back her right leg and kicked forward for all she was worth. The point of her shoe caught him directly between his bare legs.

Declan's eyes bulged from the shock and the weight of the impact, and he slowly let go of Sarah's wrist as he sunk to his knees, holding himself with both hands between his legs.

A wave of guilt swept over Sarah as she stood there watching him writhe on the sand, clearly in agony. But then she reminded herself of the reason behind her action and the self-reproach soon passed.

"You, lousy bastard!" she yelled down at the stricken man. Declan was still on his knees with his head bowed as if checking that everything below was still in order. "I never want to see you again."

With that, Sarah turned and began marching away across the beach.

She could hear Declan coughing and spluttering behind her, calling out, promising that he did not mean it and begging her to come back. But she ignored his cries and carried on, heading towards the nearest set of stone steps so that she could leave the beach.

Sarah soon realised that she would have done better had she retraced their original steps, the nearest exit in her direction was still too far away for her to see. Even so, going back would mean her walking past Declan, and she was not prepared to trust him so soon after his failed attack.

Suddenly, she heard movement coming from behind.

Sarah spun around and saw Declan stumbling towards her, hoisting up his jeans to allow hm more speed.

"Leave me alone!" Sarah shouted. But Declan ignored her cries and carried on running, gaining on her all the time.

Sarah began to run. Her heels dug in the sand with each footfall making her progress slow and cumbersome. She considered stopping just long enough to remove her shoes and carry them. But another quick glance behind showed her that even to stop for a couple of seconds might be all that Declan needed to catch her.

Sarah frantically glanced around her, desperate to seek out another human being taking a late-night walk along the beach. She knew that several dog-walkers favoured the area, but there was no one in sight.

Another quick glance and Declan was all but upon her, close enough that she could see his leering grin and wide-eyed stare.

Just then, Sarah's legs were kicked from beneath her.

She flew head-first through the air, but instead of landing on soft pliable sand, she belly-flopped onto a pair of legs.

Declan stopped, standing over Sarah he surveyed the ground around her, pulling a face.

Once Sarah caught her breath, she looked around and screamed when she realised that she was lying on top of the dead body of Michelle Calvert, her face contorted into a grizzly mask of terror.

Chapter Four

Janine Carstairs gazed across the glistening waters as she sipped her latte. The view from their vantage point outside the Pilgrims Rest Inn was idyllic, encompassing the harbour with its fishing boats, their occupants already done with their day's labours, gently

bouncing on the late-morning tide. The cliff to their right climbed so high it almost appeared as if it pierced the sky at its peak, with the cottages perched along its ridge seeming to balance on the verge as if waiting to fall into the water below.

The cacophonous squawking of gulls overhead as they swept across the sky mingled with the distant blare of a sea vessel approaching the harbour entrance, conjuring the very essence of the peace and tranquillity of the tiny piece of heaven which Janine and her daughter had discovered, quite by chance, having missed the last ferry across to the Isle of Manus the previous evening.

Janine was an independent journalist and she had been commissioned by a lifestyle glossy to write an article about the picturesque, if somewhat remote, island and its inhabitants.

The isle was renowned for the fact that the vast majority of those who lived there were all ancestors of the original settlers from the twelfth century.

The only newcomers, or blow-ins as the locals romantically referred to them, were those considered by the local council as beneficial to the island by virtue of their trade or service, such as the local doctor and priest. Everyone else had to be able to prove their lineage as directly related to one of the original island dwellers.

Taking in a deep breath of the fresh sea air, Janine closed her eyes and considered asking the proprietor of their extremely comfortable inn whether she and her daughter could extend their stay there for another night.

The quaint market town they had driven through last night on their way here appeared extremely inviting to Janine, and she knew that she could have spent some very happy hours wandering through the lanes and visiting myriad shops and stalls on offer.

Her daughter on the other hand would doubtless have a different view on the subject.

When she opened her eyes and saw Marie sitting opposite her glued to her phone, earplugs jabbed firmly in each auricle as if totally unaware of the natural beauty all around them, she remembered the battle she had been forced to engage in when her ex-husband Mike let them down at the last minute and informed her that he could no longer take their daughter to Florida for the school holidays. Opting instead to take his new girlfriend to Mexico for a boob-job.

Naturally, Janine was the one left to explain the situation to Marie, thereby leaving her to receive all the flack for the last-minute cancellation.

Things would have been easier if they had stayed at home. At least there Marie had the option to hang out with her friends and do whatever they usually did with their time-Janine had stopped asking long ago. But since she had already accepted her latest assignment Janine was obliged to come to Ireland to complete it on schedule.

This was the first time Janine had been commissioned by this particular glossy, so she was determined to make a good impression as it could lead to more work.

Cancelling the assignment because your teenage daughter was throwing a strop would not cut it.

Janine decided to chance her arm, after all, nothing ventured nothing gained.

She moved her foot forward under the table and tapped her daughter's calf with the toe of her sandal to gain her attention. She knew that there was no point in speaking to her when her earphones were in place.

Marie looked up, frowning.

Janine spoke, but kept her voice low on purpose, forcing Marie to evict one of the plugs. "Aye?"

"I said, how do you feel about spending the day here in town? We could have a mooch around the shops, visit the market, have a pub lunch. What do you say?"

"I thought we needed to get over to the island so you can start your article?"

"Another day won't make that much of a difference. And this inn is probably a darn-sight more welcoming than the accommodation the magazine have lined up for us over there. We could spoil ourselves a little, get our nails done together, do a little mother and daughter bonding."

Marie rolled her eyes. "I'd rather we just got going, the sooner we get to that place the sooner we can leave and go home."

In truth, her daughter's response did not come as any great shock to Janine.

Marie was seventeen and fast turning into one of those teenagers all parents dread.

She hardly ever spoke, unless she were being directly

addressed, and even then, her reply was often a shrug of her shoulders rather than any actual words.

Janine was as understanding as she could be with her. But even her patience was at times pushed to the limit.

She appreciated that the divorce had been a traumatic event for her daughter, as such an event was for any child regardless of their age. But Janine had done her utmost to cushion the blows and ensure the transition from living with two parents to only having one in your direct line of fire, went as smoothly as possible.

Janine was not sure if it were merely her own insecurities raising their ugly heads, but deep down she felt sure that somehow Marie blamed her for the split, despite the fact that it had been her father who decided to run off with a twenty-three-year-old cosmetics consultant who could barely string two words together without injecting the word 'like' into the sentence.

Janine knew for a fact that, initially, Mike had attempted to explain their separation to their daughter as being no one's fault and that he and her mother had just reached a point in their relationship where they wanted different things.

Marie had always been a daddy's girl, but she was nobody's fool. She soon twigged on that Mike and Tina had been more than just good friends long before he decided to leave the family home.

But even so, the way she treated Janine at times came across as if she believed that her mother could have done more to keep hold of her father, rather than allowing him to go without a fight.

What Marie did not know was that Tina was not the first indiscretion her father had to his name. There had been at least two others previously, one while Janine was heavily pregnant with their daughter.

There had been times since the divorce when Marie was

laying into her mother, blaming her for something which was in reality completely of her control, that Janine had been sorely tempted to reveal Mike's past to her, but she always managed to bite her tongue and hold back, not wanting to make Marie feel as if it was some kind of one-upmanship competition.

As a journalist, Janine had covered enough articles on the effect divorce had on children to appreciate that she needed to bear in mind that her daughter was as much of a victim as she was and that her unwarranted attacks came from a place of great sadness, not anger.

If her father chose to lie to her that was his look-out. Janine was a big believer in karma and so was happy to play the bigger person.

"You know," ventured Janine, "if you took the time to check out your surroundings you might just see how beautiful they are."

"Whatever, Mum," replied Marie, returning her gaze to her screen.

"You know, this is the land of your father's distant relatives."

"And they must have left for a reason."

Janine sighed. She knew she was losing an uphill struggle and part of her did feel sorry for Marie. After all, she knew how much her daughter had been looking forward to visiting Florida. But she refused to take responsibility for the guilt that her ex-husband deserved.

Deciding that their conversation was over, Marie moved to replace her earbud.

Janine jumped in. "You know, I bet that if you just tried a little, we could make this a happy memory we could share with my grandchildren someday."

The expression on Marie's face made her appear as if she had just swallowed pure lemon juice.

Shaking her head, she shoved her bud back in without answering.

Chapter Five

THE CAR FERRY ACROSS TO MANUS TOOK A LITTLE over twenty minutes. Although she knew the trip would be short, Janine could not help but leave her rental car and stand outside with the foot passengers so that she could enjoy the refreshing sea breeze. She took in great gulps of the salty air, feeling it infuse her lungs and blow away the cobwebs from stuffy London.

Marie on the other hand merely shrugged when her mother suggested that they stand on deck, preferring – as usual – to keep her eyes glued to her phone. Janine had given up on the idea of encouraging her daughter to take in the beautiful views and decided to just enjoy them for herself.

Whether her daughter's attitude was a result of general teenage angst, or the fact that she was being dragged out of her normal comfort zone, that was to say her bedroom, Janine did not know, but she was willing to cut her daughter some sympathetic slack due to the last- minute cancellation of her holiday in Florida.

Regardless of whether or not the teenager was willing to admit it, Janine knew just how much she had been looking forward to her holiday with her father, and she could still see the look of utter dejection on her face when Janine passed on the message that her trip had been cancelled.

Mike, as per usual, was too much of a coward to convey his decision to his daughter personally, instead opting to use his ex-wife to undertake the task.

Janine had done her best to comfort Marie when she received the bad news, but her daughter, always a daddy's girl in spite of the divorce, just slammed her bedroom door and refused to discuss the matter.

Janine had already decided that unless her husband made it up to their daughter before next summer that she was going to take Marie on that cancelled holiday herself.

Or, if her exam results warranted it and Janine could stomach the idea of her daughter being on the other side of the world without a chaperone, she had heard some of the other mothers at the school discussing the option of allowing their daughters to take their first holiday without them tagging along.

Florida had already been cast into the mix which was one reason Janine had been glad when Mike suggested it first. But now it almost seemed to her that fate was edging towards allowing Marie to go with her friends instead.

For now, however, she was keeping the idea to herself while she came to terms with the prospect.

There were only a handful of cars going across, with more people choosing to travel as foot-passengers. Janine estimated that the ferry could probably hold at least twenty cars and perhaps as many as a hundred foot-passengers when fully loaded.

When they disembarked, Janine pulled the car over to allow others to pass by on the narrow road while she checked the car's sat-nav to plot the route.

The cottage the magazine had arranged for her during her stay on the island was owned by the church, so the directions she had been given were to the presbytery where she could collect the keys.

Janine had already been warned by one of the other reporters that the Wi-Fi on the island could be a little *spotty* at best, so she was not surprised to hear Marie complaining next to her whenever her phone crashed.

The views as they meandered through the rolling abundance of lush greenery were breathtaking and Janine refused to rise to her daughter's constant whinging regarding the lack of reception or the fact that the island did not boast a single club or wine bar. These were the first of many gripes Marie had lodged having first checked out the island on Google.

Further searches did nothing to enhance her appreciation of the locale when she discovered that there were also no shopping centres, restaurants or anywhere in fact that young people could hang out to avoid the disapproving gazes of their parents.

"What the hell do young people do on the island?" she demanded having made her initial discoveries. "Is it like some sort of Amish settlement where the youngsters aren't allowed to do anything which might be deemed *enjoyable* by their elders?"

Janine had tried to assure her that there had to be something to do to keep her amused even though she too had her doubts.

Marie had never been an avid reader although she always managed to pull the stops out during exam time. The sad fact was that academe had eradicated any pleasure she once derived from reading, almost to the point that Marie refused to so much as open a book during the holidays.

The signal on the sat-nav was also as 'hit-and-miss' as the Wi-Fi Janine soon discovered, especially when the hills surrounding them enveloped the road that they were on. But as far as she was concerned the view was far too beautiful to complain about other minor inconveniences.

The church was at the end of a tiny market street and barely accessible via the only road which led to it. At first, Janine was convinced that she had taken a wrong turning and veered onto a footpath as people criss-crossed in front of her car as if unaware of the fact that she was even there. It was only when she heard the sound of horns blaring behind that she realised it was the jaywalkers who were at fault.

The stalls on either side of the road left very little space for passing cars, and the pedestrians seemed oblivious to them, their attention fully captured by the products on sale.

Slowly edging her way through, Janine finally managed to leave the market behind her before turning off the main road and into the carpark which served the church.

She drove around to the back and parked outside what she presumed was the presbytery's front door.

As she exited the car, Janine was surprised that the noise from the market seemed so far away. Considering she could walk back there in less than five minutes, it was almost as if the church formed some sort of sound barrier masking everything outside the main entrance.

Janine insisted on dragging Marie out of the car to meet the parish priest, informing her that it would be rude to stay in the car as they were his guests on the island.

Reluctantly, Marie climbed out, removing her headphones and holding them up to her mother with a feigned smile before dropping them back on the seat.

Although Janine felt sorry for her daughter having missed out on her Florida trip, it was no fault of hers that her ex had let their daughter down, so Janine knew that she was to face the brunt of Marie's attitude as she was the only parent at hand, and as such directly in her firing line. But parental guilt aside, there was only so much that Janine was willing to put up with before reading her daughter the riot act.

They stood side-by-side outside the presbytery as Janine pulled the iron bell chain.

A minute or so later the door was opened by a tall, rather

dashing young man, in his early thirties. Janine was immediately struck by his piercing blue eyes and thick black wavy hair which drooped down over his forehead from his side parting.

"Yes," he said, smiling, "may I help you?"

He was dressed in a long black cassock and clerical collar as were most priests of Janine's acquaintance but, even on first sight he exuded a smouldering quality more akin to James Bond than a parish priest.

Janine was sure that in the brief she had been provided with the local priest was meant to be in his early sixties, so either this was not the same man or, she had misread the brief.

"Mum."

Janine suddenly realised that she had been standing there with her mouth open without actually saying anything.

Feeling her cheeks redden, she cleared her throat before asking, "Father Boyle?"

The priest's smile broadened. "Not quite so distinguished I'm afraid," he replied, looking from mother to daughter, then back again. "I'm Father Wells, his curate. Father Boyle is out visiting one of his parishioners. May I do something for you?"

Janine's mind raced with possibilities, but she managed to check herself before answering with something inappropriate.

She moved forward and held out her hand. "My name is Janine Carstairs, I'm here to write an article on the island. Father Boyle was gracious enough to arrange for somewhere for my daughter and I to stay."

The priest took her hand and shook it gently.

His fingers were soft, warm and inviting.

"I see," he replied, "Well, I think I know which property he had in mind, if you'll give me a moment I'll try and hunt out the keys." He stood back and turned to one side, indicating with his hand for Janine and Marie to enter the presbytery.

Janine ushered Marie ahead of her, then followed behind.

The inside was all dark wood. The furniture looked solid and strong. The floor was stone with a red and green pattern which stretched across the floor.

At the end of the hallway, a tall grandfather clock *ticked* loudly.

There was something foreboding about the entrance which Janine put down to the automatic feeling of guilt which had been driven into her as a child while attending her local convent.

That convent with its strict discipline, adhesion to daily mass and the overbearing nature of the nuns who made up the majority of the teachers, was the main reason why she had not sent Marie to such a school. Mike was not particularly religious anyway, so he offered no resistance.

"If the pair of you would care to take a seat, I'll be back in a minute."

Father Wells signalled towards an oak bench just inside the door, and he waited until both women were seated before disappearing through the furthest doorway along the corridor.

When he was gone, Marie leaned in towards her mother. "This place gives me the willies," she confided. "Please tell me the place we're staying at is not going to be like this."

Janine gave her hand a gentle squeeze. "If it is, I think we might have to come up with an excuse not to stay after all."

Marie nodded her agreement.

A minute or two later the curate returned with a set of keys.

Janine and Marie stood up to greet his return.

He handed them over to Janine. "Here you are," he said, casually. "Do you know how to get there?"

"I'm afraid not," Janine confessed. "I was relying on Father Boyle for instructions." She smiled, weakly. Father Wells held her gaze long enough for her to feel her cheeks grow hot once more.

Janine could not help but wonder if he knew how attractive he was.

Or, being a priest, was he truly oblivious to such things?

The curate turned and walked back over to the front door, opening it for the two women to leave.

Once they were outside, he followed them as far as the welcome mat.

"You drive back out the way you came in," he said, swinging his arm to indicate that the entrance was on the other side of the church. "Head back through the market, then take the first turning on your left. It's a cul-de-sac with a large park at the end of it. The cottage is the last building on your left. You can park in front of the wrought iron railing, so long as you don't obstruct the gates."

Janine turned to Marie. "Got that?"

Marie looked shocked. "What, me? I wasn't paying attention," she admitted.

Janine laughed. "Well, it's a good job one of us was."

She turned back and thanked the curate, trying desperately not to blush this time when their eyes met.

"I hope to see you both on Sunday, if you're still here," he said, dryly.

The thought sent an involuntary shiver down Janine's back.

Chapter Six

Once they were back in the car and out of earshot from the priest, Marie 'tutted' and exclaimed, "Jesus!"

Janine turned her head slightly, still keeping her main focus on the road ahead as she negotiated the way out of the churchyard. "What?"

"Oh, I don't know, maybe the way you were flirting with that priest. I thought for a moment there that you were going to launch yourself at the poor bloke and yank his trousers down."

Janine laughed, in spite of herself. "Excuse me, I was doing nothing of the sort. I don't know what it is you thought you saw, but I was merely being polite and courteous."

"You were acting like a smitten thirteen-year-old," Marie corrected her. "It was so embarrassing. Aren't you a little old for such behaviour?"

"Hey, I'm not over the hill yet, thank you very much. Just because your father elected to forsake our marriage for the arms of a teenager doesn't mean that I'm past it." Janine could feel her blood pressure rising at the mere mention of her ex. She hated the way she spoke with such passion whenever his name was brought up, especially when she was the one who had referenced him.

Worst of all, it made her sound as if she were angry at Marie, and on this occasion a least, that was not the case.

She glanced to her side.

Marie was looking outside her window. Janine could not tell from her reflection in the glass whether she was upset. But if she was, Janine knew that it was her fault for snapping at her.

Janine left it a moment, then said. "He was kind of hot though, don't you think?"

Marie turned back to her. "Yuck! He's a priest, and a Catholic to boot. Isn't it some kind of mortal sin to lust after a man of God?"

"A girl can't dream?"

Marie burst out laughing.

It felt good to hear her laugh. Since the separation it was almost as if she had forgotten how to. Instead, she had buried her emotions away in some deep dark hole and refused to bring them to the surface.

Janine had done all she could to reassure her daughter that the divorce had absolutely nothing to do with her, but whenever the subject came up, she could see the faraway hurt in Marie's eyes.

Janine knew that children of divorce often blamed themselves regardless of their parent's reassurances. But Janine had hoped that this would not be the case with Marie.

Her daughter had always had such a strong, vibrant personality and a down-to-earth quality when it came to dealing with most matters which Janine had come to admire over the years.

Their eyes met for a moment, and Janine offered her daughter a cheeky wink.

Marie shook her head, smiling.

The cottage was only a five-minute drive from the church, and Janine was pleased that there was ample parking available.

The park which stood at the end of the cul-de-sac was a mere stone's throw from the cottage, and she could see what the priest had warned her not to block to gates as the road honed it to a point leaving very little manoeuvring room for anyone parked there.

They unloaded the car of their luggage and set about exploring the cottage.

There were two fairly large bedrooms, of which Janine allowed Marie to have her pick. The teenager chose the back bedroom, no surprise to Janine, as it seemed to have a stronger wi-fi connection.

The cottage was immaculate in appearance and gave the impression that it was regularly cleaned and hardly used. There was not so much as a smidgeon of dust on any of the worktops when Janine gave them the *finger* test.

Once they were settled Janine suggested that they visit the town and procure some supplies for their stay. Marie screwed up her face at the suggestion and stated that she preferred to stay in and catch up on her social media.

Janine decided not to push the subject and left her daughter to it.

Janine walked back through the market and sampled some of the local fayre on sale.

The stall owners seemed very friendly and more than willing to offer samples of their wares regardless of whether Janine showed an interest.

By the time she had walked to the far end of the street, Janine had purchased a loaf of freshly baked crusty bread, some eggs, sausages, cheese, chutney and a bottle of locally made wine.

The opposite side of the street, which was bathed in the afternoon sun, contained stalls which mainly sold clothes, material, wool and household items.

There were some beautiful shawls and scarf-sets on display,

so Janine chose a purple and cream combination for Marie, which she hoped her daughter would like.

Janine continued down towards the near end of the market, but her attention was soon grabbed on a large second-hand bookshop halfway down the street.

Whenever she was on holiday, even a working one such as this, Janine liked to choose a new novel to fill in the non-working hours. As she had always preferred the feel of paper between her fingers rather than one of the e-readers which everyone else seemed to have, a second-hand bookshop was just the place to discover her next good read.

A small brass bell *dinged* as Janine opened the door.

The middle-aged lady behind the counter looked up from the book she was reading and smiled at her. "Good afternoon," she said, cheerily. "Is there anything specific you are looking for, or just browsing?"

Janine smiled back. "Well, I am looking for something, I'm just not sure what it is yet. If that makes sense."

The woman placed her book face down on the counter, splayed open. "Well now," she began, glancing around at myriad shelves which covered each wall, as well as those which stood alone in the aisles. Each one was fit to bursting with books of all different sizes. "As you can see," she continued, "we have a vast selection, all of which extremely well priced. Did you have a particular genre in mind? We cover most options."

Janine followed the woman's gaze taking in the various publications, before turning back to her and shrugging her shoulders.

"Well," the woman said, resignedly, "I'm sure you'll know what you want when you see it. I'll leave you to carry on. Just give me a shout if you need any help."

With that, she returned to her own book.

Janine thanked her and began trawling the shelves.

After about twenty minutes of searching, Janine came across

an old copy of The Exorcist. She remembered seeing the film during an all-night horror fest at her local cinema when she was a teenager. They showed five films in total overnight, starting at 11 pm, with *Friday the 13th*, followed by *Happy Birthday to Me*, then *The Exorcist*, next *The Omen*, finishing with *The Texas Chainsaw Massacre*.

They were legally too young for the films, but luckily the young man selling tickets was going out with one of the girls, so there was no question of them being stopped.

Janine remembered that by the third film her other friends had started to drift off. But she was still rivetted to the screen even though she found herself covering her eyes several times, especially during the final scenes.

She too began to doze off during The Omen, but the sound of the chainsaw in the last film brought everyone back to life.

Janine read the back cover of the book which convinced her that she wanted to see how close the original novel was to the film version.

She took the book back to the counter.

The proprietor raised her eyebrows when she saw Janine's choice but did not comment on it.

While the woman rang up the receipt, Janine noticed a pile of books behind her, with a large cardboard cut-out as a stand displaying an eerie castle at night with a full moon in the background.

According to the sign, the book advertised was entitled: Local Legends and Myths from the Isle of Manus.

The woman noticed Janine's interest. "May I tempt you to a copy?" she asked, turning to wave towards the display. "It's written by a local historian you know."

Janine realised what an enormous help the book might be in drafting her article, and if the author was a local, she might also be able to arrange an interview with him.

"Yes, please," she replied, eagerly.

Chapter Seven

Janine stopped off at a corner shop on her way back from the market to purchase some essentials such as: coffee, milk, sugar etc. By the time she left the shops she felt a little laden down with all her shopping and wished now that she had insisted Marie go with her.

Fortunately, it was only a short walk back to the cottage.

The late afternoon sun was starting to wane as Janine turned into the cul-de-sac the cottage was on. As she made her way towards it, she noticed that someone was standing outside the door.

As she drew nearer, she noticed that it was a priest.

Her heart skipped a mini-beat for a moment as she remembered the dashing young curate who had given her the keys for the cottage, and she felt her cheeks blush as she remembered Marie's admonishment in the car.

From this distance, Janine could see wiry grey hair protruding from under the brim of the priest's hat, so she realised that it could not be the curate, after all.

Placing one of her bags on the ground, she pushed at the gate which creaked open on its rusty hinge.

The priest spun round, smiling. "Miss Carstairs?" he asked, lifting his hat with his left hand and extending his right.

Janine walked into the yard carrying all her bags. She placed the one she held in her right hand down on the floor so that she could shake.

"My name is Father Boyle. So sorry I was not at home to welcome when you came to collect the keys. I was visiting a parishioner in need of comfort," he explained.

"That's perfectly alright," Janine assured him. "Your curate looked after us."

"He's a good man, Jamie. A little young to devote his life to the church in my opinion, but when God calls all must answer."

"Won't you come in for a cup of coffee?" Janine offered.

The priest smiled. "Lovely," he checked his wristwatch. "I think there's just enough time for a quick one before evensong. Please permit me." He bent down to retrieve Janine's bag, allowing her to search her pocket for the key.

"I'm so glad I managed to catch you," Father Boyle said, cheerfully. "I did knock but when there was no answer I was afraid I had missed you."

Janine turned back to look at him, her key in the door. "That's odd," she remarked, frowning, "my daughter should be in."

The priest shrugged. "Not to worry, you're here now."

They walked inside and Father Boyle closed the door behind them.

Janine stopped at the bottom of the stairs and called up to Marie.

No answer came.

There was no sound of music blaring from above, which was what she was used to hearing upon her return from work. But then she realised that Marie did not have her CD player with her, so there was a good chance she was listening to music through her headphones.

They took the bags into the kitchen and Janine put the fridge items away.

Father Boyle took a seat at the table and placed his hat on the back of the chair.

Janine filled the kettle and switched it on. "I'm afraid I don't have any biscuits to offer you." She smiled apologetically. "Unless you'd care for a sandwich, or some toast?"

The priest shook his head. "No, thank you, you're very kind, but a cup of tea will suffice."

Janine set out the cups. She put one out for Marie, then excused herself while she went upstairs to see what she was up to.

As she expected, Marie was lying on her bed, headphones in, playing on her phone.

Janine stood in the doorway for a moment before her daughter realised that she was there.

"Fuck-wank!" Marie exclaimed, sitting up abruptly and clutching her chest, dramatically. "You scared the hell out of me, why didn't you knock first?"

"What would be the point, you wouldn't have heard me through those things. And when did we start using such language, young lady?"

Marie pulled out one of her headphones. "Oh, Mum, you're so dry sometimes. Serves you right for almost giving me a heart attack."

Janine rolled her eyes. "Slight exaggeration and still no excuse for swearing."

Marie pulled a face and fell back on the bed.

"I take it you didn't hear our guest banging on the door, then?"

"What guest?"

"Father Boyle from the church is downstairs having coffee."

Marie sat back up. "Not the dreamy one from the church that you were gushing over?"

Janine blushed. "Will you keep your voice down, he'll hear you."

"Whatever."

"So, do you fancy a coffee?"

"Can you bring it up?"

Janine sighed. "I can, but I won't. Get yourself downstairs lazybones and say hello to our guest, he can't say long."

"Forget it, I'll go without."

"I've bought you something," Janine coaxed. "Something I think you'll like."

Marie jolted upright. "What is it?"

"You'll have to come down and see for yourself."

"Mum!"

"Come on, kettle's on."

Janine went downstairs leaving Marie in her room.

As she poured the second cup of coffee, she could hear Marie *thudding* down the stairs in protest. Janine turned in the direction of the staircase, then looked at Father Boyle.

The priest laughed. "A little reluctant to join us, I take it," he remarked.

Marie entered the kitchen a moment later. Father Boyle rose and introduced himself, offering his hand, which Marie shook before taking a seat opposite him at the table.

Janine set the cups down in front of them.

As she sat down, Marie asked. "Any biscuits?"

"No, sorry, I forgot," replied Janine.

"Your mother was fairly laden down when she arrived home, I'm not sure that she could have managed anything else, even a small packet of biscuits," Father Boyle smiled.

Marie nodded, obviously unimpressed by the excuse.

Janine reached under her chair and picked up the carrier bag with Marie's scarf set.

"Here, not that you deserve it," she said, handing it to Marie.

Marie eagerly opened the bag and took out the matching hat, gloves and scarf.

Her eyes widened. Janine knew that purple and cream were her favourite colour combination, but even so, she was comforted by her daughter's reaction to her present.

Marie took out the items and tried them on at the table.

Satisfied with the fit, she stood up and walked into the lounge.

"Where are you off to?" Janine called.

"I want to see how they look," Marie replied, moving in front of the mirror which hung adjacent to the front door.

She came back in a moment later and gave Janine a kiss on the cheek and a hug. "Thanks, Mum, they're great," she gushed.

Sitting down, Marie lifted the carrier bag off the table. Realising that there was still something in it, she peered back inside and pulled out the two books Janine had purchased, placing them on the table.

Janine was sipping her coffee before she realised what her daughter was doing.

Before she could respond, Marie had placed both books on the table with the titles turned towards her mother and Father Boyle.

Before Janine could respond, the priest leaned forward to study the two volumes.

Janine hesitantly reached out to remove *The Exorcist* from his sight. "I'm sorry father," she apologised. "I didn't mean for you to see this."

Father Boyle winked at her. "It's a very good read. Not that I've read it for many years now. The film was also very entertaining as I remember."

His words shocked Janine, although she was not sure why. After all, there was nothing wrong with a man of the cloth reading a horror novel, or even seeing the film made from it. In truth, she realised that she felt more embarrassed at the fact that he knew she was reading it.

Father Boyle picked up the second book and perused the title.

"That was written by a local man, I believe," Janine informed him. "I'm hoping it might give me a few angles on the article I'm reading."

The priest nodded. "Yes, I know him, he's one of my parishioners, although now I come to think of it, I haven't seen him at church for a while now."

"Do you think he might be willing to agree to an interview?" Janine asked.

Father Boyle laughed. "Oh, if I know Timmy O'Brien, he'll jump at the chance. He loves talking about his work. In fact, now I come to think of it, I'm sure he's giving a talk soon at the community centre. You might want to pop along; it'll be a good chance to meet him."

"That would be brilliant," replied Janine, "I take it this is not his only published work?"

Father Boyle put the book back on the table. "No, he has several tomes to his credit, mainly on folklore and local legends."

Just then they heard the sound of something plastic *slapping* against itself.

They spun round as one, just in time to witness a black cat stroll into the kitchen.

"Ah," said the priest, "allow me to introduce you to Gypsy. I meant to tell you about her. I'm afraid she comes with the cottage."

Gypsy looked up at the intruders and sniffed the air.

Marie bent down and held out her hand trying to coax the cat to come to her.

"Please, be careful," warned Father Boyle. "I'm afraid she is feral and prone to lashing out for no apparent reason."

Marie kept her hand out, calling the cat by name.

"Be careful, darling," Janine warned. "I'd rather not spend the night in ER waiting for you to get a tetanus shot."

"Honestly, Mum, stop panicking," Marie chided. "I just want her to get my scent, I won't try and pick her up or anything."

Gypsy edged her snout closer to Marie's offered hand. Deciding there was no threat, she moved in closer until she was close enough to rub her face against Marie's fingers.

"Well, I've never seen her take to someone that quickly before," remarked Father Boyle. "You obviously have a way with you," he observed.

"I presume she doesn't actually belong to anyone?" asked Janine.

The priest shook his head. "No. We had the cat-flap installed for a previous tenant who had three cats, but when she left, Gypsy here started using it when she wanted to take shelter from the cold. She comes and goes as she pleases, so far as I know, and I'm reliably informed that if you have the log fire on, you'll often find her asleep on the hearth rug."

"She's beautiful," said Marie, keeping her hand out while Gypsy rubbed herself against it, purring.

Janine looked on. Marie had never expressed any interest in owning a pet before, but she had to admit that her daughter seemed to have a natural affinity with their uninvited guest.

"Good heavens, is that the time," Father Boyle rose from his seat, scraping his chair back along the tiled floor. "I must love you and leave you, ladies, can't be late for evensong. And then I've confession to look forward to. Always popular around these parts, although more so during the winter months, I find. Not exactly sure why."

Janine stood up to see the priest out.

Marie continued enjoying Gypsy's affectionate play. "Bye," she called, keeping her focus on the cat.

Father Boyle opened the front door and walked out into the late-evening breeze.

"Well, it was lovely to meet you both," he gushed, "and I'll look up Tim's details and give you a call."

"Thank you, Father, I'd really appreciate it."

Janine watched the elderly cleric stroll down the street for a moment before closing the door. When she re-entered the kitchen, she found Gypsy sitting on the table tucking into a saucer of milk.

"Oh, Marie, not on the table, we eat there," she groaned.

Marie looked up, smiling. "You are seriously turning into a right worry-wart these days," she replied. "I'll wipe the table down when she's finished."

Janine looked stunned. "You, actually volunteering to do some housework, this is a first. They say black cats have mystical powers. This might be the proof in the pudding."

Chapter Eight

JERRY BROOKE SAT THROUGH EVENSONG WITH HIS
usual expression of tedium etched on his face.

Although a relatively devout man, Jerry found this particular
service to always be overly long, made worse by the orchestral
arrangements of the choir mistress who insisted that each verse
of each hymn be peppered with unnecessary instrumental
infusions.

Even Father Boyle managed to lose his place in songs which
he had been singing for more years than he cared to mention,
disorientated by the sudden intrusion of yet another musical
interlude before the next verse could begin.

Ordinarily, Jerry did not attend Evensong. But it so happened
that tonight he needed to make his confession, and as the ritual
commenced directly after evensong, he knew that he needed to
be present in order to make his way to the front of the queue for
the confessional.

Those who merely arrived at the end of the mass without
first relishing the full experience of evensong were considered
close to being heathens by the tight-knit community.

In larger parishes, such things would not cause him any anguish whatsoever, but as he was considered a prominent and respectable member of the community, it was important to him to keep the illusion alive.

Jerry had been a social worker and spiritual advisor for most of his working life, starting originally in Lincoln before being offered a promotion on the mainland specialising in the care of young women whom the courts had deemed unfit to mingle in society until they came of age.

Most of the girls were juveniles who had committed some menial crime which, due to their constant re-offending, might have afforded them a prison term were it not for their age.

Instead, with the intervention of social services, they were sent to a reform school/young offenders' institution where it was hoped that they could be made to realise the error of their ways and, thus, go on to become productive members of society.

Over time, Jerry had worked his way up to become the lead advisor which allowed him to oversee the running of the institutions under his remit.

He had even turned down an offer of further promotion which would have seen him taking charge of institutions caring for both sexes, not just the females. But he declined the offer seeing little benefit for him in having to split his time, spending half of it visiting young male offenders who held no interest for him.

Even the offer of the increased salary did nothing to persuade him. His interest had always been in the welfare of girls who would one day grow into women, and in whose lives he hoped he might still be a profound influence.

As the congregation begun what Father Boyle promised was the last hymn of the service, Jerry edged a little closer to the end of his pew. He had glanced around him during the service and spotted many of the usual penitents who treated the confessional more like a social club affording them a good natter with the priest, rather than a place where they needed to have their sins absolved.

Some of them were known to take ages as they knew Father Boyle did not have the heart to rush them along.

The confessional box was situated off to one side to allow for privacy. Yet, some of these culprits seemed to almost shout out their sins at the top of their lungs, almost as if acknowledging them for all to hear were some badge of honour.

Jerry, on the other hand, wanted to be in and out with a minimum of fuss.

Ordinarily, he would attend one of the morning confessionals. There was always a smaller queue and as they started when the church opened there was no need for him to suffer through a tedious evensong service first.

But for all his faults, he was a firm believer that if he should pass away during the night without first having received absolution for his sins, then he was almost sure to end up in hell, and then it would be too late for him.

As the parishioners droned on through the last hymn, Jerry considered the sin for which he was there to confess. He knew that Father Boyle could not understand his repeated instances of sexual immorality, but then, as a priest, he had taken a vow of chastity before he ever experienced the pleasures of the flesh, so how could he possibly know what he was talking about?

As far as Jerry was concerned, the priest had no right to stand in judgement over him and merely needed to carry out his office and absolve Jerry of his moral impropriety.

That was the deal.

The sinner sinned, then confessed, and the priest absolved him.

Then life carried on for both parties.

Besides which, it was not Jerry's fault that he found himself in this position so often. He was a good, law-abiding citizen who tried to do some good through his choice of occupation, but his task was made almost impossible thanks to girls like Sorcha Brown.

She might only have been fifteen, but that little minx knew her way around men better than some of the prostitutes who worked the alleys on the mainland.

In his defence, Jerry had not made a move on her. She had been the one who instigated things. That first time in his office just after she had been sent to the reformatory, she purposely made a point of hitching her skirt up as she sat opposite him, crossing her legs to afford him a full view of everything she had on offer.

Jerry knew right away that he should report the incident to his superiors and see to it that Sorcha was accompanied by a female warder whenever they had a meeting.

But before he could prevent it, Sorcha had made a play for him. Walking seductively round to his side of the desk and kneeling before him as she fiddled with his zip.

It was not his fault!

Any man in a similar situation would have succumbed to her wicked, wanton ways.

He was only human after all.

Since then, their meetings had become a regular occurrence. Sorcha was always in trouble with the warders for one thing or another which resulted in them booking another appointment with her social advisor.

The trouble was that now she had him well and truly over a barrel. Even if no one believed her stories there was no smoke without fire, and such a circumstance could easily result in his dismissal, or possibly even a criminal charge.

So now, Jerry was forced to bring in little luxuries which Sorcha could not obtain from within the institution. Cigarettes, a mobile phone which he had to top up upon her request, Belgian chocolates, the list was endless.

For her part, Sorcha still kept him satisfied at their meetings, but Jerry could tell that she knew that she was now in charge of the situation and if he did not toe the line, she could end his career with a single word.

As far as he was concerned, it was not worth the fuss to refuse Sorcha her little presents. She would be out of the place within the year, then he could relax. He knew that once he was no longer her advisor that she would have no hold over him.

In the meantime though, he was unable to resist her advances, and why should he? The little slut was bound to end up selling her filthy wares on the streets once she was free from her incarceration, so what the hell.

As Father Boyle blessed the congregation for the final time, Jerry edged himself out of his pew and genuflected before marching towards the confessional.

He casually slotted himself into the first row and knelt on the padded runner, pretending to pray. With his eyes closed he could hear the shuffling of those gathering next to him to take their place in the queue, smirking to himself as some of the regulars muttered under their breath, clearly irritated by the fact that he had beaten them to first place.

After a moment, Jerry opened his eyes and gazed around him, smiling benevolently at any who happened to catch his eye.

Eventually, Father Boyle appeared and entered the confessional.

As the light above his name came on, Jerry moved from his pew and entered the box from the opposite side.

Closing the door securely, he began. "In the name of the Father, and the Son, and the Holy Spirit, Amen. Bless me Father for I have sinned. It has been a week since my last confession, and here are my sins."

He heard Father Boyle release a low sigh through the wooden grate.

Regardless of the seal of the confessional, and the anonymity the box was meant to provide, Jerry knew full well that the priest knew who he was.

The priest could not help but see all those gathered when he entered the confessional.

Added to which, even if he were blindfolded, Father Boyle knew his parishioners instantly by the sound of their voices.

The entire situation was farcical so far as Jerry was concerned, but if the Church insisted that this was the only procedure by which he could have his sins absolved, then so be it.

"May God be in your heart so that you make a true confession, my son."

Jerry leaned in closer to the grate so that his voice would not carry. "May God forgive me Father, but I have been weak. I have given way to the sin of lust. I was cajoled into it by another, it was not my fault. I was not the instigator, nor did I offer any encouragement. But my will was weak, and my body ruled my head. For this, and any signs I cannot remember, I humbly ask for God's forgiveness."

Father Boyle sat back in his chair, rubbing the top of his nose between the forefinger and thumb of one of his hands.

Finally, he spoke. "The sin of lust is a mortal sin, my son, and by far the most immoral. Have you confessed to this sin before?"

Jerry knew that Father Boyle already knew the answer to this. The first couple of times he confessed, it was a fairly straightforward matter. Three Hail Mary's and a good Act of Contrition and he was absolved.

But he had noticed that on the last few occasions, the old priest had almost been challenging Jerry's sincerity that he was truly sorry for what he had done.

That was not his job. He had no right to question the penitent on whether or not they were truly sorry. Priests were there to listen and absolve, not judge.

What business of his was it to stand in judgment?

Jerry cleared his throat, conscious of the fact that with Father Boyle sitting back, he might have to raise his voice for the old man to hear. "Yes, Father, I have had to confess this sin before, and you absolved me." Jerry kept his voice down to a whisper but projected it far enough so that the priest could hear.

He only hoped that no one sitting outside the confessional could make out his words.

"And was your victim on this occasion the same one as before?"

Father Boyle's words shocked him like cold water being thrown in his face.

The first time he had confessed to this sin, Jerry had made the mistake of revealing all to the priest about Sorcha, including her age and the fact that he was in a position of responsibility and trust as her mentor.

The priest had obviously been shocked at the revelation but, nonetheless, seemed to almost have pity for Jerry, assuring him that if he did not yield to such a monstrous act in the future, should a similar circumstance arise, he could be sure of God's forgiveness.

Now, his forgiveness seemed a little on the thin side.

Furthermore, Jerry hated the fact that Father Boyle referred to Sorcha as 'his victim'.

After all, Jerry was the one with everything to lose, not her.

He was the one who remained at her mercy, and she knew it. The little minx was just toying with him like a cat with a mouse trapped in a corner. She knew exactly what she was up to, it was not as if he held her down and raped her. She was every bit as willing as he was.

But how could he make the old priest understand that she was the one manipulating him, not the other way round?

"Well, my son. I need your answer."

"Yes, Father," Jerry hissed, his mouth pressed against the wooden slats.

Father Boyle took in a deep breath, releasing it slowly through his teeth. "Why do you continue to put yourself in such a position?" he asked, the annoyance in his voice obvious.

"It's not my fault, Father," Jerry whined. "It's my job, I have to go there, and this wicked woman knows that and tortures me with her sexual prowess. She knows I am not strong enough to resist her temptation."

Father Boyle moved in closer, causing Jerry to jerk back.

"Woman. Woman. She is only a girl, both in God's eyes and in that of the law. She is in no position to take advantage of you, you are the adult in this situation and must take full responsibility for your actions. You and you alone carry the burden of this evil deed, and if you were truly sorry you would report this to the police and throw yourself on the mercy of the court."

Jerry could feel himself physically starting to shake.

It was a combination of fear and anger welling up inside him and he gripped the edge of the wooden shelf in front of him to help stall the eruption of vitriol he wanted to spew forth.

How could the priest threaten him with the law?

That was a worldly matter and no business of his.

Jerry began breathing through his mouth alone. Beads of perspiration sprouted out on his forehead and dribbled down his face. Some meandered into his eyes, and he had to wipe them away with his fingers to stop the stinging.

Jerry knew enough about his faith to realise that no priest, no matter how self-righteous, would ever dare to break the seal of the confessional. For to do so would mean his instant defrocking, the church was very clear on the subject. Priests who had heard confessions from murderers risked prosecution before revealing what they had been told in confession.

Jerry began to calm down. He knew that Father Boyle held no power over him as to whether he went to the police or not.

All he needed was to be absolved, and his life could go on as before.

The next time Sorcha flaunted her filthy wares in his face, he would merely seek out a different priest on the mainland to absolve him.

"Father," Jerry continued, trying to keep his breathing under control. "I have made a full and honest confession here today, so now will you please give me absolution. God knows I'm sorry for my actions, and I will endeavour not to let the situation repeat itself again, you have my word."

Father Boyle paused before replying. "Take care, my son, God sees into your heart. Absolution is worth nothing if you are not truly sorry."

Jerry opened his mouth to speak, then closed it when he heard the priest muttering the words of absolution.

"When the old man was finished, Jerry asked. "And for my penance, Father?"

"Have you your rosary on you?"

"Yes, Father."

"Then say the whole rosary plus an Act of Contrition before you leave the church. And may God give you the strength to do what is right and just."

Jerry thanked him and made the sign of the cross before standing up and exiting the confessional.

As he opened the door, he almost knocked over old Mother Scanlan. He apologised, even though it was her fault for standing so close to the box, rather than staying in her seat to wait her turn.

She scowled at him as Jerry held the door open for her.

He could not help but wonder if she had been standing

outside the door during his entire confession. As one of the biggest gossips on Manus it would not have surprised him if she had.

If so, had she heard what he had said to the priest? There was no way of challenging her. The look she had given him was the same one she always had etched on her miserable face, unless she was about to reveal some juicy scandal, then, and then only, did the recipient see her smile.

Jerry strode down the aisle, purposefully.

He would save his penance for when he reached home.

Chapter Nine

As the evening wore on, and Gypsy had finished her milk and disappeared back out through her cat flap, Marie went back to her room and started The Exorcist.

Janine had been looking forward to reading the book herself that evening. However, she decided not to put up an argument. For one thing she was pleased to see her daughter reading an actual book as opposed to something on her phone.

Furthermore, she felt that flipping through the Tim O'Brien book might be more beneficial for her work, especially as she intended to interview him as a local celebrity once Father Boyle provided her with his contact details.

She settled herself into one of the comfortable armchairs in the living room with her note pad on her knee and began to study the author's biography which was written on the back page.

As the priest had mentioned earlier, Tim was a local man who, according to the write-up had once taught history at the local school. He had subsequently written several books concerning both the Isle of Manus as well as a couple of titles based on towns on the mainland.

His subject matter was steeped in legend and folklore-as the title suggested-going back several hundred years, and as a result of their popularity he had been able to give up his teaching position and take up writing full time.

Janine felt a tiny stab of envy for the man. Like so many journalists she too had always dreamed of writing a successful novel and subsequently turning the undertaking into a career.

Until now she had always used playing hostess to Mike's career and bringing up Marie, as well as holding down a job in her own right as her excuse for not having the time to sit down and begin mapping out her novel. But, now with Mike gone and Marie growing up faster than she would have liked, Janine knew that it was time to stop relying on outside influences and buckle down to the task at hand.

Although Tim O'Brien had not actually written any novels, Janine wondered if she could quiz him for any tips on how to start her literary journey. So many novelists began their writing careers as journalists she was confident that she already had the foundation for the task. The rest was up to her.

The first chapter introduced Manus to the reader explaining how the first settlers arrived from the mainland and how over time, as more of them arrived, the villages and finally the town were established.

It hinted at several local customs, legends and myths, each one with its own footnote promising more detail in a subsequent chapter.

Janine read about a local beauty spot called Westside Cliff, which promised gorgeous views out to sea as far as the eye could see. Further on, it mentioned that the landmark was also popular with those who decided to take their own lives resulting in some of the locals renaming it *suicide cliff*.

One such victim was a lady by the name of Molly McShane, who was one of the first documented cases, and the footnote specified that she had become known locally as *The Banshee Bride*.

There was a chapter dedicated to her further on in the book, and Janine turned to it and bent down the corner of the first page as a reminder for her to read that chapter next.

At 8 pm the clock on the mantle struck the hour.

Janine was eager to continue with her reading, but she was also aware that she had not prepared anything for their dinner and knowing Marie she would be venturing down soon in search of sustenance.

Reluctantly, Janine put down her book on the table and went into the kitchen.

She opened the fridge and studied the array of food she had purchased earlier.

Being so engrossed in her book, Janine was happy to settle for some bread, cheese and wine. But she wanted to at least offer her daughter a hot meal on their first night in the cottage.

She realised that she should have bought some baked beans. Cheese on toast smothered in the saucy pulses was a firm favourite of Marie's, but as it was, they were off the menu.

Fried eggs and sausage with bread and butter appeared to be the best option, and at least it would be hot and filling.

Just then, Janine heard the sound of footsteps descending he stairs.

A moment later, Marie entered the kitchen.

"Ah, just in time," announced Janine, "I was about to shout up to see what you fancied for dinner."

"Did you get any steak?" asked Marie eagerly. "Or steak and kidney pie?"

Janine sighed. "Er, no, the only meat I bought was sausage. I could do you a sausage sarnie, or how about egg and sausage sarnies, with the yolks running out, just the way you used to like them?"

Marie, looking unimpressed with the offer, moved in beside her mum and studied the contents of the fridge. "Not a lot of choice on offer," she remarked, sullenly.

"Well, you could have come shopping with me as I suggested," replied Janine, shouldering Marie, playfully.

Marie stood up, evidently unimpressed with what was on offer. "Don't suppose, as it's our first night here that we could go out for dinner? Find a nice pub with draught Guinness and a decent menu?"

Janine sighed. Much as she would have preferred to stay in and read her book, she reminded herself that this was supposed to be a holiday for Marie, as well as a working one for her.

A gentle stroll through the town on a summer's evening might be just the thing to keep their sense of mother-daughter bonding intact.

Janine closed the fridge door. "As ideas go, that's not a bad one at that," she replied. "Grab your coat, it's bound to be chilly on our way home."

With a shriek of delight, Marie spun around on the spot and ran back up the stairs, shouting back, "I won't be a minute."

Janine smiled. She knew her daughter only too well. Even a night out with her mother called for make-up. Marie had a natural prettiness which Janine was not the only one to comment on. As a result, she had taught her that, unlike some of the other girls she hung around with, Marie only needed a light smattering of make-up to enhance her already beautiful face.

Even without any make-up, Marie could still turn heads. But Janine appreciated her daughter's insistence on wearing some. It reminded her of when she was her age.

He sky was more black than grey when by the time they left the cottage, and the first sprinkling of stars dotted the night sky.

They walked to the end of the cul-de-sac and stood there for a while before deciding which way to go.

Down one side of the street, the market stalls stood watch over the pavements, covered over in their thick canvas shrouds to protect them from the elements.

The bleakness of their monolith-like structures seemed a million miles away from the inviting welcome Janine had experienced from their owners earlier in the day.

Behind the forgotten stalls, the steeple from the church gazed down over the town like some stern guardian keeping watch over its errant subjects.

Looking in the other direction, the girls could see distant lights which heralded life of some description, so they took off in that direction instead.

Marie shivered from a sudden gust of wind and linked arms with her mother as they walked towards the light. It was a gesture which took Janine somewhat by surprise as Marie had not offered it for as long as she could remember.

Once Marie had reached thirteen, she decided that, in order to assert her independence, one of the habits she needed to dispense with was holding hands and linking arms with her parents when they went out. Gradually, this liberation came to include hugging, kissing, and referring to her parents as mummy and daddy. Although she was not averse to using the title of 'Daddy' when she wanted something which she knew Janine would not approve of or agree to.

When they reached the end of the street, both women were struck by the array of bars and restaurants in sight. They both felt an immediate warmth flood through them as they observed couples and families meandering through the streets, gazing into the various windows of the eateries on offer, studying the menus before deciding which venue to enter for their evening meal.

A couple of the bars appeared to be full of rowdy men and boisterous women cheering and shouting at the large television screens propped high above the bar. From a quick glance, it was obvious to Janine that there was a football match on which the patrons clearly had a vested interest in.

Marie loitered for a moment outside one of them, gazing in

as if interested in the goings on, so Janine gently tugged her and reminded her that she was too young for such a place.

Marie rolled her eyes but moved on regardless. She knew that her mother at least suspected that she was no stranger to pubs. Like so many girls of her age, Marie could make herself appear much older than her years with the right clothes and a touch of make-up.

It had not escaped Janine's notice that when her daughter went out for a night with the girls, she always carried a sports bag wherein, she suspected, Marie hid the outfit she intended wearing for the evening, along with her make-up, the plan being to change at one of her girlfriend's homes so that Janine was none the wiser.

Or so she thought!

Janine believed that – although Marie might think otherwise – she gave her daughter enough freedom to enjoy her teenage years without completely releasing her grip on the reins.

At Marie's age Janine had not been afforded such a luxury from her own mother, and she always remembered the promise she made to herself that if she were ever to become a mother, she would treat her offspring with more laxity and allow them the privilege of taking responsibility for their own actions, only stepping in if absolutely necessary.

Further down the street, they came across what appeared to be a more family-friendly restaurant. As they approached, they noticed a family of four reading the menu posted just outside the main entrance, before nodding their heads and venturing in.

To Janine, his was a good sign.

The menu did indeed cater for all ages and tastes, and gazing through the window, it appeared as if there were plenty of available tables.

"What do you think?" Janine asked. "Looks nice and cosy."

"Mmn," Marie replied, still perusing the menu. "Are you

going to give me a hard time in front of the staff if I want some wine, or a pint of Guinness?" she asked, suspiciously, still keeping her focus on the menu.

"You can have one or the other," Janine replied, sternly, unable to prevent a smile creeping across her lips.

Chapter Ten

Jerry sat back against the wooden bench, throwing his head back as he took another large swig from his bottle of Bushmills.

Having left the church with a flea in his ear from Father Boyle, Jerry was too het up to go straight home. He needed to walk to burn off some of the frustration and anger he could feel bubbling up inside him.

Just who did that old priest think he was to suggest that Jerry hand himself into the police? What right did he have to accuse Jerry of abusing his position as a social worker? Did he have even the slightest idea of how demanding such a role could be? No, of course not.

No one put demands on you when you were a man of the church, sitting aloft in your ivory tower, passing judgment on those who flocked to your service week in and week out, holding onto your every word as if you were some sort of direct conduit to God himself.

Meanwhile, men such as Jerry had to live in the real world with all the trials and tribulations that came with it. His employer did not give him a free house to live in with no concern for the cost of the amenities, or where the next meal was coming from.

A job for life and a comfortable retirement to look forward to once you had outlived your usefulness, that was all the likes of Father Boyle had to contend with.

Plus, all that nonsense about staying pure and righteous, not indulging in the sins of the flesh – sheer hogwash!

Jerry had heard enough stories about priests who dishonoured their calling by abusing choirboys the moment their parents' backs were turned. They were just as bad as the rest of society, willing to succumb to the sin of temptation whilst still hiding behind a thin veneer of respectability.

Yet with all that, the old priest had the audacity to insinuate that Jerry's sin was beyond the pale and demand that he relinquish his freedom in order to redeem himself.

Meanwhile, what blame did he aim at Sorcha Brown's door? None, that's what.

That was something a priest could never understand. Even though he had never even met the girl in his mind, she was as pure as the driven snow. A young, vulnerable teenager who was in need of help, encouragement and protection from the outside world, which had conspired to bring her down and make her feel unworthy.

Even if Jerry had somehow managed to contrive a meeting between the two of them, that wicked minx would act all coy and shy as she had done the first time they had met.

Knowing that the priest would not succumb to her temptations, she would doubtless go out of her way to impress him and act as if the proverbial 'butter would not melt'.

Naturally, Father Boyle, the fine and noble Father Boyle, would swallow the she-wolf's tactics hook, line and sinker.

Therefore, a poor victim such as Jerry would stand no chance in trying to put his side forward, whether it was to the priest, his employers, or the police.

What thanks would he receive after all he had done for those bitches? He would end up with a lengthy prison sentence while Sorcha stood in the dock in floods of tears, bemoaning how Jerry, who was meant to be her social and spiritual advisor, had taken advantage of her, abusing her in an unforgivable and monstrous way.

No, the likes of Father Boyle would never understand the true way of the world.

Jerry knocked back another large swallow. The liquid fire coursed down his throat, burning his insides and hitting his stomach like a flaming arrow.

Jerry lifted his bottle and studied the remains. He had already drunk far more than he had intended when he first made the purchase. The level was already down past the halfway mark of the label. Ordinarily, he knew better than to drink so much on an empty stomach, but his dealings with Father Boyle had left him raging and in need of fortification.

Having left the church, Jerry stormed out of the churchyard, brushing past those who loitered in the grounds after the service, gossiping and putting the world to rights.

He mumbled an apology to those he actually made contact with, even though it was their fault for meandering in front of him while he was trying to make a break for the main gate.

Jerry heard a few mutterings from behind as he went, and for a moment was sorely tempted to turn back and let spew a tirade of abuse just to shock their sensibilities and give them a taste of what it was like to be on the receiving end for once.

Those church-going holier-than-thou hypocrites made his blood boil.

But miraculously, he managed to keep his tongue in check and simply walked away as quickly as he could. He spent the next half hour trudging through the streets muttering under his breath, cursing the sheer temerity of the old priest for daring to side with his charge over him.

Finally, he found himself outside an off-licence, and he knew from past experience that whiskey was the only cure for the way he was feeling. Although Jerry had some at home, he was still not in the mood to return there just yet. Not until he had his temper under control and his anxiety level normalised.

He took his purchase, clutched against his chest, to Bishop's Park on the other side of town. Cutting through some of the back streets saved him a good half hour on his journey.

Jerry knew that it was still too early for the local louts to be out, hanging around the park entrance, accosting every woman who dared to venture through after sunset. But it was also late enough so that parents who took their children there during the day to play would have left.

Other than the occasional dog-walker, it was the perfect place for him to sit in peace and enjoy his refreshment.

Jerry had climbed to the top of one of the larger hills inside the park, which afforded him a distant view of the sea off to one side. Once he was sure that there were no prying eyes watching him, he began to drink in earnest.

Alone with his thoughts and his single malt, Jerry continued to fume.

Glancing once more at his bottle, he shook it to give the remaining liquid the semblance of being higher in volume than was the case. He knew that he should leave the park before he became too drunk to stand, let alone walk home.

Jerry's anger had not sufficiently abated to allow him to feel at ease, and given the chance he would gladly have thrown his bottle with the remainder of its contents at the nearest wall in his rage. But he also knew that the temporary release that would afford him would not make up for the waste of good scotch.

Placing the bottle inside his coat pocket, Jerry stood up.

For a moment the world spun before his eyes, and he grabbed onto the edge of the bench to assist his balance. He stood there for a moment, hoping that he had not already past the point of no return. There were worse situations to be in, but even so he did not relish the prospect of spending the night on the park bench.

Once he had regained his balance, Jerry released a long pent-up breath through his nostrils and started walking towards the east side of the park, which was the closest side to his home.

In the distance he could hear the sound of the waves lapping against the beach, and the *hoot* of an owl, wakened from its slumber.

As he continued to take a few unsteady steps towards his exit, Jerry mumbled curses at Father Boyle and the office for which he stood.

He wished that the old priest was right here now, he would give him a piece of his mind and no mistake. Set him right on a few facts of life and open his eyes to the hypocritical underbelly of his calling.

Jerry fumbled in his pocket for his bottle, suddenly in need of another swig.

In the distance he could hear a far-a-way whistle like the high-pitched screech of train from days gone by. He tried to ignore it and concentrate on removing his bottle from the folds of material it was presently caught in, but the noise seemed to grow in intensity with each passing second, piercing the night and resounding in his ear drums.

As he finally manged to free his bottle, the whistle turned into a scream which sent a bolt of pain through both his ears, forcing him to release his scotch to cover them.

The bottle landed on the concrete floor shattering into a million pieces.

Jerry cursed his loss, but trying to block out the noise in his ears became his major focus. He looked around him for a cause of it, but there was nothing within sight that looked out of place or appeared to be the cause.

Jerry pressed his index fingers inside his ears to try and block out the sound.

He could feel the wind around him whipping up into a gale which caused the trees to sway above him and leaves which had fallen to the ground to fly around him in a frenzy of attack.

As he fought against the strength of the breeze, the scream seemed to rise in pitch causing him to close his eyes and cry out against the pain erupting in his head.

After a moment, he opened his eyes once more, unable to understand why he could not see where, or what, the noise emanated from.

It was then that he saw it.

Away in the distance, a billowing ripple of white, possibly a sheet which had been swept off a washing line by the rising wind. It fluttered towards him with immediate purpose, and even from this distance Jerry could tell that it was making a beeline in his direction.

The shrill screech filled the air around him and Jerry crouched down on his haunches in the vain hope that being closer to the ground might help to block it out.

His intoxicated state caused him to lose his balance. Eager not to remove his fingers from his ears, Jerry fell sideways and landed hard on his right hip and shoulder.

The shock from the fall sent a new shiver of pain through him, and Jerry lay on his side for a moment trying to absorb the blow.

The *sheet* grew closer.

But now it appeared to have taken on a more solid form.

It entered the park, floating with direct purpose over the fence.

Jerry could not take his eyes off it. The pain in his head was multiplying by the second and he believed that his head would explode if he could not find a way to block it out.

He squinted up as the white form hovered above him.

It was no longer just a figureless form.

As he stared up in terror, he could see that the thing had a face. It glared down at him the features though somewhat imprecise were twisted into a mask of hatred.

An aperture appeared where the mouth should be. As it grew wider the sound which had been deafening Jerry grew in volume until he could feel his eardrums start to burst.

A scream caught in his throat as Jerry fell back on the concrete, his eyes wide in terror.

Chapter Eleven

JANINE POURED THE LAST OF THE WINE INTO MARIE'S glass. Her daughter's eyes widened at the gesture and a huge smile spread across her face.

"Wow, Mum, are you sure?"

Janine nodded. "I know it doesn't compare with Orlando, but I have to accept-however slowly, that you're growing up too fast for me to keep thinking of you as my little girl. Even though, that's all you will ever be."

"Oh, Mum, please don't ruin it." Marie flushed red and glanced around to ensure that no one else was close enough to hear her mother's words.

They had enjoyed a wonderful meal. Marie's eyes lit up when she saw steak and kidney pudding on the menu which had been her favourite meal since childhood.

They both enjoyed a pate to start, and Janine tucked into a very well-prepared piece of sirloin. Marie had her Guinness which she savoured during the meal, knowing that she would not be allowed another.

Janine chose the house red, and when she compared the cost of the two glasses which she intended to drink she realised that it would be more economical to order a full bottle, just in case she fancied another half-glass later on.

As it turned out, even after a third glass there was still the best part of another left in the bottle, which was why she poured it into her daughter's glass, even though she did not ask for it.

The warmth from the meal made Janine feel sleepy. But she had to admit, if even only to herself, that it was more a combination of the day's events which relaxed her. The day had begun with Marie being the usual sullen teen her mother had come to accept. But since the arrival of Gypsy she had certainly perked up.

During the meal they had talked and even laughed together in such a way that Janine could not remember the last time they had done so.

For one thing, Marie had not so much as glanced at her phone once since they had sat down. The entire evening gave Janine hope that this trip was not going to be the disaster she had foreseen since informing Marie that she was not going to visit her father for the holidays.

They even shared a joke about Mike's new wife and her latest bout of plastic surgery, which, although it made Janine feel a tad wicked about, she joined Marie in her laughter with reckless abandon.

They clinked glasses and Marie took her first sip.

Raising her eyebrows, she commented, "Oh, that is nice, good choice, Mum."

"I know, I was quite shocked considering it is only the house red."

"You can really taste the fruit," Marie gushed. "We should see if they sell this in the supermarket. I bet it would go lovely with crusty bread and cheese."

"And spicy pickle, with crisps on the side," Janine agreed.

Marie nodded, excitedly, savouring her next sip.

"Would either of you care to see the dessert menu?" Their waitress appeared by the side of the table, her pad and pen in hand.

Janine glanced a Marie who shook her head. "No, thank you, not for me, that pie was lovely, but very filling."

"Is that why you couldn't finish it?" Janine enquired, indicating towards the chunks of meat and gravy Marie had pushed to the corner of her plate.

"No, actually," Marie looked up at their waitress, "I was hoping that maybe you could put this in some tin foil for me to take home?"

"Take home," replied Janine, surprised by her daughter's remark.

"Yes, for Gypsy. She's bound to be hungry when she gets in."

Janine nodded. She was glad that Marie had taken so quickly to the cat. Unlike most children she had never expressed any interest in owning a pet of her own.

"Of course," replied the waitress. "Is Gypsy your dog?"

Marie shook her head. "Our cat, a newfound friend."

The waitress winked at her. "I'll see if there's any worthwhile scraps left in the kitchen that might tempt your feline friend. How about you, madam," she continued, "anything for dessert?"

Janine shook her head. "No, thank you. That steak was lovely."

Their waitress smiled as she slipped her pad and pen back in her apron before clearing away their plates. As she leaned over the table to reach Marie's a soft moan slipped from her lips.

"Are you okay?" asked Marie, concerned.

"Oh, I'm fine and dandy, thank you. This is my first day on the job, and to be honest, my poor feet are killing me."

"I waitressed when I was at university," Janine responded. "It does nothing for your feet or your back. I sympathise, I was glad to see the back of that job."

"Is this all you could find, or are you looking for something less physically demanding?" asked Marie. "It sounds like you need it."

The waitress stood up, balancing both plates on her right forearm. "Oh, this is only a temporary fix at the insistence of my mother," she began. "Between us, she caught me out late last night with my boyfriend, or ex-boyfriend to be exact. So, this is my punishment, get a job until school starts again, or go with her and sit in the waiting room at the medical centre where she works until her shift is over, so she can keep an eye on me."

"Tough choice," Marie offered.

"I take it your mum does not approve of your choice in men?" Janine chimed in.

He waitress laughed. "You could say that. Worst of all, she was right. He was such a pig. Do you know," she leant in closer as if about to relay some secret plot. "We were walking along the beach las night when we literally tripped over a dead body."

Both Janine and Marie reeled back in shock.

"I know," replied the waitress as if answering their silent question. "The poor thing was only in her thirties. Heart attack, or so the doc reckoned, tragic really. But if that were not enough, my creep of a boyfriend still wanted to make out while we were waiting for the ambulance. I ask you, sick or what?"

"You poor thing," replied Janine. "No wonder you dumped him."

"Try telling my mother that. I kept insisting that I'd never have anything to do with him again, but she still made me take this job, so I wasn't free to go back on my word."

"As a mother, I can see where she is coming from. At least she knows where you are." Janine offered. "Perhaps after she cools down and sees what a strain this job is for you, she'll relent."

The waitress huffed. "Have you met my mother?"

Both Janine and Marie laughed together.

"Are you both here on holiday?"

Marie nodded. "Yes, my mum is a journalist and is writing a story about the island. Here, Mum, you should interview… Sorry, I've forgotten your name already." Sarah had introduced herself when she first came to serve at their table, but clearly her name had not stuck with Marie.

"Sarah, Sarah Byrne. Put-upon daughter of this parish," replied the waitress.

"I'm Marie, nice to meet you. Mum, you should interview Sarah about last night and the body she found."

Janine looked surprised. "Well, to be honest, it's not really that sort of piece I'm writing," she answered, apologetically. "It's more to do with local culture and folklore."

"Yeah, but wouldn't this be an exciting twist?" Marie added, excitedly.

"Not really," admitted Janine. "It may sell to the tabloids, but I've been tasked with a different style of journalism altogether. Sorry," she turned to Sarah and smiled.

Sarah held up her free hand. "No problem, I've already been interviewed by one of our locals, and he was a pain in the arse, to be quite frank. Oh, not that you would be I'm sure," she said to Janine, her cheeks suddenly flushed with blood.

Both Janine and Marie burst out laughing.

Chapter Twelve

When Sarah returned with their bill, she placed a small paper take-away bag on the table next to Marie. When Marie peered inside, she saw a foil carton with a cardboard lid secured by the folded edges of the container.

"There's some nice little tit bits for Gypsy," Sarah whispered. "Don't tell the boss."

Marie laughed and thanked her.

The girls continued talking while Janine fished out her credit card. She smiled to herself that her daughter seemed to have found a friend after only one day on the island.

Marie had never been the most sociable of individuals from Janine's perspective. She still remembered taking her to an open evening for her primary school when she was five. So many girls seemed drawn to Marie that Janine felt sure that she would soon make friends. But Marie seemed to have different ideas and complained on the way home in the car about what a nuisance it had been that so many girls had insisted on introducing themselves to her when all she wanted was to look around the school.

Over time, her attitude did not improve by much. Although

she was often invited over for parties and sleepovers by her classmates, she seldom attended, preferring to sit at home and read or watch television.

Janine had hoped that buying Marie her first mobile might broaden her horizons when it came to keeping in touch with friends on social media, but it soon became apparent that she was as particular about who she allowed into her virtual circle as she was in her physical one.

The one consolation-which had been Janine's biggest fear-was that Marie was never bullied at school. Or at least she never complained of it. She may have been aloof, some might even say rude, but at least the other girls did not seem to hold that against her.

Janine sat quietly listening to the two girls chatting while she held her credit card in her hand.

Eventually, Sarah noticed it and apologised for keeping her waiting.

Before she put Janine's payment through, Sarah glanced over her shoulder then leaned in towards her to whisper. "One of the other girls told me that the manager keeps all the tips that customers put through electronically," she explained. "It's a lovely gesture, but he doesn't deserve it. May I remove the gratuity amount from your bill before I put it through?"

"Yes, please," Janine smiled.

"He shouldn't be allowed to do that," Marie piped up. "Isn't there something you can do about it?"

"It isn't worth making a fuss over. This is only my first night, and some of the girls have worked here for ages, so I don't want to get them into trouble," Sarah explained, placing the card-reader back in front of Janine for her to type in her code.

"Bastard!" Marie replied, shaking her head. "Isn't he supposed to be your mother's friend?"

Sarah shrugged. "Well, more of an old acquaintance if I'm honest."

Before Janine handed back the machine, she removed a fiver from her purse and slid it across the table to Sarah with a crafty wink.

Sarah blushed as she reached for the money, surreptitiously slipping it into her apron pocket. "Thank you," she mouthed silently, tearing off Janine's receipt and handing it to her along with her card.

"Let's swap numbers," Marie announced, taking out her mobile.

Janine pretended not to be surprised by her daughter's suggestion. This was indeed the first time she had ever known her to want to make a friend this fast.

While the girls scanned their numbers across to each other, Janine put her card and receipt away and finished what was left in her glass.

Suddenly, something caught Sarah's eye. "Oh, no, that's all I need."

Janine and Marie followed her gaze towards the main front of the restaurant.

They saw a young man leering in the window, his nose pressed against the glass with a ridiculous grin on his face.

"A friend of yours?" asked Janine.

Sarah sighed. "Remember that moron of a boyfriend I told you about," she indicated towards the window.

"How did he know you'd be here?" Marie asked, curiously.

Sarah shrugged. "In this town, nothing is held sacred for long. If my mother finds out, she'll never believe it was a coincidence. She'll probably chain me to the radiator in the basement for the rest of the holidays."

Janine could not help but laugh.

Marie turned to look at her. "It's not funny," she scolded. "Stalking's against the law, we could call the police."

"Thanks," replied Sarah, "but I doubt Constable Clark would take it seriously."

"Do you think he plans on coming in and causing a scene?" Janine asked, her parental concern taking over.

Sarah shook her head. "I doubt it. We close in fifteen minutes. He'll probably wait outside until I leave, then follow me home. He knows that my mum's at work."

Janine stopped herself from asking about Sarah's father. The fact that she had not mentioned him all evening caused her to suspect that he was not on the scene.

"No problem," said Marie, "we'll walk you home, won't we, Mum?"

Janine was starting to feel the wine take effect, and if she were being honest, she was looking forward to her bed.

That said, she was so taken with Marie's concern for the girl that she knew she could not let her down. "Of course, we will," she confirmed.

"Oh, thank you both so much for the kind offer, but I live on the other side of town. It'll take you ages to make the round trip," Sarah explained. "Please don't worry, I'll just have to deal with the idiot myself." She glanced back at the window.

Janine and Mare followed her gaze once more.

Her ex-boyfriend was clearly not alone. He was now laughing and joking with two older-looking men. All three of them were drinking beer from bottles, and judging by their behaviour, they were not on their first of the night.

Janine felt an eerie chill pass down her spine.

Watching the three drunken louts push and shove each other about outside made her re-think Marie's proposal. Even with herself in tow, she no longer felt comfortable walking out at night across town with two vulnerable girls.

"Tell you what," she said, "how about we all take a cab back to our place, just to throw him off the scent. Then later I can call you another one to take you home. We can phone your mum from there to let her know what's happened. What do you say?"

"Brilliant," replied Marie, excitedly. "You can help me feed Gypsy."

Sarah looked nervous. "No, really, that's very kind of you, but I don't want to be a nuisance. And my mum will hit the roof if I tell her that Declan was waiting for me outside work."

"Why? It's not your fault the prat won't take a hint," Marie said, her temper starting to boil.

Sarah laughed. "You don't know my mother. Regardless of the circumstances, it's always my fault."

"I know that feeling," Marie agreed.

"Hey!" Said Janine. "I'm sitting right here, you know."

They all shared a laugh together.

Just then, Sarah noticed her manager watching her from the other end of the restaurant. "Oops, I'd better start to look busy, don't want to be sacked on my first night."

"When does your shift end?" asked Janine.

"Only about ten minutes to go," Sarah replied. "But he obviously wants blood."

"Okay then, once you're free to go, call us a cab, you're coming home with us, no arguments," insisted Janine.

"Too right," Marie chimed in.

Janine could tell that Sarah was about to object once more. "I'll speak to your mother, I'm sure we can sort things out amicably," Janine assured her.

Sarah thanked them both before rushing away to see what her boss wanted.

For all her bravado, Janine knew that the girl was relieved for the offer and looking out at the three men in the street, she could understand why.

"Thanks, Mum," said Marie, out of the blue. "You're a real star."

Janine smiled. "I have moments."

Chapter Thirteen

Their cab arrived within five minutes of being called. The three women waited inside the restaurant until it pulled up outside the main door.

Unfortunately, from where the cab was parked, it was still possible for Declan and his cronies to see the main door through the restaurant's glass front.

"Okay, we all ready?" Janine asked, cheerfully.

"Ready to go," replied Marie.

Sarah merely smiled, nervously.

Janine could tell from the girl's demeanour that she was not overly eager at the prospect of coming face-to-face with her ex outside on the pavement.

Janine had hoped that the driver might open the back door for them to climb in, thus making their exit smoother and with less chance of being accosted by the three men. But after a moment or two, she soon realised that the driver preferred to sit in his seat and gaze out of the window rather than demonstrate chivalry.

That would cost him his tip, so his loss.

Sarah glanced back over her shoulder towards the main

window, hoping that Declan and his mates were too busy acting up to notice them leaving. But to her dismay, she saw him nudging his friends and starting to make his way around to their side.

Janine opened the door and ushered the two girls out.

There was a sharp wind which whistled down the street as they exited the restaurant.

Janine rushed to the back door of the cab and yanked it open, keeping her back towards the three men as they rushed towards them.

Marie climbed in first so that Sarah could be in the middle, cocooned between her and her mother.

As Sarah bent down to enter the cab, they heard a cry from behind.

"Sarah, babe, where ye goin'?"

Sarah turned back, but Janine told her to ignore the call and slide over next to Marie.

Suddenly, Janine felt Declan at her back. "Sarah, oi, I'm talkin' to you," he called in a demanding manner.

Janine considered just slipping in beside the girl and slamming the door behind her. But something told her that such an action would not fit the bill. As much as she would have preferred to avoid any confrontation with the men, she realised that without it they were too Neanderthalic to take the hint.

Leaning against the jamb for support, Janine turned slowly to face the men.

Declan was so close that she could smell the alcohol on his breath. His two goons stood directly behind him, both still slugging from their cans.

"May I help you?" Janine asked, fixing Declan with a strong stare which conveyed her lack of mood for his antics.

Declan leered at her, showing a mouth with several missing teeth. "You certainly can, young lady," he drawled. "That's my girlfriend you've got there in the back, and I'm here to accompany her home, like."

Janine pulled a face and leaned back as far as she could from his fetid breath.

The action was not wasted on Declan. "What's wrong, do I stink or summink?"

"Well, your breath certainly leaves something to be desired," Janine replied, waving her hand in front of her face. "Would you mind taking a step back, please."

Her words clearly shocked Declan.

His two mates started laughing, clearly impressed.

Declan turned back to face them. "Oi," he yelled, pushing the nearest one away.

"Mum, please get in the car," Marie called from inside the cab.

"What's going on?" the driver demanded, half-turning in his seat to see what was happening. "I don't want no trouble, see."

"It's no trouble," Marie assured him, trying to keep her voice steady. "We're just about done here."

As Declan turned back to face Janine, she held up her hand to keep him at arm's length. "If you lads will excuse us, I need to get my daughter and niece home before my husband calls the police to come and look for us."

Declan appeared shocked. "Your niece," he stammered, trying to glance behind Janine. "She's your niece? I had no idea." He wiped the spittle from his mouth with the back of his free hand, the other still clutched his can of beer. "Perhaps I could cadge a lift with you, just to make sure you get home safe, and that?"

Janine managed a half-smile. "No thanks, we'll be fine. Goodnight."

Before Declan had a chance to respond, Janine slid inside the cab and slammed the door behind her.

The driver had kept the engine running while waiting at the

kerb. Now, sensing something was not as it should be, without waiting for instructions, he pulled out and sped off down the main road, leaving the three men back on the pavement.

"Thank you," said Sarah, timidly. "I'm sorry to have caused you all this trouble."

"No trouble," Janine assured her. "No wonder your mum is not keen for you to be going out with someone like him. I'm presuming you saw some redeeming qualities in him that were not immediately obvious to the rest of us?"

Sarah laughed. "I think it was the whole bad-boy image thing that did it. He was forever hanging round the school gates trying to chat up one of us. Then one night after Mum and me had an enormous fight about my grades, I just lost it and went down to the pub I knew he frequented."

"Were your grades really that bad?" asked Janine, curiously.

"That was what got me all fired up in the first place," continued Sarah. "I'd aced all my exams, well, the important ones at least, but my physics teacher, Mr Edwards, failed me because I never bothered to write down my calculations, I always do them in my head, and he knew that. I had every answer down pat, but because there was no evidence of how I came to the answers, he refused to give me a grade."

"That's not fair," Piped up Marie. "Why didn't you report him to the head?"

"I was in the process of putting in an appeal, but my mum is old school, and as far as she was concerned, if a teacher said that I'd been cheating, they had no reason to lie, and without her signature on the appeal form the board wouldn't accept it."

"That's ridiculous!" Marie shouted, her anger clearly rising at the injustice. "I would have kicked up a massive stink and plastered what I thought of your physics teacher all over social media."

"That would really have helped the situation," said Janine, sarcastically.

"Oh, come on, Mum, what would you have done if the same thing happened to me?" Marie demanded.

Janine sighed, hoping that such a lovely evening would not end up with an argument. She knew that to avoid such an incident she would have to answer tactically. "Well, for one thing, I'm not as much of a believer in the indomitability of the teaching profession as Sarah's mother. No single person, in my opinion, should be allowed to make such a decision without having to consult with impartial colleagues. It would have been easy enough for Sarah to prove her case by working out a different problem in her head in front of another teacher."

"I wish you were my mother," Sarah exclaimed. "I wouldn't be in this predicament right now if only she'd had a little faith in me."

Janine held up her hand. "Well, while I'm grateful for the compliment, it's easy for me to say how I would have acted, but I'm sure your mother had her reasons for her decision."

"You're right there," agreed Sarah. "She thinks that anyone in authority must be right about everything and the rest of us are just idiots."

This made both Janine and Marie laugh in unison. Even Sarah joined in after a moment.

The cab pulled up outside the cottage and the three women alighted.

Janine went to the driver's window and paid him.

"It's none of me business," he suddenly announced, keeping his voice low as if he did not want the two younger girls to hear. "But those blokes you were talkin' to outside the restaurant, they're a bad lot. I'd keep my distance if I were you."

Janine thanked him and told him to keep the change, deciding that after his well-meaning advice, he now deserved his tip.

They entered the cottage, and Marie made a beeline for the kitchen. When she switched on the light, she was delighted to find Gypsy asleep on the dining table where she had fed her earlier that evening.

Janine was not so impressed with finding the stray moggy on the table where they ate, but seeing the delight in her daughter's reaction, she decided not to say anything.

Sarah and Marie tentatively started stroking the feline, taking care lest the cat should go for them. Marie explained to her new friend that, according to the priest, Gypsy was a stray and possibly feral. However, the reaction from the cat to their fussing showed that she definitely enjoyed the attention.

After a while, Marie excitedly served up the tender morsels Sarah had purloined from the restaurant's kitchen, and together they watched as Gypsy eagerly tucked into her treat.

"Should we try your mother?" Janine asked, taking a seat at the table.

"Yes, good idea," Sarah replied, although her tone made Janine suspect that she was not all that eager to make the call.

Sarah took out her mobile and hit her mum's button.

After a few rings, the woman answered. "Hi, Mum, it's me... No, not yet, we had a little problem at the restaurant and I'm with a lovely lady and her daughter whom I met there... No, I'm at their house... Well, if you'll give me a minute to explain, I'll... No, I'm not in any trouble, will you just give me a minute to tell you?"

Sarah looked at Janine and blushed, clearly embarrassed that she and Marie had to witness the exchange.

"... Mum, if you'll just let me explain, Declan turned up at the restaurant to pick me up after work... No, of course I didn't ask him to, I don't even know how he knew where I'd be... I'm telling you the truth, after last night I was in no hurry to see him so soon... They're customers, the lady noticed Declan waiting for me and offered me a lift to their place so he couldn't follow me home... Don't be absurd, of course not... Will you... Will you just..."

Sighing loudly, Sarah handed her phone over to Janine.

Janine could hear her mother yelling down the receiver even though she was not on loudspeaker.

"She wants to speak to you," Sarah explained. "I'm really sorry about all this, the woman barely lets you get a word in edgewise."

Chapter Fourteen

BRIDGET DONNELLY RUBBED THE LAST OF THE HAND cream between her fingers, interlocking them to ensure that every bit of the moisturiser had seeped in. She lay back against her headboard and adjusted the pillows she had propped up to allow herself a more comfortable position while she watched television.

It had not been a particularly tiring or stressful day for the fifty-five-year-old ex-dinner lady, but she could still feel sleep creeping up on her even though it was a good hour until her usual bedtime.

The 'Z' list celebrities on her television screen were arguing at the top of their voices about their individual relationships, each one vying to make themselves heard above the others. Several of the girls had already begun to choke back tears as they waved their arms in the air, attempting to elucidate a particular point which no one else in the group seemed to understand.

Bridget laughed to herself. Watching others argue amongst themselves had always been a vice of hers, which she refused to admit to anyone she knew. That was why programmes such as the one she was watching were so important to her. The fact that no one on the screen had anything specific or interesting to say made little difference so far as she was concerned. It was more a case of the overall shambolic essence of their life stories which captivated her.

Bridget lived in a four-bedroom house she had inherited from a distant aunt several years earlier. Moving to Manus, she gave up her job back in Cork, and initially, with no mortgage or rent to pay anymore, she ran a stall in the market selling woollens of all descriptions, which she made herself. She had always had a talent for knitting, needlepoint, sewing and the like, so she was happy that she finally had a chance to show off her skills and make some money on the side.

She ran her stall for over a year but soon became bored with the mundanity of the business. Also, keeping a full-time stall in the market was an expensive ambition, and she soon found herself having to raise the price of her wares to afford such an option.

Eventually, Bridget gave back the stall and instead opted to rent one of the smaller ones, which came with a daily rate, leaving her the option of making use of it whenever she felt in the mood. Weekends naturally cost more, but Bridget found a decent enough trade on Fridays, so she often only used the stall once a week. This allowed her more time to craft her clothing without feeling rushed.

The money she made from her weekly trading was healthy, though not enough to keep her buoyant. After a while she could see her savings disappearing due to more mundane expenditure such as gas and electric, food and her shopping trips to the mainland.

So it was that she decided to seek out alternative ways of making ends meet.

Due to her connections from the school where she used to work, Bridget was able to have herself registered as a carer for pre-teens. Her home was smart enough, and she was able to put on a convincing show when the social services representative made an appointment, therefore, she was granted a licence to look after up to two children at a time.

Since then, she had fostered several children, all of whom merely needed a short time away from their parents for domestic reasons, or until a social service investigation had been completed.

The money was not exactly a fortune, but it was easy to earn. All Bridget really had to do was make sure that they were fed and arrived at school on time each day. As most of her charges were already in secondary school, they were quite capable of making their way to the local school unaided, which allowed her more time to spend watching television or making more clothes for her stall.

Even then, Bridget found her savings dwindling, and she knew that if she complained to the social services, she would more than likely have her major source of income re-homed somewhere else.

So it was that she started advertising for a different form of income of a more personal inclination. She was, naturally, careful to keep this new form of engagement a closely guarded secret so as not to raise suspicion amongst the locals, some of whom would be only too happy to report her activities to the proper authorities and have her status as a carer removed. Not to mention the stigma of being marked as a fallen women amongst the tightly knit Catholic community.

As much as Bridget did not give two figs about anyone else's opinion of her, she still had to live there, and as a Catholic she regularly attended mass, so there would be no way of her escaping the scandal if her secret ever got out.

Therefore, Bridget decided to vet each 'gentleman caller' over the internet and on the phone before agreeing to allow them to visit.

She made a point of refusing anyone who claimed to live on Manus, as a way of ensuring that none of the locals would ever suspect her. She often laughed behind the backs of some of the local women, especially the 'holier-than-thou' variety whose husbands had tried to make contact with her. Their pious sheen of respectability held no sway with her, and she often toyed with the idea of writing to them anonymously, just to let them know exactly what their spouses were up to.

But in the end, she decided to let sleeping dogs lie.

There was no point in stirring up trouble in such a small community. Sooner or later, someone was bound to point the finger in her direction as the author of such poison pen letters.

But it still amused Bridget to know their little secret, and that was enough to satisfy her for the present.

She could feel her eyelids starting to close when her phone rang beside her.

Checking the clock on her nightstand, Bridget tutted to herself as she looked at the screen of her mobile. The name emblazed across it read: Dan Trample. Dan was indeed one of her regulars from the mainland, but he knew better than to call her so late to make an appointment.

Bridget was not sure if Dan was, in fact, his real name; it was just the one he had given her when they first made contact. She did not know his surname, but she had always put her customers' names in her phone under the fetishes they liked her to perform for them.

Dean, for example, liked being walked on with high heels. He would merely lie on her bedroom floor, naked, while Bridget trod all over his body wearing a pair of stilettos.

If a customer did not have a specific fetish, then she would simply enter them in her log with their first name followed by the word 'sex'. This indicated that intercourse was all they required.

As a rule, she did not mind indulging in some of their

kinkier rituals. For a start, it meant that she could justify charging them more, whether they wanted full sex afterwards or not. Most of them seemed to accept her terms without fuss or argument, so Bridget presumed that such an arrangement must be the norm when they visited other women of a similar ilk.

There were certain requests which Bridget would not entertain, no matter how much she was offered or how hard a potential client begged. Anything to do with urinating or defecating on them was strictly off the table. As much as she appreciated that some blokes just had odd ways of growing excited, she could not envisage stunts including such bodily fluids. To her, it was just a little too disgusting.

Her only other fast rule was to practise safe sex. Again, some other clients would offer to pay her double her fee not to use a condom, but Bridget was not willing to take the risk, and that was final.

She considered letting the phone go to voicemail, but at the last second changed her mind. Dean was doubtless wanting to make an appointment for the following day, so Bridget did not want to miss out on her fee.

"What time do you call this?" she demanded, abruptly.

"I know, I'm really sorry," Dean spluttered, his voice low and timid, "I'm just really desperate to see you." He almost begged.

"What, you mean tonight!" Bridget scalded. "No way, it's far too late."

"Please, I know it's late, but I had some business in Cork this afternoon, and being so close to the ferry, I couldn't resist coming over on the off chance you'd see me."

Bridget sighed loudly, her frustration evident. "So why didn't you call me earlier before you left the mainland?"

"I know, I know I should have, and I'm very sorry for leaving it 'til the last minute, but I'm across the road from yours now, and I won't take long, please say you'll let me in."

Bridget would have enjoyed refusing him business at such an

hour, especially as Dean had not bothered to make an appointment in advance.

But the money was too good to turn her nose up at, so she decided to relent. After all, he was a regular and never quibbled about the cost.

"I'll warn you now," she stated, "I've already taken off me make-up and I'm in bed, so I can't be doing with dressing up at this late hour just for your pleasure, especially as you never made an appointment."

"Oh, that's absolutely fine," Dean assured her, the relief in his voice undisguised. "So, you'll see me, now?"

"Yes, alright. Just give me a minute. Wait until I open the door, and make sure no one sees you enter."

Bridget snapped off the call before waiting for Dean to answer.

Grumbling to herself, Bridget threw back the covers revealing her naked body. She had always slept in the nude, even on the coldest of winter nights, feeling somehow uncomfortable if she tried wearing pyjamas or a nightie.

She slid her legs over the edge of her bed and slipped her bare feet into her slippers.

Standing, she went to the door and grabbed her silk dressing gown off the hook, fastening the belt around her waist before leaving the room.

As she emerged onto the landing, she heard the sound of bare feet on the small staircase which led up to the bedrooms on the next floor. She switched on the light just as Trevor arrived at the foot of the stairs. The twelve-year-old and his twin sister Scarlett were her latest foster kids and they both occupied the two smallest bedrooms at the top of the house.

"Where do you think yer goin'?" Bridget demanded, walking towards the young boy as he stood frozen to the spot.

"I need to pee," he replied, apologetically.

"Well, you'll just 'ave to keep it in, now get back to bed."

Trevor grabbed himself between the legs, his bottom lip quivering. "I really need to go," he urged. "I'll wet myself otherwise."

Bridget sighed. "Get in there and be quick about it," she demanded, pointing to the toilet at the end of the passage. "You've got ten seconds, or you'll feel me slipper on yer backside, understand?"

Trevor nodded and ran to the toilet.

Bridget waited while the boy finished. There was no way she could let her visitor in while one of the kids was about.

"Hurry up," she yelled, impatiently.

The toilet flushed and the boy came running back out onto the landing.

The relief on his face showed when he saw that Bridget had not removed her slipper as she had threatened.

He ran past her back up the stairs, and seconds later, Bridget heard his bedroom door shut.

She made her way down the stairs. Once in the hallway, she removed her hair grip and ran her fingers through her shoulder-length dyed blond hair. Through the frosted glass of the front door, she could see a shadow loitering.

Opening the door, she let Dean enter.

He mumbled an apology as he moved past her so that she could shut the door.

Bridget ignored his request for forgiveness and held out her hand. Dan removed a pile of notes from his pocket and handed them over. Bridget slipped them into her dressing gown once she was satisfied the full amount was there.

Dean followed Bridget upstairs and into her bedroom, where she closed the door behind them. "Right then," she demanded, "remove your clothes and lie on the floor, now."

Dan obliged, his entire body trembling in anticipation.

Bridget removed her gown and hung it back upon the door.

Opening the top drawer in her nightstand, she removed an

open box of condoms and tore one off the strip, leaving it on the bed for later.

She kicked off her slippers and removed a pair of black stilettos from under her bed, forcing her feet into the pointed toes. They pinched slightly, but she knew she would not have them on for long, so it did not bother her.

Dean left his clothes on a chair by the door. Once he was naked, he lay prone on the floor as instructed, his hands out in front of him.

Bridget moved forward and, using the end of the bed for balance, she placed her feet upon his hands and bore down with her full weight.

She heard Dean release a moan of pleasure.

"Look at you," she observed. "You're a worthless lump of dirt beneath my feet. Now I'm going to show you what happens to dirt. I'm gonna tread all over your worthless body until I think you've learned your lesson."

Chapter Fifteen

IT WAS A FINE, BRIGHT MORNING AS CONSTABLE Clark stood watch over the police cordon which he had set up when he first arrived at Bishop's Park, the scene of Jerry Brooke's demise.

A group of early-morning joggers had stumbled across the dead man, much to the chagrin of several of their elderly members, some of whom even had to be sedated by Doctor Cleary when he arrived to inspect the body. They had now been transported to the local medical centre for observation, while those who had managed to remain coherent had given their statements to Constable Clark before being allowed to return to their homes.

Since then, a call to the mainland had brought an army of paramedics, scene of crime officers, forensic specialists and an assorted array of uniformed and plain clothes officers all under the watchful gaze of the Detective Inspector in charge.

Peter Clark recognised some of them from the previous day when they came to investigate the deaths of Michelle and Emmet Calvert.

As a lowly constable, Peter had learnt that it was far more

prudent – and less stressful – for him to merely stand back and allow the more self-important members of his profession to carry on with their investigation, rather than offer up his assistance as the only official officer on the island.

Doctor Cleary felt more comfortable standing to one side once he had made his initial inspection of the dead man. Although he was a practitioner of considerable experience and was not prone to feeling intimidated, he still felt somewhat overwhelmed when surrounded by the white-suited, hooded and masked forensic experts, all of whom managed to convey – without using actual words – that he was in their way and wasting their valuable time by still being there.

The doctor moved over to where Constable Clerk stood, keeping the gathering spectators at bay. The two men acknowledged each other with a knowing nod of the head.

"Well, I'm no pathologist," admitted Cleary, under his breath, "but I reckon it was a heart attack, plain and simple."

The police officer nodded. "The second one in two days," he observed. "The Chief Constable will not be happy with his end-of-month figures."

Cleary smiled. "Well, at least the corona should be able to discount poor Emmet's death as nothing more than an accident."

Constable Clark turned around to ensure that no one was within hearing distance behind the cordon. Once he was sure, he turned back to the doctor. "What about the look on his face?" he asked, nodding towards the body on the ground. "It seemed similar to that of Michelle Calvert when we found her on the beach."

The doctor thought for a moment. "Facial rictus is not uncommon at the moment of death. The face often contorts as the realisation of impending demise takes over the senses."

Clark nodded. "It was the eyes that got me, same with

Michelle. That wide-eyed stare as if they were gazing upon something grotesque before their hearts gave out."

"I know," agreed the doctor. "I tried to close Jerry's, but the lids refused to move. It was the same with Michelle. Again, not completely uncommon where heart attacks are concerned. If you don't manage to get to the body within two hours of death, rigor mortis often sets in and freezes the muscles in the face. Try as you might, once that happens, you cannot close the eyes until the imbalance has passed."

"How long do you reckon he's been lying here?"

"Maybe eight to ten hours. Certainly not more than twelve, though the post-mortem will tell us for sure."

Just then, they both heard the sound of someone out of breath approaching.

They turned together and saw Father Boyle staggering up the path, his face red and puffy. He stopped just in front of the police cordon and leaned over with his hands on his knees. Several of those gathered at the tape moved aside to allow him access.

Constable Clark walked over and raised the tape above the priest's head.

Father Boyle thanked him in between coughing and trying to catch his breath.

Doctor Cleary patted the old priest on the back, gently. "Steady on there, Father," he advised, "one corpse is enough for one day."

The priest stood up and cleared his throat. In between large gulps of air, he managed to force a few words out. "I... was afraid I might... miss the body being removed... I only just heard and wanted to ensure... that I gave the last rites."

Constable Clark moved forward. "Okay, Father, just give me a second. I'll speak to the DI and let him know what you're about, shouldn't be any trouble."

Father Boyle thanked him, clearing his throat one final time before catching his breath. The priest was not wearing his liturgical vestments but was instead in a black suit with his Roman collar visible around his neck.

He removed his stole from one of his pockets, kissed it, then placed it around his neck in preparation for administering the sacrament. He and the doctor waited while they watched the officer speaking to his superior.

The inspector was a tall, painfully thin man in his late fifties with a pencil moustache and jet-black hair, which appeared dyed. He had it parted over from the extreme left of his scalp just above his ear, and even with the vast amounts of hair oil weighing it down, some strips still rose up when the wind blew in certain directions.

The man turned back to look over at Father Boyle whilst Constable Clark spoke to him.

Eventually, he nodded his assent and asked the forensic team to stand back for a moment while the priest carried out his dutiful task.

Constable Clark signalled for the priest to move in.

While the old priest carried out his duty, the inspector walked over to Doctor Cleary, flicking through his notebook as he went. Peter Clark followed him, keeping a few paces behind. He did not know this particular officer, but he knew from previous experience that some senior officers preferred their subordinates to not crowd them.

"So, in your professional opinion," the inspector began, "this was a heart attack, pure and simple?"

Doctor Cleary nodded. "From what I can tell, yes, officer. There are certainly no outward signs of foul play, though obviously the post-mortem may suggest otherwise."

The inspector nodded, keeping his gaze on his notebook. "And what about the expression on his face?" he asked. "Is that normal for a straight-forward heart attack victim?"

Edmund Cleary rubbed his chin, thoughtfully. "That rictus

grin is not altogether unusual in such cases, it's just rigor mortis. That said…" He trailed off.

The inspector looked up from his notes. "Yes!" he demanded. "Have you something else to add to your diagnosis?"

Doctor Cleary released a long sigh. "I can't say definitively," he admitted, "but in certain cases, depending on the cause of the heart stopping, there is a symptom known as parasympathetic rebound which can also leave the face in such a state."

"Para what?" asked the inspector, holding his pen poised to add the details to his book.

"Parasympathetic rebound," the doctor repeated, emphasising the pronunciation to assist the inspector in spelling it correctly. "Of course, I cannot categorically diagnose the condition from a perfunctory glance, your pathologist will have to decide if that is the case or not."

The inspector nodded. "And just for my own personal account, what exactly causes this infliction to take place?"

Doctor Cleary glanced from the inspector over to the constable and back again, before speaking. "In very extreme instances," he ventured, cautiously, "if someone is terrified, and I wish to emphasise this is only in extreme cases, their whole metabolic system reacts automatically by trying to calm them down. Sometimes, on rare occasions, as a result, the heart stops beating, and it is known to leave the face looking like this." He indicated towards the corpse.

"So, what you're saying is the victim is actually frightened to death?" asked the inspector, incredulously.

Doctor Cleary shrugged. "Effectively, yes."

"And what could cause such a reaction?"

The doctor glanced over at Peter Clark, who dropped his gaze to the floor. It was clear that neither man wished to add speculation to the matter.

Finally, Doctor Cleary replied, "Who can say?"

Chapter Sixteen

JANINE ROSE EARLY THAT MORNING AND CREPT downstairs so as not to wake the girls. She thought it best to let them sleep in as long as they wanted, having doubtless been up half the night chatting.

Although she was forever badgering Marie back home not to waste a precious day off languishing in bed, these circumstances were unique as far as she was concerned. The two girls really seemed to get on, and Janine could not help but smile to herself when she recalled how her daughter's face appeared to light up whenever Sarah suggested something they should do together.

Janine had to admit that she too had taken to the girl. However, in her case, that was due mainly to the fact that Sarah's introduction into their lives came as a breath of fresh air revitalising Marie's otherwise stoic outlook on life.

Her father's decision to pander to his new partner's vanity rather than keep his promise to his only daughter had definitely taken its toll on the girl, but even before that episode Janine had begun to notice her daughter slipping into that bleak, apathetic attitude which so many of her peers seemed to wear like a badge of honour, bordering on depression at the plight of the future of the world they were about to inherit.

In her mind, Janine was already attempting to calculate scenarios where the two girls could visit each other on holiday and the sheer joy she could look forward to seeing on her daughter's face at the prospect.

Such scenarios gave Janine a vengeful satisfaction, which she was not proud of but nonetheless could not help but relish, imagining her ex-husband complaining that their daughter had no time for him anymore and preferred spending time with her new friend.

That would teach him not to be so flippant with his promises.

Of course, such arrangements would have to be with the consent of Sarah's mother.

Having spoken to the woman last night on the phone, Janine could see why Sarah was so reluctant to alter her initial plans to go home after her shift at the restaurant. Naively, she thought that being an adult, as well as a parent of a daughter of a similar age as her own, Sarah's mother might be willing to listen to her explanation as to why Sarah ended up back at the cottage.

But even then, it took three attempts for Janine to straighten out the story as the woman continually kept interrupting and then talking in tangents, hardly allowing Janine to get a word in edgeways.

On more than on occasion she had even had to hold the phone away from her ear as the woman seemed incapable of speaking for more than a few seconds without resorting to shouting in order to make her point.

Poor Sarah. At least her mother – reluctantly – agreed to allow her to stay the night with them. The only other positive thing which came from the experience was that Marie whispered in Janine's ear before bed about how grateful she was to have her as her mother, instead of someone like Sarah's mum.

Her daughter's words still made her smile, and she intended to use them as ammo the next time she was accused of not allowing Marie to live her own life.

Janine made herself a strong coffee and sat at the kitchen table, sifting through her itinerary for this trip. The morning sun rose above the trees in the park outside her window and brightened up the room, bringing with it a warmth which was extremely comforting.

Janine closed her eyes and stretched out her arms, bathing them in the sunlight's glow.

A sudden clatter of plastic brought her round from her reverie with a start.

She opened her eyes and scoured the area before her but could see no sign of the instigator of the sound.

Just then, Gypsy jumped up on the table and sat next to her.

The sudden appearance of the cat made Janine jump, and her hand almost knocked over her cup. Thankfully, she managed to catch it in the nick of time.

Gypsy seemed completely non-plussed by the mishap she had almost caused, and she stretched out on the table as if it were her divine right to be there, licking her paws and grooming herself in the process.

"You scared the life out of me," Janine scolded, raising her eyebrows when she realised that she was being purposely ignored.

Remembering that although both the girls had managed to tame the feral feline with the tasty morsels from the restaurant the previous night, Janine had yet to make a formal acquaintance, she gingerly slipped her hand across the table towards the languishing cat, stopping when Gypsy turned her attention to the approaching fingers.

The cat stared at Janine's hand for a moment, her tail swishing slowly through the air.

"Now, if you want some breakfast, you have to play nicely,"

Janine warned her, leaving her hand just where it was as if inviting the cat to reciprocate.

After a moment, Gypsy craned her neck forward and sniffed at Janine's fingers.

Satisfied that they held no threat to her, the moggy then started to lick them with her raspy tongue.

Janine allowed her to continue until she was finished, then she rose from her chair and went to the fridge to fetch some milk. She poured some into a saucer and immediately went to place it on the floor, but Gypsy looked up at her with disdain as if it were beneath her dignity to drink from such a level.

Janine released a long sigh. She had a feeling that once Marie had fed her on the table, the cat might think that that would be the norm from now on. Either way, she decided that Marie would have to teach the cat the appropriate place to feed; she was not going to play the bad guy on this occasion.

She placed the saucer within easy reach for the cat, and Gypsy stretched, arching her back, before moving in and lapping at the milk.

Janine resisted the temptation to stroke the moggy as she drank, not wishing to push her luck with a feral cat after her warning to Marie the previous evening.

Checking her notes, Janine scribbled a few lines to remind herself to call Father Boyle later to remind him of his promise to put her in touch with Tim O'Brien, the author of the book she picked up while shopping. Also, she decided it might be a good idea to finish reading it before they met so that she could discuss the contents with the author.

She knew from passed experience how fragile some writers could be concerning their work, and she wanted to ensure that she had him on side to assist her with her article.

Just then, she heard the girls emerging from their bedroom.

Janine heard them laughing and joking together, followed by the sounds of the toilet flushing and the taps running.

Moments later, they both descended the stairs and entered the kitchen.

"Morning," they said, in unison.

Marie came over and planted a kiss on her mother's cheek.

The action almost caught Janine off guard, it had been that long since she had been honoured in such a manner for no specific reason other than it being a new day.

"Morning, girls," she replied. "Did you both sleep well?"

"Eventually," Sarah responded, "sure this one could talk the hind legs of a donkey."

"Me, that's rich, I could hear her talking to me even after I fell asleep." Marie walked around the table and began stroking Gypsy who was busy licking her paws having just finished her milk.

"Is it okay if I make some coffee?" asked Sarah.

"Of course," Janine responded, "the kettle's not long boiled but probably needs re-starting."

"Have we got anything to give Gypsy for breakfast?" asked Marie.

"Only milk. I've already given her one saucer full."

"We need to stop off somewhere today and buy her some proper cat food," insisted Marie.

"She seemed to enjoy the chef's offerings last night well enough," added Sarah.

"You don't want to spoil her too often," offered Janine, "otherwise she'll turn her nose up at ordinary cat food."

"We need to buy her the *best* cat food on the market," Marie insisted. "No generic brands for our little precious."

Janine rolled her eyes. "Oh, so she's ours now, is she?"

Marie shrugged. "Well, she is so long as we're here. This is her house, remember."

"Anyone else for coffee?" asked Sarah, taking down a mug for herself and spooning coffee granules in it.

"Yes, please," answered Marie. "Strong and black with two sugars."

"I'm fine," said Janine, transfixed by how attached Marie seemed to have become to Gypsy.

"I think she wants some more milk," Marie exclaimed, standing and opening the fridge to take out the carton. She shook it, there did not appear to be much left. Turning to Sarah, she asked, "Do you want some for your coffee?"

"I wouldn't dare deprive our little goddess," she smiled. "I'm okay with it black."

"Goddess?" asked Marie.

"Yes, the ancient Egyptians thought that cats were reincarnated gods. If you ask me, cats today believe they should still be treated the same."

Marie shrugged and poured what was left of the milk into Gypsy's saucer.

The cat immediately moved in and began licking it up.

"Is there anything for breakfast?" Marie asked, glancing over at Janine.

Janine nodded. "Yes, there's bread, cheese, sausages."

"No bacon," pouted Marie. Janine had purposely bought sausages because recently they were what her daughter demanded for her breakfast. She could not remember the last time she wanted bacon.

"No, sorry," Janine sighed. "I'll get some while I'm out today."

Sarah came over and placed Marie's steaming mug of coffee in front of her.

She took her own and sat opposite her new friend. "I've had a brilliant idea," she announced, excitedly. "We'll go to Liam's for breakfast, you'll both love it."

"Who's Liam?" asked Janine.

"He's my cousin," replied Sarah. "He runs his own café in town. It's not far and he serves up the best full-Irish in town, if I do say so myself. He even makes his own soda bread fresh every day. It'll be my treat, the least I can do since you both saved me last night."

Before Janine had a chance to venture an opinion, Marie accepted the kind offer on behalf of them both.

Chapter Seventeen

SARAH HAD NOT BEEN EXAGGERATING WHEN SHE
described the breakfast served at her cousin's café. The food was
simply to die for. Somehow, the eggs tasted fresher and tastier
than any Janine had ever eaten before. The sausages also were
by far the most succulent and juicy that she had ever tasted, and
just as Sarah had promised, the soda bread just melted in the
mouth, smothered with butter which Liam claimed was churned
that very morning.

Even Marie, who in Janine's experience could be one of the
fussiest eaters imaginable, especially at breakfast time when
usually all she craved was strong coffee and perhaps a Danish
pastry, made short work of her full breakfast, even using the last
of her soda bread to mop up any remnants of egg yolk from her
plate.

Liam was a most charming host and took both of cousin's
new friends to his heart, making them feel as welcome as long-
lost friends he had not seen for ages.

He even refused to accept any payment for their meals,
stating that he would take it as a personal insult if Janine
refused his hospitality.

As they were leaving the café, Janine received a call from Father Boyle.

"Hello," said the priest, cheerfully, "are you okay to talk?"

"Yes, by all means, Father. We've just had breakfast. How may I help you?"

"Well, oddly enough, it's me who rang to help you. I've just got off the phone from Tim O'Brien, the author we spoke about yesterday."

"Yes, I remember," Janine replied, eagerly.

"Well, I told him all about you and the article you're writing, and he would love to be interviewed by you."

"That's marvellous."

"Oh, he's a very accommodating chap, when he's sober, anyway." The priest chuckled.

"I see," Janine added, familiar with the drinking habits of writers, having met and interviewed several during her career.

"Furthermore," he continued, "his talk at the town hall is this evening. It's sold out, has been for a while now, according to Tim, but I've managed to snag a couple of seats for us as his guests. I can introduce you both after his performance is over, maybe you can arrange your interview with him then."

"That's perfect, Father," Janine replied, heaving a huge sigh of relief. Even though it was only her second day on the Manus, she was already feeling guilty that she had not started writing her article. Usually, she began her introduction upon first arriving at a location, but what with everything from the previous evening, she had decided that a good night's sleep was more important than burning the midnight oil.

If she were being totally honest with herself, up until that moment, she had no ideas where or how she was going to construct her piece. Now, at least she had an in-road. She hoped that Tim O'Brien would be as willing to talk to her as the priest had implied.

"Well, that's all settled then," continued Father Boyle. "I'll see you at the town hall this evening. The talk is due to start at seven thirty, but I'll probably be there around seven to greet some of my parishioners. I'll e-mail you a map with directions."

"That will be marvellous, Father, and thank you again for arranging everything."

"My pleasure, I'll see you this evening, God willing."

When Janine cut off the call, she suddenly remembered that Father Boyle had not secured a ticket for Marie. In all honesty, such an event was not usually up her daughter's street, but she had been acting so obligingly since meeting Sarah, Janine wondered if she should have asked for another seat on her behalf.

The two girls were walking ahead of Janine, arm-in-arm, chatting and laughing together just like old friends.

Janine wondered if she should broach the subject now, in front of Sarah. The problem there would be if Marie wanted to attend and insisted that Sarah come with them.

That said, Sarah was scheduled to work this evening at the restaurant, so chances were that she would not be able to attend in any case.

Even more reason for trying to secure Marie a ticket.

Marie suddenly unlinked her arm and spun round. "Mum, would it be okay with you if I worked with Sarah this evening at her restaurant?"

The request took Janine completely by surprise, and before she had a chance to formulate an answer, Marie walked closer to her and continued with her suggestion.

"Sarah says that her boss was only asking her last night if she knew anyone who might want to make some extra money, as two of his regular waitresses are off at the moment. I thought it might be good experience and something I could use on future applications. What do you think?"

Janine did not need persuading. This solved two problems with the same stone. First, she would not need go back to

Father Boyle to ask for an extra ticket, and secondly, it meant that Marie would not be alone all evening at the cottage, or worse still, wandering the streets in search of excitement.

"Well?" Marie pressed.

Janine nodded. "It sounds fine to me if you're up for it. Father Boyle and I are meeting up with that author I wanted to interview, so it's actually great timing."

Marie kissed her mother on the cheek and turned back to her friend, holding up both thumbs. Sarah walked back towards her friend, and the two girls slapped a high-five.

"Thank you," Sarah said, looking at Janine. "After last night, I'll feel a lot better knowing that I have one of my saviours by my side."

That thought had not occurred to Janine.

After the previous evening, she did not feel comfortable thinking about that Declan character turning up at their shift end and loitering outside to wait for the two girls.

But now that she had already given Marie her permission, she did not want to go back on her word and leave Sarah at the man's mercy.

"Tell you what," she began, trying to think of an agreeable solution, "how about I pick you both up at closing time, just in case that bloke and his mates are lurking in the shadows when you leave?"

"Oh, I'm sure he got the message last night, thanks again to the two of you," Sarah beamed. "I doubt very much he'll be so eager to face either of you again in a hurry, you really put him in his place."

Janine smiled. "Even so, better safe than sorry, eh?"

Sarah turned to Marie, who nodded. Knowing her mother as she did, there was no way she was going to drop it, and at least this way they did not have to worry about Sarah's ex turning up and ruining the night.

"Okay then," agreed Sarah. "I feel really guilty that you have to come by because of my bad taste in men, but I really appreciate the offer. If I'm being totally honest, I was dreading what my mum was going to say about me going back to work there, but now I know she'll be on board, so thank you again."

Janine could feel the relief washing over her.

At least now she knew that she could relax and enjoy her evening without worrying about how the girls would get home.

In her mind, she was already calculating how her evening would pan out. If Tim O'Brien's little talk was due to begin at seven thirty, then allowing at most an hour and a half for the performance, it was bound to be over by nine. Add another hour or so for her to be introduced to him by Father Boyle, plus time for their chat to set up their interview, should still leave her plenty of time to make it back to the restaurant before closing.

"So, what plans do you two have for the rest of the day before your shift starts?"

"Sarah needs to go home for a change of clothes and to see her mother," announced Marie. "Would it be okay if I tag along?"

"Fine with me," agreed Janine.

"Could Sarah stay with us again tonight?" Marie added, glancing back to her friend.

Marie's face lit up at the suggestion.

"Of course," replied Janine, smiling at the girl. "So long as your mum is cool with it, I don't want to be the cause of any family rift."

"Oh, she'll be more than happy," Sarah assured her. "She'll be working tonight anyway so the mere fact that I won't be alone at home will be a great comfort to her. If you're sure I won't be any trouble."

"If you are I'll chuck both of you out and you can sleep in the graveyard with Gypsy."

"Mum!"

Janine left the two girls to make their way to Sarah's home

while she took herself off on another jaunt of the district to help work off her breakfast. She had already decided to ensure that she left herself enough time to finish Tim O'Brien's book so that she could ask some pertinent questions if the occasion arose.

She knew from experience that most authors loved having their ego stroked by readers who made enquiries about their work that only they could answer. Janine knew enough about the writing game to craft her questions accordingly.

She made her way through the streets, this time avoiding the market in case she grew distracted and lost track of time.

There was a cold wind from the North Atlantic which permeated the streets even this far inland, but the sky was blue dotted with fluffy white clouds, and when Janine walked in the sun, the heat overpowered the breeze.

After a short while, Janine found herself at the gates of Bishop's Park. She decided that a quick round would leave her satisfied enough before heading home to snuggle up with her book.

As she walked along the path, Janine could not help but notice the small gathering up ahead of uniformed police officers standing around a small area marked off by blue and white tape.

As she grew nearer, a middle-aged officer noticed her and walked over to meet her.

"Good morning, madam," he said, politely, touching the brim of his cap with his finger. "You must be new in town," he announced.

Janine nodded. "Yes, that's right, I'm Janine Carstairs. My daughter and I are over here for a short holiday. Well, a working holiday in my case, I'm writing a short piece on your beautiful island."

"How lovely," the officer smiled. "Well, I'm Constable Clark, I'm the local 'bobby' you might say." He held out his and Janine shook it.

Janine looked past his shoulder. "May I ask what happened here?" she ventured.

Constable Clark glanced behind him and quickly turned back to face Janine. He was still smiling, although not as eagerly as before. "A local man. Seems he must have had a heart attack sometime last night. Poor fellow lay here until a dog walker stumbled across him this morning."

"Oh, I see," Janine responded, trying not to sound disappointed. She had always strived to rise above those of her profession who eagerly sought out tragedy as a source for their grist. "Is it okay to walk around? I was just out for some fresh air."

The officer stood back to allow her to pass. "Of course, by all means, enjoy your walk."

Not wishing to appear like a rubberneck, Janine thanked him and walked on, casually glancing sideways as she passed the cordoned-off area.

The body had obviously been removed, and there were two men in white overalls surveying the ground.

Ordinarily, had she been sent to the scene, Janine would have started asking questions about the victim as a way of perhaps instigating a human-interest story. But as she was there for a more specific task, she doubted her editor would welcome such a divergence.

Janine exited the park by the far exit and made her way back home.

Chapter Eighteen

WHEN FATHER BOYLE RETURNED FROM BISHOP'S PARK, his first thought was a nice cup of tea with lots of sugar to warm him up and help with the shock of seeing another parishioner lying dead before their time.

His one consolation was that he had managed to give Jerry absolution for his sins through penance the previous evening which, he prayed, regardless of the heinous nature of the subject of his confession, might find favour in God's eyes now that the poor man was at his mercy.

He could not shake the frozen look of terror on Jerry's face from his mind.

The fact that Michelle Calvert seemed to have the same rictus grin and wide-open stare had not escaped him, but as nobody else seemed to be making any connections, he decided to keep the thought to himself.

He was no Father Brown, nor did he prescribe to members of the cloth acting as detectives and trying to tell those who were already trained for the task how to do their jobs.

As he gazed around the church, Father Boyle could see a smattering of the devoted kneeling in silent prayer, most of whom he recognised immediately. He made a point of keeping the church open at all times during the day for those who wished to seek spiritual comfort to help deal with the trials and tribulations of modern life.

He was well aware that the bishop had given permission for his priests to lock their doors between services to deter would-be thieves and undesirables with no fixed abode who might wish to use the church as a place of respite from inclement weather. But Father Boyle sincerely believed in God's house remaining open and welcome for all, regardless of their reason for being there.

The fact that they had never been the victim of thieves or robbers assisted with his argument when Canon Royce last visited and questioned why the priest was not locking the church doors as the bishop had suggested.

Father Boyle did not delude himself. He knew that there were, in fact, several of what the bishop referred to as 'undesir-ables' on the island. But his faith in the human spirit and good triumphing over evil could not be easily shaken.

As he walked past the back of the pews, an unfamiliar figure caught his eye.

From the back, it was hard to tell who it was, but Father Boyle prided himself on being able to recognise most of his parishioners on sight, even from behind as they sat hunched over in prayer. But this young girl was definitely not one of his regulars, and she was seated far over to one side of the church, away from the rest of those gathered.

Unlike them, her head was not bowed, and from what he could tell, she was visibly shaking in her seat.

Curious, Father Boyle walked to the farthest aisle, which led to where the girl was sitting and made a point of approaching her quietly so as not to startle her. The sound of footsteps echoing throughout the vacuous space could often sound quite menacing to those fragile creatures wrestling with their consciences while awaiting absolution.

As he grew nearer, the girl shifted round in her seat.

It was young Erin Murphy. Not a regular in the church, but the father knew her family, her mother especially, who was extremely devout and never missed Sunday service.

Her father, on the other hand, although a good if somewhat surly individual, had often expressed the view that regular attendance at mass was not necessary so long as a person made a good, honest living and tried never to do others an injustice.

Colm Murphy owned several small holdings on the island, and although he boasted about being a good landlord, Father Boyle had heard rumours that he was not above turning entire families out if they were late with their rent more than once. This he simply classed as business and insisted that there was nothing personal in his actions.

Other such rumours had reached the father's ears over time, and although he did not believe in listening to gossip, especially when spread maliciously, he had to admit – if only to himself – that there was more than a mere kernel of truth to the talk.

Colm was also suspected of beating his wife, and it was true that Enid Murphy had often been seen around town as well as in church with bruises to her face. Father Boyle had also noticed the woman wincing in pain on occasion when she was genuflecting.

When asked, like so many victims of marital abuse, she would make excuses, blaming her own clumsiness as the reason for her plight.

To his knowledge, Father Boyle had never noticed Erin with any signs of having been mistreated by her father, although he had heard that whenever she displeased him, he was quick with the rod that he kept over the fireplace in their main living room.

As the Murphys' only child, Father Boyle feared that Erin

took the full brunt of her father's wrath whenever – in his opinion – she stepped out of line.

As Father Boyle approached Erin, he could see that she was shivering in her seat.

When she caught his eye, she immediately looked down at the floor and quickly turned back to face the front.

The priest suspected that her demeanour was a result of the weather, but more to do with her hesitation at speaking to him. But regardless of the reason, in his experience a hot sweet cup of tea often performed wonders when it came to putting a parishioner at their ease.

He walked up behind her and placed a comforting hand on her shoulder.

Erin spun back around, dislodging Father Boyle's hand in the process.

"Good morning, Father," the girl whispered, her eyes shifting furtively around the church to see if anyone was sitting close enough to hear her words.

"Good morning, Erin," the priest replied, ensuring he kept his own voice low so as not to concern the girl or alert those around the other pews of his presence. There were some amongst his parishioners who always felt the need to speak to him whenever they encountered him, and right now, he felt sure that Erin needed his counsel far more than they did. "It's lovely to see you here on a weekday. How have you been?"

Erin dropped her gaze once more.

She unconsciously edged away from Father Boyle, then stopped herself when she realised how it might look to him. She certainly had nothing to fear from the priest. He had always been the personification of kindness and sympathy whenever she attended confession, so there was no reason to believe that he would act any differently this morning.

That said, what she had to tell him was far worse than anything she had ever confessed to in the past.

That was the reason she had decided not to simply turn up at the usual time and take her place alongside the usual sinners awaiting absolution.

Even so, now that she was here and the priest was standing over her, Erin could not help the build-up of fear in the pit of her stomach, which made her want to stand up and run from the priest and the church before she said anything more.

Erin turned to face the priest.

He could see immediately that she was in some distress. Not just from the dried streaks of tears down her flushed cheeks or the way she trembled as if her entire body was freezing. It was more the look of anguish bordering on fear he could see in her eyes.

Father Boyle waited for a moment for the girl to respond to his question, but he soon realised that the poor girl was in no fit state to hold a conversation right at that moment.

He leaned in a little closer. "I was just about to put the kettle on in the presbytery, how do you fancy joining me for a nice cup of tea and a chocolate hobnob?" He gave her a crafty wink.

Erin smiled in spite of herself and nodded eagerly.

Father Boyle had always had a way of calming those of a nervous disposition.

Unlike many Catholic priests of his age, he was not drawn to the Old Testament and managed to avoid giving sermons threatening hellfire and brimstone for those who displeased God.

Father Boyle held his index finger up to his lips as he signalled for Erin to follow him.

From the corner of his eye, he could already see one of his faithful flock rising from her knees and lifting her hand to catch his attention, but he pretended not to notice as he guided Erin towards the door which led to his personal apartment.

Guilty as he felt for ignoring one of his devoted parishioners, he comforted himself in the knowledge that Erin's need was greater than any other at that moment.

Once inside the kitchen, Father Boyle put on the kettle and prepared two cups and saucers. As promised, he opened a new packet of chocolate hobnobs and shook several onto a plate, setting it down in front of Erin.

As he poured their tea, Father Wells suddenly appeared at the open doorway.

Father Boyle had often found it immensely unsettling that his curate seemed to appear out of nowhere without so much as a sound of his approach. But he kept his thoughts to himself, not wishing to upset the young man.

"Father Wells, you must have heard the kettle. Can I tempt you to a cup of tea and a choccy biscuit?"

The curate glanced down at Erin and held her gaze until she began to feel uncomfortable and looked down at her hands.

"Erin and I were just about to have a little chat," continued the priest, noting the young girl's obvious discomfort, "so I can make you a tea to go if you like."

Father Wells switched his gaze to his mentor.

As usual, his expression seemed to be made up of a mix of irritability and consternation. Even Father Boyle could not remember the last time he had seen his charge smile.

He had broached the subject as tactfully as he could one Sunday after evening mass whilst trying to extol the benefit of making the parishioners feel at ease when they came to church. But it was clear from the curate's expression that he did not agree with the senior priest's idea of how to treat their congregation.

Father Wells shook his head. "No, thank you, Father, I'm going down to the archive to carry out some more research. I'll be there if you need me."

Father Boyle smiled. "Have you managed to access those papers for our friend Tim O'Brien? I'm going to one of his lectures this evening, so I could always take them with me."

"Not yet," replied Wells, curtly. "I'll see what I can find."

With that, he turned away and left the kitchen.

Erin heaved a visible sigh of relief as he walked out. There was something about that man that made her feel very uncomfortable, and she knew that she was not alone in her suspicions. Several of her friends had also confessed to finding the curate cold and unapproachable, and they prayed that there were no plans to replace Father Boyle with him any time soon.

Father Boyle brought over their tea. "Alone at last," he announced. "Help yourself to the biscuits. The more you eat, the less guilty I'll feel if I end up polishing them all off."

Erin laughed.

It felt good to laugh.

She wondered if the kindly old priest would still be willing to welcome her into his inner sanctum after she confessed what was on her mind.

Part of her still considered just carrying on and not saying anything to anyone else. Certainly not her parents and not even to Father Boyle.

But here in his warm kitchen with a comforting cup of steaming tea in front of her, Erin could feel her resolve easing away. She knew that speaking to the priest was the right and just thing to do.

She only hoped that she could find the courage to tell him everything.

Chapter Nineteen

HAVING LEFT JANINE AFTER BREAKFAST, MARIE AND Sarah decided to go shopping. Sarah was particularly excited to show her new friend some of the quaint clothes shops squirreled away throughout the lanes which lay off the beaten track away from the main hustle and bustle of the highstreets.

They spent the rest of the morning trying on different outfits and encouraging each other to buy things they felt looked fantastic on the other. Their tastes, as it transpired, were quite similar in many respects, although Sarah tended to go for the more bohemian look, whereas Marie still veered towards slightly more conservative apparel.

The main thing was that they both enjoyed each other's company and spent the vast majority of their time together laughing at the silliest nonsense.

They stopped off for coffee in the afternoon at a small café which overlooked Westside Cliff, which Sarah explained was one of the local beauty-spots most frequented by tourists in the summer.

They sat outside with their cappuccinos to rest after their morning's endeavours.

After the full breakfast they had enjoyed in Liam's restaurant that morning, neither of them was hungry enough to attempt lunch, but they both enjoyed the chance of a sit-down before setting off for Sarah's house.

"Down there is where I stumbled over the body of that woman," Sarah explained, pointing off towards the far side of the beach.

Marie looked up and strained her neck as if it might still be possible to see something, even now. "That must have been awful," she acknowledged. "I'm not so sure I could return to the scene so soon afterwards."

Sarah shrugged. "The thing of it is around here that there are so few places where we teenagers can go to get away from our parents that if we started avoiding specific areas, we'd soon run out of options."

Marie nodded. "Even so, you're coping incredibly well for someone who tripped over a corpse. It gives me the shivers just thinking about it."

"Well, if I'm being honest, it wasn't my first corpse. When I was too young to leave at home alone, I used to sometimes go in to work with my ma at the health centre. She used to set me up in one of the empty rooms to put me to sleep once I'd finished my homework, but on occasions, the commotion of ambulances coming and going would wake me up, and I'd sometimes venture out to take a peek at what was going on."

Marie pulled a face. She already had an idea where this story was leading.

"A couple of times I would sneak a look outside in the corridor and see one of the paramedics wheeling a dead body on a gurney."

"And it didn't upset you?" Marie asked, incredulous.

"Not so much as you might think," admitted Sarah. "I just think that some people are more pragmatic about it than others. To me, they were just people sleeping, there was nothing sinister or creepy about them. I've often thought I could make a living as an undertaker. You need to have a certain outlook to be able to carry out that kind of work."

Marie squirmed in her seat. "Rather you than me, girl," she offered, smiling. "I could never imagine touching a dead body, not to mention all the embalming and dressing and applying make-up that's involved, yuck."

Sarah laughed. "Horses for courses, I suppose," she reflected. "Mind you, seeing a dead body where you expect to find one and almost falling over one unexpectedly are two different things altogether. I don't mind telling you I screamed my lungs out when I first saw Michelle Calvert lying there on the sand."

"Did you know her personally?" Marie asked.

Sarah took a sip from her cup, then shook her head as she swallowed. "Not to speak to as such, her husband was very rich, so we didn't exactly mix in the same circles. But I knew of them both, and I'd seen them around town now and then."

"Did your mother tell you the cause of death?" Marie felt herself being drawn in, in spite of the morbidity of the conversation.

"They put it down to heart failure, but I'll tell you what…" Sarah glanced around before continuing to make sure that no one was within earshot. "Even in the darkness, the expression on her face made her look as if she had been scared half to death."

Marie shivered, but she was still intrigued. "How do you mean?"

"Well, for a start, her eyes were wide open, and the look in them was eerie, as if she had seen something horrifying just before she died. Also, her lips were pulled back in like a rictus grin, and the skin on her face was taut as if it had been pulled tight across her bones." Now it was Sarah's turn to shudder. "Gave me the willies, I don't mind confessing."

"I don't blame you," Marie assured her. "I'd probably still be hiding under my bedcovers if I had found her."

The two girls laughed.

"Well, hello there, ladies, and what are you two doin' out on yer own this fine day?"

The male voice came from their side, and both girls glanced over to see who it belonged to. Marie recognised the men from the previous evening outside the restaurant even before Sarah commented.

"Oh, what the fuck are you doin' here!" she demanded. "Stalking us? You know that's a criminal offence and I can get you banged up for that?"

Declan held his hands up. "Now, now, there's no need to take on like that," he assured them. "Me and the boys 'ere were just having an afternoon stroll an' 'appened to stumble across you both. No harm in that now, is there?"

Marie did not like the look of the man, nor the fact that he had his two companions from last night hovering behind him like personal bodyguards. She vaguely remembered being as vocal towards them the previous evening as Sarah was being now. But if she were being honest with herself, she knew that such bravado came with the assistance of the wine she had drunk at dinner.

Now, in the cold light of day and with nothing but caffeine for courage, Marie could feel herself shrinking back into her chair at the sight of the big men looming over them.

To add to her building panic, Declan now turned his attention directly towards her, leaning down until his face was mere inches from her own. "And where is that lovely lady you were with last night?" he asked, sarcastically. His words caused his two henchmen to turn to each other and laugh. "My but she was a feisty one and no mistake. But then, so were you as I recall."

"Just fuck off and leave us alone Declan!" Sarah shouted, obviously sensing her friend's unease with the situation.

Declan immediately stood back up. "Just making polite conversation with your new friend. Or wait, isn't she your cousin, as I recall that lady stating last night?"

"What's it to do with you?" Marie suddenly retorted, Sarah's bravery at dealing with the man, instilling her with courage of her own.

To her relief, it seemed to have the desired effect, and Declan moved back another step, holding his hands up once more in submission. "Goodness, but you're a mighty pair and no mistake," he replied, smiling. "And there's me just wantin' to know if you fancy coming to a party."

"What party?" asked Sarah, her interest piqued.

Marie was taken aback at her friend's sudden change of tone, especially as, up until now, she had not had anything positive to say about Declan.

"We're having a little celebration for one of me cousins," Declan replied. "It's his birthday today an' he's finally become a man."

"Is it his eighteenth?" asked Marie, feeling that she needed to follow suit after Sarah's change of attitude, even if it was just to avoid annoying the three men.

Declan laughed. "No, not yet, he's sixteen, that's when you become a real man in our culture. By eighteen, he'll probably be married with kiddies and everything."

"You're not," Sarah pointed out, accusingly.

Declan held out his arms. "That's because I've been waitin' fer the right time to ask you, my lovely," he said, smiling broadly.

Sarah laughed out loud. "In your dreams, bucko," she said, scornfully.

Declan held his hand against his chest. "Ow, can you not hear my poor heart breaking?" he asked, rhetorically.

"So, when's this party then?" Sarah ventured.

Marie could not be sure if her friend was genuinely considering the offer or merely playing along to keep the men sweet.

"Tonight, at the camp," replied Declan, "sure an' it's going to be a real hoot, probably an all-night affair, we've got relatives arriving from all over as we speak. In fact..." he suddenly glanced at his watch. "Me an' the lads here were on our way to the harbour when I spied you from the van. We need to get a shifty on or my cousins will think we've abandoned them." He turned his attention back to the girls. "So what d'yer say, girls, does it not sound like an evening not to be missed?"

"Can't," shrugged Sarah. "We're both working a shift at the restaurant this evening."

For a moment, Marie wished that Sarah had not divulged that information to Declan, especially remembering the previous evening's confrontation.

"Sure an' that's no problem," Declan assured her. "We'll come by an' pick yers up when you're done. The party will be in full swing by then."

Marie glanced over at her friend.

Sarah appeared to be seriously mulling the offer over.

After a moment, she said, "I'll let you know later, we might have plans with my aunt after work."

"Bring her along," insisted Declan, "the more the merrier. Have her meet you at the restaurant, and we'll all go together."

Marie shuddered. She could imagine nothing worse and she new full well that there was no way her mother would allow her to go, let alone attend with them.

"I'll call you tonight," Sarah offered. "Now piss off and leave us to our coffee."

With that, Declan and his crew turned and left, chatting to each other in a language Marie could not understand.

Once they were out of earshot, Marie turned to her friend. "You weren't serious about us going, were you?" she asked, anxiously.

Sarah chuckled. "Relax, we'll only go if you want to. I have to say, their parties are a riot. There's usually a couple of half-decent fights and the alcohol flows like water. The food's not half bad either."

Marie could not hide her shock. "My mother would never let me go," she confirmed. "I'm surprised from what you said last night that your mother would ever agree to it, either."

Sarah grinned. "Well, if we do decide to go, neither of our mothers can be any the wiser. I'm beginning to think that it's high time I brought out the rebel in you."

Marie drained her cup, concerned as to why the idea of going to the party suddenly seemed so appealing.

Chapter Twenty

FATHER BOYLE SAT WITH HIS ELBOWS RESTING ON THE table, his head in his hands. The cup of tea in front of him had turned cold twenty minutes ago, but he had not touched it. It was the second one he had made himself since Erin Murphy had left, and it would be the second one he would throw down the sink untouched.

There had been times over the years when he felt completely useless as a priest, and none more so than at this minute.

He had always felt that his calling came as a way for him to bring comfort and support to those in need and a way for him to demonstrate to others the way to live a good, honest Christian life, one that would bring them closer to God and reassure them of his love and understanding.

But having spent the best part of two hours with young Erin, he felt completely drained, and all his previous years of inspiring those in his flock to look to God for guidance and support seemed to have been in vain.

The young woman had come to him for help, and he had sent her away in floods of tears like a scolded child.

It had taken him almost thirty minutes before persuading the girl to tell him what was troubling her. He suspected it would have something to do with that over-bearing father of hers, or, possibly, that she had felt herself being drawn to that physical love which so many of her age were eager to experiment with before making their marriage vows before God.

He had been preparing himself to explain to Erin that although physical love was a great temptation, God had purposely made it so to test us in proving our willingness to follow his teachings, and that she would only reap the benefits of his love by waiting until she became a bride before taking that final step.

But he was completely unprepared for what she told him, and he knew that his shock and disappointment were both clearly displayed by his expression as she made her confession.

Initially, Father Boyle suggested that they both return to the confessional so that Erin might feel more comfortable in a familiar surrounding before she confessed. But twice during that first half an hour, Erin stood up ready to leave, too embarrassed to explain the reason for her being there and expressing her concern that too many parishioners known to her parents were already in the church and would not be adverse to mentioning to them that they had seen her go to confession in the middle of the day.

But Father Boyle had managed to calm her down and assure her that they did not have to be inside the confessional box for him to hear her and absolve her of her sins.

The important thing, he explained, was that she made an honest and heartfelt confession and confirmed before God that she wished to repent.

She would not be the first young parishioner to confess to impure thoughts, and Father Boyle prided himself on being able to sway such penitents from falling into a path of sin and vice.

Once he had calmed the girl down, he reassured her that anything she told him would be between them and God alone, just in case Erin was afraid that he might mention their meeting to either of her parents. He reiterated that the seal of the confessional was sacrosanct and that the sacramental seal was inviolable.

He could tell immediately from Erin's face that his words had done more to confuse rather than assure her.

Therefore, he explained that it was absolutely forbidden for him, as a priest hearing confession, to betray in any way a penitent in words or in any manner and for any reason, regardless of the circumstances.

Finally, he felt as if he had reassured Erin enough to trust him with whatever was plaguing her.

He placed his stole over his shoulders and closed his eyes, making the sign of the cross. Erin did likewise. Father Boyle began reciting the words, inviting Erin to open her heart and make a true confession.

Erin cleared her throat before she began.

Her timid voice cracked, and her tiny frame shook as she spoke. "Bless me, Father, for I have sinned. It has been a month since my last confession…and these are my sins."

Father Boyle waited, his head still bent, feeling that just looking at the girl might be enough to cause her to change her mind and flee from the room.

Finally, she continued. "Father, I have sinned against God, and I fear for my soul as I am about to do so again in a monstrous way."

"Be brave, my child," the priest encouraged her. "God knows what is in your heart."

"Father…I have indulged in carnal lust, with a boy, a boy I thought loved me."

"I see." Father Boyle tried to keep the exasperation from his tone. He had suspected as much but hoped that Erin had come to him prior to making such a mistake so that he might at least have the chance of talking her out of it. "And how many times have you and this boy engaged in this behavior?"

"Only the once, Father. I knew straight away that it was wrong and that I had been weak. He has pressed me several times since, but I have refused to succumb."

Father Boyle nodded. "That is good." Father Boyle assured her. "God understands that we mere mortals are weak by our very nature, but he is quick to forgive us our most severe sins so long as we understand that what we have done is wrong and we promise him never to repeat the incident."

There was a further pause.

Father Boyle waited for Erin to continue, but when no response came, he suspected that her confession was complete.

"There's worse to come, Father."

Erin's words took him by surprise.

He settled himself, then said. "What else is troubling you, my child?"

"Father…I'm pregnant!"

The revelation shocked the priest. He had presumed that Erin and her boyfriend would have taken precautions, a far lesser sin with a much more favorable outcome for both parties.

Father Boyle released a long sigh.

Knowing that Erin's mother was a devout Catholic, he suspected that she would blame herself in some way for her daughter's predicament. Added to which, he could only imagine the reaction of her bullish father when he found out.

No wonder the poor girl was in such a state.

He only hoped that the boy would do the decent thing and marry her, sooner rather than later to help curtail the gossips.

"Oh, my child," Father Boyle sighed, rubbing the bridge of his nose between his finger and thumb. "I won't ask how this happened, even an old priest knows about the birds and bees, but why did you allow it to happen? You are one of the most sensible girls I know."

Erin took out a tissue to daub her eyes as a new stream of tears trickled down her cheeks. "I'm sorry, Father. I know it was wrong, and I've regretted it even before finding out I was pregnant. But now it is too late, the damage is done, and Liam…" Erin suddenly looked up, unable to hide the embarrassed expression which shone through her tears. "I'm sorry, I mean, the boy, doesn't want anything to do with me. He says it's my problem and I have to deal with it on my own."

"This'll be Liam Mularkey, no doubt?" Father Boyle ventured. He could see from Erin's reaction that he had hit the nail on the head.

Liam Mularkey had always been a troubled boy since he hit his teens. When the father thought back to the pious young altar boy who had once confessed to him of his earnest wish to become a priest, Father Boyle hardly recognised them as one and the same.

He knew deep inside that there would be very little chance of persuading the young man to do the decent thing. Even the prospect of Erin shaming him amongst their congregation would do nothing more than shine the light of such shame directly on her.

Liam would no doubt boast about his virility amongst his own peer group, wearing it like some victorious badge of honour.

"Have you told either of your parents?"

Erin sat bolt upright. "No, Father, I can't, they wouldn't understand. My mother would never forgive me for bringing such shame upon the family. And my father…"

Father Boyle nodded.

As much as he hated to admit it, even to himself, Colm Murphy was not the kind of man to show sympathy and support at such a time, even to his only child. More than likely, he would find solace in a bottle, which in turn would give him an excuse to take his anger and frustration out on both Erin and her mother, for Colm would doubtless blame his wife for not tutoring their daughter properly in the responsibilities of women.

"Would you like me to try and talk to Liam? Perhaps it is not too late to show him the error of his ways and encourage him to take his share of the responsibility."

Erin shook her head, sadly. "There's no point, Father, I've tried. He was so nasty. He told me he would deny the child was his and start spreading rumours amongst my friends that I was little more than a tart who slept with anything in trousers..." Erin trailed off again as another batch of tears arrived.

Father Boyle's heart ached for the girl's predicament.

But some situations were easier to fall into than they were to escape from.

After a moment, he asked. "So, what are we going to do about all this, Erin? Do you think you are capable of bringing up a baby by yourself, possibly without the assistance of either of your parents? Or have you considered giving up the child for adoption? You know the church has its own adoption agency on the mainland. They will see to it that your child is given to a loving and caring Catholic couple who perhaps cannot have children of their own."

Erin's hands trembled.

She shook her head, slowly. "Father, I cannot let my parents know that I'm pregnant." She admitted, her voice croaky and almost unrecognisable through her tears.

"But, Erin, you know that it won't be long before you start to show," Father Boyle replied. "What are you planning to do then? Go away on holiday? What will you tell your parents? You cannot hide this from them, no matter how desperate you become."

Erin wiped her nose with her tissue and cleared her throat.

She looked at him through tear-stained eyes. "Father, I'm

going to the mainland to arrange an abortion," she admitted. "It's the only way."

The sudden shock of her words hit Father Boyle like a slap in the face.

He reared up in his chair, almost sending himself over.

He could not control his anger. "What are you saying!" he demanded, his voice no longer soft and gentle. "Are you aware that you put your very soul in peril if you concede to such an act?"

Erin dropped her head once more.

Her narrow shoulders heaved up and down as she continued to sob.

Father Boyle immediately regretted the harshness of his tone, but Erin's announcement had taken him completely by surprise. Never in a million years did he suspect that she would consider such a vile action.

He waited for a moment to allow himself to calm down.

When Erin finished her latest round of tears, she slowly raised her head to look at him, but her shoulders remained slumped, proving that she had no fight left in her.

"You won't be on your own in this," Father Boyle assured her. "The church and your parents will all rally round to support you, you'll see."

Erin dropped her hands into her lap, palms up. "They won't, Father, you know my parents, my mother will never be able to look me in the eye again, and as for my father…" she trailed yet again. There was no point going over it all again, it would never change anything.

After a long pause where neither of them spoke, Erin asked, barely louder than a whisper. "Can you give me absolution, Father?"

Father Boyle felt his anger rising.

He did his best to quell it, forcing himself to remember the vulnerability of the penitent before him.

But what Erin was considering could not be forgiven by a simple act of contrition.

This was not an errant schoolgirl confessing to masturbating for the first time.

Father Boyle leaned over the table. "You cannot ask God to forgive you for something you are intent on going through with when you know that his teachings do not allow it. It is a terrible sin you are planning to commit, and you know it is wrong. There is plenty of time for you to reconsider your position. It is not a foregone conclusion yet."

To his surprise, Erin stood up, almost knocking back her chair in her haste and ran from the room.

Father Boyle resisted the temptation to chase after her. For one thing, it would only serve to alert those within the church that something was wrong, and it would not take them long to put two and two together.

The last thing he wanted was to cause Erin further anguish, and he would feel responsible if the gossips started speculating and word of it reached Erin's parents.

Instead, he sat at the kitchen table and searched his heart for a way to help the poor girl. He knew that he was constrained by his position, but there had to be something he could do for her.

So lost in thought was he that he did not notice his young curate emerge from corridor and pass by the open door.

Chapter Twenty-One

JANINE GLANCED AT HER WATCH. SHE JUST HAD TIME for a sandwich and a shower before leaving for the lecture with Tim O'Brien. Father Boyle had sent her the details as promised and had left word at the door in case he was running late.

Janine had spent the afternoon skimming through Tim's book on the island, making notes for her article and placing sticky notes on certain pages to jog her memory should she wish to ask any questions at the session.

She hoped that the author would be open to arrange a separate meeting with her to delve further into the history of the island at a later date, and to that end, she was relying on Father Boyle to introduce her to Tim that evening.

From what she had managed to ascertain so far, his book was very well researched and written not so much as a guide for those wishing to visit the island, but more from an academic angle going back as far as present records allowed.

Janine stretched out her arms and untangled herself from the blanket she had wrapped around her. She ensured that all her notes and scribblings were slotted in the correct order before slipping a paperclip over the top left-hand corner to keep them together.

She closed Tim's book and placed it on the table on top of her notes so that she would not forget it this evening.

Making her way into the kitchen, Janine put on the kettle and began making herself a cheese and tomato sandwich. After that morning's breakfast, she had not been in the mood for any lunch, and even now she was not exactly starving, but she thought it prudent to eat something now to avoid her stomach rumbling during the talk.

As she turned back towards the table, two paws suddenly emerged from the chair opposite her, and Gypsy lifted her head and yawned, stretching out her body and glancing towards Janine as if her presence were no more than an intrusion.

The cat jumped up on the table and began sniffing the air.

When Janine had returned home earlier that day, she had found the cat asleep on the table, curled into a tight ball.

Her initial instinct was to pick the animal up and place it back on the floor, but it being feral, she decided to try and coax the cat off using her words, rather than her hands.

Janine had bought some of the more expensive cat food on her way home, as it appeared her daughter had already adopted the stray.

She opened one of the cans and turned it upside down over a plate, allowing the mouse-like substance to slide out of the tin by itself. Glancing over her shoulder, Janine noticed Gypsy raising her head in anticipation, the pungent aroma of the meal evidently reaching her nose from across the room.

Janine placed the plate on the floor next to the water bowl Marie had set out earlier.

Gypsy looked down at the plate, then straight back up towards Janine as if curious as to why her meal had not been placed on the table in front of her.

Janine urged the cat to jump down to eat. Gypsy strolled

over towards the edge of the table then stopped short and looked back up at her provider as if trying to communicate that it was beneath her dignity to eat from the floor level.

Janine held firm. Her hope was that if she could convince the moggie that the floor was the correct place for her meals that she could then persuade her daughter likewise.

Finally, Gypsy seemed to get the message and she jumped down and began to devour her food, ravenously.

Now that a certain order had been determined, Janine was determined to set it in stone. She opened another can of cat food and placed it on a fresh plate, swapping it with the one Gypsy had used earlier.

This time there was no sign of objection, and the cat jumped to the floor and went to work on her dinner.

Janine smiled to herself, pleased at her little victory, and prepared her sandwich and coffee. She ate at the table, glancing down at Gypsy while the cat finished her plate.

Before Gypsy was done Janine took a picture of her eating, zooming out far enough so that it was clear the feline was eating at floor level. She sent the pic to Marie, informing her that this was how to train a cat.

Marie replied with several emojis of laughing faces.

Once she was done, the cat jumped back up on the table and began licking her paws and washing the backs of her ears, before stretching out and resuming her slumber.

Janine did consider ordering the cat back down but decided that baby-steps were the order of the day.

Having showered and changed, Janine grabbed her coat and handbag, slipping Tim's book inside it, and made her way out to her car.

The sun was on the wane, and the eastern sky had already begun to darken with the faint glimmer of stars flecked across it. Janine had already estimated that the journey would take less than ten minutes, and on such a beautiful evening, she was tempted to walk. But she decided that, as she had to pick the girls up after their shift, it made more sense for her to have the car with her, rather than have to trudge back to collect it later.

Before setting off, Janine checked that she had a pad and pen in her handbag so that she could make notes during the evening. She usually preferred to use her hand-held recorder as a speedier way of chronicling her thoughts, but at such an event, she realised the use of such a contraption would be annoying to other members of the audience, not to mention disrespectful to their host.

The drive took longer than anticipated due to the queue for the car park at the village hall. Janine was impressed that a local writer could command such an audience, and she felt a sudden jolt of excitement at having been invited to the event.

Fortunately, the hall had a huge car park, and an elderly gentleman in a navy blazer directed drivers as to where they should park. Janine was not sure if the man worked there or had just volunteered his time for the task, but from the way he remonstrated at anyone who ignored his directions, it was clear that he took the post very seriously.

Janine waved a 'thank you' when it was her turn and followed his directions.

The wind had picked up a bit by the time she exited her car, and Janine was glad she had decided to bring her coat. As she walked towards the entrance, she was relieved to see Father Boyle there, welcoming guests and cheerfully guiding them inside.

Without holding a physical ticket, Janine had anticipated the chance of having to negotiate her way in past some old busy-body of a ticket collector who took their task way too seriously for such an event, so the sight of the priest was most welcome.

Janine waited a few feet away from him as he finished speaking to a middle-aged lady who was holding onto his arm, clutching the sleeve of his coat as if she were afraid to let go for fear of falling.

Janine tried to look uninterested in their conversation, but she was already too close to be out of earshot.

The woman was indeed in a state of panic, begging the priest to intercede with her husband concerning their daughter. The woman's voice rose several times in volume as she spoke, causing those who walked past to glance in their direction.

It was only when Father Boyle explained to the poor woman that everyone could hear their conversation that she finally stopped talking and reluctantly let go of his arm, rushing inside the hall whilst attempting to cover her embarrassment beneath her head scarf.

The priest released a long sigh and smiled at Janine. "A troubled parishioner, I'm afraid," he explained, apologetically as if he were to blame for the woman deciding to pick that moment to launch herself at him.

Janine smiled. "That's okay, Father, I suspect you often get stopped in the street by those who feel that your time is theirs."

"You'd be amazed," he whispered. "Shall we take our places? I've spoken to Tim, and he is looking forward to being grilled by you after his talk. I've managed to secure us front row seats."

"That's wonderful, thank you so much for arranging this for me, it will really help with my article."

On route to their chairs, Father Boyle kept his head slightly bowed as he explained to Janine how eager Tim was to have a rummage through the church archives for new material for his next book.

Janine wondered if he was making conversation as a way of not being stopped on his way to his chair by another overzealous member of his congregation.

"Unfortunately," he continued, "my curate informs me that the archives are far from ready for anyone other than members of our order to search. I must confess I have only been down there a couple of times since I took over the parish, and it is in an almighty state. Bringing it back into some form of order may well be a full-time job. Luckily, Father Wells seems more than willing to undertake the mammoth task, so I feel I must bow to his authority when he says allowing anyone else down there at the moment is tantamount to an accident waiting to happen."

Janine was impressed by the fact that there were at least one hundred chairs set out at stage level, and most of them were already occupied.

She glanced around and noticed that there was also an upper tier, which also appeared to be full of eager attendees.

"He's obviously very popular," she remarked, taking, out her mobile and switching it off for the talk.

"Oh yes," Father Boyle agreed. "Tim doesn't do many of these. He once told me it was better to keep the audience wanting more than saturating them with facts, even if they are about their own island."

"It certainly seems to be working, this place is heaving. I'm so glad you managed to secure me a seat, let alone in the front row."

"You know what they say about it not being what you know, but who you know," the priest smiled. "If I'm being perfectly honest, I had already asked Tim to reserve me two seats a couple of weeks ago. I was due to bring an old friend Sandra O'Leary, she's the housekeeper for Emmet Calvert, one of our more prominent members of society. Regrettably, he died unex-pectedly a few days ago, and poor Sandra is still under the local doctor as a result, so she was in no fit state to come along tonight."

"How sad," Janine replied. "If you don't mind me asking, how did the gentleman die?"

Father Boyle turned to her and said, keeping his voice low. "He had an accident, fell down the stairs at his mansion. Very sad."

"Was he a young man?"

The priest shook his head. "No, but he was in good health according to the doc. He had a young wife, too; they'd only been married about five years."

"She must be devastated," Janine observed.

Father Boyle checked around them to make sure no one was following their conversation before he continued. Still keeping his voice down, he said. "Well, talk about a tragedy, Michelle, his wife, passed away the same night from a heart attack. Her body was discovered on the beach beneath Westside Cliff by a local girl. Scared the poor child to death. Well, not literally, you understand."

"Was that Sarah Byrne?" Janine asked.

Father Boyle looked shocked. "Yes, it was as a matter of fact. How on earth did you know that?"

Janine smiled. "My daughter and I met her the other evening at the restaurant where she waitresses. They seem to have hit it off like a house on fire. In fact, Sarah has managed to secure Marie a shift tonight. I'm picking them both up later."

The priest nodded. "Small world. Well, small island anyway. Yes, Sarah is a lovely lass, her mother is a pillar of our little congregation."

"Not too keen on her choice of boyfriend, though, from what I understand."

"You can say that again," Father Boyle replied. "The Higgins bunch are an odd lot to say the least. I've tried several times to strike up a formal acquaintance with them, but they tend to prefer to keep to themselves. I suppose centuries of being moved on by successive landowners must take its toll in the long run, so perhaps they are rightly suspicious of anyone outside their own circle trying to make friends."

Just then, the lights dimmed, and a man walked onto the stage and introduced that evening's host.

Janine was suitably impressed by the applause which greeted him.

Chapter Twenty-Two

"And our specials for this evening are on the blackboard over there," Marie turned to one side and pointed towards the large board which hung on the wall behind her.

"And are you by any chance on the specials menu for tonight?" replied the man nearest to her, winking at his three mates seated around the table. "Or are you only for dessert?"

Before Marie had a chance to move away, the man flung his arm around her waist and pulled her in closer to him so that her waist was rammed up against the side of his head.

Marie could feel him tightening his grasp as his hand slid down just far enough to squeeze her left cheek.

"Get off me," she protested, trying to keep her voice down so as not to alert any of the customers seated nearby.

The last thing she needed on her first night was to cause a scene and not be invited back tomorrow. This gig paid cash-in-hand, and the owner had been more than generous in his offer, especially when another one of the staff had called in sick.

But, desperate or not, Sarah had warned her that he stood for no commotion, so Marie intended to be on her best behaviour.

That, however, was before she found herself being groped.

She tried to pull away, discreetly, but the man just tightened his hold even more.

"Will you please let go of me?" Marie asked, starting to sound pitiful.

"Okay, okay," replied the man, "but it'll cost you a wee kiss first." He closed his eyes and puckered his lips, looking up at her.

Marie felt sick. Whatever he thought of himself, he was no God's gift. His face was pock-marked, and it looked as if he had not bothered to shave for at least a couple of days.

Added to which, now she was this close to him, there was a definite stench of unkept body odour emanating from him. This, mixed with his whiskey-breath, made the thought of having to kiss him not worth her job after all.

She wrinkled her nose and screwed up her face in disgust.

Her expression was not wasted on the man. "Oh, so yer think yer too good fer the likes of me, eh?" He scowled.

To Marie's relief, Sarah appeared from the side. "And how would you like your arm, sir?" she asked, politely. "Fried, roasted, broiled, sautéed in butter?"

The four men all turned towards her.

She stood smartly to attention with her hands behind her back.

"What?" asked the man with his arm around Marie. His brow knitted. "What're yer talkin' about?"

"I said," she repeated slowly, keeping her voice to just above a whisper. "How would you like your arm cooked?" From behind her back, Sarah produced a large kitchen knife. It had a thick curved blade and looked to Marie like one of those blades used by serial killers in the movies when they were eviscerating teenagers in a small town.

Sarah moved in a little closer until her face was only inches away from his.

The man instinctively pulled back, but he kept his arm wrapped tightly around Marie.

Sarah placed the point of the knife on the table in front of him and leaned on it so it punctured the tablecloth beside his tablemat. "What I mean is, sir, if you don't remove your arm from around my friend, I'm going to slice it off and give it to our chef as tonight's special, then we're both going to watch as he serves it to you in the basement, understand?"

The look of sheer terror on the man's face as he let go of Marie and held both his arms aloft in surrender almost made Sarah burst out laughing, but she managed to maintain her composure so as to make the men suspect that she was for real.

Marie moved away and came to stand behind her friend.

Sarah kept her expression straight as she slowly turned to look at each man in turn.

The nearest one shuffled back away from her, knocking his chair into his friend's.

None of them spoke. They just stared back at the waitress, wide-eyed.

Finally, when she was satisfied that the group had received her message loud and clear, Sarah said. "Right then, gents, I'll be back in a moment to take your orders, please take note of our specials board as you decide." With that, she smiled and turned away, taking Marie with her.

When they were out of earshot of the table, Marie squeezed her friend's arm.

Sarah turned to her. "How're you doin' now you've met some of our more colourful clientele?" she asked, sympathetically.

"You were just brilliant," Marie gushed. "I was ready to do something stupid and lose my job. If you hadn't have come along when you did…"

"You'd've thought of something," Sarah assured her. "It's your first time encountering pigs like them, so don't worry.

Blokes like that are all noise and no impact, they'll push fer all they can get. You just have to show them you have their measure."

"I still think you were wonderful the way you dealt with them."

"It comes with the territory, I'm afraid. I did some summer shifts in a café on the front last year, that was rough. The first time a punter tried it on with me, I nearly burst into tears. Luckily, we had a waitress there who knew exactly how to deal with those types. Before I realised what was happening, she 'ad the bloke in an armlock and marched him out the door, throwing him out on the pavement before he knew what day of the week it was. She trained me well, bless her."

"She certainly did," Marie agreed, smiling.

Sarah patted her hand. "Now, don't you go worryin' about those lads, I'll take over their table."

Marie shook her head. "No, don't worry. Now you've put them in their place, I'll know how to deal with them if they try something like that again."

Sarah smiled. "Are you sure?"

"Yep," Marie nodded. She clenched her right hand into a fist. "If any of them tries anything again, I'll give them what for."

"That's my girl. We'll make a fighter out of you yet." Sarah glanced over her shoulder to check that no one else was within earshot. "Have you decided about tonight?" she whispered.

"Oh," Marie had not given the proposition much thought since they had discussed it between them after meeting the lads at the café earlier in the day.

Sarah had assured Marie that there was no pressure on her to attend if she did not feel comfortable about it. But she promised her that if they did go, she would look after her and make sure she did not come to any harm.

After watching Sarah deal with the men at the table just now,

Marie was in no doubt that she could rely on her friend if such a situation arose at the campsite.

The main problem was that she knew that her mother would not allow her to go.

Her only option there would be to lie to her and make up something. Sarah had suggested she could say she was staying round her house that night, and as her mother would be away at work, no one need be any the wiser.

Sarah had even suggested that if Marie fancied anyone at the party that she could invite them back to her place, so long as they kicked them out before her mother returned from work in the morning.

From what Marie had seen of Declan and his mates, that prospect did not exactly appeal, as she suspected that the majority of his friends would be of the same ilk.

Even so, nothing ventured, as her grandmother had always been fond of saying.

Marie wondered if the old lady would have felt so blasé about this particular situation.

Sarah had made it clear that if Marie did not wish to go, then she was happy to stay home too. But deep down, Marie could not help but feel that her friend really did want to attend, even after the incident with Declan on the beach.

Marie was in no doubt that Sarah could handle him if it came to it, but she was still a little surprised that the girl was willing to take such a chance so soon after the event.

The other problem, which Marie would not admit to her friend, was that she felt bad about having to lie. Naturally, over the years, she had told the odd white lie to appease her mother about one thing or another. But even then, she always felt a terrible stab of guilt in the pit of her stomach, which took ages to dissipate.

She suspected it might have something to do with the look of disappointment on her mother's face whenever she suspected such a deception, even though she always said that she believed her in the end and never brought it up again.

Somehow, her mother's faith in her made the guilt worse.

Marie looked back at Sarah.

The girl was waiting anxiously for her answer, and Marie could tell from the expression on her friend's face that she was hoping Marie would be up for the experience.

Marie bit her bottom lip.

After a moment, she nodded. "Okay then, I'm in."

Sarah slapped her across the shoulder. "Good girl, we're going to have a marvellous time tonight," she said enthusiastically. "You've never partied until you've been to one of these affairs, gypsies really know how to enjoy themselves."

"I'd better text my mum during my break," offered Marie. "I'll just say we're staying at yours, okay."

"Yep, brilliant, and I'll text Declan to make sure they're hear at closing to pick us up. That way he won't get too smashed to drive when it's time."

Marie was tempted to ask her friend one more time if she was sure that tonight was a good idea. But, before she had a chance, a customer signalled for service and Sarah went rushing off to see to them.

Marie released a huge sigh.

It was too late now to turn back, and besides, Sarah was so excited by the prospect of a good night out Marie knew that she would not have the heart to back out now.

Marie could already feel a knot beginning to form in her stomach at the thought of sending the text to her mother.

She tried to suppress it as she continued with her work.

Chapter Twenty-Three

JANINE WAS PLEASANTLY SURPRISED AND A LITTLE overwhelmed by Tim's talk.

For one thing, he was far more than just a good orator. He was also a gifted storyteller, poet, musician and singer, all of which he combined into his show, keeping his audience enthralled and entertained throughout the entire performance.

Tim regaled the crowd with a potted history of the island going back as far as records allowed. This he interspersed by reciting works from poets known to have been born on the Manus, along with some of his own, which in Janine's opinion were not half bad.

He played his banjo and sang songs about life in the early days of Manus right up to the struggles and the effect it had on those living on the island. Although some of the songs were a little grim, as was to be expected considering their subject matter, Tim did not allow the evening to ever dip into melancholy.

He knew how to work an audience and when to change the mood to bring them back around. This he managed to accomplish with great aplomb while taking crafty swigs from a silver hip flask, which he assured the audience contained chicken soup made by his old aunt Mary to help keep his throat free from ailments.

He received a laugh each time he announced: "I must remember to thank Aunt Mary for this heavenly brew."

The ninety-minute show flew past without Janine having to glance at her watch even once.

When the show was over and Tim had received a richly deserved round of applause which seemed to go on forever, he took questions from the audience. Several hands shot up when he opened-up the floor, and Tim answered each one graciously-even those which Janine felt had already been addressed during the course of the evening-with the same jovial manner he had maintained throughout his performance, never once making the asker feel foolish for not having realised that their question had already been addressed.

The last hand held aloft belonged to a middle-aged lady sitting in the third row.

"Yes, dear lady," invited Tim.

The woman's voice was shaky as if either speaking in public made her nervous, or the subject matter of her question caused her some concern. "Would you mind telling us the story of The Banshee Bride?" she asked, nervously, her cheeks blushing from the effort.

Several voices around the hall affirmed their wish to be told the tale also.

Janine recalled the title of a chapter from Tim's book, and although she had not had time to read it, she had earmarked it for later.

Tim smiled, understandingly.

He took another gulp from his flask and cleared his throat, this time leaving out the joke about his aunt.

He adjusted his microphone. "The story of Molly McShane is a tragic tale, as dark as any," he began, "and not a proud moment for the island. We're going back to a time centuries ago, before British protestants first subjugated Ireland's native Catholic population. At the time, Manus had a tiny population compared to today, but the people were content with their lot and generally there was no crime to speak of other than the odd dispute over livestock, or when someone's dog decided to steal another man's chicken for dinner."

There was a general tittering throughout the hall.

"At that time, there was no need for any official legal intervention, and most disputes were cordially resolved between the parties concerned, with a little help from some mountain dew to seal the deal.

"Molly McShane was a native of the island, and although there are no surviving paintings or drawings of her, she was renowned for being a great beauty, with a heart of pure gold to match. She worked predominantly as a schoolteacher, looking after what we might term as kindergarteners now. There are stories of her leading the children around the island like the infamous Pied Piper of Hamelin, only she used a guitar as her instrument of choice, and her intentions were far less malevolent than his.

"She believed that through music and song, children could be taught about the wonders of our Mother Earth, as well as how best to take care of it. She sang of the magic of animals and how they were God's greatest creation, which he gave to us in order that we might take care of them and treat them with respect and compassion. Several of her songs were inspired by the changes of the seasons and the wonders of nature.

"Fortunately for us, some of her songs have managed to survive through the mists of time thanks to some rather talented troubadours who made a point of writing them down for posterity."

With that, Tim took up his banjo and played a lullaby which

most of the audience seemed to recognise. Some even *hummed* along to the melody.

It was certainly a beautiful song, and the words appeared to Janine to flow together seamlessly.

When Tim finished, he received another resounding round of applause.

Tim took another bow before continuing. "Just after young Molly turned sixteen, she met and fell deeply in love with a young farmer whose family had recently moved to the island. His name was Dan Brennan, and he was only a couple of years older than Molly at the time. They were a perfect match according to legend and were seen daily walking along the edge of the cliffs at Westside Point, what we now refer to as Westside Cliff. They were betrothed within three months, and the date was set for their wedding in the summer of that year. This, as you can imagine, caused a certain amount of resentfulness amongst other young men, and some not so young, from the island who themselves had tried to woo the young Molly without success.

"At the time, as I have already mentioned, there were no official legal authorities on the island, however, we were still subject to the same laws as those dwelling on the mainland and to that end there was a magistrate seconded to the island who used to visit three to four times per year to adjudicate over any on-going disputes amongst the locals. His name was Connor Brady, and although, as I say, he was only a magistrate on the mainland, when he visited us, he insisted on being addressed by the title 'Judge'.

"At that time his powers, so far as the law of the land was concerned, were somewhat limited in that he only had the discretion to refer serious crimes such as those which demanded a proper trial and potential incarceration, to the authorities on the mainland, but as the vast majority of our inhabitants had very little knowledge of the workings of the law at the time, they accepted his word as incontestable.

"It was on one such visit that Brady set eyes on young Molly, and although he was at the time in his mid-fifties with daughters from a previous marriage older than her, he decided that, as a rich widower, the schoolteacher would not be able to resist his advances. So confident was he of his prowess that he approached Molly one morning in front of half the community whilst adjudicating over the application of an easement across someone's land.

"As proceedings were something of an event in those days, there was never a free seat in the old town hall that was used as a court during Brady's visits. Spotting Molly sitting at the back, Brady no doubt decided that it was the perfect occasion to announce his intentions to all those in attendance – including her – as, at the time, he had the power to marry couples during proceedings. He doubtless believed that Molly would be so overcome with emotion at the prospect of becoming his bride that she would run into his arms and accept his generous offer to become his blushing bride.

"As it turned out, young Molly was said to be both mystified and horrified in equal measure that this man-old enough to be her father-had decided to take her as his wife. Being a well-brought-up and respectful girl, she apologised most sincerely to Brady in front of the court, explaining that she was already betrothed and, as such, not free to accept his 'kind' offer.

"This, according to legend, did not go down well with the old magistrate. Unperturbed by her rejection, Brady began to berate the young girl in front of the gathering, informing her that she was nothing more than a silly young girl who should be grateful that an influential and powerful man such as he would even look at her twice, let alone grant her the honour of being his bride.

"It is said that Molly managed somehow to maintain her

composure and merely apologised once more for not being able to accept his offer. By now, the rest of the audience had started to whisper and snigger behind their hands at the magistrate, and when he demanded they be silent, it had the opposite effect as some of them actually laughed so hard that they fell off their chairs.

"Humiliated by this outburst, try as he might, Brady was unable to regain order and eventually, faced with a crowd of unresponsive revelers, he stormed out of the hall with the sound of their raucous laughter ringing in his ears. It is said that as he left, he shot Molly a glance of pure malice bordering on hatred, which made her bow her head in fear to avoid further eye contact with him.

"To a man such as Brady, such humiliation before a group who were meant to respect him was beyond the pale. His dignity and reputation had been maligned to the extent that he felt he could no longer carry out the duties which his position required. Unable to merely shrug the incident off in good humour and keep face, he decided that revenge was his only option. He sent word around the island, making enquiries as to anyone else who had been dishonored and humiliated by the young schoolteacher. Naturally, there were several young men who had had their pride dented by Molly's refusal at courtship, and eventually, Brady learnt of her engagement to Dan Brennan.

"Bribing those who had come forward, a false charge was made against Molly's intended of theft of certain livestock belonging-coincidentally-to those whom Molly had rejected. Poor Dan was dragged before the magistrate forthwith and was pronounced guilty of all charges by Brady without so much as a proper hearing. Now, as I mentioned earlier, the magistrate had no authority with regards to dispensing anything higher than a fine. But he ordered Dan be taken from the court and hanged from the nearest tree for his alleged indiscretions. Those who had assisted him in bringing these erroneous charges were only too happy to comply, and poor Dan was literally strung-up in double-quick time.

"It is said that poor Molly, in the process of been fitted for her wedding dress, only heard of these circumstances after the event, and although she rushed to the court to try and intervene on her beloved's behalf, by the time she arrived it was to find her fiancé's dead body dangling from the tree. The locals who had gathered did what they could to comfort the poor child, but she was inconsolable. Still in her white bridal gown, she desperately tried to climb the tree to release Dan, her mind evidently not able to cope with the fact that he was beyond her reach and already with God.

"As the crowds dispersed, Molly's cries could still be heard throughout the vicinity, until eventually, a group of parishioners banded together to take her from that awful scene so that they might retrieve Dan's body and arrange a proper Christian burial. But as they approached her, their wives at hand to assist in calming the girl down, Molly turned on them, accusing them – somewhat unjustly considering those now in attendance – of conspiring with the judge to murder Dan. The story has it that her face was wild with anger, her porcelain white skin stretched back to resemble a rictus grin with her eyes turned black and exuding a menacing stare of pure hatred and malice, which caused some of those present to move back in terror.

"Before they could stop her, Molly ran from the place and out of sight from the crowd. No one had the courage to go after her, presuming she would calm down in time, so they began the unenviable task of removing Dan from his place of execution. Little did they know that Molly, deranged with grief, had decided to end her own life so that she could once again be with her beloved. But the closer she grew to the Westside Cliff where she intended to meet her fate, the more her mind was wracked with the notion that to take her own life would mean that God would not allow her to see her Dan because of her immortal sin.

"By the time Molly reached the highest point of the cliff, the same place where on the previous evening she and Dan had strolled together, confessing their love to one another, Molly's mind must have been in a turmoil of grief bordering on madness. Unable to reconcile with the prospect of having to carry on living without her betrothed, Molly is said to have stood at the end of the cliff and screamed out at the sea, demanding that Lucifer take her soul and allow her to bestow revenge on those who had wronged her.

"By now, many of the locals had heard the commotion and came running to see what was happening. They heard Molly making her pact with the Devil just before throwing herself from the cliff down into the unforgiving waves below. But there are those present who swore that instead of Molly slamming into the water, her body was hoisted up and carted off by an evil spirit which carried her away over the horizon until she was lost from sight."

Tim paused and glanced around the congregation, many of whom were so riveted by his tale that they were literally sitting on the edge of their seats.

"Well now," he continued after a moment. "I believe that most of you know how the story ends…if it ever has. From that point on, the ghostly figure of Molly McShane was often seen in spirit form, though usually only from the corner of one's eye, as she swooped across the land, her white dress billowing in the wind, her pitiful cries rising to a crescendo which could pierce an eardrum. For it is written that to hear her cry or see her face means instant death. So, whenever it was suspected that her Banshee-spirit was about the land, men, women and children would close their eyes and ram their fingers in their ears to block out the sound for fear that she would carry them back with her to hell itself.

"But it is also said that if the Banshee has been summoned, she cannot return to hell emptyhanded; she must therefore take back a soul with her. Now, usually this would be the soul of the individual she has been called forth to destroy. But, if for some reason that person happens to die before she arrives, then instead she will take back the soul belonging to whoever summoned her to begin with. So have a care any of you who decide you wish to call upon the Banshee Bride's services, for you may well be placing your own immortal souls in peril."

There followed another resounding round of applause.

"What happened to the magistrate and his cronies?" came a cry from the back of the hall.

"Ah," continued Tim thoughtfully. "Well, curiously enough, the morning after Molly's suicide, Brady and all those who had assisted him in killing Dan Brennan were found dead in their beds. Their faces stretched in a torment of agony with their eyes wide open and staring as if they had seen something that their brains could not comprehend."

Tim paused and scanned the room. "I'll leave it up to you all to decide what they died of. But I know what I think."

Chapter Twenty-Four

ONCE TIM'S PERFORMANCE WAS OVER, HE WAS surrounded by a group of mainly women, all clamouring for autographs and selfies, which he happily obliged them with.

Some of the group merely wanted to chat to him, which again Tim was gracious enough to accommodate them without any outward signs of fatigue or irritation, even though from her vantage point, Janine could hear that once again some of the questions being asked had already been covered during Tim's speech.

Father Boyle, too, seemed to attract a few well-wishers who hovered over him, shooting the breeze until he excused himself to Janine and stood to one side next to the stage in case she was starting to feel a little hemmed in by his gathering flock.

Janine took the opportunity to glance through Tim's book. She turned to the chapter entitled 'The Banshee Bride', having already decided that it would form part of her assignment. As she skimmed through the chapter, she glanced up and noticed that Tim was making eye contact with her over the heads of his fans.

He smiled a broad, cheeky grin, which Janine could not help but respond to.

She was looking forward to their official meeting once the audience had dispersed.

Father Boyle had arranged with Tim for them all to go out for a drink after his performance so that the priest could formally introduce him to Janine.

Janine was confident having heard him speak that Tim could offer her a wealth of knowledge about the island, and she wished more than ever that she could have recorded his show, but out of respect, she had not even asked, just in case, for some reason, he took umbrage at the prospect.

Janine knew only too well from past experience how some individuals reacted to being asked if she could record their performances to assist her with her follow-up piece. From what she had seen, she suspected that Tim was not one of those, but even so, it had seemed a trifle discourteous for her to ask to record his session when the two had not even been introduced.

She felt more confident now that he would not object to her taping their interview later on.

Reaching into her bag, Janine retrieved her mobile and switched it back on.

The screen came to life, showing a text from Marie. She opened it, hoping that there had not been any trouble at the restaurant that evening. Even with Sarah there, Janine was still concerned that her ex might turn up out of the blue as he had the previous evening, and without Janine there to take charge, she could not help being concerned that he might not be willing to take 'No' for an answer.

Janine felt her anxiety subside as she read the message. Marie was merely asking if it was okay for her to spend the night at Sarah's. Apparently, Sarah's mum had already said it alright with her.

Janine wondered if she should ask Sarah for her mother's

number so that she could thank her for letting Marie stay, but after hearing the woman rant and rave over the phone the previous night, Janine was ashamed to admit-even to herself-that she was in no hurry to converse with the woman again.

She texted back, asking if the girls wanted her to pick them up after their shift to drop them at Sarah's. She realised that it might be pushing things timewise, especially as Tim's crowd seemed unwilling to disperse just yet, but Janine knew that she would not be able to relax unless she knew the girls were safe.

Father Boyle strolled back and took his seat next to Janine, his loyal fans having now left the hall.

He leaned in to whisper, "I see Tim is as popular as ever, especially with the ladies."

Janine smiled. "So I see. It looks as if some of them might be a tad reluctant to give him up for the evening."

"Are you okay to wait until he is free?" the priest enquired. "He is too well-mannered to dismiss his fans out of hand, but he'll be thirsty after his talk and wanting his pint of ale before too long."

"On top of his aunt's soup?" joked Janine.

Father Boyle held a hand in front of his mouth to stifle a laugh.

Tim noticed the priest's reaction to Janine's reflection, even though he had not actually heard what she had said. It was clear from the look on his face that Father Boyle was right about him needing his drink.

Tim managed to roll his eyes without the last couple of ladies badgering him for information noticing.

Janine caught the movement and smiled back at the author.

Eventually, Tim placed his arms around the shoulders of the final two women and made his excuses, nodding towards where Janine and Father Boyle were sitting, and stating that he was late for an interview with someone who had travelled over from the mainland to meet with him.

The two women shot Janine a sideward glance, clearly unimpressed with the fact that they were being replaced by someone who did not even live on the island.

The porter in charge of locking up the hall had been waiting patiently at the back by the exit, and he glanced purposely at his watch as the final party began making their way towards him.

Tim apologised to the man whom he seemed to know by name as he stood back to allow Janine to exit ahead of him.

The Golden Crown pub was just across the road from the hall, and the minute Tim, Janine and Father Boyle entered, they were warmly greeted by the lady behind the bar.

"This is Mary," Tim said, leaning over the counter and kissing the woman on the cheek. "She serves the finest pint of ale on the island."

"And the mainland," the woman added, crabbily.

"Of course," replied Tim, apologetically. "In fact, I've travelled over much of this great land of ours and never have I supped such a welcoming brew as served by our lovely hostess here."

"Oh, get on with yer," the woman laughed, slapping him playfully on the arm. She looked over at Janine. "And what will it be for my lovely lady?"

Janine smiled. "Thank you, a gin and tonic please."

The woman nodded. "Father?"

"Just a half for me, please, Mary, I have an early start for a change," the priest replied jovially.

The three of them found a table in a relatively quiet corner and sat down.

The pub was relatively busy, but not to the extent that they had to raise their voices to be heard.

A young girl came over carrying a tray with their drinks.

She smiled at Father Boyle. "Good evening, Father," she said, politely.

Before the priest had a chance to respond, Tim interrupted.

"And how is my bonny Nancy doing this evening, breaking hearts as usual?"

The girl flushed but kept on smiling as she placed the glasses down, before scurrying away back towards the bar.

Tim raised his glass in salute. "Here's to you both," he announced, "may any troubles which come your way be small and insignificant."

They all *clinked* and took a mouthful.

Janine pulled a face; her drink was definitely more gin than tonic. She would have to pace herself if she was going to drive later.

Tim managed to finish half his pint in one go, holding his half-empty glass up in front of him afterwards as the froth slipped slowly back down the insides. "Now there's a fine pint and no mistake," he exclaimed. He leaned in a little towards Janine. "Mary's family own the brewery that makes this gorgeous nectar, you must try some before you leave."

Janine smiled. "I've never been much of a beer drinker," she confessed. "Is it strong stuff?"

"Strong," added Father Boyle, keeping his voice low. "It's barely legal."

Tim laughed heartily and took another gulp, managing to virtually finish his pint.

He placed a hand in front of his mouth, managing to suppress a belch. "Manners," he announced, rhetorically.

He signalled towards Mary for another pint. "Now then," he began, turning his attention back to Janine. "The good father here tells me that you're writing an article on our fair island for one of those bigwig papers back in England?"

Janine nodded. "Well, it's a glossy magazine, actually. They specialise in stories concerning quaint towns and villages all over Britain. They have a fairly decent readership I believe, although to be honest, I've never worked for them before."

"Ah, so did they seek you out?" asked Tim.

Janine laughed, shaking her head. "I wouldn't go that far. Being freelance, I have my details registered with dozens of agents, all of whom make their money by marrying up writers with relevant stories and taking their cut directly from the publication. The trick is to never turn down an assignment, that keeps you relevant and employed simultaneously."

"Sounds quite brutal," Tim observed. "I suspect that from what you're saying, if you turn down too many offers, you slide off their books."

Janine nodded. "It can be a little like that, but at least most agencies allow you to set a profile stating that you are prepared and not prepared to do. So, for example, because of my daughter, I cannot travel to any far-flung part of the globe for weeks on end. Even on this assignment, her father was supposed to take her on holiday with him, but, as per, he let her down at the last second, so she's here with me now."

"You have a daughter, how wonderful," mused Tim, "and where is she tonight. You haven't locked her up in the basement just so that you can meet me, I hope?"

Tim's question took Janine unawares just as she was sipping her drink.

She quickly placed her glass back on the table and stifled a choke as best she could.

Tim leaned over and gently patted her back. "I'm sorry," he said, apologetically. "The good father here should have warned you about my sense of humour."

"There's only so much a person can say about you without taking a full year to explain all of your caprices," Father Boyle interjected. "Janine is only here for a week."

Recovering her composure, Janine waved aside the comment. "No problem, I'm usually more adept at understanding people's sense of humour. You just caught me a little off guard there, but don't worry, I'm prepared now."

She and Tim exchanged a knowing glance which did not escape the priest's notice.

"Are you sure you can be trusted with this reprobate?" he asked Janine, grinning. "I'd hate to leave you in his company if you're going to fall for his usual blarney. He has a reputation with the ladies, to be sure."

Tim slapped a hand to his chest. "You do me a great disservice, Father; ask any poet and they will confess how easy it is for them to fall in love. It goes with their territory."

"Huh, love indeed," announced Mary, suddenly appearing by their side with Tim's fresh pint. "Shag anything with a hole this one, and don't let him tell you otherwise."

"Mary!" Said Father Boyle, clearly shocked by her statement.

Mary blushed. "My apologies, father, I was just warning this young lady here to beware of Tim's old flannel. But I'm sure she is too sensible to fall for any of his nonsense."

"Your words wound me like no sword or dagger ever could," Tim replied, dejectedly, keeping his hand on his heart. "Sure, and what will young Janine here think of me hearing your hurtful comments?"

Mary rolled her eyes and glanced down towards Janine. "You've got to love the man for trying. God loves a trier, doesn't he, Father?"

"He does indeed, my child," Father Boyle agreed, raising his glass in salute.

Chapter Twenty-Five

BRIDGET DONNELLY SLUMPED DOWN IN HER favourite armchair, taking a sip from her glass of whiskey before placing it on the occasional table next to her. This was her third glass of the evening, but she felt it justified. It had been an awful day from start to finish, and she was looking forward to her bed.

To start things off, Trevor had dropped an entire pint carton of milk on the kitchen floor at breakfast. The top was open from the previous evening, so the contents spilled out over the linoleum, drenching the fluffy mat Bridget used to stand on while at the sink in her bare feet.

To be fair, Bridget had been the one to use the milk last, so there was every chance that she was responsible for not securing the stopper. But even so, that did not excuse the boy's clumsiness. He should have been paying more attention to the job at hand instead of mucking around trying to impress his sister with one of his stupid impersonations.

Bridget had wacked him hard across the back of his head whilst yelling at him to clean up his mess. She was especially angry because that was the last of the milk, and she had to drink her morning tea black.

It took him so long that in the end, he ran out of time for breakfast and had to go to school on an empty stomach. But in her mind, that would teach the boy a valuable lesson to be more careful in future.

Next, she received a call from the school halfway through the morning informing her that Scarlett had been vomiting and needed to be collected. This was a major inconvenience as Bridget had one of her regulars booked in for that afternoon, and she hated cancelling, especially as she needed the money.

In the end, Bridget decided that on this occasion it would be safe enough with Scarlet tucked up in bed. This client only ever wanted straight intercourse, so at least the noise level would be minimal. She would suggest that they did it on the sofa downstairs, just in case Scarlet was still awake. It was big enough for the job, and comfortable enough for her trick to still enjoy himself.

Bridget had always warned the kids that when she had a 'friend' over that they had to make themselves scarce and stay in their bedrooms. Even so, she preferred it if they were asleep at the time, or better still, at school, which was why she saw most of her clients either during the day or after the kids went to bed.

Typically, upon returning home, Scarlet suddenly felt fine and wanted to stay downstairs and watch telly.

This was too much, so Bridget told her in no uncertain terms that if she was too ill for school, then she was too ill for watching telly. She sent the girl upstairs, warning her that if she made so much as a peep before Bridget called her for dinner, she would rue the day.

Then, just to add salt to the wound, her client cancelled at the last minute, citing some cock-and-bull story about his wife deciding to join him to visit relatives on the island at the last minute. He insisted that he could not risk making an excuse to get away from her, not even for half an hour.

Although he was extremely apologetic, Bridget lost her

temper with him and claimed that she had refused another client to visit based on the fact that she was expecting him.

Finally, the man promised to pay her an extra twenty quid on his next visit, which Bridget informed him she would hold him to.

The final straw came when Trevor arrived home, and Scarlet came downstairs. Both of them claimed they needed to use Bridget's computer for their homework and began arguing with each other over which one needed it first. Why they could not use their fancy phones for what they needed, Bridget did not know, but their arguing blew her last fuse and she laid into both of them with a plastic spatula.

Finally, they shut up and carried on with their homework in silence while she made their tea. Because of the way they had behaved, Bridget sent them straight to bed after they'd finished eating. Neither complained as they knew from her mood that Bridget would not entertain any complaints.

Once they went upstairs, she hit the bottle.

Bridget was partway through watching a documentary on one of her favourite comedians as he gave his view on the joys of taking his family on a world cruise, when her phone went off. She glared at the screen and saw that it was John Camper calling.

John was a regular whom she referred to as 'camper' because he had an outdoor fetish when it came to sex. His 'kink' was to do it in a sleeping bag inside a tent. Not a particularly weird fantasy when you consider that people all over the world on camping holidays were doing the same thing. But nonetheless, Bridget had a rule about keeping her business inside the secrecy of her own house, so she charged John double her usual rate to incorporate his fetish.

This he paid willingly. Bridget never asked any of her clients about their private lives; she really only wanted their money. But from the way John spoke and the posh car he drove, she suspected that he was not short of a bob or two and wondered if she should have asked for triple instead.

It was something she considered every time he phoned.

"Hello, John," she said, turning down the volume on her telly with the remote.

"Oh, hello," he replied, almost apologetically. He had a very soft way of speaking and was by far her most nervous client. Bridget suspected that he either suffered from Catholic guilt, or he was married and felt bad about cheating on his other half.

"Do you want to book an appointment for the usual?" Bridget asked.

"Well, actually, I'm on the ferry now and was hoping you could see me tonight."

Bridget considered the invitation.

It would certainly make up for the client who bailed on her earlier that day, and as the kids were already in bed, she could easily slip out for an hour or so without anyone being any the wiser.

Even so, John usually called at least a day in advance, so she decided she could use his obvious desperation to her advantage.

"Sorry, John," she said sympathetically, "I've had a rough day and I'm in for the night now."

"Oh, right, I see." Bridget could tell from the disappointment in his voice that she had him on the line. Now she just needed to reel him in.

Knowing he was already on the ferry made it that much easier.

"I wish you'd called me before I sat down with a drink, I'd've been up for it then, especially on a lovely night like this."

There was a short pause before John continued. "I'm really sorry for the short notice, I was going to call you before boarding, but then I received another call from work which I had to take, so I just drove onto the ferry so as not to miss it. I was really looking forward to seeing you this evening."

Bridget sighed. "And I'd like to see you too, but it takes a lot for me to leave the 'ouse once I've settled down for the evening. If only I'd known in advance that you were coming over."

Another short pause followed. "There's nothing I can say to maybe change your mind?" The desperation in his voice was palpable. Now Bridget knew that she had him hook, line and sinker.

Bridget let out a deeper sigh, not of annoyance, but more of weight to signify that she was reconsidering his request.

She allowed the silence to hang in the air, hoping that it would urge John into making the next move. If it failed, she was more than willing to mention the money, but Bridget felt it would be far better if he thought it was his idea, then she could reluctantly agree as if to enforce the fact that she was doing John a massive favour.

Finally, it worked. "Look, as it's such short notice, how about a little bonus as compensation?" John urged, his voice trembling even more than usual. He was clearly afraid of annoying Bridget in case she refused to see him again because of his persistence.

"How do you mean?" Bridget asked, sounding intrigued.

"What if I gave you an extra, say, twenty quid because of the inconvenience?"

She had hoped for fifty, but there was still room for more play.

"Oh, John, you are making this hard on a poor working girl," Bridget replied, sweetly. "But to be fair to you, I'm all set for an evening at home with me feet up in front of the telly, and like I said, I've already had a drink to relax me."

"How about fifty? Please don't be cross with me for trying to persuade you. If you say no, then no it is. But I really would like to see you. I promise I'll never ask at such short notice again."

Bingo.

"Ahhh, you really are a little Devil and no mistake," Bridget kept her tone gentle, emphasising the reluctance with which she felt obliged to agree to his terms. "Go on then, you've convinced me, an extra fifty it is."

"Oh, thank you, Bridget." The relief in his voice was clearly genuine. "I'll see you in the usual place in, shall we say, an hour? That'll give me enough time to disembark and set the tent up. And thank you again, I really appreciate your under-standing."

"Just you make sure that the ground sheet is folded over. Last time my back took three days before it stopped hurting."

"I will, I promise, and I've bought a padded blanket too, so that should alleviate any uncomfortableness."

"Okay then, one hour from now. And make sure no one sees you setting up shop. I can't afford for any local busybody to trip over us while we're conducting business."

"I promise, and thank you again," John said, gratefully. "I'll make sure that the coast is clear before I start. See you in an hour."

Bridget placed her phone back on the table and lifted her glass to her lips.

That extra fifty quid was going to come in very handy.

If only she had more regular clients like John, she could pack in looking after ungrateful little brats like those two upstairs and concentrate on her craft work.

On the other hand, she knew that she could not carry on selling herself forever. Eventually, the clientele would search out fresher meat, then she might actually be grateful for the fact that she kept her hand in with the fostering.

She knocked back her whiskey and checked the time.

Another short measure would help to ward off the night chill when she left.

Chapter Twenty-Six

IT HAD CERTAINLY BEEN A BUSY NIGHT IN THE restaurant, and Marie really felt as if she had earned her money. Fortunately, the four miscreants she had had trouble with earlier were the only unpleasant customers for the night, and after Sarah had intervened, they left quietly once they had finished their meals. They even left a decent tip, which Marie was not expecting.

Not all the customers, pleasant or otherwise, were so generous in their gratuities, but Sarah explained that such behaviour was par for the course and that although the tips were nice to receive, she had learned from the other girls working there not to rely upon them.

The safest bet was just to be as helpful and pleasant to all their customers and hope for the best.

Breaks were allowed on a 'when and if' basis, which basically meant that if they were fully staffed, everybody could expect at least one during their shift. But, on a night such as this, with such few waiting staff, the girls had to the free cups of tea and coffee prepared by the kitchen staff, which they drank on route to collecting dishes once they were prepared.

Fortunately, the girls did have moments when they were waiting to hand in customers bills at the till together, and this was the only time they really managed to talk.

"Well?" asked Sarah, eagerly. "What's your decision. Are we going, or not?"

Marie had thought of little else since her mum texted her with an offer of a lift to Sarah's after work.

She could see from the expression on Sarah's face that her friend really wanted to go, which made her feel too guilty to say no. "Are you sure it will be okay?" Marie asked, tentatively.

"Of course it will," Sarah assured her. "What are you worried about?"

Marie bit her bottom lip. If truth be told, the more she thought about it, the more unsure she was about being anywhere alone with Declan and his cronies, let alone on their territory where help, if needed, would be nowhere at hand.

But she kept in mind that he had been Sarah's boyfriend until a few nights ago, so she did not want to insult her new friend by casting aspersions against him and his family.

"It's just, well, we'll be all alone with them all, and up until this afternoon, you didn't want anything to do with Declan anymore, and now…"

Sarah laughed. "I still don't want him as a boyfriend, that hasn't changed. But these get-togethers are something else. These travellers don't stint when it comes to entertaining. There's tons of food and drink, music, dancing, and even the odd fight now and then. It really is an all-inclusive party and not everyone gets invited."

Sarah could see that Marie was still not convinced.

If she was being honest with herself, she had never attended one of these shindigs on her own, and she would not want to now, either. The only reason she contemplated going was because she had Marie with her, and together they could watch each other's backs in case things became uncomfortable.

Besides which, the elders would all be there, and Sarah had met some of them at previous events. The women, especially, would keep an eye out for any untoward behaviour from Declan and his crowd.

Even so, if Marie really did not want to go, then Sarah would stand by her friend and they could just go home and watch a DVD or something instead.

"Look," Sarah began, placing a comforting hand on Marie's forearm, "if you're really concerned, we don't have to go. The last thing I want is to make you feel uncomfortable. We can always let *wild* Marie out another night."

"Hey, are you two going to do some work, or what?" The manager had crept up beside the cashier without either of the girls noticing.

Marie blushed at being caught out.

"All right, all right, we're moving," Sarah shot back, cheekily. "Bloody slavedriver, there are laws to deal with the likes of you."

The two girls split up and returned to their respective tables.

Marie had never had a friend quite like Sarah.

The girl was not only sweet and kind, she was fearless too. The thought of the party did not seem to faze her one little bit, and Marie could not help but feel a trifle foolish for being so apprehensive.

She knew that Sarah was far too lovely to hold it against her should she pull out, but her deep-rooted guilt at making such a decision was fighting beside her inner voice, which was egging her on to break a few rules for once and to stop being such a goody-goody.

This could well be a night to remember, even if she never told her mum about it.

The next time Marie had a quiet moment, she texted her mum back, thanking her for the offer of a lift but stating that the restaurant owner was springing for a cab for them.

It was only a small white lie.

When she caught Sarah's eye across the room, she lifted both thumbs.

Sarah could not contain her excitement and disappeared a moment later into the cloakrooms. When she re-emerged, she beckoned Marie over to her, carrying two menus as if to show anyone looking on that they were still working.

As the two girls met, Sarah made a point of showing Marie something on the menu.

"I've texted Declan to pick us up after our shift," she informed Marie, excitedly. Hopefully, I've caught him before he's had too much to drive."

"Are we going in our uniforms?" Marie asked, looking down at the plain white blouse, black skirt and ballet pumps she had worn at Sarah's recommendation.

"No way," replied Sarah. "I'll get Dopey to drop us off at my place first so we can change, then we'll go on to the party. I'm so glad you changed your mind. Tonight's going to give you a real taste of Irish hospitality, with a little danger thrown in for good measure… Nothing that we girls can't handle though, am I right?"

Marie smiled, but deep down she was still unsure about the night's festivities.

Her mother had always been strict with her when it came to attending events that she felt uncomfortable about. Concerts with her friends were okay so long as Janine or one of the other parents were arranging to pick them up afterwards.

It was the same thing with late-night showings at cinemas, which Marie had always found a bit of a bummer, as she and her friends often felt like going out to eat afterwards. It had been the cause of numerous rows between them, but for the most part, her friends' parents felt the same so the argument was pretty futile on that front.

Marie had noticed that her mother had eased up a little on her when she passed sixteen, although she drew the line at

Marie going to clubs where there was a minimum age limit of eighteen. Entering such places was easy for girls of Marie's age, all it took was a little make-up and the right outfit and the bouncers let them right in.

She and her friends had tried it out a couple of times just to see how easy it was to gain entry. But they never stayed past their curfew so as to avoid any awkward questions when they arrived back home.

Knowing that her mother would never agree to her going to the party this evening was causing Marie more anguish the closer it grew to leaving time.

She could feel a knot in her stomach growing bigger with each passing minute.

But Marie knew that it was already too late to pull out. For one thing Sarah had already made arrangements for them to be collected, and she knew how much her friend was looking forward to going, so to say she had changed her mind this late in the day no longer seemed like an option.

Besides, Marie had something she needed to prove to herself, even if her mother was not willing to admit it. She was old enough to start making her own decisions, at least about certain things, and something as simple as a party with a friend should not have been cause for a confrontation.

After all, her grandmother had told Marie stories of how her mother used to sneak out as a young girl to do the exact same thing, so if it was good enough for her why not Marie?

They could both have a good laugh about it years from now.

So why was she still feeling so apprehensive?

Was it really because this was the first time she could remember lying to her mother?

Was this years of Catholic guilt personified?

Honour thy mother and father.

Yeah, right, because her father had shown her immense

honour when he cancelled their holiday together just so he could pander to the whims of his new woman.

How many times had he told her that she was his girl and that no one would ever come before her? If she had been with him on the island, she would not have felt the slightest twinge of guilt about lying to him about the party.

But she knew deep down that his behaviour had nothing to do with her mother. She had been hurt and let down just as much as Marie had by his selfish actions so she did not deserve to be on the receiving end of such deceit.

"The boys are on their way," Sarah said, excitedly, sidling up to Marie and nudging her with her elbow. "Sure, I can almost taste the mountain dew from here."

"Me too," replied Marie, smiling, although she had no idea what mountain dew was; she presumed it was some form of cocktail.

Well, it was certainly too late to pull out now unless she wanted to risk losing her only friend on the island.

Marie took a deep breath and attempted to dismiss from hand growing trepidation.

Tomorrow she would probably look back and wonder what all the fuss was about.

Chapter Twenty-Seven

BRIDGET CLOSED THE DOOR BEHIND HER, MAKING sure it did not slam. Although she was fairly confident that the kids would not dare to disobey her orders for them to stay in bed, she still did not wish to alert them to the fact that she was going out and leaving them home alone.

The wrong word in the wrong ear at social services might well see her lose her little nest egg.

The sun had set several hours earlier, and now there was a brisk wind moving in from the sea. Dressed only in a flimsy summer dress, Wellingtons and a light cardigan, Bridget questioned her choice of garments on such a night but decided that the walk to and from the park would suffice to keep her warm enough.

Not to mention the four shots of whiskey she had enjoyed before leaving the house.

She strode briskly across the grass, cutting a path through the houses which surrounded her own, making her way by the quickest possible route to her destination.

Her light dress clung to her legs, forced to remain there by the chill wind.

She had not even bothered with underwear, removing hers along with her stockings before she left the house. Her client this evening was not fussed by such apparel. So long as Bridget was willing to slip naked into his sleeping bag, he was more than happy; therefore, she always wore as little as modesty would allow to help speed up the process.

As she reached the peak of a small hill, Bridget saw one of her neighbours meandering along the path, carrying two heavy bags of shopping.

Bridget had known the woman for years. They had often nodded to each other when waiting in line for confession, but other than the odd conversation upon seeing each other in town, they were not what anyone would consider friends.

One thing Bridget did know about the old woman was that, for a good Catholic, she was an unmitigated gossip who seemed to take a particular delight in trashing anyone whom she decided was 'up to no good'.

Bridget crouched down behind a bush and waited for the woman to pass.

Typically, she was taking forever, doubtless because of the two burdens she had balanced on either side, and her crippling arthritis which she was only too happy to bemoan about to anyone who would listen, as well as several people who were just too polite to excuse themselves and move on with their day.

The last bus of the evening had already been and gone, and Bridget could not help wondering why the old biddy did not catch it and save herself such an effort.

Then she suspected that her neighbour was probably talking to some poor, unwitting fool and lost track of time.

Bridget glanced at her watch. This delay was something she had not anticipated, but there was no way she could risk being seen by the busybody, so she had no alternative but to stay hidden until the coast was clear.

The old woman seemed to be stopping every three or four

steps to put down her bags and take a breather. Bridget wished that the old bag would just have a heart attack and drop dead on the spot. That way at least she could carry on with her business uninterrupted.

She suspected that there were quite a few people in town who, although doubtless not willing to admit it, would be glad to see the back of the old trout and her gossiping ways.

It was just typical that she had to be here on this night of all nights, making a nuisance of herself.

Just then, Bridget saw a shadowy figure looming over the horizon, heading in the same direction as the old lady. Bridget crouched down even further to ensure she could not be seen from the path.

When the new arrival came into view, Bridget recognised her, again from the church, but she was sure that the woman did not live on this side of town. Perhaps she was out visiting someone. Either way, Bridget hoped that she would give the old woman a hand and speed her on her way.

She waited for the younger woman to catch up.

When they met, it was obvious that they knew each other, but instead walking off together, the stupid women decided to stay put and strike up a conversation.

Bridget could feel her blood boiling. She had no other option other than to cut back across the estate and make her way to the park via the main road, which would add a significant amount of time to her journey.

What was wrong with these people? Why stand out in the cold in the middle of the night when they could both doubtless benefit from making their way to their intended destinations?

At that moment, Bridget could feel her mobile vibrating in her sling purse.

She peered through the bush, convinced one of the women must have heard it, but to her relief, neither seemed to take any notice. Bridget surmised that the wind was on her side, blocking out the noise from this distance.

She carefully unzipped her purse and removed the phone, keeping her hand over the screen to prevent the light from giving her away.

As she suspected, it was John informing her that he was in situ and that everything was ready.

Bridget turned her back to the women to keep them from noticing any glare from her screen. Gently, so as not to make a sound, she texted John that she was running late, but assured him to wait and she would be along shortly. Before pressing 'send', as a caveat she added in large caps, 'DON'T TEXT ME BACK, JUST BE PATIENT'.

Finally, the penny dropped, and the younger woman took one of the bags, and they both set off back along the path.

Bridget waited until they were both out of sight, then checked that it was clear in both directions before emerging from her hiding place and continuing on her way to her rendezvous.

Her legs were aching by the time she reached the park. Bridget put it down to a combination of having to stay squatting for so long, as well as making the journey in her Wellingtons, as they were very old with not much support left in the sole.

Such a journey required more rugged footwear, but alas, all Bridget had back home were stilettoes with pointed toes, which were even less suitable for such a journey.

She remembered the last time John came over to the island she had promised herself a new pair of walking boots before his next visit, but with everything else going on in her life, it had slipped from her mind.

Bridget made her way across the park, deliberately keeping to the shadows and avoiding the reflection from the lights scattered around the path. A couple of times, she heard voices from young couples meandering through on their way into town. But she managed to keep hidden long enough for them to move along.

Finally, she reached the clearing which led to the remote area behind a row of hedges where she and John always met.

Sure enough, as she cleared the first hedge, she could see his tent set up in the distance. By now, Bridget's feet were sore enough to bleed, so she limped the last few yards before reaching the veritable safety of the canvas covers.

John appeared from one side of the tent, causing Bridget to jump.

"You silly bugger, what did you 'ave to leap out on me like that for?" she demanded.

John looked shocked. "Sorry," he replied, apologetically, "I was just checking one of the tent pegs was properly fastened. I didn't mean to frighten you."

Bridget took a few deep breaths to calm herself down.

"Come on then," she said, curtly, "let's get on with it. 'Ave you got me money?"

John glanced around to check that no one else was watching before removing his wallet from his back pocket. He took out a wad of notes and handed them over.

In the dim light, Bridget could not see properly what she was counting, but the feel of the notes gave her the confidence that John was not trying to pull a fast one. Plus, he knew if he ever did, it would be the last time she would be willing to play his little games, so that in itself was enough of an incentive for him to be straight with her.

Bridget tucked the notes into her purse. "Come on then," she said, moving towards the open flap.

"You're limping," John remarked, following her in. "Are you alright?" There was genuine concern in his voice, although Bridget did not acknowledge it.

"It's these bleedin' boots. They've got no cushion left in the soles. I usually only wear them fer the gardin', but you an' yer bleedin' camping fetish, they're the only things I've got to walk over this terrain."

"I'm sorry, I feel terrible," John responded, "I didn't realise."

"Yea, well, I'm 'ere now," muttered Bridget. "Make yerself useful," she sat down and lifted one of her legs towards John. "'Elp me take 'em off."

John did as he was instructed and took hold of the offered leg, grabbing the Wellington by the heel and toe and gently pulling.

Bridget's leg slowly slipped out of the rubber confines.

"Ow, that bleedin' hurt," she complained.

John apologised once more and lifted her other foot, trying in vain to be more careful with this one.

"Argh!" Bridget winced. "They've done me feet in well and proper. I shall 'ave to walk 'ome in me bare feet at this rate."

John squinted in the poor light at Bridget's bare feet. "They do look awfully sore," he noted. "I haven't got any cream or anything useful with me, but would it help if I massaged them for a bit?"

Bridget eyed him suspiciously. "Is this another one of yer fetishes, because if it is, I'll want more money?"

John flushed. "No, no, I assure you, nothing like that. I just thought it might ease the soreness in your poor feet, that's all."

Bridget narrowed her eyes.

She already had a couple of foot fetishists on her books who would be in their element at the chance of massaging her bare feet. But to be fair to him, John had never requested anything in that direction before, and from what she could remember he had never so much as tried to touch her feet during their past encounters.

So perhaps he was being genuine after all.

"Okay then," Bridget agreed, "but be careful with 'em, they're the only ones I've got."

John knelt down and rubbed his hands against his trousers

as if to remove any lingering dirt or dust. He carefully lifted one of Bridget's feet by the heel and gently began to rub it between his fingers.

Bridget immediately pulled her foot away. "Oi, stop that, it tickles. Can't you do it without ticklin' me?"

"I'm so sorry," John apologised, yet again, his cheeks still flushed. "Would it help if I rubbed them a little more firmly?"

"Go on, try that," Bridget retorted, not attempting to keep the irritation from her voice.

John tried again, this time using a firmer action.

It seemed to do the job. Other than the odd flinch from Bridget, she lay back on the sleeping bag and closed her eyes, letting John continue without further interruption.

If she was being honest, the feeling was quite pleasurable. Most of her regulars spent more time sucking her toes than massaging her feet. Not that she complained, that was quite a nice experience too, even though she always made a point of making them aware that she was letting them do it for their pleasure, not hers. Just in case they started asking for cheaper sessions.

She let John continue for about fifteen minutes before telling him to stop.

Pleasant as the experience was, she needed to keep an eye on the time because of those blasted kids.

"Come on, that'll do fer now," she announced, pulling her foot back. "Let's get on to the main event, shall we?"

Without speaking, John pulled down his trousers and underwear and pulled his shirt over his head without bothering to undo any of the buttons.

Bridget could see that he was already aroused, which was usually the case with him.

She slipped off her cardigan and dress and, removing a condom from her purse, she zipped it closed and placed her clothes on top of it, next to her. She slid into the sleeping bag, which John had already laid out, and propped herself up on one arm, waiting for him to join her.

John moved forward and pulled back the top flap of the and eagerly climbed in next to Bridget. His protrusion brushed against her belly as he slid further down into the soft duvet cover.

He began to zip the sleeping bag shut.

"'Ang on a minute," Bridget hissed, almost menacingly. "Haven't we forgotten something?" She held up the unopened condom wrapper and shook it before John's eyes.

"Oh, yes, of course, silly me." John unzipped the cover and pulled it back. A sudden shock of night air wafted into the tent, rippling the canvas sides and causing John to take a sharp intake of breath.

Bridget opened the foil wrapper with her teeth and slid the condom out, feeling the slippery rubber between her fingers until she had decided which was the right way up.

Moving down John's naked torso she slipped the rubber tunnel onto his fully erect penis, and used her fingers to guide it down until his entire shaft was covered.

Once the zip was refastened, Bridget used her hand to guide John inside her.

He was no time waster.

John began sliding back and forth inside Bridget, grunting with a mixture of effort and pleasure as he worked. He managed to manoeuvre his hands down behind her naked torso until he could cup her buttocks in both hands.

Bridget stared behind her into space as John worked.

She could feel his wet slippery tongue lapping at her nipples before taking them into his mouth and sucking on them.

He came with a full body *shudder,* and Bridget allowed him to lie on top of her for a couple of minutes to prolong the ecstasy for him.

Eventually, she patted him on the shoulder, which was his signal to remove himself from her.

With a load sigh, John extricated himself from between her legs and reached down to unzip the sleeping bag. He climbed out first, then held out his hand to help Bridget to her feet.

They dressed in silence.

Bridget's feet began stinging again the moment she put her Wellingtons back on.

John witnessed her pain. "Why don't you let me drop you home?" he asked, genuinely concerned. "It won't take me long to dismantle this lot and carry it back to my car, fifteen minutes at the most."

It was certainly a tempting thought, but Bridget did not want to waste the time.

So long as she did not come across anyone she knew on the journey, she could be halfway home by then.

"Nah, don't worry," she replied, "I'll be okay, I'll give them a nice long soak when I get home." She crouched down to exit the tent. "See you soon," she said, not bothering to look back.

"I'll look forward to it," John called after her.

When she emerged from the clearing Bridget scanned the area to make sure on one was about before setting off back across the park. When she was some distance away from her rendezvous spot Bridget relaxed, at least if anyone saw her now, she would just be a person on a late-night walk. Nothing suspicious about that.

The main concern still was encountering anyone who might recognise her. But she doubted that any of the local busybodies would be out at such an hour, so she just concentrated on where she placed her feet, trying to avoid uneven rocks, stones or anything protruding from the ground which might cause her pain.

As she emerged from the park, Bridget felt the full force of the sea breeze. No longer protected by the high bushes and hedges, she wrapped her cardigan around her and held it in place with her crossed arms.

Her purse, laden with her earnings, swung reassuringly against her hip as she walked.

It had been a good night's work, and she deserved the scotch and foot bath she planned on having when she arrived home.

Crossing the first path towards the estate, Bridget heard a faint cry carried on the wind.

She stopped in her tracks for a moment to listen.

Was that a woman crying for help?

She waited a moment.

Nothing.

Probably just a seagull or the wind playing tricks.

Shivering, she carried on along the grassy verge.

Then, she heard it again, more distinct this time. That was no seagull, and it sounded too loud for a trick of the wind.

Bridget spun round. She wished now that she had brought out some form of weapon to defend herself with. She kept a hammer by the back door in case of intruders and an old cricket stump under her bed. Either right now would have been better than nothing.

If some woman was being attacked, there was a good chance that she could scare the attacker off with just a shout. Knowing that he had been seen by someone else might just do the trick. After all, most of these bastards were cowards who would run a mile if challenged.

She strained to listen above the sound of the wind.

There it was again, sounding closer this time but seemingly from a different direction.

Bridget turned around, then back again.

Where was it coming from?

It almost seemed as if the sound was all around her, attacking her ears from all sides simultaneously.

That was no cry for help!

If someone was playing silly buggers with her, they would be sorry.

Bridget wanted to shout out, telling whomever it might be in no uncertain terms that they had chosen the wrong victim to play a prank on this time. But she stopped herself. Screaming out now could possibly raise an alarm, which may have consequences.

She was too close to the estate to risk drawing attention to herself.

Bridget carried on, her head bowed against the wind, no longer concerned with some stupid adolescent pranks.

The cry came again. This time close enough that Bridget felt that it had to be made by someone directly behind her.

That was it.

She spun round, her fist clenched, ready for a fight. "Right, you fuckin' bastards, you've picked on the wrong bitch this time."

There was no one there.

She squinted into the distance. Something odd had caught her eye. It appeared almost as if something white was fluttering in the breeze, heading her way.

Bridget pulled back. Although the object seemed to have no specific form, it floated on the wind with purpose, managing to avoid any overhanging trees in its path as if it was being controlled or piloted.

Could it be one of those drone things she had seen on the telly?

Covered in a white sheet to scare decent folk late at night?

A prankster's trick.

The cry came again, so loud now that Bridget was forced to cover her ears with her hands. The sound pierced her eardrums and made her feel as if her head were about to explode.

For a moment, she closed her eyes in pain.

When she opened them again, she saw the full horror of

what was now hovering directly over her. The white apparition had taken on a form all its own with black eyes which seemed to bore into Bridget's very soul and a gaping maw which opened wider as the pitch of the cry grew in intensity.

As the thing lowered itself onto her, Bridget tried to release a scream, but it stuck in her throat and only emerged as a raspy croak.

Her reason and sanity deserted her as she felt her heartbeat *thudding* in her ears, growing louder and louder, battling with the unearthly cries which emanated from the floating figure above her.

Mercifully, Bridget was dead before she hit the ground.

Chapter Twenty-Eight

MARIE AND SARAH SAT SIDE-BY-SIDE IN FRONT OF Sarah's dressing table mirror, adding the last touches to their make-up.

In truth, Marie still had an uncomfortable knot sitting in the pit of her stomach at the prospect of the night ahead, but she had decided earlier on at the restaurant that she could not change her mind about going and disappoint her new friend.

Sarah *hummed* a tune to herself as she applied her eyeliner, clearly excited about the party. She looked completely different made-up and, although Marie had been sitting beside her during the transformation, she could barely recognise her from the waitress she had just shared a shift with.

Declan, as promised, had picked them up from the restaurant at the end of their shift.

Sarah had instructed him to wait in the car around the side of the restaurant so that the manager would not see them leaving with him. After recent events, she was afraid that he might decide to contact her mother and let her know what was going on if he saw them together again.

But Declan, being the half-wit that he was, ignored his

instructions and made a fool of himself by standing outside in front of the restaurant's main window and pulling faces at the remaining clientele, while simultaneously performing a drunken jig on the pavement.

It took Sarah three attempts to usher him away by signalling animatedly at him through the glass before he finally took the hint and moved out of sight.

The 'carriage' that awaited the two girls when they left work looked, to Marie at least, as if it belonged more in a breaker's yard than on the road.

It was a beaten-up old hatchback with two doors, both different colours, neither of which matched the rest of the rust-eaten body. The passenger window was made of polythene secured around the outside with black masking tape, while the driver's side one was missing altogether. Judging by the shards of broken glass which stuck out from the frame, it was obvious that the window had been smashed, rather than removed.

Declan had arrived with two friends, one of whom Marie recognised from earlier. The other, the driver, appeared to be no more than thirteen or fourteen, and when he climbed out of his seat to usher the two girls into the back, Marie immediately turned to Sarah with a look of astonishment in her eyes, which she hoped conveyed her concern at the boy's age.

Fortunately, her silent protest had the desired effect.

"Wait on a moment," Sarah declared. "Who's this?" she demanded, indicating towards their potential driver.

Declan swung his arm around the boy's shoulders. "This 'ere is my cousin Sean."

The young man offered his hand to Sarah. "Pleases to make your acquaintance," he announced, shaking her hand.

Before he had a chance to offer it to Marie, Sarah cut him off. "And how old might he be?" she asked, eyeing Declan, suspiciously. "Certainly not old enough to be in front of the wheel of this thing, that's fer sure."

Declan laughed, loudly, throwing his head back with the effort. "Now don't you be worryin' your pretty heads about Sean here, he's one of the safest drivers on the road today."

"Not to mention the only sober one left at the party," offered Declan's companion from the passenger side.

Declan gave him a stern look, then turned back to face Sarah. "Now you just get your beautiful little butts in there, and Sean 'ere will whisk you off to your place in comfort and safety like you was on yer own magic carpet. Ain't that right, Sean?"

The young driver nodded, eagerly. "Sure, I've never had an accident in all me life," he said, reassuringly.

"And how long's that been?" Sarah asked, dismissively. "Fourteen years?"

The three men laughed in unison.

Sarah turned back to face Marie, raising her eyebrows. "Well?" she asked. "Shall we?"

Reluctantly, Marie climbed in the back seat, putting her faith in her friend's judgement.

Before Sarah had a chance to climb in after her, Declan moved around her and slipped in beside Marie. "Now this will make for a more comfortable ride, don't yer think?" he asked Marie, stretching his lips back to reveal his missing teeth. "Come on now, don't be getting' jealous on me," he continued, turning back and reaching out to grab Sarah by the hand.

Sarah climbed in beside him and Sean slid back his seat.

Declan's other mate climbed in his side, and they set off.

The old car blew thick black smoke out of its exhaust as the engine roared into life.

Sarah noticed that the lads kept to the back roads, doubtless to avoid encountering the island's one and only full-time police officer on route. The old banger heaved and jerked each time Sean put it into second gear, but once they were back in third, everything seemed to calm down again.

Declan insisted on putting his arms around the girls' shoulders, making Marie want to vomit whenever he squeezed her shoulder and made a crude comment.

The passenger passed back a large glass bottle with no label, having taken a long swig from it. To Marie's relief, Declan removed his arm from her and grabbed the bottle, helping himself to a large swallow.

"Ahh, that's just what the good doctor ordered," he announced. "Here, now give this a try, it's homemade and full of everything a body needs," he said, offering the bottle to Marie.

Marie had no idea what the contents of the bottle were, but the pungent odour emanating from it reached her before Declan dangled it in front of her face.

"No, thank you," she said, politely. "It smells a little strong for my taste."

The three men all laughed, heartily.

Declan passed the bottle over to Sarah. "Now you won't be so rude as ter refuse a drink from your host, will yer?"

To Marie's surprise, her friend took the bottle and wiped it with her sleeve before putting it to her lips and tilting it back.

She took a small gulp and screwed her face up once she had swallowed the clear liquid.

Marie pulled a face, feeling her friend's pain whilst being more than a little astonished that she had accepted the drink in the first place.

Sarah shook her head, her eyes clamped shut, as she waited for the liquid to burn its way down her throat. She refused a second offer of the bottle just before Sean turned the car into her street.

The two girls emerged from the car outside Sarah's gate. Declan and Sean stood on the pavement and both took a step towards the house when Sarah planted her hand firmly in the middle of Declan's chest.

"Oh no you don't, mister, get back in the car, the pair of yer, I don't want the neighbours seeing and reporting back to me mother know, do I?"

The two men did not argue, doubtless realising the futility of such a conversation, and both climbed back inside the car to wait.

Once inside and out of earshot, Marie asked, "What was that stuff you drank out of his bottle?"

Sarah laughed. "That was good old mountain dew, made the traditional way. Some call it Irish Moonshine, or more popularly Poitín. Do not mention to your mum that they brought some with them," she stated, earnestly, "and for the love of God, don't ever mention it to my mother. That stuff can be up to ninety per cent proof."

Marie screwed her face up. "Then why did you drink it? It sounds horrible."

Sarah shook her behind as she began to climb the stairs. "Just to get me in the mood," she laughed.

Both girls changed for the party. Sarah offered Marie some of her skirts, but Marie decided to stick with the jeans she had brought with her. The thought of having her legs on display in front of Declan and his cronies did not sound at all appealing so far as she was concerned.

Having her legs securely clad in thick denim sent out a much firmer message that it was 'hands off' to all concerned. Sarah's choice of short black mini skirt and fishnet tights made Marie cringe inside at the thought of all those leering lads who were doubtless waiting for them to join the party. If they were anything like Declan and his mates, Marie worried that Sarah would spend the night slapping their wandering hands away.

She was tempted to say something, but in the end decided that her friend knew what she was doing. After all, this was her territory, and she doubtless knew what to expect.

Having checked themselves out in the full-length mirror on the landing they were ready for the off.

Declan and Sean both hopped out of the car to allow the girls to enter.

Declan gave a loud wolf whistle when he saw them emerge from the front door.

Marie could not help but notice that his eyes were transfixed on Sarah's stocking-clad legs, but she was in no way jealous of her friend. In truth, she preferred it this way.

The drive up to the encampment took a little over twenty minutes with Sean yet again avoiding all the main roads.

Before they could see the camp, the sound of the music, laughter and singing wafted in through the car's open windows, causing the men to cheer loudly as if to announce their arrival.

The car spluttered to a halt on the outskirts of the camp, where Marie estimated there must have been close to a hundred vehicles of all shapes and sizes parked on the grass verge.

As she climbed from the car, she could not suppress the feeling that the knot in her stomach from earlier was growing ever larger by the minute.

Chapter Twenty-Nine

"GET OUT OF ME BLOODY WAY, WILL YER!" LIAM Murphy screamed at the car in front of him, which was taking far too long, in his opinion, to make a three-point turn. The Fiesta had already taken five turns, and it was still facing the wrong way.

Lima chose to ignore the green sticker on the bumper announcing that the driver had only recently passed their test. So far as he was concerned, either they could drive, or they could not, and he had already made his mind up about the middle-aged lady at the wheel.

As the Fiesta reversed once more, hitting the kerb with both back tyres, Liam saw his chance and was not prepared to let it go. He revved his Audi and screeched around in front of the smaller car, slamming on his brakes once he was sure that he had it blocked in.

He turned in the direction of the driver.

The poor woman at the wheel was a nervous wreck, and her eyes could not hide the sheer terror that she felt, convinced that she was about to become the latest victim of road rage.

Liam pressed the button on his side door panel, which lowered his passenger-side window.

He stared at the other driver, his eyes conveying sheer menace. "Bloody woman, you and yer lot should not be allowed on the feckin' road, yer a bloody nuisance."

He continued to glare at her for a couple of seconds, proud with himself for the fear in her eyes which he had caused. Then he turned back to face front and sped away.

He was already in a bad mood as a result of the day he had suffered at the office.

Four boring meetings spread across ten hours with nothing productive to show for any of them. As one of the recently promoted senior managers, he had been tasked with taking control of four smaller offices within the company. This was something which he felt confident that he could do, as he explained to the senior board panel at his interview.

Little did he know at the time the true state of those offices which were to soon come under his command. Their figures were by far the worst in the company's history, and none of the junior officers below him seemed willing to take any personal responsibility for the ineptitude of their staff.

Part of his new duty was to make a quarterly report to the board on the progress amongst his teams. To date, he had already faced them on two occasions with nothing to show for it but falling sales and the loss of several large contracts, some of which had been with the firm almost from day one.

Liam could tell from the expressions of board members who had promoted him that they were now beginning to regret their faith in him. One more bad quarter and it could mean his dismissal, or worse still the offer of demotion with the embarrassment that would bring, knowing that he had screwed up his one and only chance.

Therefore, today he had laid it firmly on the line with each of his staff that if he went, he would not go alone. He made it clear in no uncertain circumstances that they would all be held personally responsible for the failings in their groups and that he was not prepared to protect them from the repercussions.

His main hope now was that his actions today might finally force his team managers to realise the seriousness of the situation and start kicking some serious arse to make things happen.

His personal view was that there were too many women in senior positions amongst his teams. Women were a necessary commodity in any office, but only for something to gawk at when their skirts were nice and short and to fondle at the firm's Christmas party. None of them – in his opinion – should ever be granted any real power. Women just did not understand the fundamental workings of business, and that was all there was to it.

He had managed to reduce some of the female members of his teams to tears that afternoon when he began berating them for their poor performance and if that was not all the proof necessary to show that they were in the wrong position, he did not know what did.

Far better that they married and started raising a family.

Resume their proper place in society.

At least his wife Enid knew her place. She may have taken on a part-time job on the switchboard of the local tourist office when their daughter grew old enough to make her own way to and from school, but she never used it as an excuse for not having his dinner on the table when he arrived home. Or for allowing their house to be anything but pristine.

Yes, she certainly knew how to behave, and he hoped that she had distilled some of that knowledge into their daughter, Erin.

Colm pulled the car into the driveway and switched off the engine.

Thinking of dinner reminded him that tonight was his wife's famous steak and kidney pudding. You could say what you liked about Enid, but her pudding was the envy of all who ate it. He had lost count of how many members of the parish had asked for her recipe.

It was indeed something she could be proud of. Not that she was ever the type to boast.

Colm opened his front door and waited for the delicious aroma of suet pudding and cooked meat to assail his nostrils.

He breathed in deeply. There was certainly a 'meaty' waft of something, but it did not smell of steak and kidney to him.

Upon hearing his key in the lock, Enid Murphy rushed out into the hallway, wiping her hands on her apron. "Good evening, darling," she said, nervously. "How was your day?"

She walked behind him and began to help him off with his overcoat.

"Your slippers are warming by the fire, and I've just poured you a large whiskey; it's sitting next to your paper."

Her routine as a dutiful wife was something which Enid took very seriously. Colm had his ways and certainly a temper which could rise like a helium balloon without warning, but over time, she had learned that so long as she made certain efforts to please him there was a good chance that she could calm any approaching storm.

His nightly glass of whiskey upon arrival from work, which he enjoyed in his slippers in front of the fire while her perused his evening paper to discover what had been happening in the world, usually set the scene for an evening free from his temper.

"What am I smelling?" Colm responded, not bothering to acknowledge his wife's greeting.

Enid stopped in her tracks; her husband's coat inches away from its usual hook.

"I'm sorry," she replied, apologetically. "I was late from work and Mr Green had run out of kidneys. He's promised to have some in tomorrow and to save me some."

She nervously placed Colm's coat on the hook and began to

dust it down with her hands, purposely not looking round to see her husband's expression.

Colm let out a pent-up breath. "If he didn't have any, why didn't you try somewhere else?" he demanded.

Enid kept her back to him, busying herself with straightening and brushing down the other garments hanging next to her husband's coat, none of which actually needed tidying.

"Well, I know how much you like the ones from Mr Green, so I thought it best to wait until I could get some there. I bought you some lovely sausages from him and I've prepared your favourite thick-cut chips, and there's a loaf in the oven so you can have some hot fresh bread and butter with it, just the way you like."

Enid was purposefully talking as fast as she could to convey all the information to her husband, therefore not giving him a chance to lose his temper.

As she turned to face her husband, she smiled sweetly, confident now that she had placated any anger that might be rising in her husband's chest from his disappointment at not having his usual meal that night.

Without warning, Colm raised his hand and struck Enid across the face.

The force of the blow sent her reeling back against the wall, her legs almost collapsing underneath her from the shock.

Colm grabbed her by the front of her blouse and yanked her towards him, sending a couple of buttons spinning across the floor. Before Enid had a chance to respond or protect herself, the back of Colm's hand slapped her hard against her other cheek.

Enid squealed out in pain, unable to prevent the sound from leaving her lips. Her biggest fear was that their daughter Erin might hear what was going on and venture down to investigate.

Colm grabbed her roughly by the hair and yanked her head back.

He seemed almost overjoyed by the sight of the tears now

streaming down his wife's cheeks. Keeping a firm hold on her hair, he raised his hand once more as if ready to strike.

"No!" The cry came from above them.

Looking up, Colm could see Erin standing at the top of the stairs. Her mother's attempt at not alerting her to what was happening in the hall had obviously failed.

Erin, like her mother, had tears in her eyes. This was not the first time that she had been exposed to such a scene, quite the opposite, but the distress it caused her never seemed to shake her reserve to protect her mother from such a brutal attack.

She ran down the stairs holding onto the banister for support. Erin could feel her body trembling as she came closer to the bottom, where her father still held her mother with a tight grip on her hair.

Enid's worst fear had come to light. Over the years, she had grown accustomed to her husband's rages and the consequences she had to suffer as the norm. But she was more than happy to feel the full force of Colm's attack so long as he kept his hands off their daughter.

"No, please go back to your room, darling, everything is alright." Enid uttered the words through the pain and tears, knowing that her daughter would not be convinced, but praying nonetheless that she could persuade her to return to her room and at least pretend that nothing untoward was taking place.

Instead, Erin launched herself at her father, grabbing his free hand to prevent him from striking her mother again. She held on for all she was worth, but her father was good deal taller and stronger than her, and he managed to manoeuvre his arm around and grab Erin by the hair, tightening his grip until she too began to yell out in pain.

"Leave her alone!" Enid demanded. "She's only a child."

Colm turned back towards her. "A child that lacks the discipline to know how to respect her father," he spat.

Both women had their hands behind their heads, desperately trying to relieve some of the pain caused by Colm's grip.

After what seemed to the two females as an eternity, Colm released his hold on them, and the two women fell together in each other's arms, sobbing.

Unrepentant, Colm slid his leather belt from the loops of his trousers and wrapped the buckle end around his hand, leaving the vast majority of it dangling by his side.

Without speaking, Colm lifted back his arm and brought the belt down with all his might, hitting Erin across her behind.

The poor girl yelped in pain and shock at the sudden blow.

Before either woman had a chance to respond, the belt came down again, this time lashing against a protective arm which Enid had wrapped around her daughter.

Colm continued with his assault, not needing to take any specific aim as he knew his weapon of choice would make contact with either of his targets, regardless.

Enid and her daughter slid slowly to the floor, huddled against each other for safety, crying out whenever the leather belt made contact, until Colm had worn himself out from the effort. He stood for a moment, towering over his wife and daughter, his breathing hard and perspiration streaming down his face.

He stood there with the belt still gripped firmly in his hand until he was satisfied that both women had learned their lesson, then he strode purposefully into the lounge and knocked back the large whiskey his wife had poured him earlier.

He smiled cruelly at the sound of the women's sobbing coming from the hallway.

Chapter Thirty

MARIE'S HEAD WAS STARTING TO POUND. THEY HAD only been at the party for a little over an hour, during which time she had only consumed the equivalent of two drinks with plenty of food to soak them up.

The music was incredibly loud, but certainly no louder than any club back home, and with it being an outdoor event, Marie thought that the effect on her eardrums would feel less intense.

The people, at least the women, certainly were welcoming, and made Marie feel as if she was one of the family. They piled homemade food high up on her plate, insisting that she return for more when she was finished.

She was told the names of some of the dishes, but she could not pronounce, let alone remember, what they were called. Instead, she chose to just smile sweetly and thank everyone for their generous hospitality.

There was one dish in particular which contained yellow rice and meat of some description. Marie could not make out what animal it was, but it was one of the tastiest she had ever tried.

Sarah dragged her up for a dance when a particular tune was played, which she liked.

They were soon surrounded by at least a hundred people of all ages, becoming lost in the moment. Marie noticed that the men seemed more than willing to stand up and display their talents on the dancefloor as much as the women, which made her smile, as most of the parties she had attended usually saw most of the men all standing together at the bar watching the girls dance together.

This group certainly knew how to enjoy themselves.

After dancing for a while, the girls found somewhere to sit just outside the huge ring of revellers. Upon arrival, they had each been presented with a large plastic tumbler they were told to fill up with whatever they wanted to drink.

The bar, which was just a long bench the size of three dinner tables, groaned with all manner of beverages, and there were several crates and boxes underneath, which no doubt the table could not support.

Every so often, someone would come round and pour something into the girls' cups and say 'cheers' or something similar in a language which Marie did not understand.

Initially, she was reluctant to take a drink from a stranger, especially a man, but Sarah informed her that it was all part of making a stranger feel welcome. Sarah certainly did not seem at all hesitant about drinking whatever was poured into her tumbler, so that made Marie a little less suspicious.

Even so, she ensured that she only sipped at her drinks to try and make the unknown contents last as long as possible.

"Are yers having fun?" The girls turned back to see Declan leering over them, his arm around the shoulders of a younger man. It was not altogether clear to Marie which one was holding the other up as they were both clearly intoxicated. The younger of the two looked barely old enough to be drinking, but having met Sean earlier in the evening, she suspected that age was not a concern amongst the travellers where such things were concerned.

"Yes, thank you," Sarah called back, trying to make herself heard above the sound of the music.

"Told yer, yer would, didn't I say so, best crack on the island," Declan announced, triumphantly. "This 'ere's me cousin, Eamon," he indicated to the young man beside him. "This bash is fer his birthday. 'E becomes a man today, don't yer, son?"

The other man blushed and half pushed his cousin away. "Shut it, will yer," he shouted.

"Ah, it's nothing to be ashamed of," Declan assured him. "Now, which one of you lovely ladies want to give me cousin a birthday kiss?" Eamon looked extremely embarrassed by his cousin's suggestion, and he looked skyward as if to avoid the girls. "Come on now," continued Declan, tightening his grip around his cousin's shoulders. "Whilst yer have the chance, 'efore yer get crushed in the stampede."

The two girls exchanged glances.

It was obvious to them both that neither wanted to comply. Not that Eamon was not a pleasant enough looking lad, but both girls imagined that, if Declan had his way, he would demand a kiss too once they had passed on their birthday wishes.

Marie could feel her own cheeks starting to redden. She was starting to feel bad for the birthday boy who had been put in such an embarrassing position through no fault of his own.

Just then, Sarah threw back what was left of her drink, stood up and grabbed Eamon by the sides of his head, then pulled him in for a kiss.

To Marie's astonishment, the kiss lasted far longer than she supposed it might.

Eamon's eyes were wide open in shock, but he did nothing to dissuade Sarah from her task. Marie felt sure that the kiss was turning into more of a snog, so she looked down at her drink, feeling somewhat uncomfortable.

"Hey now, that's enough, leave the poor fello' alone." From the sound of his voice, Declan was feeling more than a little putout that Marie seemed to be enjoying herself so much. Whether he had initially made the suggestion just to embarrass his cousin or the girls Marie was not clear, but from the look of things he was already regretting it.

Finally, Sarah let go of her prize and slumped back down next to Marie, clearly out of breath from the effort.

"Phew!" she exclaimed, turning to Marie. "Your turn."

Now Marie could really feel her cheeks turning crimson.

Sarah had put her on the spot with nowhere to go without causing some major embarrassment to the poor lad.

Sighing, she handed Sarah her cup, stood up and turned to face the two men.

Eamon was looking equally shocked by Sarah's actions, though Marie could tell that he was trying his best to hide it from his cousin because he probably thought that he needed to show that he could take such things in his stride.

Marie reached out and gave Eamon a hug and a quick peck on the cheek as she wished him a happy birthday.

The birthday boy smiled and thanked her, sincerely.

"Now then," said Declan, licking his lips, "where's mine?"

Marie pulled a face and sat back down.

Sarah was in the course of draining her friend's drink when Declan made his announcement, and at the sound of his words, she choked on the last swallow and spewed the drink out through her pursed lips.

After coughing to clear her throat, Sarah began laughing, hysterically.

Unable to stop herself, Marie joined in, although she at least made an effort to cover her laughter behind her hand.

The two girls grabbed each other as if to stop themselves from falling off their seats.

"What the fuck's so funny?" Declan asked, all humour now gone from his voice.

Sarah turned to face him. "Is it your birthday too?" she enquired.

Declan looked annoyed. "What's that got to do with things?"

"When it's your birthday, you can have a kiss," Sarah assured him. "But not until then."

Declan snorted through his nostrils. Marie looked back. She was starting to feel as if her friend had gone too far with her ex-boyfriend. When he was riled, as he clearly was at that moment, he looked like a man who was capable of anything in retaliation for being humiliated.

His attention was firmly fixed on Sarah, his eyes burning. Spittle started to dribble from his lips as his breathing intensified.

Unfortunately, Sarah burst into another fit of giggles.

Clearly, she was not intimidated by Declan in the slightest, which was all well and good, but the angrier he grew, the more afraid Marie became.

Thankfully, doubtless seeing Marie's unease, Eamon broke the tension. He patted his cousin on the back. "Come on," he said, jovially. "Obviously, these are ladies of good taste, so why would they want to waste their kisses on a dirty reprobate like you?"

Declan's eyes were still boring into Sarah as Eamon dragged him away.

Marie felt her heart flip. That was an experience she would rather not repeat.

Once the lads were out of earshot, Marie turned to her friend.

"You really pissed him off then," she noted. "If looks could kill, I wouldn't hold out hope for either of us right now."

Sarah finally managed to control her laughter. "Oh, don't you worry about him, he deserved it and more besides. God alone knows what I saw in him in the first place, but I'm well shot of him now. Come on," she continued, rising to her feet a little unsteadily. "You're in need of a refill."

"No thanks to you," Marie retorted, playfully.

Sarah nudged her as they set off for the bar area.

Marie glanced around at the happy revellers as they walked. She could not help but notice a group of girls staring at the pair of them from across the field. From this distance, it seemed to Marie as if the girls were scowling at them, and the way they talked to each other without ever turning their focus away from her and Sarah made Marie feel particularly uncomfortable.

She attempted a smile in their general direction, but it was not acknowledged.

Turning back, she saw that Sarah had been looking in the opposite direction, waving to some people in the crowd whom she obviously knew.

Marie decided to ignore the girls and not bother to bring her suspicions to her friend's attention.

As they approached the bar area, the two girls were approached by an elderly lady wearing what Marie would have described as traditional Gypsy dress. The woman smiled at them before taking Marie by the elbow and directing them towards the food area.

Marie turned to Sarah. "She doesn't speak English," Sarah informed her. "She is one of Declan's aunts, she only speaks Romany." Sarah moved around her friend and gave the woman a big hug, which she reciprocated, warmly.

The woman turned to Marie, who, not wishing to cause any disrespect, did the same as Sarah. The woman smelled of herbs and spices, and there was a distinct odour of strong alcohol on her breath.

The woman pointed towards the food area once more.

"She wants us to eat," Sarah announced. "It would be rude to refuse even you're not hungry. A couple of bites should do."

Marie nodded, and the three of them made their way over to the huge food table.

The woman signalled to one of the women serving and said something to her in their mother tongue.

The woman nodded, then turned to Marie. "I hear you're not feeling well," she announced. "You have a headache."

Marie was stunned by the revelation.

She had not even mentioned her headache to Sarah, let alone the old woman.

The shocked expression on her face did not escape the lady behind the table.

"Don't look so concerned," she assured her. "Marta can see things others cannot. She can even feel your pain." She nodded back to the old woman, who looked at Marie and tapped her head as if to confirm that she knew where Marie's pain was.

"That's incredible," Marie exclaimed, unable to hide her surprise. She had heard of such people and read about them in books and magazines, but to actually be in the presence of such a person had really taken her off guard.

The younger woman turned her back and began fiddling with some bottles and jars on a table behind her.

Marie looked at Sarah, the disbelief still etched on her face.

Sarah leaned in to whisper, "She can even tell fortunes, but I have it on reasonable authority that she mainly sees the bad stuff, so I've never been brave enough to ask her to read mine."

Marie was not sure how to react to such information, so she merely turned back to the old lady and pointed to her own head, nodding.

"Here, try this," offered the younger woman, tuning back to face them. "Your headache will be gone in a moment." She held out a small glass beaker filled with a light brown liquid, which still swirled around inside from being vigorously stirred.

Marie took the glass without hesitation but then paused as she considered drinking the contents.

The woman laughed. "It's quite harmless, I assure you, and far better for your headache than anything you can buy in a chemist."

Marie smiled, hesitantly.

She looked at the old woman, who indicated to her to drink.

"It's best knocked back in one," the young woman suggested.

Marie turned to Sarah, who nodded.

She threw back the drink and swallowed. It tasted a bit like weak tea with a peppery undertaste, which made Marie pull a face and run her tongue against the roof of her mouth to clear her palate.

The old woman laughed and patted Marie on the back before turning and walking away into the crowd.

By now, the woman behind the counter had served up two plates of food, which she held out towards the girls. Sarah handed Marie back her plastic mug, which she had held onto since they left their seats. She took one of the delicious-looking plates on offer and thanked the lady.

Marie did likewise, handing back the glass beaker first and thanking the woman for her medical intervention.

"Come on," said Sarah, "let's go and find something to wash this lot down."

Chapter Thirty-One

ERIN HAD BEEN RELUCTANT TO LEAVE HER MOTHER alone with her father after the terrible beating he had given them, but her mother assured her that now he had calmed down and had a couple of strong drinks, he would be a different man after his dinner.

In truth, Erin had been glad her mother insisted that she go out for the evening. She desperately needed to speak to Liam face-to-face with no one else around.

She walked down the path towards one of the more secluded parts of Westside cliff where they usually had their night-time liaisons, like so many young lovers. The white cardigan she wore over her summer dress covered the welts and bruises left by her father's beating from earlier. Like her mother, Erin still did all that she could to keep the truth of their family away from prying eyes.

Erin knew of the body of Michelle Calvert being discovered further down the coast, and the thought made her shiver, but at least their rendezvous spot was nowhere near there.

Erin was desperate. She knew that it would not be long before she started showing, and once people began to notice, there would be no going back. In spite of her insistence with Father Boyle that she intended to have an abortion, in reality, she was far more afraid of God's wrath on judgement day than she was of even her own parents finding out about her situation.

She had always considered the thought of having children, but not so young in life.

Erin knew that if she decided to keep her baby that all her dreams of university and a successful career would be kissed goodbye. It would definitely mean her having to settle down to being a teenager mum and, although she knew that in spite of what would be her initial distress and horror at the situation her mother would stand by her and help her out in every way she possibly could, she did not think that her father would be so forgiving.

In his eyes, everything was a matter of perception, regardless of what the true situation might be.

Colm Murphy stood proud each Sunday outside church with his wife and daughter by his side as he acted out the epitome of the loving husband and father. If only the parishioners knew the truth, they would see what a sham his exterior shell was and the true kind of man it concealed.

Erin could only imagine the kind of beatings she would have to endure when her father learnt of her situation. It even crossed her mind that he might *do* something to her to make her lose the baby, rather than live with the shame of having a pregnant daughter out of wedlock.

His temper and cruelty knew no bounds as he had proved to both Erin and her poor, long-suffering mother on countless occasions.

In fact, so far as she was concerned, there was only one possible way that her parents might welcome her situation without cause or fuss, and that was if she could persuade Liam to marry her before her belly started to protrude.

Knowing his view on the subject, Erin was already aware

that convincing her boyfriend would be an uphill battle, but the way she looked at it, she had very few options left open to her.

She had always considered Liam to be an intelligent, sensible and above all a decent human being, and in truth, that was the impression he had always given until she announced that she was pregnant. Then, all of a sudden, his mask slipped, and he showed a side of himself that Erin had never seen before.

During their courtship, he had never so much as raised his voice to her. They had never had an argument, and to be fair to him, Liam had not exactly pressured her into sleeping with him. It all happened quite organically when their petting went too far.

In that respect, she could not blame him for what happened, she felt that she was just as much to blame. The difference was that now that she was pregnant, she felt that she had very few options left open, whereas Liam still believed that he could deny everything and just carry on with his life.

Erin's sincerest hope was that Liam's attitude was merely as a result of shock at learning about her pregnancy, and that perhaps now that he had had a while to reflect, he might be more willing to accept his responsibilities and make a life with her.

Perhaps once he saw how desperate she was, he would relent and take pity on her.

She could but hope.

Erin descended the stone steps which led down to the beach. She glanced around, but she could see no sign of Liam, and for a moment she feared that he had chickened out and decided not to meet her after all.

Her heart sank.

Taking in a deep breath of sea air, Erin began walking towards the boardwalk further along the beach, under which they shared so many romantic moments together.

In the dim glare cast by the streetlights on the road above, it was hard for her to make out any specific shadows up ahead, but she continued on her way, desperately hoping that Liam would appear.

She moved her lips in silent prayer that her boyfriend would not let her down, although, having spoken to Father Boyle the way she had done earlier, she feared that God might not be willing to listen to her.

Suddenly, in the distance, she saw a tall figure move out of the shadows and wave to her. It had to be Liam. Even at this distance, Erin could make out his broad shoulders and slim waist.

She ran to him, whispering a thank you to God as she went.

Liam wrapped his arms around her in a tight embrace, kissing Erin on the side of the neck until she turned to face him, then pressing his lips against hers and urgently seeking out her moist tongue.

They stayed like that for a while, their hands exploring each other's frames, squeezing, fondling, rubbing themselves against one another until Erin could feel Liam's erection pushing against her through his jeans.

Erin pulled back.

"What's wrong?" Liam asked, his hands still on her shoulders, his tone a mixture of hurt and surprise.

Erin looked into his eyes. "You know what's wrong, Liam," she declared, fixing his gaze. "We need to discuss what we're going to do about it."

Liam immediately released his hold and turned away.

After a moment, he replied. "I thought we'd already agreed. Why are you bringing this up again?"

"Because we haven't agreed on anything, that's why," Erin stated, her voice already starting to crack under the pressure of the situation. For a brief second, when Liam had embraced her so passionately, she imagined that perhaps he had already decided to stand by her and make an honest woman of her.

But now it was evident that that was not the case.

Liam spun back around. "You said that you were going to get rid of it. What's suddenly changed? You haven't told anyone about it, have you?" he demanded.

"IT!" Erin screamed. "IT! Is that what you call our baby? IT!"

Liam spun around and quickly surveyed their surroundings as if desperate to ensure that no one else was close enough to hear Erin's outburst. Once satisfied that they were indeed alone, he slapped his hands against his ears as if to block out her words. "It's not even a baby yet, what are you saying? It's barely an embryo; otherwise, the law would not allow you to get it sorted."

"Liam Mularkey, you know full well that in the Lord's eyes our child is already living inside me, regardless of what the law says," she replied, defiantly.

"Will you please keep your voice down," Liam pleaded, reaching out to Erin.

Erin slapped his hands away and took a step back out of reach. "Is that all you care about, someone finding out? What about when my belly starts to protrude, people are going to know my condition soon enough."

Liam stayed where he was, afraid that if he tried to move in closer Erin would create a scene. She was right about one thing; it was his biggest fear that someone would find out about Erin's pregnancy before she had time to arrange an abortion.

He knew that if word of her condition reached either of his parents, he would be forced to do the decent thing, and that would mean the end of his life so far as he was concerned. He was too young to consider becoming a father, let alone being married and settling down.

An abortion was the most obvious solution, and he could not understand why Erin was being so obstinate about it. After all, neither of them was in love with the other, even though Erin had mentioned it on a couple of occasions, Liam felt sure that it was merely said in the heat of the moment.

Liam closed his eyes and took in a deep breath. "Please just tell me that you haven't told anyone about this yet."

Erin could feel her temper rising. "I've told Father Boyle," she replied, folding her arms. "I had to speak to someone, and you weren't listening. You can't expect me to deal with this all on my own, I'm terrified."

Liam raised his arms and interlinked his fingers behind his head.

What the hell was the girl doing telling their priest?

Was this her way of holding him to ransom? Start by telling the priest, then moving on to her parents, their friends, his parents.

"Why the hell would you do that?" he snarled, spittle bubbling at the corners of his lips. "What if he decides that he needs to tell your parents, or mine, what then?"

Erin could feel the tears starting to well up inside.

She fought the urge to start crying and stubbornly turned her dejection and sorrow into defiance. It was obvious to her now that Liam would never change his mind about the baby. What she had ever seen in him was a mystery to her now. He was clearly not man enough to do the right thing, and certainly no gentleman.

But the sad truth was that he would always be the father of her child should she decide to go through with the birth, either alone or with him being forced to stand by her.

Right now, Erin wished she had never allowed Liam anywhere near her, let alone being the one who took her virginity.

"Father Boyle won't say a word to anyone," she insisted. "He would not break the seal of the confessional regardless of the circumstances."

Liam's face suddenly cleared. "You told him in confession?

Oh, my good God, thank heavens, you really had me going there for a moment."

He moved back in as if to hug her, but Erin slapped him away again.

Liam could not disguise his astonishment at her behaviour. Erin's revelation that she had told Father Boyle during confession brought a wave of relief which Liam could not help but embrace.

So why was Erin reacting in such a way to his delight?

Surely, she did not want others to know their business.

Liam held his hands up as if to demonstrate his resignation.

"Okay, okay, I know you're upset with me," he offered, gently. "But try and be reasonable. You know that what I'm saying makes perfect sense. Neither one of us wants to be saddled with marriage and a baby at our age. If there was any other way, I'd be happy to consider it, but you know an abortion is the only answer."

Erin bit her bottom lip. "It's easy for you to say that," she retorted, bitterly. "You're not the one who has to go through with it, I am. Can I even trust you to be there with me when I go to the clinic?"

Liam moved forward, prepared to risk another slap. "Of course you can, you know you can," he replied, keeping his voice low and soothing.

"Can I?" Elin demanded. "You haven't exactly been forthcoming with help and advice thus far."

Liam nodded. "I know, and I'm truly sorry, darling, but now we're both on the same page, we can work together to solve this issue and get back to living our old lives."

Just then, he heard a cry in the distance.

A high-pitched, lonesome wail pierced his eardrums and caused him to jam his index fingers into his ears. "Ow," he exclaimed, "what the hell is that?"

"What's what?" Elin asked, dumbfounded by Liam's actions.

"Can't you hear it?" He cried. "It's getting louder."

Erin shook her head. If this was one of his tricks to avoid discussing their predicament any further, then she was not falling for it. Now that she had him here, Erin was adamant that she was going to keep him with her until they had made all the arrangements necessary to carry out her procedure.

There was no way he was going to be allowed to back out and leave her to it again.

"Liam, will you stop playing the fool, for the love of God. We've got important arrangements to make, and you're just being an idiot."

But looking at his face, Erin could see that he was not joking.

There was definitely something distracting him, and whatever it was, it was obviously causing him severe pain.

Erin strained to hear what her boyfriend was complaining about, but there was nothing. Apart from the gentle sound of the tide washing against the shore, the night was still.

She reached forward and grabbed Liam by both arms. "What's the matter, Liam?" she pleaded. "Tell me what's wrong."

Now it was his turn to pull away. "Can't you hear it? It's everywhere."

The sound in his head began rising in a crescendo of waves, each one more deafening than the last. He spun around back and forth, desperately trying to locate the source of the noise, but there was nothing to indicate the direction it was coming from.

Before Erin had a chance to offer her support, Liam cried out and ran away from her across the beach, his fingers still lodged tightly in his ears.

Erin watched in disbelief as Liam disappeared from view around the boardwalk.

She considered running after him but decided that this stunt was nothing more than an excuse to avoid making arrangements for the termination with her. The truth was obvious to her now; she was on her own, and Liam had no intention of stepping up.

Erin stamped her foot in frustration.

It would serve him right if she decided to tell the world about her condition, starting with his parents. Then he would truly be sorry for the way he had treated her.

His parents would force him to do the honourable thing, regardless of whether he wanted to or not.

Erin waited for a moment, hoping against reason that Liam would reappear from behind the boardwalk and return to her full of apologies.

But it never happened.

Finally, Erin turned and started on her way back home.

This time she was unable to stop the tears from falling.

Chapter Thirty-Two

IT HAD BEEN AT LEAST A COUPLE OF HOURS SINCE THE incident with Declan.

The lady who gave Marie the headache cure had been spot on; her pain diminished within a couple of minutes of her taking it, then disappeared altogether five minutes later.

The girls had made their way over to the drinks selection and filled their beakers up with beer. One of the older men serving poured a small cupful of something clear into their beer, winking at them as he did so.

Marie looked over at Sarah questioningly, but her friend assured her that it was nothing more than a shot of mountain dew and that the beer would dilute it so that both the taste and the smell would not put her off.

She was right, too. Marie could not taste the added shot in her beer, and being so thirsty, she downed half her beaker in one go.

They went back to their seats to eat. By now, Marie had forgotten about the girls whom she had seen staring at them on their way to the food tables. That was until the same group suddenly appeared in front of them while they ate.

At first, Sarah did not seem to notice the girls crowding around them, her concentration focused on opening an oyster shell, so Marie nudged her gently, as she was feeling intimidated by the menacing stares from the group.

Sarah looked up. "Oh, hi, Eve, how's it going?"

It was obvious to Marie that her friend knew the girl who stood directly in front of them, so she breathed a silent sigh of relief. Somehow, she would have felt more uneasy if they were just a random troop of strangers.

"Not all that," the girl replied, eyeing Marie. "Who's yer mate?"

"This is my good friend Marie," Sarah replied, still wrestling with the shell. "This is her first time on the island, so I thought I'd give her the full experience."

Marie smiled weakly, but Eve did not reciprocate.

Marie quickly scanned the faces of the rest of Eve's gang. The other girls all had similar harsh expressions on their faces as if preparing to go into battle.

Marie felt a sudden *churn* inside her.

It was well known that Travellers could be violent for any number of reasons, some of which would not spark concern amongst ordinary people. However, until this moment, it had not occurred to Marie that such a situation could also refer to the women amongst them. Until that moment, all the people she had met at the party, with the possible exception of Declan, had been nothing short of gracious and charming.

Marie wished that they had stayed closer to the food area. She was sure that the kind ladies there would not allow anything to happen to them.

As it was, they were way too far away to call for help should the situation demand it, and along with the noise from the music and the singing, their cries would be lost in the ether.

Marie turned back to face Sarah. Her friend still appeared completely nonplussed by the girls gathered around them. They had shuffled themselves into a semi-circle with Eve in the middle, cutting off any chance of escape should either of them try.

Marie considered what it would take to make a break for it by spinning around in her seat and trying to make a dash in the opposite direction. There was always a chance that the two girls could lose themselves in the crowd to escape whatever Eve and her gang were planning.

But she knew she could never leave Sarah behind, just as she was sure that her friend would never do the same to her.

Still, Marie could not fathom why Sarah did not seem more alarmed by the situation.

There were six girls in total, including Eve, so short of Sarah being a martial arts expert, there was no way that Marie could envisage them evading a beating when it would be three against one.

"I saw you talkin' to Declan earlier," Eve said, a distinct accusatory edge to her tone.

"Yeah, that's right," replied Sarah, nonchalantly. "He came over to introduce his cousin whose bash this is. Seemed like a nice fellow."

Marie glanced up at the girl.

Eve's expression still conveyed menace. "I know all about you an' Declan," she snapped, "so don't bother denying it."

Finally, Sarah stopped fiddling with her shellfish and turned her attention towards Eve. "I'm not denying anything," she answered, shrugging her shoulders. "Why should I, he and me had a thing going, but it's all over now."

Marie casually placed her plate on the seat beside her. In her heart, she felt that things were about to grow very ugly, and although she would do anything she could to calm down the situation before it led to a fight, somehow, she had the impression that that was exactly what the girls were gunning for.

She was not sure if it was mere paranoia taking over, but

Marie was sure that since they had been standing there, some of the girls had slipped their hands into the pockets, and the more she stared at them the surer she was that she could see their hands closing around weapons through the material.

If things kicked off, this was going to grow ugly very soon.

"All over now," Eve mimicked Sarah's tone. "Just like that yer expect me to believe it's all over now. Then why, when I challenged him earlier, did Declan say he was still with you?"

Sarah put down her plate, giving Eve her full attention. "Because he's a liar, that's why."

This was not the way Marie had hoped the conversation would go.

It was almost as if Sarah wanted to goad Eve into a full-on confrontation.

She cleared her throat. "It's true," she murmured, desperately trying to keep her voice steady. "When I met Sarah, Declan was loitering outside the restaurant where she works, waiting for her, but she would have nothing to do with him. She told him in no uncertain terms that they were done, but he wouldn't take no for an answer. In the end, my mum had to take her home in a taxi just to get away from him."

Eve turned her attention towards Marie. "So how come he ended up inviting yer both 'ere tonight then?"

"We were just sitting at a café near the beach when he appeared out of nowhere and invited us to his cousin's birthday bash. Sarah didn't even want to come, but I kept badgering her because I'd never seen a proper travellers' party other than on the telly, and they always looked amazing."

Eve considered Marie's explanation for a moment before turning back to face Sarah.

Her expression still maintained that she was not altogether convinced, but after a while, she said. "You do know that when I come of age next year, me and Declan are going to be married?"

"No, I wasn't aware of that, congrats," answered Sarah,

cheerily. "But please do not think for a moment that I am someone you should be concerned about. In fact, had I known this, I would never have entertained going out with him in the first place."

Marie's stomach still held a tight knot, but she felt it release when Eve said something to her gang in their own tongue, and the girls removed their hands from their pockets.

"If the little bastard goes anywhere near you again, just you make sure you tell me about it, okay?" Eve stated.

Sarah nodded. "You have my word, and what's more, I'll tell him that I'm going to tell you, that should scare him off."

"That an' all," agreed Eve. "Come on," she turned and the girls around her moved aside to let her pass, then followed her back into the crowd.

Marie released a huge sigh of relief. "Jesus, I thought we were done for then."

"Me too," agreed Sarah. "And I've seen some of those girls fight before, we'd have been lucky to walk away in one piece after they laid into us."

Maire looked shocked. "Hang on, if you were so sure they'd kill us, why were you so calm and collected while that Eve was grilling you?"

Sarah shrugged. "That was all on the outside, inside I was wetting myself, but you can't let them smell fear or they turn feral. Come on," she urged, standing up, "I don't know about you, but I need another drink."

They were stopped halfway to the drinks area and dragged into what appeared to Marie to be a kind of conga line. The two girls danced around holding onto the waist of the person in front of them for at least ten minutes before splitting off from the unending dance and heading back for the bar.

Again, they ordered beer, and once again, someone added a shot into their beakers.

Although Marie had always been wary of anyone trying to

slip something *dodgy* into her drink, the fact that it was done openly in front of both her and Sarah, not to mention the fact that Sarah seemed quite at home with the custom, lowered Marie's suspicions.

She raised her glass in salute to the man behind the bar, and the two girls walked back to their seats to enjoy their drinks.

They watched the dancing, marvelling at how energetic some of the older participants were. Sarah whispered that some of those on the dancefloor were nearing their hundredth birthdays, which Marie found incredible. But looking at some of their faces, she could well believe her friend's supposition.

As the night continued, Marie began to feel the effects of the booze taking hold.

Even so, she found herself with an incredible thirst and therefore could not help herself, knocking back her beer and mountain dew combination.

She turned in her seat and leaned back against Sarah, closing her eyes as she listened to the tuneful music.

That was the last thing she remembered until she woke up in the medical centre.

Chapter Thirty-Three

THE SOUND OF HER MOBILE VIBRATING IN THE distance cut through Janine's dreams and brought her back to reality.

She opened her eyes and tried to focus on the patterns embossed on the ceiling above her. For a moment, her mind was clouded with images of wild stallions racing majestically across an open field, their manes flowing from the speed of their gallop.

Janine often dreamed of horses when she was in a deep sleep. It was a reflection from her childhood when she had an aunt who kept horses and who encouraged Janine to ride whenever she visited. It grew into a passion, but alas, when her aunt died, her partner decided to sell the stables and emigrate to Australia.

Her dreams often returned her to those halcyon holidays of her youth.

Janine blinked several times and tried to sit up. The movement caused the room to spin momentarily, so she closed her eyes once more and rubbed them vigorously with her index fingers before trying once more to open them properly.

Her head ached, but at least she could now see the room around her.

Her mobile *buzzed* twice more before the device switched to answering mode.

Sitting upright, Janine glanced to her left at the sleeping figure of Tim, snoring softly with his face almost completely buried in a pillow.

Her memory was somewhat unclear from the drink, but deep in her subconscious, Janine remembered walking along the road with Tim beside her, their arms slung across each other's shoulders, singing an Irish folk song which Tim had taught her in the pub.

Janine also had a vague memory of everyone in the bar standing and applauding Tim as he recited a poem just before closing time.

She had never intended to stay drinking for that long.

Nor, for that matter, did Janine imagine returning to Tim's flat with him and spending the night. But her present situation told her all that she needed to know concerning the previous evening, and she considered herself old and wise enough to know that regret was a wasted emotion and not worth her energy.

Not that she particularly regretted their brief encounter, it was hard to regret something you barely had any recall about.

Besides, no one forced her to try the pub's under-the-counter speciality.

Janine slid her bare legs out from underneath the covers.

Sitting on the edge of the bed, she glanced around the room in an attempt to familiarise herself with her surroundings. Tim's flat appeared to reflect the chaos of his mind, as he had admitted during their drinking session that he found it unnerving almost to the point of insanity when engaged by a publisher who insisted on imposing a deadline for his work.

The poetic mind had to be free and create only when the muse descended, he informed Janine.

It seemed to have worked for him as he had a considerable output to his name, although he confessed to having lost the interest of many publishers over the years due to what they perceived to be his lack of dedication to conformity.

Janine glanced around at the various piles of books, magazines and notepads which littered the room, along with an array of rolled-up posters still waiting for their turn to be displayed. As the walls were already crammed with a series of drawings, paintings, posters and several sketches of the local countryside, Janine surmised that their wait might be some time in coming.

Janine rubbed her eyes and yawned, covering her mouth with the back of her hand to help stifle the sound.

Although Tim seemed dead to the world, she decided that, under the circumstances, a quick exit might be the best option.

It was then that she remembered her phone. Having received the text from Marie the evening before stating that she and Sarah already had a lift organised, Janine had not switched her setting back to loud, hence the vibrations.

She stumbled over to the dresser where she had discarded her jeans the previous night and retrieved her phone.

As she listened to the message, her heart sank.

'Hello Miss Carstairs, this is Officer Clark, I believe we met the other day in Bishop's Park. Anyway, this is to inform you that your daughter Marie is here with us at the local health centre, I'm afraid that she had a tad too much to drink last night and is now very much in need of her mother.

I'll text you the address. See you soon'.

Automatically, her mothering instincts cut in. Janine, no longer concerned about whether or not she woke her sleeping lover, stumbled around the room retrieving her clothes and struggling into them in the semi-darkness.

There was no sign of her shoes in the bedroom, so once she was dressed, Janine ventured out into the hall and found them sitting atop an occasional hall table next to her handbag.

Once dressed, as time was pressing, she did not bother to write Tim a note. She checked that her car keys were in her bag before leaving the flat and closed the door as gently as she could behind her.

Fortunately, as soon as she exited the building, she remembered that Tim's flat was only a stone's throw from the pub, and that the village hall was across the road from there, so locating her car was relatively simple.

The walk to it, on the other hand, took a little more concentration.

The sky was still dark, and the cold rush of the wind helped to sober her up, although her legs still felt a little unsteady. Janine knew that legally she was in no fit state to drive, but the chances of finding an Uber on the island were doubtless impossible.

She checked her phone for the text with the directions to the health centre and typed them into her sat nav. It showed that the drive should not take more than ten to fifteen minutes at that time of the morning, but it was still too far for her to consider walking.

Officer Clark had specified that Marie was okay, but even so, Janine needed to see her as soon as possible to make sure for herself.

She cursed herself for not insisting on driving the girls home from work herself, but in reality, she knew that had she done, so she would doubtless have been labelled as overbearing by Marie.

Besides, you had to give your children some freedom when they reached a certain age so that they could at least experience making mistakes for themselves.

The fact that the first time she actually allowed Marie some leeway she went out and became plastered was neither here nor there.

After all, she was no one to talk after her session last night.

Once in her car, Janine started up the engine and turned on the heater. She searched in her handbag for the minty breath freshener she always carried and sprayed it liberally around her mouth. Mixing the liquid with saliva and flushing it between her teeth before swallowing.

The fact that she was about to be confronted by an officer of the law had not escaped her, but she hoped that, given the circumstances, he would be willing to give her a break if he managed to smell alcohol on her breath.

She turned on the voice activation signal and followed the directions, ensuring that she kept to the speed limit even though she appeared to be the only driver on the road.

When Janine arrived at the health centre, she parked up as close to the entrance as possible, ensuring that she did not obstruct the spaces dedicated to emergency vehicles.

She ran her fingers through her hair in the mirror and sprayed her neck with perfume. Before opening the door, Janine took in another couple of shots from her freshener, pulling a face as she swallowed. On her walk to the entrance, Janine took in a large lungful of air to try and give herself a fighting chance of not smelling like a brewery in front of the police officer.

As she reached for the door, Janine recognised Constable Clark heading in the opposite direction. She held open the door and waited for him to reach her.

"Hello again," he said, solemnly, his mind clearly on something else. "You must forgive me, but I have to rush off, just had an urgent call. Your daughter is inside, she's in very good hands." With that, he raced past her and took off in his patrol car.

Janine breathed a small sigh of relief. At least he had not stayed long enough to consider breathalysing her.

Once inside, Janine informed the receptionist of why she was there, and the lady directed her down the corridor to the room where Marie was.

When Janine walked in, Marie was sitting slumped in a chair with her head in her hands. She was only wearing a thin tee-shirt, but she had a carrier bag beside her which Janine imagined contained the rest of her clothes.

She could hazard a decent guess as to why they had been removed.

Marie looked up at her.

Janine had never seen her daughter look so ill, even when she had that serious bout of flu a couple of years before. All the colour had drained from her face, and it was clear from her stained cheeks and puffy eyes that she had been crying. Her usually beautifully crafted hair was bedraggled and hung around her face as if she had been dragged backwards through a hedge.

Any thoughts Janine may have harboured concerning reading her the riot act melted away in an instant. All she wanted to do was go to her and hold her.

Before she had a chance, a man in a long white coat appeared behind her.

Janine spun round. "Oh, hello," she said. "I'm Marie's mother."

The doctor smiled. "Lovely, I'm afraid your daughter is still a little worse for wear, but I think she's already purged most of what was causing her discomfort. We've given her a little something to help calm her tummy, but I'm afraid there's every possibility that there's more to come."

"She's going to be alright, though?" Janine asked, tentatively.

The doctor nodded. "Oh yes, for sure, a little too much partying, that's all." He reached into his pocket and took out a silver foil packet, which contained two tablets, and handed it to Janine. "If she does end up bringing back the medication we've given her, then these dissolved in a little water should do the trick."

Janine took the foil parcel and thanked him.

Smiling, he turned and walked away down the corridor.

Chapter Thirty-Four

CONSTABLE CLARK PULLED UP IN THE FIRST SPACE HE came to on the ridge overlooking the southern tip of Westside Cliff. This was about as close as possible for any vehicle to reach the beach from this direction, and he could already see the ambulance with its blue lights still flashing, parked up towards the steps which led down to the shore.

He also noticed Doctor Cleary's car parked at an angle across from the ambulance.

Clark felt reassured that, for once, he was not the first official on the scene and hoped that, due to the hour, there would be no trouble with onlookers crowding in and ruining any chance of forensic evidence being captured.

He exited his vehicle and made his way down to the beach.

Doctor Cleary was already on his way back towards the stairs, and they met halfway.

The doctor shook his head, slowly. "I can't believe what I'm seeing," he confessed, evidently shocked by what he had witnessed. "A young boy like that, dead before he even had a chance of living."

"Who is it?" asked Clark. Having received his initial call

from someone walking their dog across the beach, the officer had alerted the doctor and the paramedics on his drive over there.

The witness did not recognise the body, and from the state of her phone call, she was too distressed to try and take a closer look. She did, however, agree to wait nearby until the police officer arrived on the scene so that he could take a witness statement from her.

"Young Liam Mularkey," Doctor Cleary confirmed. "What was he, sixteen, seventeen?"

"What are we looking at?" asked Clark, glancing around the doctor's shoulder to ensure that no one was crowding in around the body.

The doctor shrugged, wearily. "I'd say a heart attack at a guess, but naturally we'll need a post-mortem to ascertain that for definite." He shook his head, thoughtfully. "But I'll say one thing, he has the same horrific expression on his face as Jerry Brookes and Michelle Calvert. If I didn't know any better, I'd swear they were frightened to death, but my medical head refuses to accept such a theory. Especially for such a young, fit, healthy young man as poor Liam."

"Has there been any official word yet about the others?"

"Not yet, the pathologist back on the mainland is a bit of a lone wolf. To my knowledge, he hasn't had an assistant since the last one left five years ago. He prefers to work alone unimpeded, which is great for him so far as consistency is concerned, but it does mean that in situations such as these, we end up with a bit of a backlog."

"Can't they get hold of anyone else to speed things up, I mean, under the circumstances, surely there's some protocol to follow?"

"Well, that's down to the coroner. But I know for a fact that he and the pathologist are old golfing buddies, so he'll probably be allowed to have his own way."

Officer Clark sighed. "Terrific," he said, dejectedly. He glanced around the area, a curious look on his face. "Have you seen my witness, the lady who called it in?"

Doctor Cleary nodded. "Yes, she was still here when I pulled up. It was Rose Mullins. I sent her home; she was obviously in shock and in need of a strong cup of tea. I doubt she'll be much use to you tonight. You know where she lives?"

The officer nodded. "I'll speak to her tomorrow, thanks for that. Well, I suppose I'd better inform the mainland and sort out a cordon for the area. Not that I suspect they'll be much to find if it was a heart attack, but you know these mainlanders, they love their procedure no matter how pointless."

The doctor smiled. "That inspector at Bishop's Park certainly seemed like the belt and braces variety." Cleary observed. "Doubtless he'll be on his way with his forensic team before daylight. Well, I'm off to fill in my report. See you around, no doubt."

The two men parted company, and Officer Clark made his way along the sand to where the paramedics were securing Liam's corpse to a stretcher.

Clark pulled back the sheet covering Liam's face just to ascertain for himself the boy's identity. It was not that he did not trust or believe the doctor, but for his own peace of mind before he informed the boy's parents.

It was at times such as this that he longed for the prospect of having a couple of deputies to help carry the burden. Not that he would task them with breaking such tragic news to grieving parents, but at least they could assist him with cordoning off the area and, when necessary, interviewing witnesses.

Due to the island's general lack of crime, it had been deemed that only a part-time force was needed on the island, and that if warranted, more officers could be dispatched from the mainland within the hour.

By part-time, of course, what it boiled down to was one full-time officer on twenty-four-hour call.

For his part, Clark was happy enough with the status quo for now. Community policing was usually the main part of his duty, and having so many unexpected deaths in such a short space of time was definitely unusual, to say the least.

But he had to admit, whether it was just him growing older or the job starting to take over, there were times when sleep felt like a distant memory.

Once he had cordoned off the area, Constable Clark drove over to where Liam's parents lived. On the way, he called the mainland to report the boy's sudden demise and was assured that a senior officer and forensics team would be over at first light.

As an afterthought, Clark called the presbytery and woke Father Boyle. He knew that as Liam's parents were both members of his flock, he would doubtless wish to offer them comfort at this tragic time. The father promised he would leave at once and see the officer at their house.

Informing Liam's parents went just the way he had expected.

Neither of them could believe what they were hearing, and who could blame them. After all, their son was a young, fit teenager with his whole life ahead of him.

Liam's mother, a devout Christian, could not accept what God had done to them and kept, through her tears, insisting that it was all some terrible mistake.

Liam's father, too, could not accept that his football-loving son could have a heart attack at such a young age and kept insisting that there was no history of heart problems in the family.

Constable Clark thought it best not to mention the terrified look on their son's face when he was found, at this juncture. Better, he thought, just to allow them to grieve and wait for the shock to sink in.

He was relieved when Father Boyle arrived to help look after the couple.

Unlike some members of the cloth who only knew how to suggest that God had a plan for everyone and that it was his will and should not be questioned, Father Boyle's approach was far more personal and empathetic. As part of his training, Constable Clark had attended umpteen seminars hosted by experts in the subject from around the globe on how best to deal with grieving relatives and loved ones. But he knew from experience that Father Boyle could give all those alleged professionals a run for their money when it came to what to say, how and when.

After a while, Liam's mother insisted that she needed to see her son in order to accept that he was really dead. This was a fairly common response under such circumstances and Clark knew that he had no right to stop them from attending the morgue.

However, as with victims of traffic accidents, he advised against it for the moment, suggesting that they might want to wait until morning. But both parents insisted that they would not be able to rest until they saw their son with their own eyes.

Constable Clark took Father Boyle to one side and explained the situation concerning Liam's frozen expression. The priest appeared taken aback by the news but soon recovered to focus on the grieving parents.

The officer phoned ahead to warn the staff at the medical centre where the body was being kept until it could be transported to the mainland the following day.

Liam's father insisted on driving them himself, so Clark led the procession, followed by Father Boyle, then the Mularkeys brought up the rear of the solemn procession.

Once they all arrived at the medical centre, one of the doctors was waiting for them in reception. Constable Clark took the doctor to one side and admitted that he had not divulged the state of the boy's body to his parents. The doctor nodded his understanding and assured the officer that he would explain all once they were in the waiting room attached to the morgue.

Father Boyle offered to go in with the Mularkeys, and they gratefully accepted his offer.

While he waited in the foyer for the three of them to return, Clark received another call on his mobile informing him that Bridget Donnelly's body had just been discovered on the other side of town.

For a moment, he found himself unable to take the information in.

Two bodies in the space of one night on an island where most of the residents lived well into their dotage was a little much to accept.

He left a scribbled message for Father Boyle and Liam's parents at reception, apologising for having to rush off so suddenly. He gave the receptionist the details of where to send the ambulance and jumped back into his patrol car to make his way over there.

Clark contacted Doctor Cleary en route. The poor man had only just fallen asleep, but like Clark, he knew that duty demanded he respond immediately, so he informed the officer that he would be five minutes behind him.

The officer felt guilty for the thought, but at least he knew that Bridget had no living relatives on the island to inform, so that was one task he did not have to face straight away.

The switchboard operator had not given him any specific details regarding the state of Bridget's body. But he could not help but wonder if this was going to be another mysterious heart attack victim.

Chapter Thirty-Five

By the time Janine arrived home, she had sobered up considerably. Having seen her poor daughter looking so distraught and vulnerable back at the health centre, she immediately transformed into 'protective parent' mode, and all her own problems seemed to melt away with the concern for her daughter.

The guilty look in Marie's eyes when she first saw her mother enter the room at the clinic told Janine all she needed to know about her daughter's state of mind. This was the first time that Janine had ever been called out in the middle of the night to collect her, which in itself was a miracle compared to some of the stories she had overheard being discussed by single mothers in bars and cafés when she was out and about.

In general, Marie, in spite of her occasional attitude outbursts, was a good kid who, whether for her own reasons or because she genuinely did not want to add to her mother's burden, kept to the straight and narrow and avoided some of the teenage traps her friends and peers had slipped into.

That alone, in Janine's eyes, meant that she was entitled to be cut a little slack.

Added to which, judging by the state her daughter was in, Janine felt confident that it would be a long time-if ever-before Marie allowed herself to end up that wasted again.

When Janine placed her arm around Marie's shoulders and hugged her, Marie leant into the hug and allowed her head to rest against her mother's bosom, something it seemed to Janine a lifetime since she allowed herself to seem so vulnerable.

Finally, Janine asked. "So, did you have a good time, kiddo?"

Marie laughed, in spite of herself, then immediately clamped her hand across her mouth and sat upright. She grabbed the plastic bin, which had been provided by the clinic staff when she first came, and vomited into it.

Coughing and spluttering, she eventually came back up for air, wiping her mouth with a tissue before discarding it into the same plastic receptacle.

She moaned loudly before saying, "Please take me home, Mum, I just want to go to bed."

Janine helped her to her feet and retrieved the bag, which contained her bile-stained clothing. The smell from the bag was overwhelming, so Janine tied the handles together to keep it contained, placing her other arm around Marie's waist as they made their way out of the room and back not the corridor.

As they were leaving the clinic, they heard the sound of shouting coming from another room to their left.

They turned to each other. "That's Sarah's mum," Marie informed Janine. "She's been screaming at her off and on since we came in."

Janine's heart immediately went out to the poor girl, who she suspected was probably not in a fit state to defend herself.

As they passed the room in question, through the open door, Janine could see Sarah slumped on a chair, much the same as Marie had been when she arrived, with her head in her hands. The door had been closed when Janine first arrived, which explained why she had not seen her daughter's friend when she walked past it.

They stopped for a moment, hovering outside, both women unsure whether or not to intervene and try to calm Sarah's mother down. But it was clear that she was in full tyrant mode and probably not in the best frame of mind to accept some well-intentioned advice.

Just before they continued on their way, Sarah raised her head and looked at them.

Her mother had moved to one side, still berating her child at full steam while she aimlessly folded some towels, which allowed Janine and Marie to make eye contact with Sarah without her parent knowing.

The minute she saw them, Sarah smiled weakly and mouthed the word 'sorry'.

Whether she was apologising for the state she had allowed Marie to find herself in, or for the noise her mother was making was unclear. But Janine winked at the girl and smiled back as if to convey that she did not blame the girl for anything that had happened that night.

Marie managed to complete the car journey home without needing to expel whatever was left inside her.

Once inside, on her mother's suggestion, she took a shower to eradicate any lingering odour of vomit from herself. She sat under the hot spray for ages before finally acquiring the strength to shampoo her hair and scrub her body.

When she emerged from the bathroom in her white dressing gown, with her damp hair wrapped in a towel, her eyes were half closed, and the drawn and weary expression on her face did not correspond with someone who had just enjoyed a refreshing shower.

Janine met her on the landing with a cup of hot, strong black coffee and a couple of the pills the doctor at the clinic had given her.

They went into Marie's bedroom. Marie lay on her bed, propped up by several pillows while she took her meds and sipped her coffee. She smiled when she tasted the strong liquid. Janine, who usually chastised Marie for putting too much sugar in her coffee, had made it extra sweet.

Marie gulped down her tablets. The sweetened beverage made the task more palatable than a mere glass of water would have done.

Marie glanced over at her mother. "Sorry, Mum," she mumbled, her head slightly bowed. "I guess I made a right fool of myself tonight."

Janine smiled. "Won't be the last time, kid, I'm sorry to tell you. There's no age limit on that."

Marie laughed, then held her side. Her stomach hurt from the strain of purging the vast majority of what she had consumed earlier in the evening.

"Does it still hurt?"

Marie nodded. "Only when I move," she said, jokingly.

Janine sat next to her on the bed. "Do you remember much about what happened?" she asked, trying to keep the concern from her voice. There had been no mention from either the police officer or the doctor about her daughter being molested in any way. But Janine still wanted to hear it from her daughter's own lips before she completely relaxed.

She had read way too many stories concerning young girls being lured into drinking too much by men out to have their way with them by any means available, including drugging their drinks until they were too incapacitated to fight them off.

She had even reported on instances where the girls had been so out of it that they were not even aware that they had been sexually assaulted during a drunken stupor, such was the potency of the drugs used.

Marie thought a moment before answering. "I remember us going to the party," she admitted. "I really didn't want to go, but

Sarah was so excited by the idea that I felt too guilty to say no."
She held up a hand. "Not that she forced me," she confirmed.
"In fact, she told me several times that the decision whether we
attended or not was totally up to me. But I could see how eager
she was, so I just said yes, and that was that."

"Was it what you expected?" Janine asked, her voice still
calm.

Marie nodded. "Sarah was right about that, at least. It was a
Traveller's party for someone's birthday. Everyone was so nice,
except a couple of girls who wanted to kill us because Sarah had
gone out with that dickhead Declan. But Sarah managed to calm
them down and assure them that they were no longer an item.
Then, of course, Declan himself made an appearance. He and a
couple of his cronies had driven us there, so I suppose it was
inevitable that he felt entitled to sit with us for a while." Marie
laughed. "But Sarah soon got rid of him, she's really a feisty
one, that girl, I wish I could be more like her."

"So, what was it, just one too many over the eight?"

Marie nodded, her eyes displaying the remorse and guilt for
the fuss she had caused.

"What were they serving?" Janine continued.

Marie shrugged. "We stuck to beer. The food was to die for,
so we ate plenty to soak up the alcohol. Oh, but then I stupidly
tried something Sarah referred to as 'mountain dew', boy did
that stuff have a kick like an angry mule. I think it was that that
finally did for me. Sarah seemed to be able to handle it without
any bother, I think maybe I was just trying to keep up with her
and prove to myself that I was capable. It made me feel like a
proper grown-up for about ten seconds, then, according to
Sarah, I just suddenly passed out, so she asked one of the travellers to drive us to the medical centre, and that was that."

"She must have known that her mother would be on duty
there tonight," Janine observed. "She sounds like a devoted

friend willing to dive straight into the lion's den to save you like that."

Marie nodded. "She was, love her. The minute I came around, all I could hear was her mother screaming at her, blaming her for everything and threatening to ground her for life. I wanted to intervene and say something on her behalf, but I was feeling so lousy and kept on throwing up, so in the end I just stayed in my room feeling pathetic."

"By the sound of it, there wasn't much else you could do," suggested Janine, relieved by the fact that there did not seem to be any evidence of anyone trying to take advantage of her daughter while she was under the influence.

"I know," agreed Marie, dejectedly. "But I hated having to leave Sarah there to face the music, especially after looking after me and making sure that I received medical help for my stupidity. I can think of several girls at school who would have just left me to sleep it off on a bench and carried on enjoying themselves, regardless of how sick I really was."

"She's obviously made of better stuff," agreed Janine. "Don't forget to call her in the morning and thank her for looking after you. Friends like her can be hard to find."

"If her mum ever gives her back her phone," Maire responded. "She was so mean to her."

"I know, darling, it's just some parents' way of expressing their concern. I'm sure she has her good points too."

Marie looked Janine in the eyes. "Mum, why didn't Dad want to take me on holiday with him? He promised, and I had been looking forward to it for so long, and then he just dumps me because 'Barbie' suddenly needs to have her body infused with even more plastic. Do I mean that little to him?"

Now Janine understood the real reason behind her daughter's behaviour.

Her sullen. Moody, teenage angst was a cry of injustice for

the way her father had treated her, and Janine could not blame her. After all, she was supposed to be his little girl, the father-daughter bond was supposed to concrete a special relationship which all fathers longed for and dedicated their lives to fulfilling.

Instead, he had deserted her for someone who only stimulated one organ in his body.

It was bad enough that he had left Janine for the little 'airhead', abandoning their marriage without so much as a second thought. But Janine had always expected him to honour his role as father and ensure that he did his utmost to keep his relationship with his only daughter sacrosanct.

Marie deserved so much more, and although Janine was used to being on the receiving end of her daughter's feelings of betrayal for no reason other than she was an easy target, she had always tried to maintain a certain amount of dignity when referring to Marie's father, even to the point of making excuses and protecting him, regardless of the way he had acted towards them both.

But now, she tired of her role as the loyal ex-wife.

Although she refused to assume the disgruntled caricature of the scorned woman, ranting and raving against her ex at every opportunity and to anyone who happened to be within earshot. She was, however, no longer prepared to try and justify his reasons for such intolerable behaviour.

Even so, Janine would always assure her daughter that she was in no way to blame for her father's callous treatment of her. That was a burden which he had created for himself and for which he would have to justify when-if-he was ever brave enough to confront his daughter with the truth.

But right now, Marie needed at least one parent to show that they cared and put her above all else.

Janine moved closer to Marie and wrapped her arms around her, holding her closer than she had done in too long.

Marie responded in kind, for once not pushing her mother away and making one of those disgruntled noises which teenagers reserved for their parents whenever they grew too close. Instead, she nestled in against Janine, closing her eyes and inhaling deeply as if trying to staunch the flow of tears.

They sat like that until Marie finally fell asleep.

Chapter Thirty-Six

ONCE MARIE WAS SOUND ASLEEP, JANINE TOOK herself off to her own room to try and catch up on some lost sleep. But, after staring at the ceiling for almost an hour, she decided to do something more constructive with her time.

She went back downstairs into the kitchen and sat at the table with her laptop and all her notes and tapes from her interview with Tim from the previous evening.

When she heard his voice on tape, she blushed at the thought of their time together after the pub. Janine still could not fathom exactly why she went home with him, the idea was certainly not on her radar at any time during the evening.

Perhaps, she thought, there really was something in the notion of Irish charm.

In many ways, she was glad of the fact that she could not sleep. She needed to send something to the magazine editor by the end of the day, and as yet, she had not even created the outline for her article.

Janine began with that as a starting point. She constructed her layout around the information she had gleaned from the internet concerning the history of the island, interspersed with some of the details from Tim's talk.

Some of the poet's stories were so well crafted that Janine had to ensure that she did not steal his prose directly, although she doubted that he ever read the publication she was working for, as a journalist, she had her own code of conduct which she adhered to for the sake of integrity.

Whilst formatting her article, Janine's mind kept returning to the story concerning Molly McShane, the lady Tim referred to as 'The Banshee Bride'. There was enough material there for an entire article by itself, and Janine considered mentioning it to her editor as an option for a further piece, researching Molly McShane's life on the island and delving into the myth and legend of what the poor woman subsequently became.

Tim had let slip that he too was contemplating an entire book on the story, but that he had been stumped by the new curate refusing him access to the church archives on the grounds that the basement in which they were stored was unsafe, and the church would be liable if he fell or had an accident while down there.

According to Tim, it was all nonsense. He had, in fact, been down there twice before the new curate put in an appearance, and so far as he could tell, the foundations were as solid as the day they were laid.

Tim believed that the curate had his own agenda for keeping people out, but as yet he was unable to fathom what it was.

He told Janine that while he was down there, he had come across a ledger which had been written by a local priest at the time of Molly's suicide. According to Tim, the priest was extremely knowledgeable on the legend behind the Banshee, including how to call one forth, what the consequences were if you summoned one unnecessarily, and how to deflect the power of the Banshee should one be called against you.

Tim admitted that he wished he had spent longer in the

archives before the new curate took up his position, but with the poor lighting down there, he began having headaches after an hour or so, and sometimes they would last for days.

Janine wondered if, given the go-ahead, she could perhaps persuade Father Wells to allow her access into his domain. She knew that, as a priest, he would not be charmed simply by the fact that she was a woman, but he was still a man and, as such, possibly open to a little complimentary flattering.

It was worth a try if she could find the ledger Tim spoke of.

Janine switched the tape back on to listen to Tim's account of how the wicked magistrate contrived to dispose of Molly's true love in order to have her for himself.

The sudden sound of the cat flap made her spin around on her seat.

As she gazed down, she saw Gypsy emerge from outside, letting the flap swing back and forth behind her. The cat jumped up on the table and looked at Janine as if she was waiting to be served.

"You made me jump, mischievous moggy," Janine said, clutching a hand against her chest and taking in a few calming breaths. "I suppose you want feeding, is that it?"

Gypsy continued looking up at her without moving.

Janine opened a can of cat food and forked it out onto a quarter plate. She turned to see the cat still sitting on top of the table, only now it was straining its neck to see what was on the plate.

"We've had this conversation already," Janine reminded her, bending down and putting the plate on the floor.

The cat did not need any convincing. It jumped down and immediately began devouring its meal.

Janine poured a saucer of milk and placed that down next to the food.

She decided to fix herself an early morning coffee. The sky

outside was no longer dark but instead had taken on a light blue hue, which summoned the arrival of the dawn.

Janine took her coffee back to the table, careful to place her cup on the other side of her just in case Gypsy decided to jump back up and knock it over.

While Janine sipped the hot liquid, Gypsy finished the last of her milk and, as expected, hopped back up on the table next to her. She sat there for a moment, licking her paws and grooming herself whilst purring contentedly.

Janine considered reaching out and stroking the cat, but although Marie seemed to have built a trust with the feline, Janine was not so sure that she was considered to be in the same club, regardless of the fact that this was not the first time she had fed the stray.

Returning to her notes, Janine tapped in some side-bar issues for later consideration in case they slipped her mind. This was a process she had found invaluable over the years as a memory-jogger.

As she worked, Gypsy became increasingly interested in one of her notepads and began pawing at it, aimlessly.

Janine allowed the cat to continue for a while, but then the moggie, no longer content with just pawing at the paper, began to tear little shreds off at the corner.

Eventually, Janine moved the pad out of reach.

Gypsy glanced up at her as if questioning why she was ruining her fun.

"If you want to make yourself useful, why don't you go up and comfort Marie. She's not feeling too well."

To her amazement, Gypsy jumped down from the table and casually strolled out of the kitchen into the living room. Janine leaned back in her chair and watched as the cat meandered towards the stairs, then began climbing them.

For a brief moment, Janine was concerned that the cat might pee or defecate somewhere on the upper floor. But then she surmised that a feral cat would do its business outside, not being used to the comforts of being indoors.

She listened from her chair but could hear nothing that sounded untoward coming from above, so she decided to continue with her work.

After another hour, Janine had settled on the format of her story and e-mailed her editor to glean his take. She included a separate file detailing the legend of Molly McShane and her idea to make more of the story for a separate issue.

Leaning back in her chair, Janine rubbed the back of her neck, twisting it from side to side to ease the tension. She glanced at her phone and saw that it was just coming up to six o'clock, and now she could feel sleep catching up with her.

There was still time for a good couple of hours before Marie was likely to wake up, so Janine closed down her laptop and made her way upstairs.

She stopped outside Marie's room and peered inside.

Marie was still sound asleep, her hair, now free from her towel, lay across her face and nestled beside her Gypsy also appeared to be fast asleep.

Seeing them together, Janine knew that the possibility of them taking the cat home with them after their break was increasing by the minute. Marie would not want to leave her behind, and as she had no owner, there was really nothing stopping them.

Janine decided to leave the decision until Marie mentioned it in earnest.

She turned away and went back to her own room, crashing on the bed in her clothes, deciding there was no point at this stage in undressing.

Within seconds, Janine joined her daughter in blissful slumber.

Chapter Thirty-Seven

FATHER BOYLE RUBBED THE SLEEP FROM HIS EYES. IT had been a very long night, and by the time he eventually made it back to the priory, he barely had time for a quick catnap before having to open the church to admit his army of volunteer cleaners.

He had stayed with Liam's parents after accompanying them home from the morgue.

Naturally, Liam's mother was inconsolable and did not stop crying right up until the moment her husband finally convinced her, in spite of her protestations, to lie down and try to go back to sleep. Sheer exhaustion accompanied by grief and a lack of rest from the previous night finally claimed her, and she dozed off on the sofa, refusing to go upstairs to bed.

Liam's father ushered the priest into the kitchen, where he poured them both a stiff shot of single malt. Ordinarily, Father Boyle would not partake when he knew he was driving, but he sensed that the man needed someone to raise a glass with him to his son, so he accepted graciously.

"To my boy," stated Sean Mularkey, raising his glass to heaven, "may he rest in eternal peace by the side of the Lord."

"Amen," responded Father Boyle, lifting his glass before lowering it to take a sip.

The malt was certainly welcome on a cold night, and Father Boyle felt its warmth careening through his body.

They both sat down at the table, and Sean, who had drained the contents of his glass in one swallow, refilled it and leaned over to offer a top-up to the priest. Although Father Boyle had barely touched his, he felt he could not refuse the man's offer under the circumstances, so he smiled politely as the man poured.

Again, Liam's father knocked back his drink in one go. He placed his hand in front of his mouth to stifle a loud belch, apologising for his rudeness.

Father Boyle watched the man refill his glass once more. He was concerned that Sean's grief was driving his actions, and although perfectly understandable in the circumstances, he feared that too much too soon might lead to another heart attack.

Siobhan Mularkey had confided in the priest when her husband had his first attack two years earlier that the specialist on the mainland had instructed Sean to curtail his drinking, especially spirits. The poor woman had been so sure that she was going to lose him at the time that she spent almost every spare minute when she was not by his side in church on bended knees praying to God to let him live.

Now, having lost her only child, it would be cruelty beyond belief if her husband were to follow him through overindulgence.

With all that, Father Boyle still felt himself unable to suggest that the man curtail his drinking. He had suffered a parent's worst nightmare, and as such, if he found comfort in the bottle, then so be it.

Father Boyle decided that he would stay with Sean for as long as he deemed necessary, even if it took the rest of the night. If he left him alone and anything happened to him, the priest knew that he would never forgive himself, nor be able to look Siobhan in the eye again.

As it was, Liam's father passed out after his next drink.

Resting his arms on the table in front of him, Sean had placed his head on them, facing away from Father Boyle as he began sobbing for the loss of his child.

Within a couple of minutes, the priest heard the man start snoring.

Father Boyle remained there for a while, ensuring that Sean Mularkey was breathing soundly. Then he rose from his seat, poured what was left in his glass back into the bottle and replaced it in the cupboard from which Sean had retrieved it.

He went back into the living room to see if Siobhan was still asleep, and when he was satisfied that she was, he left, taking care to shut the front door as quietly as he could.

Once back at St Mark's, Father Boyle said a prayer for the soul of Liam Mularkey. He had already administered the last rites over the young man's body in the morgue, but as he felt that was more a duty than a personal plea, he always liked to say a separate, more personal, prayer when one of his parishioners passed over.

He had barely closed his eyes before his alarm startled him back into life.

As he approached the front door, he could already hear the chatter of his volunteers through the sturdy wood. He opened the door to welcome them in, noticing immediately that Enid Murphy was not among them.

Not wishing to raise any undue concern, Father Boyle smiled broadly and ushered the other four women inside. "The kettle's on, and there's a new packet of chocolate digestives which needs attention," he announced, cheerfully.

While the women took off their coats to hang them up on

the hooks provided, Father Boyle stared out into the early morning to see if there was any sign of his missing cleaner.

He waited for a moment, but as there was no sign of her, he closed the door and followed the others to the kitchen.

It was unlike Enid not to telephone if she were unable to attend her cleaning duties, and Father Boyle wondered if her absence had anything to do with the death of her daughter Erin's boyfriend. Although the incident only took place a few hours earlier, word could spread like wildfire in such a small community, so it was highly probable that Erin would already know.

Father Boyle made polite conversation with his cleaners, although his mind often wandered back to his concern for Enid's absence.

There was, of course, another, more sinister reason why she had not appeared for work that morning. The priest knew only too well that the woman's husband had a foul temper, which he often unleashed on his wife and even his daughter.

If, for whatever reason, that was the reason Enid was not here, then the priest also knew that she would not attend the local health centre for fear of news about her condition spreading.

Several years earlier during one such onslaught, Colm Murphy had bruised his wife's ribs so badly that Enid was in extreme pain whenever she took in a breath. But even in that condition, she had refused medical attention, insisting that she did not wish to make a fuss over nothing.

Father Boyle had often prayed for the safety of Enid and Erin, and although Colm paraded as a good Catholic, when he admitted to his assaults on his family in confession, he never sounded truly remorseful in the priest's eyes. It was more a case of him just going through the motions in an attempt to clear his own conscience.

"Father, did you hear about young Liam Mularkey?"

The question took him by surprise and shook Father Boyle from his reverie.

He turned towards the woman who had asked the question. "Yes. Actually, I was called out last night by Doctor Cleary to administer the last rites and try to bring some sort of comfort to his poor parents. A great tragedy."

"But that's not all, Father," offered another of the cleaners. "This morning on my way in, there was a police cordon near the estate. I spoke to a young constable who had been shipped in from the mainland. Apparently, poor Liam wasn't the only victim last night."

The woman's words hit the priest like a cold splash of water. "Who else?" he asked, fearing that he already knew the answer.

Would it be Enid or Erin?

His heart raced, urging the cleaner to speak the name.

"Sure, it was Bridget Donnelly. According to the officer, she must have gone out for a nighttime stroll when she was struck down by a heart attack."

Father Boyle heaved a huge sigh of relief, then immediately felt guilty for it.

Bridget was still one of God's children and, as such, deserved his prayers.

He wondered why neither Constable Clark nor Doctor Cleary had called upon him to administer the last rites to the poor woman. He would need to make that a priority this morning before her body was taken to the mainland.

"A midnight stroll, I should coco," offered one of the other cleaners, dipping her digestive into her tea. "We all know what she was up to, even the good Father here."

The others all turned to the priest.

They could tell from his face that he knew exactly what was being asserted, but by the same token, he clearly did not appreciate the insinuation. "Now then, ladies," he began, turning to them all in order, leaving the accuser until last. The woman looked down at her cup, obviously now regretting her comment. "Bridget was a member of our community and as such deserves a little more respect, especially in view of her demise. Don't you think?"

The women all nodded in agreement, mumbling apologies beneath their breath.

They finished their tea in silence.

"Right then," announced the priest, rising to his feet. "If you ladies wouldn't mind carrying on without me, in view of what we've just heard, I need to go down to the mortuary to administer the last rites to poor Bridget. I trust you'll hold the fort in my absence."

The women assured him of their co-operation, glad now that any tension in the air was broken.

Father Boyle called through to the health centre to ensure that Bridget's body was still in situ. The young girl on the other end confirmed that she was but warned him that some police officers from the mainland were also on the premises and that their forensic officer was still inspecting her corpse.

Father Boyle thanked her and collected his hat and coat.

As he made his way towards the front door, he saw a shadow looming up at the stained-glass panel. He opened the door to see Enid Murphy loitering on his doorstep.

The minute she saw him, the woman immediately dropped her head and placed her hand over her left cheek. "Sorry, Father," she stammered, "I was just about to knock. I'm so sorry to be late, our Erin had some bad news this morning, so I had to console her before coming out."

Father Boyle sighed. "I know, I was there when they found poor Liam. I know young Erin was very fond of him."

"Oh, Father, she's in a terrible state," admitted Enid, still covering the side of her face. "To be completely honest, I wasn't aware until she received the news just how close they were. She's devastated, I've never seen her in such a state. I felt bad about leaving her, but eventually she fell back to sleep, so I thought it best to come over, but I may call in at work and ask for leave, I'm not sure she should be left alone all day."

The priest nodded. "That sounds like a good idea," he agreed. "And if you'll permit it I might call in on her later this morning, just to see if there's anything I can do to help."

Enid looked, momentarily forgetting about her face. Realising her mistake, she quickly slapped her hand back over her cheek. "Oh, thank you, Father, that would be most appreciated, I'm sure."

Father Boyle stared down at Enid, smiling warmly. Even with her hand covering almost half her face, he could still see that she was blushing, no doubt from the realisation that she had allowed him, however briefly, to see her bruised cheek.

Finally, he asked. "And how are you?"

Enid slowly lowered her hand to reveal the damage her husband had inflicted on her the previous evening.

Father Boyle took a deep breath. He could feel his temper rising, but he managed, outwardly at least, to keep it under control.

Enid began to cry, snatching a tissue from her handbag and using it to daub her eyes.

Being battered by her husband was a situation she had grown used to over the years, and she was prepared to take the brunt of his aggression so long as he did not unleash his temper on their daughter.

But recently, more and more it appeared to her, Colm had begun to also let fly at Erin without hesitation, especially if she tried to defend her mother against his wrath.

Enid felt torn between her duty to her husband and the safety of their only child.

Any thought of calling the authorities was an alien concept to her. She had been brought up to believe that a wife must stand by her husband no matter what.

Childhood memories of her own mother receiving beatings from her father whenever he returned home from the pub still resonated in her mind. But her mother had told her that such behaviour was merely a part of married life, and no matter how brutish her father might appear when he was intoxicated, he still loved them all and would do anything for them.

Just like her father, Colm always appeared friendly and unthreatening when he was in a good mood. To the majority of the outside world, he was a fine businessman, husband and father.

Only Enid, and now Erin, knew the truth.

For now, though, Enid was more embarrassed that the priest had seen the state of her face than she was afraid of her husband's temper.

Father Boyle stepped down to her level and escorted Enid into the hallway, closing the door behind them.

Enid wiped her eyes and nose with her tissue and apologised to him for making such a fuss.

The priest assured her that no apology was necessary and guided her into the kitchen.

The other cleaners had already tidied up, and their cups and saucers were now displayed on the dishrack by the sink.

Father Boyle sat Enid down and made her a cup of tea.

She thanked him, apologising over and over for the state she had allowed herself to get in.

"You know that I'm always here should you wish to talk," the priest informed her, his voice calm and consoling. "And anything you say to me will remain between us and God."

Enid nodded. She could feel a fresh batch of tears building up inside.

She placed her elbows on the table and let her head slump into her upturned hands.

The idea of unloading her feelings certainly appealed, and she knew that Father Boyle was always true to his word.

Telling the priest did not seem the same as reporting her husband to the police or social services, and Enid realised that she desperately needed to speak to someone.

Taking a deep breath, she blew her nose once more and then began, in a hushed tone, to inform Father Boyle of the situation with her husband.

Chapter Thirty-Eight

FATHER BOYLE WAS GRANTED ACCESS TO PERFORM THE last rites over Bridget Donnelly's corpse soon after he arrived at the health centre. He recognised the tall, thin officer from the mainland who had been present in Bishop's Park when they discovered Jerry Brookes' body and nodded politely to him after Peter Clark had ascertained that it was okay to let the priest inside the morgue.

Once the ceremony was complete, Father Boyle managed to have a quiet word with Constable Clark away from prying eyes and out of earshot of the other officers milling around. "I couldn't help but notice the expression on her face," Father Boyle commented. "Are you working on the assumption that the cause will be the same as that with the others?"

Constable Clark checked over his shoulder before answering. "Well, I've just been told that the post-mortems on Michelle Calvert and Jerry Brookes suggest heart attack in both cases. According to the pathologist on the mainland, rictus facial disfigurement is not uncommon in such instances. Though to be fair, I've never seen anything like it before, and I've been present at my fair share of heart attack and stroke victims."

The priest nodded. "Me too, I'm sorry to say. So, there's nothing suspicious being considered in either case?"

The officer shook his head. "Nope, seems your man over there," he indicated back towards the Detective Inspector, "seems quite satisfied with the outcomes from the PMs."

"But now there's another two suspected heart attacks, both in the same evening, surely that raises a few red flags?"

Clark shrugged. "Well, he made a couple of jokes about there being something in the water over here, but other than that, there's no outward evidence of any foul play, so again we'll just have to wait until the report comes back."

Father Boyle shook his head, thoughtfully. "Surely four heart attack victims in so short a time span requires some form of investigation?" he ventured. "We're usually a healthy lot here on the island, and all four victims were very young, especially Liam."

Officer Clark sighed. "I know what you mean, Father, but if the pathologist doesn't raise any concerns, then we've really nothing to go on. They just end up being sad statistics."

"Let's just pray that they are the last," Father Boyle offered. He turned to leave, then stopped. "By the way, wasn't Bridget looking after a couple of foster children?"

The officer nodded. "Yes, that's right, one of the locals alerted an officer at the scene. We called social services and they've now been taken back into care."

The priest nodded. "Poor little mites, being shifted from pillar to post like that."

Clark moved in closer. "Well, not wanting to be one who speaks ill of the dead, but from what the officer on duty told me the two youngsters looked delighted when they were informed that they were leaving. They both packed up their stuff and were waiting by the front door within minutes, smiles all over their faces."

The priest frowned. "Well, I suppose none of us really knows what goes on behind closed doors, do we?"

When he left the health centre, Father Boyle drove straight over to Erin's house.

Having seen the state of Enid at church earlier, he could not help but wonder what condition poor Erin would be in when he called. Obviously, the poor girl would be desolate about Liam's death. But he wondered if she had also had to face the wrath of her father into the bargain.

Under normal circumstances, Father Boyle would have preferred either seeing her at church or at home if one of her parents were present. But on this occasion, they had something specific to discuss, and now that Liam was no longer a consideration to be taken into account, he suspected that poor Erin felt very alone and isolated.

He could feel the conflict inside him churning up inside.

Although the Catholic church had very strict rules concerning abortion, and he, as a priest, had a duty to impose those teachings upon all members of his flock, deep down he could not help but feel that under certain extreme circumstances, there was sometimes no other solution.

Poor Erin had landed herself in a no-win situation.

Pregnant, unmarried, Catholic with extremely strict parents. Even Enid, being as devout as she was, would not entertain the prospect of her daughter having an abortion, and her father would doubtless not entertain the prospect of his daughter having a child out of wedlock.

Living in such a closed community did not help matters either. The minute Erin started showing, the gossip's tongues would be wagging so hard some might be in danger of falling off. That was what came of living on an island, your business automatically became everybody else's.

Father Boyle could even imagine Colm Murphy keeping his daughter locked up in her bedroom until after the baby was born, rather than face the shame. He would probably force Enid to pretend that she was the pregnant one, then, when the baby came, he would insist that they brought it up as their own, with Enid as the sister rather than the mother.

At least, the priest surmised, the child would still be alive.

But even then, what terrors awaited both Enid and her daughter at the hands of Colm Murphy? That morning, before he left to visit the health centre, Enid had confided in him the truth of how she had come by her bruises. The poor woman spent most of their conversation in floods of tears, evidently fearful for her safety as well as that of her daughter.

Father Boyle could feel the guilt eating away at his insides as he sat there listening to her tale of woe, knowing that he knew more about her daughter's condition than she did and the subsequent distress and sheer dread that she would no doubt feel when, or if, her husband ever found out.

At one point, his curate had entered the kitchen where they were having their discussion, but sensing the atmosphere, he made his excuses and left. The poor man probably only wanted to make his breakfast, but by the time Father Boyle had finished with Enid, his curate had disappeared back down to the archives, so he hoped that he would resurface after a while to partake of some sustenance.

Between his concern for Enid, Liam's parents, Colm's treatment of his wife and daughter and Erin's pregnancy, Father Boyle was not sure if he was coming or going.

The mix of thoughts circling inside his brain was starting to give him a headache.

First things first, he had to try and convince Erin that abortion was not the answer to her problem.

Although he feared his argument might fall on deaf ears.

As he pulled up outside the Murphy residence, he noticed that Colm's car was not on the driveway. This was a relief. Even though he knew that Colm should be at work, he still worried that the man had returned home for some reason or another which would in turn mean that he could not speak to Erin about her condition as her father would doubtless want to listen in.

At least now he had some time with the girl alone.

He knocked on the door and waited.

Initially there was no reply, so he tried again. Enid had informed him that Erin was in bed so there was every chance that her grief and anxiety had caused her to fall into a deep sleep.

Father Boyle moved back out onto the driveway so that he could look up at the upstairs windows, just in case one of them was Erin's bedroom and she happened to glance down to see who it was.

But there was no sign of life.

The priest waited for a moment or two longer, then turned to leave.

He decided it would not be prudent to slip a note through the letterbox just in case Erin's father saw it first and started demanding to know what it was about.

Of course, it was perfectly reasonable that Father Boyle wished to know how Erin was after finding out about Liam, and he had already informed Enid of his intention to call on her daughter, but even so, the last thing the priest wanted to do was cause any unnecessary friction between Colm and his wife and daughter, so he decided it was best to leave things alone and try to call back another time.

As he reached the gate, he heard the front door open.

Turning back, he saw Erin draped in her dressing gown, peering at him through the crack in the door.

It was obvious, even from this distance, that she had been crying. Her eyes were red and puffy and her cheeks stained with dried tears.

Father Boyle walked back towards her. He intended to stop outside the door and ask her if she was up to talking with him, not wishing to force her if she did not feel strong enough. But before he had a chance to ask, Erin moved back, opening the door wider to allow him entry.

They sat in the living room. Erin slumped down on the sofa, tucking her legs underneath her, while Father Boyle sat opposite her in an armchair.

She offered him tea, and although the priest was gasping, he politely declined, preferring to take advantage of their time alone to discuss matters.

"A stupid question, I know," the priest began, "but how are you feeling?"

Erin shrugged. "I'm not sure I feel anything at the moment, Father," Erin confessed, "other than drained."

Father Boyle nodded his understanding. "You've been dealt a massive blow, proof positive that life can be exceptionally cruel sometimes."

Erin removed a couple of tissues from a box on the table next to her.

She daubed her eyes before blowing her nose.

The priest noticed her wince with the effort. From the raw state of her nose, he presumed that she had blown it to the point of tenderness.

"Have you had a chance to speak to Liam's parents yet?" he asked, softly.

Erin looked up; her cheeks reddened. "No, Father, what's the point?" she uttered, solemnly. "He never told them about us or the…" Her voice trailed off.

"I see." He had hoped that with the possible support of Liam's parents, Erin might at least have had someone on her side when she revealed her condition.

Father Boyle had even considered that, in light of losing their son, the chance of having his child to help keep his memory alive might just convince Erin's parents to embrace the situation as well and try to make the best of it.

As it was, if Erin now approached Liam's parents with news of her pregnancy, would they even believe her, considering their son appeared to have kept their relationship a secret.

This was a mess, and poor Erin, as young as she was, had the world on her shoulders.

"I know you have an awful lot to think about at the moment," Father Boyle ventured, tentatively, "but have you managed to give any more consideration about our talk?"

Erin's eyes began to well.

She placed a hand in front of her mouth and cleared her throat, choking back a fresh batch of tears. "I met with Liam last night," she confessed. "I was hoping to appeal to his better nature and convince him to do the decent thing, but he wasn't having any of it. He made it quite clear that he didn't want to be saddled with me or his child."

"You were with Liam last evening?" asked Father Boyle, taken aback slightly by the revelation. "Were you with him when he had his attack?"

Erin focused on her bare feet sticking out from under her dressing gown.

She tucked them under her. "I…I'm not sure, to be honest. He was fine one minute, arguing with me, then suddenly he began saying that he could hear something, and he began acting all weird, slapping his hands against his ears and complaining that the sound was growing louder."

"Did you hear it?"

Erin shook her head. "No, I couldn't hear anything except the sound of the waves. I thought that he was making it up as an excuse not to have to carry on with our conversation. I'm afraid I grew really angry with him, then he just ran off."

"Did you follow him?" Father Boyle enquired; his interest piqued.

Dejectedly, Erin shook her head. "Like I said, I thought he was just being an idiot. Now, perhaps, it seems it might have been his heart attack coming on. Perhaps if I hadn't been arguing with him, insisting that he take responsibility for my condition then, maybe he'd still be alive."

Erin broke down. She held her hands against her eyes as tears flooded from them.

Her entire body shook with the effort of her sobs.

After a moment, Father Boyle stood up and offered her the box of tissues.

She took a couple more and thanked him.

Although he was not a parent, his paternal instinct made him want to hold the poor girl and comfort her until her tears subsided. But he remembered the warning passed down from the bishop last year when one of his flock was reported to the police for allegedly becoming too tactile with a young parishioner.

The case was subsequently dropped, however, the publicity that it gleaned was particularly prejudicial against the church, and Catholics in particular, so the bishop had made his opinion quite clear on the subject that any similar incidences, regardless of the outcome, would not be looked upon favourably and may well result in the priest in question being defrocked.

With the threat still ringing in his ears, Father Boyle went back to his chair.

He massaged his temples, feeling the onslaught of a headache. "You mustn't think like that," he offered, trying to bring Erin a modicum of comfort. "No one could have known that someone as young and fit as Liam was going to have a heart attack. Doubtless the post-mortem will disclose some under-lying cause which was undiagnosed. You cannot blame yourself."

Erin looked back up and nodded, slowly.

Father Boyle could tell that she was unconvinced by his argument, but he hoped to reassure her some more before their talk was over.

Then he had another thought. "Did you inform the police that you were with him last evening?"

Erin looked shocked. "How could I, Father, without everything coming out?"

Upon reflection, he understood her reasoning. "Of course, you're right," he admitted. "Forgive me."

He could see Erin visibly relax.

After everything else that she had been through, now did not seem like the appropriate moment to ask Erin if she had made any firm decisions concerning her unborn child. But Father Boyle knew that such an occasion might not present itself in the near future, so he felt that he had little choice in the matter.

Soon it would be too late.

Either Erin would start showing or she would take herself to the mainland and have an abortion in secret.

The priest knew that he had to try and convince the girl to do the right thing.

But, under the circumstances, what was the right thing?

Chapter Thirty-Nine

For the second time, Janine was woken by her phone buzzing. She turned over and reached for her mobile on the nightstand. Glancing at the screen through sleep-blurred vision, she saw that it was her editor calling.

"Hello."

"Hi, Janine." The woman sounded excited almost to the point of hysteria. Either she had just received some good news, or she had drunk too much caffeine that morning.

"Hi, Sam," answered Janine, stifling a yawn. "Did you receive my e-mail?"

"Yep, very excited, it looks like the start of a great cover. I like the idea of you delving further into this 'Banshee Bride' mystery, too. Sounds like they have a terrific folklore angle going on there."

Janine sat up in bed. "Wonderful," she replied. Any time an editor sounded this enthusiastic about an outline was cause for celebration. "I think that I can do both articles simultaneously if you're prepared to stretch my advance on the original story, I may have to stay over here a little longer than originally anticipated."

"I think we can stretch to that," Sam gushed, "but listen, something else has come to my attention which I'm hoping you'll jump at."

"What's that?" Janine asked, curiously. With two stories on the go, she was surprised that her editor was not concerned about stretching her too thin.

"I received a call this morning about several unexplained deaths on the island in the last few days. Have you heard anything about them?"

"Well, I know there was one the night before we arrived, my daughter actually knows the poor girl who stumbled over the body. Then there was another in the local park, I just happened to be passing when the forensic team were checking the area."

"That's amazing." Janine could hear the enthusiasm rising in Sam's voice. "And you say your daughter actually knows someone who found the first body? Do you think you could arrange an interview with her, maybe take some shots?"

"I suppose I could ask, but to be honest, this isn't really my area of expertise." Janine knew from past experience that such a story could well grow legs very quickly and that interviewing Sarah would only be the start of the expedition.

Soon, she would be expected to try and interview the families of the bereaved, encroaching on their grief and having to ask awkward and personal questions merely to construct a decent story.

Editors could easily become overzealous, not to mention downright ruthless in pursuit of such a story, and they cared very little for the position which they put their reporters in.

Janine had been glad to leave such reporting behind her when she stopped covering crime. The mental stress alone had taken its toll on her temperament to the extent that she barely recognised herself, and what she did recognise, she did not like one bit.

The young journalists fresh out of university were the eager beavers willing to throw themselves wholeheartedly into the depths of deprivation, bloodshed and violence, whatever it took to get a story, and words such as integrity held little meaning for them in their quest.

But Janine had no intention of ever dipping her toe back into that cesspool.

"To be honest," she admitted, "I'd rather not embark on such a venture. Couldn't you send someone from your crime department to cover it?"

Sam laughed. "What crime department? We're a glossy, we don't usually cover such things as this, but an ex-colleague from one of the tabs called me this morning when he heard I had you in the field already. You don't need to sink too deep into the mire, just start the ball rolling. If the story grows legs, he'll send one of his more experienced scribblers over. He just wanted you to suss out the lay of the land, and he's willing to pay big bucks for your assistance."

Janine pondered the idea.

Sam was making it clear that she was not expected to sell her soul for this story, but editors often began such conversations like that, then sank their teeth in if the story took off.

"I promise I won't hang you out to dry on this one," Sam assured her. It was almost as if the editor had read Janine's mind. "It's just that he is an old friend and I owe him a couple, but I've already told him that this is not your cup of oolong."

Janine sighed. "Okay, I'll see if the girl wants to talk to me, but I don't know anything about the other guy who died, so that might take a little longer."

"Excellent," Sam replied, sounding relieved. "Plus, there's apparently been two more such incidents last night, a prostitute and a teenage boy, do you think you could make some enquiries from the local constabulary?"

"The local constabulary, so far as I know, boasts all of one man, I was with him in the early hours as it happens…" Janine regretted revealing that fact the minute the words left her lips. She could feel Sam's curiosity burning her ear through the phone.

"You were? What was that all about?"

"Nothing really, my daughter went to a party and had a little bit too much to drink. They took her to the local health centre and when I went to pick her up the officer happened to be there. On an unrelated matter."

"So, you know him?" Janine could imagine Sam leaping from her seat, unable to suppress her excitement.

"I don't know him as such, he introduced himself to me as I was walking through the park when they found the second victim. We barely spoke a dozen words."

"It's a start," enthused Sam. "Do you think you could squeeze him for some details about the other two last night? A hooker and a teenage boy, sounds like there may be some legit human-interest brewing."

"I know," agreed Janine, "but encroaching on the grief of relatives isn't really what I'm good at, so please don't expect too much from me on this one."

"No problem," Sam assured her. "I'll tell you what, just find out what you can and send me something by six tonight, whatever you have will be great. As I said, if my friend thinks it has legs, he'll send his own team over, no pressure on you, okay?"

"Thanks, Sam," Janine replied, feeling slightly relieved by her editor's reassurance.

After their call ended, Janine sat up in bed and swung her legs over the side.

Part of her still regretted agreeing to this latest assignment, but she was prepared to hold Sam to her word if things became too uncomfortable for her, or she just could not persuade Constable Clark to co-operate.

At least her interview with Sarah should be a shoo-in. So long as her mother did not have any objections to it.

Pulling on her dressing gown and slippers, Janine made her way across the landing towards Marie's room. Her daughter was still fast asleep, and to her surprise, Janine saw that Gypsy was still snuggled next to her as well. It looked as if the two of them had not stirred since she looked in on them before retiring.

Janine showered and dressed, then made her way downstairs for a strong coffee to perk her up. She scribbled some ideas as to how best to proceed with the new story while the kettle boiled.

Considering what she now knew concerning the other two deaths the previous night, Janine surmised that Constable Clark may well have managed very little sleep, and possibly none at all. Therefore, she thought it prudent to try him a little later in the day, when hopefully he was better rested.

Sarah was her most obvious first port of call.

As she sipped her coffee, Janine heard the sound of footsteps descending the stairs.

She turned to face the door and waited for Marie to emerge.

Her poor daughter looked as if she had been dragged backwards through the proverbial hedge. Her hair, usually her pride and joy, resembled Medusa's snakes when they were taking a nap, as it draped down across her face in thick bunches.

"And how are we this morning, my little party-animal?" Janine asked, jokingly.

"Ha ha," replied Marie, evidently feeling more than a little sorry for herself.

"Sit down," ordered Janine, sympathetically. "I'll make you a strong coffee and an Alka-Seltzer to take the edge off that hangover."

Marie slipped in behind one of the chairs and slumped her head on her folded arms.

Gypsy jumped up on the table and gently began to nudge her with her snout.

Janine prepared the effervescent liquid and placed it on the table in front of Marie.

"Try and drink it down in one, it'll do you the power of good," Janine advised.

Marie raised her head and scowled at the fizzy drink in front of her. She picked up the glass and threw her head back, guzzling the contents as instructed.

"Yuck!" she exclaimed, pulling a face.

Janine came over and poured a little water into Marie's glass. "Swill that around to catch the remaining bits," she suggested. "Then finish it off."

Marie looked up at her mother as if she had just suggested that she swallow a live worm from the garden. But she knew that the advice was sound, so she complied without complaint.

Gypsy stood up on her front paws and surveyed the empty glass once Marie put it down. The cat moved forward and sniffed at the rim, then pulled away.

"You're not wrong there, Kemosabe," said Marie, reaching out to stroke the moggy behind her ears. Gypsy closed her eyes and began purring, loudly.

Janine brought over a steaming mug of coffee. "Stupid question, but would you like some breakfast?" she asked, gingerly.

Marie shook her head. "No thanks, but I think someone else might appreciate some." She nodded towards Gypsy who, seeming to understand that they were discussing her, raised her head and smacked her chops.

Once Janine had placed a plate of food on the floor for the cat, she made herself some toast and marmalade. Feeling guilty, she asked Marie once more if she was sure that she did not want anything. Marie shook a weary head and stared into her coffee trying to focus on the bubbles which formed at the side of the cup.

Janine sat back down and crunched into her toast. As she licked the tangy, sweet marmalade from her lips, she asked. "Do you think Sarah would mind if I asked to interview her?"

Marie looked up, intrigued. "About what?"

"About that dead woman she found on the beach the other night. You know, the one she told us about."

"What made you change your mind? I suggested that at the restaurant."

"I know, but I received a call this morning from my editor, and she has asked if I could make some enquiries concerning these recent heart attack victims, apparently there were another two last night."

"Seriously?" Now she had Marie's full attention. "Not anyone from the party I was at?"

Janine took another bite of toast. Shaking her head, she replied. "No, not that I'm aware of. One was a local woman and the other a teenage boy, but Sam didn't mention anything about them being attached to the Romany camp."

"How many have there been in total?"

"Well, according to Sam, last night's couple make four in the last few days."

"And they all died of heart attacks, even the teenage boy?" Gypsy, her plate now licked clean, jumped back up on the table and strode purposefully over to Marie, ignoring the woman who had actually fed her.

The cat rubbed her head against Marie's arm.

"From what I understand, the post-mortems for the latest two have not been carried out yet, but from what Sam heard, they are both suspected heart attacks. I guess we'll know more after the PMs have been completed, if I can persuade the local copper to share some info."

"Did you get their names?" asked Marie, aimlessly stroking Gypsy with one hand as she lifted her mug with the other. The Alka-Seltzer was already beginning to take effect, and the coffee helped to take the taste away.

"No, Sam didn't have them. She was only obtaining the info second-hand. I think that was one of the things she wanted me to find out. Perhaps Sarah might even know who they are, especially if she went to school with the young boy."

"You should call her," Marie pulled her mobile out of her dressing gown pocket and scrolled through to find Sarah's number before forwarding it to Janine's phone.

"You don't think she'll mind?" Janine asked, desperate not to wear her journalist hat when dealing with one of her daughter's friends. That kind of pushy, get the story at all costs attitude was something she refused to unleash on Sarah. After last night, she figured the poor girl was probably still reeling from the tongue-lashing served up by her mother.

Janine carried on eating her toast while she stared at Sarah's number on her phone.

Would the poor child even be awake by now?

"You don't think it's too early considering what time she must have eventually gone to bed?" she asked Marie, hoping that she would say no. Janine really wanted to get the ball rolling so that she could cover as much ground as possible before her deadline that evening.

Marie reached over and grabbed Janine's second slice of toast. Taking a huge bite, she chewed thoughtfully as she pondered her mother's question.

"Maybe I should try her first," Marie offered. It might be less intimidating coming from me."

"Thanks a heap."

"You know what I mean." Marie chuckled, clearly amused by her mother's response.

"Go on then, if you think it's best," agreed Janine.

Chapter Forty

Father Boyle pulled up outside the presbytery, switched off the engine and sat there slumped in his seat. Closing his eyes, he revisited in his mind his conversation with Erin.

Things had certainly not gone the way he would have wished. It was enough for the poor child to have to deal with the sudden death of her boyfriend, but then he had just made matters worse by insisting that they discuss the situation concerning her unborn child.

His duty to God demanded that he make his position clear to her and reiterate the teachings from the scriptures regarding those who elected to abort their children.

But by the same token, he realised that instead of reading Erin the riot act he should have concentrated more on her well-being as a member of his flock and offered her what comfort he could under the circumstances.

His constant berating of her decision to have an abortion ended with her crumbling in a heap, sobbing her little heart out, and swearing that she rejected the church and all its teachings if it could not offer her even a modicum of compassion at this desperate hour.

Finally, she ran from the room and straight upstairs, slamming her bedroom door.

Even from downstairs, Father Boyle could hear the girl sobbing into her pillow. His initial reaction was to go up after her and apologise for the harshness of his words, but he knew that his interference would not be welcome.

He had ruined a perfectly good chance to commiserate with Erin and try to ease some of her sorrow. But instead, he had left her in a worse condition than he had found her.

"Stupid, stupid man," he said, rhetorically, slamming the palm of his hand against the steering wheel.

Opening his eyes, he gazed up through the windscreen at the imposing structure of St Mark's, desperate for inspiration as how best to proceed after his latest debacle.

The problem was that he felt as if he had no one else to turn to for guidance.

The church dictated that in such circumstances Father Boyle should contact his Canon for help, but alas his previous dealings with Canon Royce had shown the man to be somewhat unsympathetic when it came to parishioners not adhering to the teachings of the Catholic church.

No doubt his advice would be to shame poor Erin into not having an abortion, regardless of the situation or consequences of such an action.

Father Boyle knew that the bishop, in spite of his position, would lend a more sympathetic ear. For a man in his eighties, he was remarkably progressive in his thinking. But he knew that questions would be asked as to why Father Boyle had not sought instruction from his canon initially before disturbing the bishop.

The preconception that all canons would act with the voice

and the blessing of the bishop was a sad misconception which he himself had fallen victim to in the past.

That situation was a particular can of worms the priest had no wish to open.

His feeling of isolation only made him feel more guilty as he suspected that, like him, Erin had no one else to turn to either. He was the only one she had confided in beside Liam, and instead of offering her comfort, he had rebuked her in a monstrous way.

Father Boyle gripped the steering wheel so tightly that his knuckles began to turn white with the pressure. He desperately wanted to turn around there and then and return to Erin's house to apologise for his behaviour. Even if she was not prepared to forgive him on the spot, and who could blame her, at least she would know that she was not alone.

Even if she slammed the door in his face, Father Boyle was prepared to shout his apology through the letterbox if need be, just to ensure his message reached her ears.

With renewed determination, the priest turned the key in the ignition and restarted his engine.

Just as he was about to pull away, he saw Erin's mother appear from the presbytery door. Her cleaning slot should have finished hours ago, so he could not help but wonder what the poor woman was still doing at the church.

At least, he suspected, she had taken his advice and decided not to venture into work in her present state. Hopefully, by tomorrow, her bruises would have settled down enough so that she was not ashamed to show her face.

The fact that she had bothered to turn up for her cleaning shift demonstrated her dedication to the church, and to him in particular.

The fact that he had just left her daughter in such a state only increased his feelings of guilt. There was no way now that he could drive back to see Erin without offering her mother a lift. But by the same token, if he dropped Enid off at home, he could not go in and speak to her daughter without her mother hearing what they had to say.

The burden of his quandary weighed heavily on his shoulders.

The priest wound down his window as Enid approached his car. "How are you feeling now, Enid?" he asked, realising the question was a little inane but not knowing how else to start the conversation at this juncture.

The woman glanced around as if concerned that someone might be within earshot.

Once she was sure that the coast was clear, she bent down closer to the open car window. "I'll be alright, Father, thank you. I stayed on a little longer as a couple of the other ladies needed to leave early. I took your advice and called work to say I wouldn't be in today." Enid unconsciously pulled her headscarf a little further around to help cover the bruise on her cheek.

"I dropped in on Erin," admitted the priest. "I'm afraid I wasn't much comfort to her. At her age, they don't want to hear an old man telling them that their friend is in a better place and under the protection of the almighty. I sometimes think that the bishop should employ a younger model for such occasions."

Father Boyle felt guilty about not revealing the truth concerning his discourse with Erin. But he comforted himself with the knowledge that to do so would break the seal of the confessional, and as such was unconscionable.

"I'm sure your words were a great comfort to her father," Enid replied, respectfully. "Youngsters today, no matter how hard you try, seem too focused on the here and now to consider the bigger picture."

The priest nodded. "I appreciate that, thank you. But I think she could do with her mother's comforting arms around her more than the intrusion of an old priest. May I offer you a lift home?"

Enid shook her head. "No, thank you, Father, I need to go shopping for my husband's tea. No rest for the wicked."

"If everyone in this world were as wicked as you, what a wonderful world we would live in."

"You're very kind, Father," Enid responded, blushing.

"I'd be more than happy to help you with your shopping and then drop you home," Father Boyle offered. In truth, he felt sorry for the poor woman having to venture through the high street with the results of her husband's brutality on show to the world.

No matter how hard she tried to hide her bruises, someone would notice, and in such a small community, gossip would abound.

Enid shook her head again. "No, thank you, Father, I'll be fine. But thank you again for your kind offer, I won't take up any more of your time."

"My time is your time, Enid," he assured her. "And my door is always open anytime of the day or night should you need it."

Enid thanked him once more, then stood up from the car and began walking away down the path towards the high street.

Father Boyle watched the woman until she exited through the main gates before climbing out of his car. As he entered the presbytery, his curate, Father Wells, was just leaving the kitchen. When he saw the old priest, he nodded in his direction, a smile almost creasing the edges of his lips.

"You just missed one of your cleaning ladies, Father," the younger man pointed out. "The one you spoke to in the kitchen this morning, I think she was waiting to see you, but I suppose she changed her mind."

Father Boyle smiled. "Yes, thank you, Jamie, I spoke to her outside before she left."

The curate nodded. "From what I overheard this morning when I was passing the kitchen, and judging by the state of her face, I concluded that she is a victim of marital abuse."

The younger man's words were more of a statement rather than a question.

Father Boyle had still not managed to come to terms with his curate's *sledgehammer* mannerisms when it came to discussing what to others would automatically be considered a sensitive subject.

He worried that if the man did not manage to find a more sympathetic approach when dealing with individuals who sought his help or guidance, his future parish might soon start to exhibit a dwindling flock.

But, Father Boyle considered, he was still young and relatively new to his office, so there was still time to work on his mannerisms. For his part, the priest knew that it was expected of him to instil such values into his curate as part of his tutoring regime.

Father Boyle had often wondered if Canon Royce had specifically chosen Jamie for his parish because he and his superior had clashed on so many issues in the past. It had become obvious over the years that he and the canon shared very little in the way of mutual understanding when it came to matters of the church and how the priest chose to run his parish.

But he always remembered his own teachings when he was at seminary school, and how hard he had found adhering to the virtue of humility, especially when all around him he saw nothing but greed and avarice, even amongst his fellow seminarians.

Turning the other cheek was one thing. Turning a blind eye seemed-for him at least-that much harder.

Father Boyle sighed. "Yes, I'm afraid that Enid is often on the receiving end of her husband's temper. But she is a good and loyal wife and refuses to report him to the authorities. Clearly, her marital vows are sacred to her. Far more so than her own safety."

The curate's facial expression gave nothing away. "All we can do is pray for God to intervene and show her husband the error of his ways before it is too late. I'm sure you've already done everything within your power to help her in her great need."

"It amounts to precious little, I'm afraid," Father Boyle admitted.

"Such worldly matters are not our concern," Jamie suggested. "We must all be answerable to God in his own good time."

"But what of compassion, mercy, guidance, surely we have a duty to try and educate our parishioners to lead good Christian lives without the threat of harm or violence?"

The old priest could feel his blood beginning to boil at his curate's blasé approach to the situation. He took in another deep breath to try and calm himself down before he uttered something he would later regret.

Whether Jamie noticed his mentor's discomfort or not, he did not give any sign of acknowledgement. "What happens between a man and his wife behind closed doors cannot dictate how we administer God's teachings. After all, we're not social workers. God sees all and waits. If there are any repercussions heading towards that woman's husband, they will take place at God's behest and in his own good time. We have no right to interfere in such earthly situations."

Father Boyle decided for his own sanity to let the issue lie.

It was obvious that his curate was never going to accept an alternative point of view, regardless of what argument was offered.

"Remember Enid in your prayers," the priest suggested.

Jamie suddenly looked deep in thought at the prospect.

It was almost as if Father Boyle's idea had never occurred to him.

He let slip the merest trace of a smile before excusing himself and walking away.

Chapter Forty-One

MARIE ASKED TO ACCOMPANY HER MOTHER WHEN SHE visited Sarah. Ordinarily, such an arrangement would have been deemed unprofessional by her editor, but under the unique circumstances of her latest project, Janine felt that having her daughter along could only encourage Sarah to open up about her experience.

When they spoke on the phone, Sarah made it clear that her mother was upstairs asleep, not particularly extraordinary considering the woman worked nights. But it did mean that they would have to keep their voices down so as not to disturb her.

Marie suggested that they meet outside at a coffee shop, but Sarah informed her that she was grounded for the foreseeable future and that she knew better than to disregard her mother's instructions.

Sarah's turning led to a very quiet cul-de-sac, so Janine decided to park around the corner so that the engine noise would not disturb Sarah's mother.

She felt guilty about entering the woman's home without her express permission, especially as this was not exactly a social visit, but she decided that should Patricia Byrne wake up while she and Marie were there, then she would make out that she came round to ensure that Sarah was okay after the previous evening.

It was a trifle lacklustre as an excuse, but it still sounded better than the actual reason.

Janine had no way of knowing how Sarah's mother would react to her interviewing her daughter, but from what she had seen, and heard, of the woman thus far she suspected that there might be some opposition. Therefore, Janine decided that it would be far more prudent to conduct the session away from prying eyes.

Once they were outside Sarah's front door, Marie texted her that they had arrived so as not to risk disturbing her sleeping parent.

Sarah guided them into the kitchen and slid the door shut to help block out the sound.

She made them coffee and placed a large coffee cake on the table next to a stack of quarter plates. As neither Janine nor Marie had eaten much at breakfast, they both accepted a slice of cake gratefully.

Looking at Sarah, Janine could see straight away that she was faring far better than her own daughter. Other than an obvious lack of sleep, there was no sign of the lingering hangover which Marie still wore.

The interview went extremely well. Sarah was more than happy to talk about her grisly find on the beach, and she even managed to fill Janine in on some related information. She knew of the victim, Michelle Calvert, and her millionaire husband Emmet. She confided in Janine that local gossip had it that Michelle only married the man, who was years older than her, for his money, and that she could not wait for him to drop off the twig.

Furthermore, she informed Janine of the curious demise of Emmet on the same night that she had discovered his wife's body, and that Sandra O'Leary was the name of the housekeeper who lived in and was still there so far as she knew.

Janine made a special note to visit the Calvert home to see if the housekeeper was up to giving an interview.

Sarah admitted that she did not know Jerry Brooke, the victim found dead in Bishop's Park, but she suggested that Janine speak to Constable Clark or Father Boyle for any further details.

"Oh, and I sent out some feelers concerning the two victims found last night," Sarah added, excitedly. "Liam Mularkey was only one year above me in school, I cannot believe that he had a heart attack, he was so young and fit. He played football and all sorts. Anyway, if you want info on him, you should try Erin Murphy. I'll text you her address. She's lovely, though a bit, well, drippy, I suppose would be the best word to describe her. I don't think I've ever even seen her at a party in all the years I've known her. A devout churchgoer, you know the sort. Oh, and here's something juicy," Sarah leaned in closer even though she was already barely speaking above a whisper. Janine and Marie did likewise. "There's rumours around town that her father, Colm, is a bit *handy* with his missus, if you get my meaning?"

Janine nodded absentmindedly while she scribbled down the notes.

Although it was not part of the actual story, and the link between Liam's demise and his girlfriend's father's behaviour was tenuous at best, she kept it in the back of her mind, just in case.

"Thanks, Sarah, this is great, you've really got your finger on the pulse of things here."

Sarah blushed slightly. Smiling, she said. "Thanks, speaks volumes for the fact that there's not much else going on around here."

They all laughed together, keeping the volume down.

"Any word on the other victim?" asked Janine, hopefully.

"Bridget Donnelly," replied Sarah, glancing around furtively as if she was suddenly afraid that someone else might be listening in on their conversation. "Well, word there is that she did not only earn her keep by taking in foster kids. Suspicion has it that she also entertained a certain class of man at her home."

Janine and Marie both clicked on to her meaning.

From what Sam had told her earlier, she hoped that it might lead somewhere.

"I suppose your local constable will have the dirt on her?" Janine asked.

Sarah thought before answering. "Well, to my knowledge, she was never formally charged with anything, but you're right, Peter Clark will be your best option there."

"What you really need is to corner some of her clients," Offered Marie. "Then you could get the juice on her by threatening to publish their names in the article if they didn't come across with the goods."

Janine glanced sideways at her daughter. "Where'd this sudden ruthless streak come from?"

Marie shrugged. "Isn't that the way reporters obtain results, with cajoling, bribery and the threat of exposure?"

"Such a high opinion you have of me, it's so touching," Janine responded, sounding a little hurt, though proud at the same time. She had never considered a career in journalism for her daughter, but from the sound of it, she had the fortitude that even some of her more seasoned colleagues lacked.

But that was a discussion for another day.

They thanked Sarah for all her help, and Marie promised to call her later.

"Where to now?" asked Marie once they were back in their car.

Janine bit her lip. "Well, I think that I should speak to Father Boyle before approaching Liam's girlfriend. No doubt she'll be

291

inconsolable with the news of his death. Plus which, juggling with my other articles, I'd really like to arrange a visit to the church's archives to try and locate some books on this Banshee cult of theirs. Tim reckoned that they have several on the subject, none of which are available anywhere else."

"Who's Tim?" Marie asked, curiously.

Janine felt her cheeks blush. Was that really only last night?

"He was the poet Father Boyle, and I went to see last night, remember?"

"And you're on first-name terms already?"

"Behave, woman."

"Is he cute?"

"What, how should I know. I guess. That's no kind of question to be asking your mother."

"So, he is then?" Marie smirked.

"Children should be seen and not heard, otherwise they risk being grounded forever."

"You can't hide the truth from me," Marie assured her mother. "I can always tell when you're getting hot for someone. Like you did that day we arrived with the young priest."

"Will you please stop," Janine insisted, feeling the heat in her cheeks. "I think I preferred you hungover."

"Hey, I'm not judging, it's perfectly normal, even at your age."

"You cheeky little…" Janine looked across at her daughter. It was good to see her laughing and joking again. She had always known that Mike, leaving them had a huge impact on Marie, even though she acted quite pragmatic about the incident. But last night was the first time that Marie had ever revealed her true feelings on the subject, and Janine now realised just how raw her emotions were.

They turned into the main gates for St Mark's.

"Best behaviour now, please," Janine pleaded. "Remember we're in a house of God."

"Okay," agreed Marie. "Just so long as you remember that when you're talking to priest dishy. He's already spoken for."

Father Boyle answered the door looking extremely tired and more than a little exasperated. When he saw that it was Janine and Marie, he immediately brightened up and ushered them inside.

The two women declined coffee as they had just had some at Sarah's.

The priest took them into his living room. It was furnished in mostly dark brown furniture. Bookcases lined one entire wall, filled to the brim with leather-bound texts, the covers of some showing signs of having been read many times over.

A grandfather clock stood guard in the far corner, its loud ticking echoing through the room.

Father Boyle sat behind a regency desk, which sat at the far end of the room with the only window behind it. Janine and Marie sat opposite in the two chairs provided.

"Well now," began the priest, "what can I do for you ladies?"

Janine gulped. "Well, Father, to be honest, this isn't a social call. I received word from my editor this morning about the tragic deaths that have recently plagued the island. She has asked me to write an article detailing the circumstances surrounding them, and I was wondering if you'd be prepared to help me with some of the facts."

Father Boyle looked taken aback by the revelation. Evidently, this was not what he had expected Janine to ask him about, and he shifted uncomfortably in his chair before answering. "Oh, I see. Well, I'm not sure exactly what I can do to assist you," he replied, clearly feeling anxious. "I knew all the victims naturally, they were all members of my congregation, but other than that..."

Janine flicked through her notepad. "I've already spoken to Sarah Byrne; she was the young lady who discovered the body of Michelle Calvert lying on the beach. She's been extremely helpful filling in the names of the victims. I was hoping to inter-view some of the relatives or friends of the deceased, specifically Erin Murphy, the girlfriend of young Liam Mularkey."

Father Boyle cleared his throat. He placed his fist in front of his mouth and turned to one side as a fit of coughing followed.

Janine suspected that she had hit a sore point.

The priest apologised for his fit, then readjusted himself in his seat once more before answering. "I visited young Erin myself this morning," he admitted. "I'm afraid that she is quite inconsolable at present. I barely managed to extract any conver-sation out of her."

"Oh, I understand," Janine replied, not wishing to push the issue, although such an interview could have been the crux of the entire story. "Well, Sarah mentioned the names of the other two victims: Jerry Brooke and Bridget Donnelly. She didn't know if either of them had any relatives here on the island that I could talk to, so again I was wondering…"

"No, I'm afraid not," Father Boyle cut in. "Neither of them, to my knowledge, has any kin on Manus."

Janine nodded. "Is there anything you can tell me about either of them. Just for background?"

Father Boyle released a long sigh. "Not really," he confessed. "Mr Brookes was a civil servant on the mainland, I believe, and Bridget ran a small stall in the market. She also fostered chil-dren through social services, but I doubt they'll allow you to speak to any of them."

"No, I suppose not," Janine agreed, scribbling down the meagre details the priest had provided. "There was just one other person Sarah mentioned," Janine flipped back a few pages. "A Mrs Sandra O'Leary, the Calvert's housekeeper. Apparently, she was there the night the couple died."

Father Boyle nodded. "Yes, poor Sandra was in the house when I called round that evening. But Emmet Calvert was not the victim of a heart attack. Tragically, he fell down the stairs and broke his neck."

"On the same night his wife died on the beach?" asked Janine, her brows furrowed.

"Yes, coincidentally it was. A double tragedy, you might say."

Janine thought for a moment. Then asked. "So, neither of them knew that the other had died. Is that right?"

"Exactly. Such a sad situation for all concerned. After Sandra called us to the house, that's the police constable, Doctor Cleary, and me, we were all waiting around for Mrs Calvert to return from her evening walk. That was until young Sarah came across the woman's body, as you know."

"That's awful," offered Marie.

"Yes indeed," agreed Father Boyle. "But then, I suppose it saved each of them the grief at learning about their spouse's demise. There may be some small comfort in that."

Janine waited a moment before continuing, but judging by the circumstances, she felt that she already knew what the priest's answer was going to be. "So, do you think it would be alright for me to call on this Mrs O'Leary? Again, it would just be to secure some background on the couple. What they were like to work for, etc."

The priest considered the request for a moment, then said. "I'll tell you what, I was planning on visiting her myself later. Perhaps if I call ahead and ask her, you could accompany me. If she's agreeable, of course."

"That would be wonderful, thanks, Father," replied Janine, gratefully. "In the meantime, I was wondering if I might be granted access to your archives. There are a couple of books which Tim O'Brien mentioned the other evening which I would like to examine as part of my original article."

Just then, they heard the sound of footsteps echoing outside in the corridor.

A moment later, Father Wells stuck his head around the door.

Seeing that Father Boyle had company, he apologised and began backing away.

"No, just a minute, Jamie, could you come back in?"

The curate reappeared and stood just inside the doorway.

"Miss Carstairs here was wondering if she might have a quick perusal of the archives. Do you think you could arrange that?"

Janine turned in her chair to glance at the young priest.

His expression was dark and brooding, and Janine could tell at once that he was not pleased with the request. Tim had already warned her that the curate was fiercely protective of his archive, but she hoped that with Father Boyle asking on her behalf that it might help to grease the wheels.

The curate looked straight back at Father Boyle, purposely not looking in Janine's direction. "I'm afraid that would be quite impossible at the moment," he replied. "There're books everywhere down there, all over the floor, and the lighting is very poor. It's a complete trip-hazard waiting to happen. Once I manage to sort things out, then of course I would be only too happy to show the lady around down there."

The priest nodded. "Any idea when that might be?" he asked, sincerely. "Miss Carstairs is not planning on being with us for long."

The curate kept his gaze fixed firmly on his mentor. "I really couldn't say," he confessed. "I'm working as fast as I can, but as you can appreciate, the archive has been in a state of disorder for such a long time now that there's no way of knowing when my work will be completed."

"How about if you escorted me down there?" asked Janine, determined to force the young priest to acknowledge her presence. "I would be very careful and promise not to venture out of your sight."

Her ploy did not work. Jamie kept his gaze on Father Boyle. "I really couldn't recommend it, Father," he said, apologetically. "If there were to be an accident, I'm sure that the diocese would hold us accountable. Far better to err on the side of caution, just until I can sort things out."

Father Boyle nodded, slowly. "I'm sorry, Miss Carstairs, I'm afraid that I must agree with Father Wells, the bishop would certainly take a dim view if anything were to happen to you whilst you were under our roof. I'm terribly sorry."

Janine kept her gaze on Father Wells. Although he never once glanced in her direction, she was sure that she detected a slight grin on his face as he listened to the priest agreeing with his assertion.

She turned back to face Father Boyle. "That's okay, Father, I understand."

Janine heard the sound of the curate leaving the room behind them.

The old priest picked up the receiver of the phone on his desk. "I'll just give Mrs O'Leary a call and see if it's convenient for us to visit her this afternoon."

Before he finished dialling, the doorbell sounded.

The priest replaced the receiver in its cradle. "Excuse me just a moment," he said, apologetically, rising from his seat. "I must see who that is."

Chapter Forty-Two

"WELL, THAT WAS RUDE," MARIE OBSERVED ONCE Father Boyle was out of earshot.

"He had to answer the door," replied Janine, shocked by her daughter's comment.

"Not Father Boyle," corrected Marie. "The other one, priest dishy. You were speaking to him and he was ignoring you. He didn't even acknowledge that we were here."

Janine shrugged. "Perhaps he's just shy. When you take a vow of chastity, the opposite sex can become quite a force of nature without even trying."

"Well, I still think it was just bad manners. It was obvious from the way he spoke that he did not want you going anywhere near his precious archive. What's he got hidden down there that he doesn't want anyone to see?" Marie leaned in a little closer. "Perhaps he's got his own sex slave chained up in the basement. You read about such things going on all the time these days."

Janine chuckled. "That's quite an imagination you've got there. Ever thought of a career as a writer?"

Marie pulled a face. She knew that her mother only meant it tongue-in-cheek. "Well, just you wait and see, one day we'll be reading about him when one of his 'Brides of Christ' escapes to tell the tale."

"Brides of Christ?"

"That's what the headline will read, and it will be someone else's story because you didn't want to take me seriously. I'll expect a full apology."

"Okay," agreed Janine, "if you say so."

They could hear Father Boyle in the vestibule talking to someone.

Their voices were both too low to make out what was being said.

Janine glanced at the time on the grandfather clock. She hoped that whoever had just arrived would not keep the priest busy for too long, she really needed to go and visit the house-keeper so that she had something worthwhile to send back to Sam by close of play.

It was a shame that Father Boyle believed that Liam's girl-friend was too traumatised for a quick interview. As the other two victims had no near relatives to speak to, her report was going to need some padding out to be worthwhile.

At least she had managed to gain some valuable insight from Sarah.

Janine swept over her notes, adding, annotating and editing as she went along. It would save time later when she emailed her final report.

They could still hear the priest whispering outside. "Do you reckon we'll be here a while?" asked Marie. "Sounds as if the father is taking confession out there."

Janine shrugged. "Your guess is as good as mine. I only hope that we still manage to visit that Mrs O'Leary. I need some more substance for my report."

"Can't you just go anyway, even if the father can't make it?" Marie enquired.

"Well, I can, I suppose, but she might be a lot more willing to open up with the priest there with me. Otherwise, it's almost like cold-calling, and nobody ever responds well to that, so I tend to do it only as a last resort out of desperation."

"When you were a reporter, I mean on the tough suburban streets, did anyone ever slam the door in your face?"

Janine smiled. "More often than you've had hot dinners, child of mine."

"Really," Marie sounded intrigued almost to the point of excitement. "That must have been so disheartening. Were you ever tempted to shove something nasty through their letterbox to teach them a lesson?"

Janine clamped a hand over her mouth to suppress a laugh.

Her daughter's question had really taken her by surprise.

"No," she replied, still smiling. "You learn to take such things in your stride. And besides, I was a professional. You learned on the job that, on occasion, someone slammed the door because they were afraid, not because they were being rude. And sometimes those same people felt so guilty when they thought about their actions that they invited you back in for tea and cake and your best scoop ever."

"I get it. Still, you must have had to grow a fairly tough skin to keep going back again and again, day after day?"

"Yes," Janine agreed. "But it came with the territory. It was the adrenaline pump that kept you coming back for more."

Marie considered her response. "Don't think I'd have the temperament for it," she observed.

Just then, they heard Father Boyle approaching from outside.

He stood in the doorway with a young girl by his side, about the same age as Marie. It was obvious that she had been crying.

"Miss Carstairs, would you mind accompanying me to the kitchen for a quick chat?"

Janine rose to her feet. "No, not at all," she replied, glancing down at Marie. "Will you be okay for a moment?"

Marie nodded and looked past her at the girl.

"This is Erin Murphy, young Liam's girlfriend," explained the priest. "She's just popped by for a chat. Do you think that you two girls could keep each other amused for a few moments?"

Erin walked into the room, gingerly.

"This is young Marie, Miss Carstairs' daughter, I'm sure that the two of you will get on like a house on fire."

"Hello," said Marie, smiling.

Erin responded in kind, and Janine and the priest left them alone.

Father Boyle took Janine into the kitchen, closing the door behind them for the sake of privacy. "I've just had a quiet word with Erin," the priest began. "Her arrival is somewhat fortuitous as she has agreed to being interviewed by you concerning the night of Liam's demise."

"Really," Janine could not believe her luck. Such an addition to her report would doubtless give it enough substance to fulfil Sam's request. "I take it she came over to speak to you though, not me?"

"Well, if I'm being honest, we had a few cross words earlier today, my fault, of course, I'm afraid I allowed my religious zealousness to get the better of me. That said, the lovely girl came round to apologise to me, bless her. I've assured her that the blame is all mine, and since she was here, I offered her the chance to speak to you."

"Thank you, Father, I really appreciate that," replied Janine. "I promise I'll go easy on her, just the facts and how she's feeling, if she's willing to discuss that."

Father Boyle smiled. "I knew you'd understand," he said, the relief in his voice evident. "The only thing is the poor girl is going through quite a lot at the moment, aside from her boyfriend's death. I cannot go into details concerning what she has told me in confidence, I'm sure you understand."

Janine nodded. "Naturally, the seal of the confessional. I appreciate that and I won't pry," she promised.

Father Boyle heaved a sigh of relief. "I knew that I could rely on your discretion. Under normal circumstances, I wouldn't expose her to such an idea, but, as it's you, I know she'll be in safe hands."

Janine felt herself blush. "Thank you, Father, I promise I won't betray your trust."

Father Boyle patted Janine gently on the shoulder.

"There is just one thing, Father," Janine continued, not wishing to push her luck but still needing to know. "Do you think we will still have time to visit Mrs O'Leary this afternoon?"

The priest slapped his palm against the side of his head. "Bless me, I'd almost forgotten, and we were only discussing it moments ago." He felt around in the pocket of his suit, then pulled out a small leather book. "I'll give her a call right now, I'm sure she won't mind a visit, but as with Erin, I must give her the choice concerning your request."

"Naturally, Father, I understand completely," Janine assured him.

The interview with Erin went as well as could be expected.

Janine stuck to her word and tried not to pry into anything personal, other than Erin's relationship with Liam, and most importantly, their last evening together.

Erin confirmed that she was happy for Marie to stay in the room during her interview. When Janine first re-entered the sitting room, the two girls were actually giggling about something on their phones. When Janine asked what the joke was about, both girls dismissed the question out of hand.

Erin was clearly upset by what had happened to Liam, and she could not help tearing up as she revealed the details of their final night together.

Janine handed the girl some tissues, which she accepted

gratefully, and at one point, Marie leaned over and placed a comforting arm around the girl's shoulders.

Janine could not help but feel a jolt of pure, unashamed pride at her daughter's reaction. Especially considering that whenever Marie spoke of one of the girls at school showing such emotion, she always rolled her eyes and stated that they were just being dramatic for the attention.

It may just have been parental pride, but Janine was really starting to believe that Marie had matured emotionally during the few days they had spent on the island.

Considering that she only came under duress to begin with, it was a surprising and delightful surprise.

Janine listened intently as Erin explained Liam's odd behaviour just minutes before he ran off into the darkness, leaving her alone on the beach.

She was particularly interested in the noise that the boy claimed he could hear thundering through his head, especially as Erin insisted that she could not hear anything.

Erin admitted that at first, she believed that Liam was making it all up as an excuse to run off because he did not wish to continue their conversation.

Erin stated that they were discussing the prospect of marriage and settling down, which apparently, they had discussed on numerous occasions since they had been together, both agreeing to wait until Erin reached eighteen. However, now as the time grew closer, she felt that Liam was backing out of their agreement.

Janine listened and jotted notes on her pad. The recorder on the table was catching the whole conversation, but she still liked to make her own notes for reference when she typed up her report.

Although Erin explained away the potential reason for Liam's reluctance to finish their conversation, Janine felt instinctively that there was more to it that the girl was not willing to reveal.

As per her promise to Father Boyle, she did not force the issue, instead concentrating on Liam's description of the deafening sound he could hear just before he ran off.

The investigative side of her brain made Janine wonder if the other heart attack victims might have heard a similar sound just before their demise.

Regrettably, there was no way of confirming that as none of the other victims, to her knowledge, were in the company of anyone else prior to their hearts giving out.

She remembered something that Tim had alluded to during his talk at the hall.

His assertion that legend spoke of victims of the Banshee Bride hearing a piercing scream, loud enough to burst an eardrum, just moments before she came to take their souls away.

Could there be anything in the folklore after all?

Being of a rational persuasion, Janine could well believe the tragic story about Molly McShane, including the unjust hanging of her fiancé and of her throwing herself off the cliff out of despair and grief. But the other part about her spirit returning in the form of a Banshee who, once summoned, came back down to earth to rip people out of the world, took a little more faith than she had in such a tale.

That said, if the locals genuinely believed it, then there was still a sound foundation for her other article concerning the poor girl.

Father Boyle re-entered the room just as Janine was finishing off. He could see immediately that Erin had been crying, but when he glanced at her, she smiled back at him, so he decided not to interrogate Janine for the reason behind the girl's tears.

Deep down, he had always considered himself as a good

judge of character, and he genuinely believed that the reporter would not betray his faith in her.

"So how is everything going in here?" he asked, sitting beside Janine.

"All good, Father," Erin assured him.

"She's been wonderful," Janine added. "My story is all but written. Did you manage to get hold of Mrs O'Leary?"

"I did indeed, just caught her. As a matter of fact, she was on her way out to drop something off at a friend's house."

Janine felt her heart sink. "Ah, I take it that means she cannot see us today?"

Father Boyle shook his head. "Not at all, she reckons she'll be back home in an hour or so, and personally I got the impression that she would appreciate some company."

"Did you tell her about me?" Janine asked.

"Yes, and the reason for you wanting to visit, she's happy enough so long as I'm there too. She can be a little nervous around strangers, but I'm sure that she'll warm to you in no time."

"Do you need me for anything else?" Erin asked, looking from Janine to the priest.

"Well, I have all I needed," replied Janine, "and thank you again, you've been extremely helpful."

"Okay then," said Father Boyle, rising to his feet. "I have some boring paperwork which demands my attention," he turned to Janine, "so if you'd like to entertain yourself for an hour or so we can meet back here and go to Mrs O'Leary together, if that's okay?"

"That's brilliant, Father, and thank you again for intervening on my behalf. I promise I'll tread carefully with the old lady."

"I know you will," the priest assured her. He turned back to Erin. "Will you be alright getting home on your own?" he asked, concerned. "My paperwork can wait if you need a lift."

Before Erin had a chance to answer, Marie stepped in.

"That's no problem, we can drop her off," she replied, glancing towards her mother for confirmation.

"Of course, we can," agreed Janine, "it'll be our pleasure."

"I don't want to be any trouble," Erin offered, not wishing to be a burden. "I can make it home by myself."

"I won't hear of it," Janine smiled. "It's the very least I can do after all your help."

Chapter Forty-Three

On the drive to Erin's home, Marie asked if they could stop off for lunch. Now that her hangover was officially a distant memory, she found her appetite had returned with a vengeance.

Janine glanced over her shoulder at the two girls riding in the back. "How about it, Erin, do you fancy joining us for burger and chips?"

Erin hesitated before answering, then said. "That's alright. If you like, you can drop me off anywhere and I'll make my own way home."

"Nonsense," replied Marie, defiantly. "I need someone my own age there to help me roll my eyes every time Mum says something Karen-ish."

"And what does that mean, exactly?" asked Janine, turning back to focus on the road ahead. "Karen-ish?"

Both girls laughed. It was a joyous sound, and Janine wanted more.

"Oh, Mum, you are such a Karen sometimes, and you know it."

"I've never even heard the expression before," Janine insisted. "What's it mean?"

The girls were still laughing.

"Next time you say or do something Karen-ish, I'll remind you," Marie assured her.

"Charming," replied Janine. "Erin darling, if you really would rather not accompany my rude daughter and me, I can take you straight home, no problem. But I would love to have a witness to prove that I am no Karen."

Marie linked arms with Erin. "Burger and chips twice, please," she ordered, then turned to her friend. "You're not a veggie, are you?" The idea had only just occurred to her, and she wondered if that was why Erin had not wanted to join them.

Erin shook her head, smiling. "God know, if I don't eat meat at least once a day, I'll pass out."

Janine found a burger restaurant in town with a veranda which offered marvellous views of the ocean. She had managed to stop herself just in time from suggesting that they go to Sarah's cousin's café, where they had eaten breakfast the previous morning. The thought of taking Erin to a place named after her dead boyfriend would have been callous, to say the least.

The two girls stuck with their orders of burger and chips; Janine had a salad instead of fries. The girls drank cokes while Janine opted for a fruit smoothie.

As she placed her order, Marie nudged Erin and mouthed the word 'Karen', making it obvious enough so that her mother could see.

"What?" demanded Janine.

"A smoothie, Mum, really," replied Marie, shaking her head.

"What's wrong with that?" Janine asked. perplexed, looking from one girl to the other.

"It's fine, Miss Carstairs," Erin assured her, "we're only teasing."

"Thank you, Erin, and it's Janine, please. When a teenager calls me 'Miss', it makes me feel so old," she jabbed a finger in Marie's direction as soon as she saw her open her mouth. "And one more word from you, young lady, and you'll be travelling home in the trunk."

The three chatted aimlessly while they ate. The cool ocean breeze wafted over them from their vantage point, deflecting the heat from the sun.

Janine avoided mentioning anything to do with Liam, deciding that Erin had already been through the trauma of remembering their last night together, and the wound was obviously still raw.

But when Janine asked what Erin's parents did for a living, she could not help but notice the youngster glance down at her plate and aimlessly push a chip around with her fork when she spoke about her father.

Janine wondered if he was the reason behind her seeming uncomfortable when she was being interviewed in the presbytery earlier. There was evidently something worrying the poor girl, and as much as Janine did not wish to pry, whether it was the reporter in her or merely the parent, she could not help being intrigued.

Marie noticed Erin's reaction to Janine's question, so she immediately changed the subject to something more age-related and light, which seemed to do the trick, and Erin perked up at once.

Either that, or she was just putting a brave face on.

The rest of their meal passed without incident.

Janine drove the girls to Erin's house to drop her off.

As she pulled up outside, Enid was in the front garden weeding the borders. The woman did not notice Janine's car contained her own daughter and carried on with her task without giving them a second glance.

Janine and the two girls alighted from the vehicle at the

same time, each using a different door. They all clustered around the gate with Erin leaning on it whilst keeping the latch in place. "Mum," she called out.

Enid spun round, almost knocking herself over in her haste.

She stood up but stayed where she was several feet in front of the trio.

"This is Janine and her daughter Marie," Erin explained. "Janine is a reporter, and she interviewed me about what happened to Liam."

Enid's brows furrowed. She began to take a step towards the gate, then stopped herself and turned to one side so that Janine and Marie could not see the bruise on her cheek.

She turned back, momentarily, then quickly looked away again, before bending down and retrieving her gardening tools. Enid shot back up, this time turning her back to the three women and started walking towards the front door.

Janine expected the woman to drop her equipment back inside her house, then come back outside to meet her and Marie. But instead she simply called over her shoulder for Erin to come back inside the house, before disappearing through the front door.

Erin turned to face the other two women.

Her cheeks glowed with a dark shade of red, and she found it hard to hold their gaze.

"I'm… I'm really sorry about that," she muttered, her voice shaking. "My mum is not always good when it comes to meeting new people, I should have phoned ahead to warn her."

Janine moved in and gave her a hug. "Not to worry," she said, reassuringly. "We Carstairs women can be a lot to take in on first meeting."

Erin smiled, weakly. "Thank you so much for giving me a lift home, and for such a scrumptious lunch. It was such a treat."

"You're more than welcome," Janine assured her. "Thank you for being such a good sport about the interview."

Marie moved in and put her arms around the young girl, squeezing her tightly.

When they broke off, she said. "I'll call you before we leave the island if that's okay. Perhaps we can meet up for the day if there's time?"

Erin smiled, broadly. "I'd like that," she admitted, but then her smile faded. "So long as it's okay with my mum and dad. They can be a bit strict about me going out."

"Of course," Marie agreed. "This one can be exactly the same," she indicated towards Janine. "She's such a Karen when it suits her."

"Oi," said Janine, leaning back and placing a kick with the side of her foot against Marie's behind.

"And she's violent," Marie added, rubbing her bottom, exaggeratedly.

Her joke made Erin smile once more.

"Erin, I said now!" Her mother called out from behind the door.

Erin's face dropped yet again. "I'd better go, thank you both again." With that, she turned and pushed through the gate, turning back once more when she reached the front door to wave and smile.

Janine and Marie climbed back into the car.

They waited until they had reached the end of Erin's road before either of them spoke.

"What was all that about?" asked Marie, turning to face her mother.

"Well, I suppose you noticed the huge bruise on Erin's mum's cheek? I imagine that was the reason for her behaviour towards us."

"Do you think Erin's father knocks her about?" Marie enquired, her voice raising slightly in volume for emphasis.

Janine shrugged. "One thing you learn as a reporter is that no one truly knows what goes on behind closed doors."

"Do you think her dad knocks Erin about, too?"

Janine sighed. "It's possible. Men who indulge in such behaviour often unleash their anger against anyone in the family they consider weak enough to take it without complaining."

"That's so wrong. Why don't they report him to the police? A crime is a crime, even on a small out-of-the-way place like this."

Janine could feel her daughter growing hot under the collar.

She admired her passion and sense of justice and shared them both, but under the circumstances, she had to remain the distant voice of reason in order to calm her down.

The last thing she wanted was Marie to call Erin and start demanding that she report her father to the authorities. The poor girl seemed to have enough on her tiny shoulders as it was.

"There are all sorts of reasons why victims of domestic abuse do nothing," she began. "I've investigated enough incidents to know that you can't force someone to inform on a loved one, regardless of what they are suffering in private."

"Loved one," Marie replied, evidently shocked by her mother's term. "You don't treat those you love like that. There's no excuse for it. We should report him to the police on their behalf, then he'll know."

Janine turned to her. "And what happens when the police turn up at their door and both Erin and her mother deny that anything is taking place?"

Marie looked fit to explode. "How can they? Why would they? It's obvious from the state of Erin's mum's face that she is a victim."

Janine turned back to focus on the road ahead. "And we know that how?" she offered. "We have no evidence to offer the police of any wrongdoing. Erin's mum could have received that bruise anywhere. We're merely speculating that her husband is the perpetrator. The police would be very reluctant to act on a hunch, especially as we've not even met the woman yet."

Marie slumped back in her seat, breathing heavily.

She thought for a moment, then said. "So why was she so embarrassed about it unless she got it as a result of her old man slapping her?"

"Because some people just are. Don't you remember not wanting to go to school each time you saw a spot in the bathroom mirror? I'll grant you that her reaction to our sudden appearance was a little odd, but like Erin said, perhaps she is not very good when meeting new people. It might just be extreme shyness."

Marie turned back to her. "Do you honestly believe that?" she demanded.

"What I believe, or think, or suspect is a world apart from what I can prove. So for now, we should at least give Erin's father, who may be entirely innocent of what we're accusing him of, the benefit of the doubt."

Marie was not satisfied, there was no doubt in Janine's mind of that. But at least she had given her daughter some food for thought.

They carried on in silence until they reached the other side of town.

"Now then," said Janine. "Would you like to accompany me to visit the housekeeper of the first heart attack victim, or would you rather I drop you home?"

Marie sighed. "I think I'd like to have a walk around town, help clear my head and work off what's left of my hangover. Is that alright?"

"Of course," Janine assured her. "Do you need any money in case you spot something you cannot live without?"

Marie smiled; the tension now broken. "It's okay, I've got some, thanks."

Janine pulled over at the first available space to let Marie out.

As her daughter made to exit the vehicle, Janine grabbed her arm, lightly. "Please tell me you're not going to do anything rash, or heaven forbid, stupid?"

Marie leaned over and placed a kiss on her cheek. "You're such a Karen sometimes," she said, opening her door and climbing out.

Chapter Forty-Four

ON HER WAY BACK TO THE PRESBYTERY, JANINE HAD A sudden thought. She pulled over and switched off the engine.

Grabbing her mobile, her fingers hesitated for a moment, then she swiped through her screen until she landed at Tim's number.

Taking a deep breath, she hit it and held the mobile up to her ear while it rang.

"Hello, my sweet lady," Tim answered, his voice sounding as if he had already enjoyed a couple of drinks. "I wasn't sure that I'd hear from you again, especially as you disappeared into the night without so much as a goodbye kiss."

"I know, I'm sorry about that."

"Don't be silly, we're both adults, we know how the game's played."

"I received a call from the police," Janine continued. Regardless of Tim's easy-going nature, she still felt that she had to explain her actions out of courtesy if nothing else. "My daughter was taken to the local health centre having enjoyed herself a little too much at a party."

"Lord, is she okay?"

"Oh, she's fine now," Janine explained. "A good night's sleep and some strong coffee did her the world of good."

"Well, that is good to hear. Was this her first taste of the deadly brew?"

Janine laughed. "Her first big taste, yes. I think she just became a little overwhelmed by the experience and overindulged. Not sure she'll do that again in a hurry."

"Ah, the drinker's lament, we've all been there, some of us more often than we'd care to mention," Tim chuckled at his own line. "Now then, to what do I owe the pleasure of this call? Do you fancy a drink? I was about to saunter over to the pub as it goes. Or would you rather come round? I've got a lovely bottle of single malt that I've been waiting for an excuse to open."

"I'm sure you don't need me to create an excuse," Janine said, jovially. Inside, she relaxed. Initially, she had felt bad about calling Tim for a favour, having run out on him the previous night.

Even though she had a perfect, and truthful, reason, she herself knew from past experience that sinking feeling of waking up alone, having gone to bed with a new lover.

"Well, if I'm being honest," Tim replied. "I'd love you to be my excuse to open each new bottle from now on. What do you say? A writer and a journalist, a dream match made in heaven."

Damn, she hoped that he was not falling for her after one night.

Not that there was anything wrong with Tim, but the circumstances were a little awkward with Janine potentially leaving the island in a few days. Long-distance relationships often worked, but she had not been looking for one when she fell into his bed.

Janine knew that as a writer and a poet, Tim could easily cover any feelings he had with lyrical rhyme or flamboyant prose. But the last thing she wanted to do was hurt the man. He had been perfectly charming the previous evening, and even if some of it was a carefully rehearsed act, she was the one who decided to go to bed with him.

There had certainly been no coercion on his part.

"Tim," she began, thoughtfully. "I had a wonderful evening with you, and again I'm sorry I had to rush off like that, but…"

"Say no more," he cut in. "I'm big enough and ugly enough to face the truth. We created a memory which will remain with me till the day I die, and for that I'm truly grateful."

"Oh, stop it," Janine said, laughing. "You'll have me in tears in a minute."

"And how I'd love to have the chance to kiss them away and replace them with sighs and smiles."

"Enough, Casanova. Look, I know that this might seem a bit of a cheek, but I'm on my way to interview the Calvert house-keeper with Father Boyle. I remember you saying that Mr Calvert had some books in his library concerning the legend of the Banshee. I wondered if you knew which books?"

"You crafty old Devil. How did you manage to arrange an interview so soon after the couple's demise? I was going to wait for at least a week before requesting one myself."

"It is all thanks to Father Boyle," Janine admitted. "He called her this morning. I get the impression that if he was not accom-panying me, then she'd refuse to entertain the idea."

"So, I piqued your interest with my little story then?"

"If I'm being honest, my editor is interested in me writing an article about it, and the legend that goes with it." She felt a twinge of guilt knowing that Tim was the recognised expert on the subject, and here was she picking his brains for information so that she could steal his thunder.

"You could just quote directly from my book," Tim offered, so long as you don't plagiarise it.

"No way, I wouldn't do that," Janine assured him. "It's just that you could be a real help if you pointed me I the right direc-tion and save me wasting unwelcome hours sifting through the library. I promise I will acknowledge your work if I quote anything from it."

"I believe you, thousands wouldn't. Did you try asking Father Boyle if you could venture down into the church archive?"

"Tried, and failed," Janine admitted. "That curate of his wasn't having any of it. Apparently, the archive is too dangerous for anyone, other than him, to peruse until he has had a chance to sort out the shelves and clear away the trip hazards."

Tim laughed. "He protects his secrets like a June bride, that man. Makes you wonder what he has hidden down there that he doesn't want any of us to know about."

"Oh, don't," shivered Janine. "My daughter already thinks that he has a bunch of women tied up in the basement."

"She sounds like a very astute girl, your daughter; I think I'd like to meet her."

"If there's time before we leave, perhaps we could all go out for a drink?" Janine offered. "So long as you don't try and force any of that mountain dew stuff on us."

"Ha, the nectar of the Gods, and no mistake."

"Listen, I hate to sound rude, but Father Boyle is waiting for me. Would you give me those titles, please?"

Tim recited the titles that he felt were the most crucial for her article.

Before they rang off, Tim asked her to put in a good word for him with the Landlady. "Come on," he said, cheekily, "surely after all my help it's the least you can do."

Janine made no promises but said that she would see how the interview went and take it from there.

Father Boyle was waiting outside the church when Janine arrived.

She lowered her window. "I'm sorry I'm late, Father," she offered, sincerely. "I had to drop Erin off after lunch then got stuck on the phone."

The priest waved her concerns away. "Don't reproach your-self, please, it's only a matter of minutes." He crouched down at the open window. "There's been a slight change in plan, Father Wells had borrowed the car so do you think I could ride with you?"

"Of course, Father, come around." Janine collected all her paraphernalia from the passenger seat and threw it in the back.

Father Boyle let himself in the car and settled comfortably, having re-adjusted the seat belt.

The priest guided Janine through the town and down a slip road which ran alongside the cliffs. The view of the water from here was spectacular, and Janine had to make sure that she did not veer her eyes off the road for too long at a time.

It meandered left and right with some of the corners being so acute she felt it necessary to slow down and *bib* her horn to warn others who might be approaching from around the bend.

They chatted aimlessly in the car until Father Boyle raised the subject of Erin.

He was naturally curious to know what she might have revealed to Janine and her daughter after they left the presbytery.

Janine was not sure how much to reveal. As she had reminded Marie, she had no real proof, just a suspicion, and the evidence of Erin's mum's appearance.

Did the priest already know?

In such small rural communities, it was hard to keep anything so horrendous under wraps, especially when you carried the bruises for all to see.

Janine glanced over. Father Boyle was looking straight at her, expectantly awaiting an answer to his enquiry.

She swallowed, hard. "If I'm being honest, Father, and please don't think I'm spreading gossip, but when we dropped Erin off home, her mother was outside in the yard and we could not help but see the bruises on her face. She tried desperately to hide them from us and ran inside, screaming for Erin to join her."

"I see," replied Father Boyle, turning back to face the windshield.

"I imagine you know more than we concerning their domestic situation, but from an outsider's perspective it looked very much as she had been on the receiving end of some brutal violence from, I suspect, her husband."

The priest did not answer for a moment.

Janine had not mentioned anything about Erin's condition, which meant that there was a good chance that she had not revealed her pregnancy to either of the women.

Deep down, Father Boyle hoped that meeting someone her own age and with a much more understanding mother than her own accompanying them, she might have let slip her troubles to a friendly ear.

That would have least started the ball rolling.

No one of Erin's age wanted to hear advice from an old priest. But from a peer, it might help her to put things into perspective.

But it appeared that the chance had passed.

"Father?" Janine asked, rousing him from his reverie.

"I'm afraid that your assumptions are quite correct. Poor Enid is indeed a victim of her husband's temper. I've tried to comfort her and offer what little advice I can, but such worldly matters are a little out of my league."

"Have you suggested that she seek help? From the authorities, social services, women's refuges?"

Father Boyle smiled, wryly. "She won't hear of any of it. Enid takes her marriage vows very seriously and accepts whatever comes with the territory as par for the course. It's an incredibly sad situation, but all I seem to be able to offer her is an occasional shoulder to cry on."

"Has no one else in the town said anything? Surely she must

have friends and work colleagues who have witnessed the results of her husband's abuse. Have none of them ever insisted that she seek professional help?"

"Quite possibly, but as I say, she is a staunch Catholic and her marriage vows are sacred to her."

"Until he kills her!" Janine shot back. She regretted raising her voice immediately. She knew that the priest had his own rules and regulations to adhere to, so to an extent, his hands were tied. But even so, it annoyed her that religion could be used as an excuse to protect a serial abuser from being prosecuted.

"Oh God have mercy," replied the priest, making the sign of the cross. "I pray daily that it will never come to that."

"Alas, Father, in my world it happens all too often. Men like that only ever seem to grow worse, and the more they get away with it, the more they think that they're untouchable."

Father Boyle nodded, slowly, and released a long breath. Janine could tell that there were undertones of frustration in his actions, and she wondered just how tortured he felt inside trying to please his God whilst still trying to protect one of his flock.

She was in no place to judge, and she realised that.

Janine was glad that Marie was no longer in the car.

Had she still been present when Father Boyle confirmed their suspicions, no doubt she would have lost her temper with him, and that could well have jeopardised the trip to see the housekeeper.

Janine decided that, under the circumstances, it was probably best to either change the subject, or at least ensure the priest that she appreciated his position.

She decided that the latter might prove more profitable in gaining his support to assist with Mrs O'Leary.

"I imagine that such a situation puts you in a very difficult dilemma?" She offered, keeping her voice low and completely non-judgemental.

Father Boyle turned back to her. "I'm so glad you understand," he smiled. "Those outside the church often can't appreciate our position. We may be priests, but we're still human beings and not exempt from having feelings."

The Calvert residence was the next turning on the left, according to Father Boyle, so Janine indicated and took the turn carefully as there was a slight blind-side obscured by an overgrown tree near the junction.

"I really do appreciate you arranging this, Father," Janine assured him, once more. "With the information I've gathered from Erin and Sarah this morning, plus whatever I glean from Mrs O'Leary, I think they'll be enough for my article."

"You will go easy on the old dear, won't you?" Father Boyle asked, a light edge of concern in his tone. "She is rather old, and she has just suffered a major shock."

Janine nodded her understanding. "I'll look to you for guidance, Father, I'm totally in your hands with this one."

Father Boyle physically relaxed in his seat at her assurance.

Although he kept in mind that Janine was a journalist, he somehow, especially after her treatment of Erin, felt that he could trust her implicitly.

Chapter Forty-Five

THE HOUSEKEEPER GREETED FATHER BOYLE WITH welcome arms, ushering them both in.

Once inside, the priest made the introductions and Mrs O'Leary led them to the lounge where she had already laid out a huge tray with a pot of tea, a plate of biscuits and a large fruit cake, both of which she informed them that she had baked that morning.

Still full from lunch, Janine made her polite excuses and accepted a cup of black tea with lemon and, after much protesting from the housekeeper, a biscuit which she slid next to her cup on the saucer.

Father Boyle, who claimed to have missed lunch altogether, opted for tea and a large slice of cake.

Once they were all comfortably seated, Father Boyle explained once more to the old lady the reason for Janine's visit. He assured her that Janine would not pry into any personal details and explained that he vouched for her implicitly if the housekeeper would allow the journalist a chance to peruse Emmet's library.

Janine could tell immediately that Mrs O'Leary was still sceptical concerning allowing her access to her deceased employer's books, so she did her best to placate her by promising to treat them with the utmost care and consideration.

The housekeeper glanced over at Father Boyle, who nodded his reassurance, then she turned back to Janine and smiled. "I'm sure that will be alright, dear," she said, graciously. "I know that Mr Calvert is no longer with us, but he was so proud of his books, you must understand…"

With that, she began to tear up.

Father Boyle removed a clean hankey from his pocket and passed it over to her.

The old woman took it, gratefully, and began to daub her eyes, mopping up her tears.

This reaction put Janine on guard concerning how she intended to proceed with the interview. Now that she saw how easily the woman became upset, she knew that she would have to tip-toe on eggs in order to keep her promise to Father Boyle.

Once the old lady had dried her tears, she offered the priest more cake, which he gratefully accepted. She held up the cake slicer in Janine's directions, but she still had to refuse. It seemed impolite, but she knew that if she forced a slice of the cake down, she would only feel sick later on.

Janine took out her tape recorder and placed it on the table, hitting the record button.

Mrs O'Leary looked at the object with mild suspicion, so Janine explained that she often used the gadget so that she did not miss any important details when she was writing her notes. The housekeeper leaned in to study the recorder for a moment, then sat back, apparently willing to allow its use.

Janine kept her questions very broad, which helped to ease her way into the interview.

Once she began, the old lady actually seemed to enjoy the experience of being interviewed, and Janine had to stop herself more than once from butting in when the old lady went off topic and began another completely unrelated story.

Oftentimes, the housekeeper would include the priest in her tales by saying things such as: "And do you remember so-and-so, and the way she used to dress to Sunday service?" This, in turn, would encourage Father Boyle to join in, once more taking the conversation off on another tangent.

At times, it was painstaking, but Janine decided that she had no choice if she wanted the interview for her piece. Plus which, the way she saw it, this was a precursor to her being allowed access to the library.

After the best part of an hour, Janine announced that she had all she needed from the interview. She made sure that she chose the time for her interjection with great care so that she did not interrupt the housekeeper in mid-flow.

Having managed to nibble her way through the biscuit for the sake of manners, Janine asked Mrs O'Leary if she might now be shown into the library.

Father Boyle stayed put while the housekeeper led Janine down the corridor to a locked room at the far end. She fumbled with a bunch of keys, which she removed from her apron, until she managed to locate the correct one, but even then, she seemed to struggle with the lock until Janine offered her assistance.

"Thank you, dear," Mrs O'Leary replied, taking a step back. "It's definitely the correct key, but that lock has always been stiff, and my arthritis doesn't help matters."

Janine appreciated her predicament as even she struggled to make the key turn.

Eventually, after a great deal of jiggling, she managed to force the lock open. She removed the key from the lock and handed it back to the housekeeper, who, before putting it back in her apron, leaned past Janine and turned the handle, forcing the journalist to stand back to allow the old woman to enter the room first.

Once inside, Mrs O'Leary switched on the lights. Janine stood there in awe as she took in the impressive sight of the room. All but one wall had floor-to-ceiling shelves, and each one was stacked to groaning with books of all different sizes.

The remaining wall had a large bay window with an oak desk in front of it. But even then, bookshelves had been slotted in on either side of the window, ensuring that the maximum amount of storage space was being utilised.

As they both stood there taking in the view, Janine heard Mrs O'Leary sniffle.

She placed her hand on the woman's shoulder to comfort her, now feeling guilty for having asked to see inside. "He must have been awfully proud of his collection," Janine offered, comfortingly. "I've never seen such a huge private collection."

The housekeeper wiped her eyes with the hankey Father Boyle had lent her earlier.

She let out a deep sigh. "Mr Calvert was sinfully proud of his collection, miss. But even then, he would not allow just anyone in here; that's why the lock is so stiff. And when he was in here, he always left strict instructions not to be disturbed."

"I'm very grateful to you for allowing me the chance to appreciate all this," Janine repeated, feeling that she had to hammer the nail home just in case the old lady decided that she was not worthy to see the collection.

"Even his wife never used to come in here," Mrs O'Leary continued, almost as if she had not heard Janine's comment. "She was never much of a reader. Least, not these sorts of books. She claimed that Mr Calvert loved these books more than her. She often used to tease him that one day he would come home and find that she'd sent them all to the jumble."

Janine laughed. "That would definitely have been a reason to cite for divorce."

The old woman turned back to look at her. "That's what Mr Calvert used to say."

From the sternness of her expression, Janine had the impression that the woman was not joking.

Janine waited. She was painfully aware that time was not on her side in order to meet her deadline that evening, but somehow, she felt unable to start her work while the old housekeeper was still there.

Eventually, Mrs O'Leary released a huge sigh and spoke. "Right well, if there's anything you, just sing out, I'm going back to see if the good father wants any more tea."

Janine thanked her and watched her walk down the corridor and back into the lounge.

She walked into the room and stood in the middle, turning around so that she could take in the magnitude of volumes which graced the walls.

Janine wished that she had more time, and Tim. He would doubtless know exactly where the tomes she was after were housed. Even if he had never set foot in the room before, she suspected that he had an instinct for such things.

It was a pit Emmet Calvert had not had the foresight to list all his treasures and the position they took on the shelves. Or. If he had, there was no sign of the map anywhere in the library.

Janine considered going and asking Mrs O'Leary, but somehow she felt that it would just be a waste of precious time.

She scrolled through her pad until she found the list of books which Tim had suggested. Glancing up at the first wall of books, she cast her eyes along the rows but could not see any of the ones on her list.

Bending down, Janine scouted the bottom two rows together, stopping whenever she felt that her eyes were playing tricks on her. She made her way around the room like that, dismissing each volume as she went.

At the end, she stretched her back out to try and relieve some of the cramp.

Something made her look up, and there she was sure she could see the first title she was after. There was a rolling wooden set of steps in one corner. Janine moved it into position and then climbed so that she could see the upper shelves more clearly.

She was right, the first volume concerning a history of arcane knowledge was right there in front of her. Reaching out, Janine carefully pulled the weighty tome towards her. It was even heavier than it looked, and she had to hold it firmly with both hands to avoid dropping it on the floor.

She could just imagine the furore that would cause. The housekeeper running in, followed by Father Boyle with cake crumbs on his chest and a look of disappointment etched on his face.

No doubt Mrs O'Leary would have a fit that one of her former employee's precious books had been treated so cavalierly and would demand that the priest remove Janine from the house immediately.

With that thought in her mind, Janine carefully descended the stairs, clutching the book in both hands. Once she reached the bottom, Janine carried it over to the desk and placed it in front of the leather armchair, which sat at one side.

She stood there for a moment, wondering whether to begin studying the book in front of her, or to try and locate the others on Tim's list for comparison.

Glancing at her list, she remembered Tim suggesting two other volumes which he believed would contain more succinct information concerning the legend of the Banshee, so she left her prize unopened and went back to perusing the shelves.

It took her the best part of fifteen minutes to locate the other two books.

Once she had them in front of her, she sat down at the table and began to leaf through the pages of the third one she had located. According to its title, it covered several well-known stories about witches, ghosts, poltergeists and spirits. Checking the index, Janine found the chapter dedicated to the history of the Banshee.

Keeping an eye on the time, Janine read deeply. The book was by a professor of folklore from a university in Detroit. According to the jacket, he had travelled all over the globe in order to glean the specific information he needed for his book.

The writing was not exactly to Janine's tastes. She found it a tad too dry and lacking in decent a narrative thread to assist the reader.

There were, however, some pertinent facts concerning both how to call and how to dispel a Banshee once summoned. Janine began to scribble down the details, but then switched to using her phone to snap the pages so that she could have more time later on to devour them on her own.

Next, she tried her first choice. The pages, like the book, were extremely thick and hard to turn. Some seemed to be stuck together, whether by age or as the result of something being dropped on them she could not fathom, but she was so afraid of tearing them that after a while she gave up trying.

This one had no actual chapter dealing with Banshees, but the subject was mentioned briefly in the chapter concerning spirits of the dead.

Again, she photographed the relevant pages and moved on to her second choice.

This one actually had a very detailed description of the story of Molly McShane.

As Janine skimmed the lines, she soon realised that Tim's recitation at the town hall was equally as detailed, and so she decided that she would probably discern the same information from the copy of Tim's book she had back at the cottage.

Even so, just to cover the bases, Janine snapped this chapter as well.

Just as she replaced the last book back on its shelf, Janine heard the sound of voices echoing from the corridor outside.

"So, how did you make out?" asked Father Boyle, standing in the doorway with Mrs O'Leary positioned just in front of him.

"Fine, thank you," replied Janine, reaching the final step of the ladder. "I'd love to have more time, but I think I've managed to find most of what I'm looking for."

"Wonderful," said the priest. "Perhaps we can arrange another visit someday," he ventured, glancing down at the housekeeper.

The look on the woman's face told Janine that she was not altogether overjoyed by the prospect, but she managed to maintain a slight smile as she turned back to face Father Boyle.

Janine walked over to them. "Thank you again," she said, offering her hand. The old woman looked at it as if checking that there was nothing threatening about it before she reached out and clutched it gingerly with her fingers.

"You're welcome," she replied, glancing around the room, inspecting the shelves to make sure that there were no suspicious gaps.

"Are we ready for the off?" Father Boyle enquired, looking over the housekeeper at Janine.

She nodded. "Yes, please, I have my deadline to meet."

The priest frowned. "Will you still have time to drop me off first?"

"Of course, no problem," Janine assured him.

Janine thanked the old woman once again at the front door. Then, to her dismay, Father Boyle and the housekeeper began discussing future events at the church. Janine did not wish to be rude, but she really needed to be on her way.

"I'll go and wait in the car," she called out, smiling to try and hide her frustration.

"Okay. I'll be there in a minute," the priest assured her.

It was almost fifteen minutes before he finally managed to tear himself away from Mrs O'Leary, and even then, it looked almost reluctant from where Janine was sitting.

She wondered what they still had to talk about, considering how long they had together while she was in the library. Even so, she smiled and waved back as she started the engine to take them both home.

Chapter Forty-Six

COLM MURPHY HAD JUST FINISHED ONE OF HIS LEAST successful days. Two of his most reliable clients had given him their notice to quit, and even the incentive of reducing their rents did nothing to dissuade them.

If there was one thing that he hated, it was having to find new tenants for his properties.

He knew that an easier option would be to employ a third-party agent to deal with such matters, but Colm could never justify their exorbitant fees for doing precious little. Besides which, he preferred to look his future tenants straight in the eye to decide whether they were going to be decent, respectable tenants or not.

Also, he had his own list of rules and regulations he expected them to adhere to, and agents were renowned for just wanting to force people through the door so that they could earn their percentage.

None of them, in his opinion, could be trusted.

He was a decent landlord, at least to those who paid on time and showed some consideration for his properties. But now he would have to start the on-going headache of interviews, reference checking, liaising with banks and building societies, and worst of all trying to ascertain that the person in front of him was actually who they said they were.

These days, with forged documents being so expertly created, people like him had to jump through hoops to ensure that potential tenants were not fraudsters.

He could feel a headache already coming on at the thought of the trials ahead.

To add to his frustration, Colm had missed the first ferry home from the mainland because the idiot who counted on the vehicles had miscalculated. There was more than enough room left for his car, but the man insisted that they were at capacity and that he would have to wait for the next one.

It was the old bugger with the curly ginger hair sprouting out from under his flat cap.

Colm had had dealings with him before. The bloke was as thick as mince and by far the slowest of all the operators.

Clearly the man had never heard of multi-tasking. If someone asked him a question, he had to stop checking tickets while he pondered an answer. Then he would take forever and a day to either explain his answer or the reason why he could not offer one. Meanwhile, the queue behind was growing by the second.

It was just his luck to have him on duty this evening.

Colm counted the vehicles on board as the ferry pulled away, and lo and behold, he was right, there was ample room for him as well.

Were it not for the fact that he would doubtless be on the receiving end of a lecture on health and safety, Colm would have reminded 'curly' of his inability to count properly next time he saw him.

Colm could feel himself growing hard as he drove off the ferry on his way home.

Frustration had always made him horny since he reached

puberty. Back then, he used to masturbate constantly whenever he was cross or angry as a way of relieving the tension.

Now that he was married, of course, he expected Enid to do her job and satisfy him whenever he had suffered such a day at work. But since she had given birth to their daughter, her interest in sex seemed to have dwindled until each time they had sex she made him feel as if she was doing him a favour as opposed to carrying out her wifely duties and affording him his conjugal rights.

She had always hated giving him oral, even before they were married. That should have been a red flag to him then. But her father promised him the money to start his business if they married, so it was almost as if Enid's dad had bribed him into marrying his daughter.

Colm was not above forcing himself on Enid if the need arose. After all, it was his right, and she should have been more compliant. God knows it was not as if he expected her to moan and make noises like those women in the films. All she had to do was lie there and open her legs until he was spent.

How bloody hard could it be?

Women had it easy so far as he was concerned, and his wife more so than a lot of others. He had often been tempted to stray during their marriage. There were plenty of girls on the mainland who had given him the eye in pubs and restaurants while he was having his lunch, and young Connie at his local bank had often flirted with him over the counter, saying things that would make a sailor blush.

But Colm took his marriage vows seriously, and he knew that he would not be able to reconcile with himself if he ever ventured down that road.

Therefore, it was doubly important that Enid knew how lucky she was and did not complain or put up any resistance when he came home wanting.

The sudden thought of Connie, the bank clerk, caused

Colm's member to press hard against his trousers. So much so that while he was waiting for a red light, he slipped his hand inside his waistband to release it from the uncomfortable confines of his underwear.

He hoped that their daughter Erin would be out this evening, galivanting around town with some of her friends, so that if Enid was in one of her awkward moods, he could drag her upstairs without their daughter making a fuss.

Feeling the way he was right now, Colm was prepared to bend his wife over the sofa and just take her from behind to release his anxiety, and if he slipped in his haste and entered her rectum, then she would just have to put up with the discomfort until he was done.

It would be her fault for not guiding him in like a good wife should.

Colm parked up outside his house and looked up towards his daughter's bedroom window. He could hear the distant sound of her music playing, which meant that she had not yet left for the evening.

No doubt that business with the Mularkey boy dying the previous night had something to do with it. Erin would probably be moping around the house now for days to come, crying on her mother's shoulder, which would prevent her from seeing to his needs.

Colm did not know what all the fuss was about. Erin hardly knew the boy, and she knew better than to be courting at her age without his permission.

Feeling his temper rising at the prospect of having to keep the noise down because of his inconsiderate child.

Well, not tonight.

If need be, he would demand that she go out and see one of her friends from school. A young girl like her should not be spending all day in her bedroom crying over a love that never was.

Colm turned his key in the lock and pushed open the door.

He could hear Enid pottering about in the kitchen.

At least his daughter was still upstairs, and from the muffled sound of her music, he suspected that she had her bedroom door closed, so it looked as if he would have to instigate plan B.

Colm threw off his suit jacket and left it dangling over the banister.

As he entered the kitchen, he found Enid bending down looking in through the oven glass door. "Hello, darling," she called back. "Your steak and kidney pudding will be ready in about half an hour, so you've plenty of time for a drink and to peruse the newspaper."

Colm crept up behind her and placed both hands on her rump.

Enid was wearing a cotton summer dress, so he could feel the fabric of her panties through the flimsy material.

Before Enid had a chance to turn around, Colm slipped his hand under the hem of her dress and grabbed the waistband of her underwear, yanking them down in one swift movement and leaving them to collect around her ankles.

Enid knew from experience what such an action meant.

Colm started kissing her on her neck whilst moving his hands up her body until he was cupping her breasts in both hands, squeezing and kneading them, then tweaking her nipples through her bra.

As usual, he was being too rough with her, and Enid tried desperately not to call out in pain as Colm pressed her nipples between his thumb and forefinger.

"Not now," Enid pleaded, her voice just above a whisper. "Erin's upstairs, she's still very upset about her boyfriend's accident."

Colm ignored her plea, sinking his teeth into her neck like a hungry vampire.

Enid squealed. The sharp pain in her neck was too much to bear.

Grabbing her round the waist, Colm spun Enid around so that she was now facing the kitchen table. He placed a hand in the middle of her shoulders and pushed her forward until she was bending over, her hands now flat on the wooden tabletop.

Enid could already feel the inflamed size of his member pushing into the small of her back. She knew that she did not have the strength to fight him off so all she had was her power of reason. But tonight, Colm was obviously in no mood to listen to that.

"Please, Colm," she whispered. "Let's wait for Erin to go out. She might come down at any minute."

Such protestations fell on deaf ears. "She needs to learn her place, that girl," Colm growled into her ear. "Yer too bleedin' soft with her, that's the problem. If she tries coming downstairs, I'll shout at her to get back to her room. She won't dare disobey me if she knows what's good fer her."

Colm slid his hands down Enid's waist and grabbed hold of the hem of her dress, yanking it up above her waist, revealing her bare behind.

Pressing himself against her, Colm undid his belt and the clasp which held his trousers together. Lowering the zip of his trousers, he let them fall to the floor, followed by his underwear.

He positioned himself behind his wife and, using one hand, guided his erect penis to find her opening.

As usual, she was unwilling and therefore too dry to comply.

Dammit, he would just have to force his way in, and serve her right if it hurt. She needed to learn to be more compliant when it came to his needs. He was a good provider and was entitled to having his desires satisfied.

Enid screamed as he forced himself inside her. Not wanting to alert their daughter, she bit down hard on her bottom lip to help absorb her pain.

Colm, oblivious to his wife's discomfort, forced himself inside further until she had enveloped him completely. Now he could really concentrate on releasing all his pent-up anger and aggression.

He placed one hand in the middle of her back, and his other one on the side of her head, forcing it against the hardwood of the table.

He ignored her pleas for him to stop.

This was his time.

Lost in his venture, Colm did not hear his daughter descending the stairs, nor was he aware of her entering the kitchen and yelling at him to leave her mother alone.

Suddenly, he felt a hefty *thud* on the back of his head as Erin grabbed a steel saucepan from the sink and swung it with full force at him.

The blow sent him reeling.

For a moment, Colm was convinced he was about to pass out.

He had slipped out of his wife without even realising it, the shock of the blow completely disorienting him.

Colm slapped both hands against his head, his fingers reaching round to cover the back as if to protect it from another potential attack.

By now, Erin had run to her mother and collapsed in her arms. The two women held on to each other tightly, both sobbing uncontrollably.

Enid kissed her daughter tenderly on the forehead and assured her that everything was alright. She was uncomfortably aware that her knickers were still encircling her ankles, and she desperately wanted to retrieve them, feeling somewhat ashamed and bare without them in their proper place.

But before she had a chance to see to them, Colm launched himself at the two women.

Sufficiently recovered from the assault, he grabbed Erin by

the hair and threw her across the room, sending her crashing into their fridge-freezer. The force of the blow made a huge dent in the appliance and knocked the wind out of the girl. Choking while trying to catch her breath, she slid down the front of it, one hand at her throat and the other pressing against her diaphragm.

Ignoring her distress, Colm advanced on his daughter, hiking up his trousers and fastening the catch before removing his belt through the loops. He wrapped the broad leather strap around his fist, leaving enough dangling to make a lash.

Seeing what was coming, Erin held her arms up to protect herself as her father began to hand out her punishment. Colm raised his hand and struck down at the cowering girl, catching her across her lower body with his first blow, then lifting his arm back again and striking her across her arm.

The sound of the leather strap echoed in the kitchen as he whipped her repeatedly, all the while either ignoring her cries of pain, or relishing them.

This time it was his wife who, having retrieved the utensil her daughter had used to save her, slammed it against the side of Colm's head with full force.

Her effort caused Colm to fall sideways against one of the kitchen units, smacking the other side of his head against the wooden door front.

He lay there for a moment, moaning. The leather strap still fastened around his fist.

Enid rushed to her daughter and gently helped her to her feet. Erin was still very unsteady as a result of being winded, but she managed to stay upright with the aid of her mother's help.

The two women carried each other out of the kitchen and made their way along the corridor towards the lounge.

Once inside the room, Enid lowered her daughter into an armchair, gently brushing the hair from the front of her face.

She held her head in both hands and used her thumbs to wipe away the tears from under the girl's eyes.

Enid could feel her heartstrings being tugged.

She knew deep down that she was incapable of protecting her daughter from the man who was meant to love them both, and the sensation made her feel helpless and pathetic.

Mother and daughter had both said some harsh things to each other that afternoon after Janice and Marie had left, and now Enid regretted every one of them.

Just then, Colm appeared at the door, blocking the entrance with his huge frame should either of them attempt to escape.

Enid could tell from the look on his face that her husband's mind had only one thought in it, revenge.

Purposefully, he walked not the room, the leather strap swinging by his side, his menacing eyes fixed on the two women cowering on the armchair.

As he reached them, Enid knew that no amount of pleading or appealing to his good nature would have any effect. Her one thought was to protect her child from the brunt of the oncoming attack.

She manoeuvred herself onto the chair, using her own body to cover as much of Erin's as possible.

The two women hugged each other for all they were worth, while Colm began raining blows upon them.

Chapter Forty-Seven

JANINE SIPPED HER COFFEE WHILE SHE WAITED FOR Sam to reply to her e-mail.

She had managed to send it in with barely minutes to spare, but she was still glad that she took the time to read and re-read it over twice, as she managed to catch some errors in the text on both occasions.

Finally satisfied with the finished product, Janine posted it with a message asking her editor to confirm that it was suitable for printing.

While she waited, she went into the kitchen to make herself a coffee.

As she entered, Gypsy appeared through the cat flap and plonked herself on the floor next to her water bowl, meowing pitifully.

"I take it you're ready for dinner, madam?" asked Janine, taking a fresh tin of cat food from the cupboard and prising open the lid. She emptied the contents onto a plate and added some chopped ham which Marie insisted Gypsy was very fond of.

She watched the cat scoff down the lot while she boiled the kettle and made her coffee.

Once the cat was finished, she jumped up onto one of the dining chairs and began licking her paws.

"Hungry, were we?" enquired Janine, leaving Gypsy to her pampering routine while she made her way back to her laptop to await her response from Sam.

To help pass the time, Janine opened her original article concerning the island and read through what she had completed thus far. The latest report about the strange phenomenon of the locals suddenly succumbing to heart attacks had taken away her focus from the reason she first came to Manus, but keeping your editor happy was what the game was all about, especially when you worked freelance.

In her latest report she had only been able to suggest that the latest two victims from the previous evening had both been the victims of heart failure as she had not been able to reach Constable Clark for confirmation that the post mortems had both been completed with the same results, but it seemed pretty obvious to her taking into account all the circumstances that both Liam and Bridget had both suffered the same fate.

As for a reason behind the sudden wave of attacks, that was something only the pathologist on the mainland could discover, and Janine knew that Sam had already despatched another reporter to try and interview him for his opinion.

Janine turned when she heard the sound of Marie coming down the stairs.

Her daughter yawned and stretched as she reached the bottom step, and by the look of her *morning* hair, it was obvious that she had been asleep.

"Evening, sleeping beauty," Janine called, smiling. "How was your nap?"

Marie nodded. "It was good, I've never felt so tired in all my life before. I think it must be the fresh sea air. I took a short detour after you dropped me off and sat on the beach for a while. I almost dropped off there," she admitted.

"Well, with one thing and another, I'm not surprised you were tired," agreed Janine. "I've just boiled the kettle, fancy a coffee?"

"I'll get it," yawned Marie. "Gypsy should be in soon for her dinner."

"I've already fed her," Janine replied. "She wolfed down the whole plate in the time it took to boil the kettle."

"Did you give her some of that ham she likes?"

"Yep, cut it into small pieces just the way she likes it."

"Thanks, Mum."

Marie made her way into the kitchen. Janine could hear her greet the cat, and the subsequent *thud* she heard she presumed was the animal jumping up on the kitchen table to welcome her usual food-giver.

Janine was pleasantly pleased by the way Marie had taken to the feline. She genuinely seemed attached to her, and secretly Janine had already resigned herself to the fact that they would doubtless be taking her home with them.

Father Boyle had already confirmed that the cat had been a semi-regular visitor to the cottage and no doubt she was feral, but Janine knew that to be absolutely sure, she would have to take the cat to a vet on the island and check to see if it had been chipped.

If she already had an owner, as unlikely as it seemed, it was only right that they contacted them first before kidnapping her, just in case there was some little girl or boy out there still grieving for the loss of their kitty.

Janine knew that such an outcome would be a wrench to Marie, but she knew her daughter would approve of doing the right thing.

Just then, Janine heard a *ping*. She glanced down and saw the reply from Sam pop into her inbox. Opening it, she felt the usual tenseness in her stomach, which she always did when receiving a reply about one of her articles.

Past experience had taught her that, no matter how proud she was of her written efforts, there were times when editors had a different opinion, and their decision was what counted.

Janine skim-read the reply just to be sure that Sam liked what she had sent in.

She clearly did and did not even ask Janine for any rewrites.

The one observation she mentioned, which in truth Janine had expected, was that she try again to speak to the local police to confirm the results of the latest two PMs.

Janine heaved a sigh of relief and read the response once more, this time in detail.

She quickly sent off an e-mail of thanks to Sam, confirming that she would contact her as soon as she heard anything more about the latest two victims.

"Are you sure you fed her, Mum?" The cry came from behind her.

Janine stood up and walked back into the kitchen. Marie was sitting on one of the chairs, leaning down and petting Gypsy while the cat eagerly pawed at her empty plate.

"Cheeky minx," exclaimed Janine. "She's literally just finished a full plateful."

Marie looked back over her shoulder. "You don't think she has worms or something?" she asked, sounding fretful.

Janine shrugged. "Well, I was thinking, if we are planning on taking her home with us we should really have her checked out by a vet first, just in case she actually belongs to someone."

Marie's eyes lit up. "Take her home? Do you mean it?" she gushed.

"Well, the two of you do seem to have grown pretty close over the last couple of days, so I presumed you wanted to keep her."

Marie jumped up from her seat and gave Janine a big hug.

"Thank you, and I'll look after her, don't you worry, I'll even find a part-time job to pay for her vet bills."

Janine hugged her back and pecked her on her forehead. "I'll remind you about that," she promised. "But first, we must ascertain if she actually belongs to anyone."

Marie pulled back. "Well, Father Boyle seemed to think she was feral."

"She could well be, but sometimes cats just travel too far away from their homes and lose their scent. We have to consider that some poor child might be missing her right now."

Marie frowned. "I suppose so," she agreed, reluctantly. "Can we take her in tomorrow?"

Janine nodded. "Tell you what," she offered, "you find a local vet and book an appointment. Don't make it too early because we'll need to go out and buy something to carry her in."

Marie turned to look back at Gypsy. "Wouldn't a cardboard box do in a pinch?"

"Yes, but they sell purpose-built ones with handles and air holes drilled into them. It'll be safer in case she panics while we're carrying her."

Marie bent down and lifted Gypsy into her arms, cradling her against her neck.

For a moment, Janine felt nervous. Even though Marie had handled her before, if she were feral, she might take exception to suddenly being swept up in such a fashion.

But the cat immediately began purring and rubbed its head against Marie.

When Marie placed her back on the table, Gypsy jumped straight down and went to sit by her empty bowl once more. She looked up at both humans and meowed.

"She really is still hungry," Marie observed. "Can't I give her a little more food? I can't bear to let her carry on like this."

"You'd better get used to it," Janine warned. "Cats are known for being particularly manipulative once they know they have their owners under their belt. What is it they say? Dogs have owners, cats have staff."

Marie laughed. "That's funny. But a little more food can't hurt. And besides, we want her to know that she is loved; otherwise, she might not stay in when we're ready to leave for the vets tomorrow."

"Go on then," Janine agreed. "And while we're on the subject, what do you fancy for dinner this evening?"

Excitedly, Marie opened the fridge door and took out some more ham. "Oh, I don't mind, whatever," she replied, aimlessly.

Now that she thought of it, Janine really fancied a drink.

She considered the pub which Tim had taken her to after his talk. They served food, and the clientele seemed friendly enough. Of course, there was every chance that Tim would be there. From what she gathered, he made it a regular haunt for both lunch and dinner.

It might seem rude for her to just turn up there without inviting him, or at least informing him of her intention. Although she was still concerned that he might have fallen for her, if she took Marie with her, it would be a clear sign to him that she was not intending to spend the night with him again.

Poets had a reputation throughout time of falling in love with virtually every woman they met, so Janine supposed that she should not be so surprised with his reaction when they spoke earlier.

Having said that, she also knew that she might just be reading way too much into what was merely a horny bachelor trying it on.

Either way, she was sure that he was enough of a gentleman not to try or say anything untoward in front of Marie.

Also, she had promised to share what she found at the Calvert residence with him, and this would be a good opportunity to collaborate.

"How d'yer fancy a pub dinner with a pint of Guinness to wash it down?" she asked.

Marie stood up straight having just emptied another sachet of food into Gypsy's bowl.

She pulled a face. "I'm not sure I could handle a pint right now," she confessed. "Last night is still too fresh in my mind, and I've still got the taste of that awful stuff I drank in my mouth." She slumped back down on her chair to watch the cat eat,

"Oh yeah, I forgot," Janine admitted. "Well, do you think you could stand being in a pub for the nosh with everyone around you drinking?"

Marie thought for a moment. "I suppose I could handle it. Why, do you have somewhere specific in mind?"

"I do as it happens. The pub Father Boyle and I visited yesterday with that Poet. They seemed to have a pretty good bar menu, and the ambiance was conducive with dining as well as drinking. What do you say?"

Gypsy finished eating and immediately jumped up on Marie's lap.

"Okay," Marie agreed, just give me a moment to sort out my hair.

Marie carried Gypsy upstairs with her to her bedroom.

Meanwhile, Janine sent Tim a text informing him of their intention to eat at the pub.

Tim called her back. "Hello, pretty lady," he slurred into the phone. "And will it be the pleasure of your company I can look forward to this evening?"

From the sound of his voice, Janine suspected that he had been drinking since lunchtime. She wondered now if perhaps it was not such a good time to introduce Marie to him. "So long as you behave yourself," she warned. "I'm bringing my daughter down for dinner, so please no mention of what happened last night."

"Tim O'Brien is nothing if not a gentleman," he assured her. "My lips will remain sealed throughout the encounter, I promise you."

"Okay then," Janine replied, hesitantly. "I've taken some photos from the books you told me to search for in the Calvert library. I'll send them over to you and perhaps we can go through some of them, if you're feeling up to it?"

"That's a wonderful idea," Tim agreed. "I knew you'd be able to charm your way in past that old biddy of a housekeeper."

"Well, if I'm being honest, it was more thanks to Father Boyle. He arranged the meeting and accompanied me to the house. Without him, I doubt I would have managed to even gain access to the house, let alone the library."

"You're too modest," Tim laughed. "When may I expect you and your charming daughter? I'll have drinks ready and waiting on the table."

"Thanks for the thought, but I think it might be better if we both take things slowly this evening. I'll be driving, and Marie had a heavy night last night, so she might only be in the mood for a coke."

"You could always catch a cab," Tim suggested.

Janine paused. "I could, but to be honest, I'm not in the mood for a skinful, just a glass of wine or two, so I'll save the money and drive. We freelancers don't eat off gold plates, you know."

Tim laughed again. "Too true, and don't I know it. Okay then, I'll await your arrival with great anticipation, and rest assured, I promise to be on my very best behaviour in front of your charming daughter."

In spite of his assurances, Janine still felt a slight twinge in her belly at the prospect of the meeting. But as they were probably going to head home over the next couple of days she desperately wanted to pick Tim's brains concerning the details she had amassed from the books in Emmet's library, and this might be her last chance.

So long as he kept to his word and did not mention the previous night, she would be happy. He was hardly going to make a pass at her in front of Marie.

Or, if he did, they could always leave the pub. He certainly did not come across as one to make a scene.

Chapter Forty-Eight

FATHER BOYLE LOWERED HIMSELF ONTO THE PADDED
cushion rest which ran along the bottom of the pew. Tonight's
confessional session had been the usual run-of-the-mill regulars
confessing to acts and thoughts which barely warranted them
turning up.

Such was the mundanity of their sins that the priest sometimes felt like a doctor whose patients only ever came to them
with minor ailments and imagined illnesses which they had
suspected as a result of seeing something on the television or
reading about it online.

He checked himself for being so unappreciative of his role as
spiritual advisor and confessor for his flock. After all, they had
been indoctrinated since they were old enough to understand to
come to church and seek absolution for fear that God might call
them before they had a chance to unburden themselves of their
heinous sins.

What was really bothering him was those parishioners who
had not attended that evening. Specifically, Erin Murphy. When
they had spoken briefly earlier that afternoon before he handed

her over to Janine for her interview, Father Boyle had reminded the young girl that they really needed to talk again concerning her proposed abortion.

He had apologised for losing his temper with her the first time she had mentioned her condition but emphasised that she was not alone in spite of her refusing to reveal her pregnancy to either of her parents.

In fairness to her, Father Boyle could well understand why she was reluctant to admit to that brute of a father of hers that she was with child, out of wedlock. Especially as with Lima's untimely demise, there was no chance of a rushed wedding to cover the unfortunate situation.

The sad thing was that young Erin did not even feel safe in confiding with her mother.

As good and loving a Christian as she was, Enid Murphy was not a woman best equipped with such a notion as a teenage pregnancy. There was no doubt in anyone's mind that she loved her daughter and would never willingly see any harm come to her, but by the same token she was a woman who had been brought up to accept that a woman's place was by her husband's side, and that she must remain subservient to him at all times.

Therefore, Father Boyle was of a mind that upon hearing of her daughter's condition, Enid would feel obliged to inform the girl's father and allow him to make the decision as to what action was best.

Poor Erin seemed to be caught between the proverbial rock and a hard place.

The priest felt a wave of guilt wash over him as he remembered the tone he had used with the young girl when she turned to him, the only person alive whom she believed would not judge her harshly.

Regardless of his teachings and the rules of the catholic church, Father Boyle knew that the poor child needed help, guidance, and most of all reassurance, and he knew that he failed her, and God, but not providing it.

His automatic instinct now was to go and see Erin at home and offer her the comfort he denied her when they first met. But he also knew that Erin's parents would be there, and that there was no way he could explain his presence and wish to speak to their daughter alone without raising their suspicions.

No, Erin had to decide to visit him again herself.

All he could do now was pray that she decided to give him one more chance before taking any unretractable action.

Even if he was unable to convince her not to terminate her unborn child, he would see to it that he put her in contact with a charitable agency on the mainland where she would be professionally guided and, if necessary, operated on in the strictest confidence.

Under the circumstances, he was even willing to give Erin an alibi for her time spent at the clinic, informing her parents that he had asked for volunteers to help out at the orphanage his church was connected to. They, at least, would both be proud and willing to let Erin take part in such a noble and Christian endeavour.

She could then return to the island a week or so later, and no one need ever be the wiser for her absence. Father Boyle would, of course, absolve Erin of any sin attached to her decision.

He, on the other hand, would have to make his own peace with God for failing in his duty to persuade Erin not to go ahead with such a procedure. But it was better that he carried such a burden than place it on her narrow shoulders.

First, though, before any of that could be instigated, he needed to meet up with Erin, preferably at church away from prying eyes, and sooner rather than later.

His mobile in his cassock pocket began gently vibrating. Usually, he would leave it in the vestry during services and confession, but these days, he noticed he often forgot. The onslaught of old age, no doubt. But at least to his credit, he always kept it on vibrate to avoid any embarrassing interruptions during service.

Having looked around and satisfying himself that he was alone, Father Boyle squinted down at the screen and saw Constable Peter Clark on the tiny window.

"Hello, Peter, I hope you're well," he asked, cheerily. After the previous evening, the priest suspected that the constable had barely been able to grab forty winks with all the reports and witness statements he would have had to complete following Liam and Bridget's untimely demise.

"As well as I can be Father," Clark replied. The tiredness in his voice was evident whether he was trying to conceal it or not.

"Please don't tell me we have another victim with a suspicious heart episode?" Father Boyle was beginning to fear the worst every time he received a call from either the police constable or the doctor.

"No, thankfully, nothing like that," Constable Clark assured him. "I just thought you might like to know that the pathologist has finished his report, and yet again it appears as if both victims died from heart attacks, as we suspected."

"Nothing suspicious?" the priest enquired. "Not even with young Liam?"

"Nothing showed up that was untoward according to the report, that said, the pathologist did suspect perhaps there might be some underlying hereditary heart defect with regards to Liam. He's passed his findings over to Doctor Cleary so that he might institute some tests on his parents, but he confided in me that there was no evidence of such a complaint concerning any of the family that he knew of."

Father Boyle thought for a moment. "So again, we're just putting it down to exceptional circumstances, and moving on?"

The police officer sighed. "Seems so, at least for the moment. According to the pathologist, the main cause of heart attacks amongst the young is stress, if you can believe it. I've no idea what youngsters have to be stressed about these days. It's not as if there's a war on or they have to look forward to working twelve hours a day down the pit for next to no money like my father did."

"We must be tolerant of the young, officer," Father Boyle scolded. "They have stresses and anxiety to deal with on a daily basis, which fortunately we were born too long ago to be affected by."

"What, like posting a selfie and not receiving as many likes as they anticipated? My heart goes out to them."

"Each generation must carry their own burdens. Now, we're you planning on dropping in for a quick snifter before finally crawling off to bed?"

This time, the police officer laughed out loud. "I wasn't to be fair, but now you've mentioned it, I take it you have some of the good stuff at hand?"

"Naturally, or I wouldn't have suggested it. What'd yer say? A swift one before being enveloped by the sweet arms of Morpheus."

"Careful, Father," Clark said, cheekily. "I shall have but one God."

"Well said, that man," the priest agreed, chuckling. "And if that doesn't deserve a fine glass of single malt, then I don't know what does."

"I'll be there in ten minutes," promised the police officer, "so long as the phone doesn't go off," he remarked, solemnly.

Having disconnected the call, Father Boyle said one last prayer, asking God to provide him with the chance to make amends where Erin was concerned. The officer's admission regarding Liam's heart attack possibly being caused by stress, made him fret at just how much stress poor Erin must feel under right at that moment.

With the church on one side and her parents on the other, it was up to him to intervene and be the shoulder she needed to weather the storm.

He made a solemn vow that tomorrow he was going to initiate whatever concocted story he had to put into place to help Erin once she had made her final decision.

Her well-being was now his utmost priority.

Chapter Forty-Nine

THE PUB WAS HEAVING, FAR MORE SO THAN IT HAD been the previous evening. Fortunately, Tim had managed to secure a table for them and waved Janine and Marie over through the crowd.

Tim greeted Janine with a kiss on the cheek and held his hand out as he was introduced to Marie. Much to her surprise when they shook, he then pulled Marie towards him and planted a kiss on both of her cheeks.

Noticing the surprised look on her face, he asked. "Did your darling mother not inform you that I was a poet? Sure, an' we all welcome new friends in the same manner."

They took their seats while Tim signalled a very fraught-looking Nancy, who was in the middle of placing a couple of plates of food in front of some other patrons, over to them.

The poor girl was obviously flustered, and perspiration was beaded along her forehead, which she wiped away on the back of her sleeve as she approached their table. "Evening folks, what can we do you for?"

"You certainly seem to be rushed off your feet," Janine observed. "Is there something special going on this evening?"

Nancy shrugged. "If there is, we weren't informed of it," she admitted. "It's like all our regulars, some of whom only appear at weekends, have decided to descend on us at the same time. Plus which, we're two down in the kitchen, hence the reason I'm helping out here. Mary even had to drag those no-good sons of hers behind the bar to assist her," she leaned in a little closer. "Though between you and me, I think they've been helping themselves to more than they've been dishing out."

"I've done some waitressing," Marie announced. "I know how you feel."

Nancy's eyes widened. "Are you serious?" Before Marie had a chance to answer, Nancy continued. "If you want to help out tonight, Mary will pay you cash in hand. She's already asked a couple of the more sober locals, but they both turned her down."

Marie glanced over at Janine. "Would you mind, Mum?" she asked, tentatively.

Janine shook her head. "I don't mind at all, but what about your dinner?"

Nancy held her hand out towards Marie. "Don't you go worrying about that, kitchen staff never go hungry."

Marie stood up and took the barmaid's hand.

"Let me quickly introduce her to Mary, then I'll send her back with your drinks. Same again, Tim?" He nodded, smiling. "And for you, madam?"

"Dry white wine, please," replied Janine.

Nancy whisked Marie over to the bar where a hot and bothered Mary was busy serving drinks. Janine watched as the barmaid seemed to talk over her before indicating towards Marie.

Mary looked up, smiled at her, and said something which Janine was too far away to hear. The next minute, Nancy led Marie to the kitchen, where she reappeared moments later wearing an apron and carrying a pad and pencil in her hand.

"She looks quite the part," Tim suggested. "She's certainly one to take advantage of a good situation."

"She is that," agreed Janine, feeling proud of her daughter for being willing to jump in and help at a moment's notice. True, the extra money she would earn would help replace the money she was expecting from helping Sarah out at her job. Naturally, since the party, Sarah's mother had put a firm stop to that, no longer trusting her daughter to so much as leave the house at night.

It crossed her mind that, as she was not yet eighteen, Marie might actually be breaking the law by working in a pub, restaurant in the back or not, it was still mainly a pub. But she decided not to mention it after all. From what she had seen of Manus thus far, it seemed a very laid-back affair, and she doubted that any of the regulars were about to report the landlady to the only constable on duty.

True to her word, Nancy sent Marie over with their drinks.

Janine could see how cautiously her daughter balanced the two glasses on the tray provided, and for a moment, she had to look away almost as if she were afraid of jinxing the poor girl by staring.

Marie placed the tray down on their table and handed them both their choice of refreshment. "Mary says that these ones are on the house," Marie informed them. "It looks like you're in with the staff."

"How are things back in the kitchen?" Janine asked.

Marie blew air through pursed lips. "Hectic would be an understatement, but everyone seems to be pulling together, so that helps."

"Waitress?" called a man a couple of tables away, smiling in Marie's direction.

"Duty calls," she said, before turning and making her way over to him.

"Looks like she's got this sussed already," Tim remarked,

emptying the remnants from his original glass before taking a sip from his new one.

"Oh, she's a quick learner when she wants to be," Janine answered.

"So now, tell me what you managed to glean from your visit to the Calvert Library? I've had a squint at the pics you sent me, but to be honest, my screen doesn't expand as much as I'd like, so I really need to read them on my laptop."

Janine took out her own phone. She scrolled through until she found the photos she had taken earlier. "Like I said over the phone – it was all a bit rushed – that housekeeper, Mrs O'Leary, guarded the books like they were the crown jewels themselves."

"Wonderfully loyal these housekeepers are," Tim observed, "even after their employers have departed this mortal coil."

"Like I said on the phone, if it hadn't have been for Father Boyle, I doubt I'd have even managed to set foot in the place. Even with him there, she was still obviously on edge. Lord knows what she's protecting, or thinks she is."

"Maybe her old boss had a secret stash of porn which she was afraid that you might stumble upon."

Janine turned and gave him a quizzical look.

"Well, you never know, especially these days," Tim concluded.

"Anyway," continued Janine, "of the books you suggested, two of them didn't seem to have much to offer, at least not in the time I was allowed. But this one," she expanded her screen and held her phone in front of Tim, "specifically mentioned the legend of the Banshee, including the traditional spells from folklore depicting how to summon one."

Tim took out his reading glasses and slid them onto his nose.

"May I?" he asked, indicating that he wished to hold the phone himself.

Janine handed it to him. He studied the small screen through his lenses, still having to squint at times to read the minute text.

Janine sipped her wine while he read.

After a moment, he said. "This is wonderful stuff, especially considering how little time you had to view the weighty tomes."

"You mentioned something about the tradition regarding how to summon a Banshee and how to dispel one once called in your talk, as I recall."

Tim nodded, absentmindedly, not taking his gaze off the screen. "Yes, but that was more a combination of speculation and guesswork as opposed to actual writings. Remember, I had a chance to have a brief look through some of the church's archives, before the arrival of 'curate friendly'."

"I would have thought that their ledgers would be at least the equal of any in a private collection such as Mr Calvert's."

"Oh, I've no doubt of it," Tim agreed. "But first we need to gain access, and depending on how assiduous the new curate is, actually finding what we're looking for could take an age by itself. When I went down there, it is no exaggeration to say that it looked undisturbed for centuries. The dust alone must have been ten inches deep, and the volumes were just stacked one on top of the other with no consideration as to order, date or even subject."

"Maybe the new curate is being honest when he says why he doesn't think it's safe for anyone to venture down there until he's sorted it all out," Janine mused.

"It's certainly possible," Tim replied, reaching out for his glass while still focusing on the screen. He took a sip of his ale and replaced the glass on the table like one who was practised in doing so without having to look. "But even so, if he weren't such a miserable bugger…" he glanced up, momentarily, "forgive me Lord. Then perhaps I'd be more willing to take him at his word."

"Well, I tried using my womanly charms today, they fell on stoney ground," Janine admitted.

Tim turned to face her. "I cannot believe that any man, in holy orders or not, would be able to resist such charms."

Their eyes met for a moment.

Tim's wolfish grin was accompanied by a slight twinkle in his eyes which immediately made Janine feel weak at the knees.

Perhaps she had been too hasty to warn him off that afternoon.

"So, what d'yer fancy, it's all good?" Marie's sudden appearance by her side brought Janine round from her temporary reverie.

She turned round and smiled up at her daughter, who was holding out a couple of menus. She handed one each to the couple.

"Can you recommend anything?" Janine asked, mischievously.

"Well, since I've been working here all of five minutes, the fish and chips seems very popular, and I overheard chef say that the haddock was only brought in this morning."

Janine handed back her unopened menu. "Sounds scrumptious, thank you."

Marie scribbled on her pad, then looked over at Tim. "Not for me," he responded, handing back his menu. "I'd just finished enjoying one of the house specialities when your darling mother called to say that you were both coming to meet me. Couldn't eat another morsel."

"Thank you," replied Marie, sliding both menus under her arm. She turned and walked back towards the kitchen.

"Now, where we?" asked Tim, sliding his hand around the back of Janine's chair.

Janine looked at him, sharply. "You were reading my findings at the library this afternoon," she answered, jabbing her index finger at her phone, while keeping her voice steady and assertive to ensure that he received the message.

Tim pulled a face and removed his arm from her chair.

He returned his attention to the phone screen.

Janine checked herself. She could not blame him for reacting as he had done. After all, she had held his gaze after his comment about her 'womanly charms'.

She should know by now that Tim was an incorrigible flirt and act appropriately depending on what message she wanted to send.

The problem was, she was now in two minds concerning what that message was.

Tim returned to concentrating on the pages captured on Janine's phone.

Scrolling back and forth, he did not speak for at least the next ten minutes other than allowing a "Ah," or a "Oh, okay," to escape his lips.

Nancy came over with Janine's meal. Her fish and chips came with two slices of bread and butter, a small pot of mushy peas and a choice of tomato or tartare sauce.

"Could I fetch you anything else?" the girl asked, smiling.

Janine shook her head. "No, thank you, this looks wonderful."

Brought round from his reverie, Tim asked. "Could you ask Mary to pour me a small drop of God's own nectar to wash my beer down?"

Janine suspected that he was after more mountain dew.

The mere thought of it brought the taste from last night back to her mouth.

"Any for you?" Nancy asked, expectantly.

Janine shook her head. "No, thank you, I'm driving," she confessed. "But a glass of mineral water would be lovely."

"Bring her some mountain dew just in case," announced Tim. Janine spun round to scowl at him for contradicting her choice to remain sober. He winked at her. "If the young lady doesn't fancy it, then I'm sure that I can find a good home for it."

Nancy shook her head and left the table.

Tim turned back to the screen.

Janine tucked into her dinner. The food was indeed as delicious as it looked. The batter was crisp and flavoursome, and the chips had been fried to a golden brown. Chewing the fish, Janine could well believe that it had only been brought into port that morning.

Nancy arrived with their drinks and knowingly placed both glasses of mountain dew in front of Tim.

While she ate, Janine looked up to see how Marie was doing.

Her daughter seemed perfectly at home serving her customers, and Janine could not help but be amazed at how effortless she made the task appear.

"This is quite incredible," Tim announced out of nowhere. "Have you had a chance to read these in detail?" he asked.

Janine swallowed a mouthful of food. "No, not yet," she answered. "I needed to send in my piece for today about the recent spate of heart attacks, so that was my priority."

Tim knocked back his first glass of poteen in one swig.

He pulled a face before continuing. "This is fascinating stuff," he revealed. "In the wrong hands, this could even be considered dangerous."

"How do you mean?"

"Well, if these pages are authentic, summoning a Banshee," he quickly looked around them to see if anyone might be listening in. Satisfied that no one was, he carried on but in a whispered tone. "According to this, summoning a Banshee is as simple as reciting a couple of ancient words and naming the person you want it to kill. There is no way under such circumstances that anyone could link the person who performs doing the summoning to the victim's death. What's more, it says that the victim has very little warning that they are about to die."

"Really, so what, the Banshee just appears and that's it?" asked Janine, fascinated.

Tim washed down his shot with a gulp of ale. "Well, if I'm reading this right, the victim usually experiences the approach of the Banshee via a high-pitched whistling sound which no one else can hear. Once they hear that, they're usually dead within a couple of minutes."

Janine placed her cutlery by the side of her plate. "Does it mention if any symptoms are detectable after death?"

"Not as such," Tim replied.

"Nothing at all?"

Tim shrugged. "There was something, oh, here it is: *The victim may show signs of one who has seen the face of God.*"

Janine scrunched up her nose. "Okay, does it offer any elaboration?"

Tim shook his head. "Not on these pages, but I'm willing to bet there's more inside the book you took them from."

"Forget that," answered Janine, "there's no way on earth that I can see the excellent Mrs O'Leary allowing me to re-enter her master's hallowed library."

"The only other option is the church archives," noted Tim. "I wouldn't care to speculate which would be easier to gain access to."

Janine made her wine last for the rest of the evening. With a full meal inside her she considered it might be safe to risk a second glass, but instead she decided to play it safe and sipped mineral water between nips of wine.

She realised that she was there for the duration with Marie having volunteered to waitress for the evening, but once again, she found Tim to be captivating company, so the time passed relatively quickly.

As the bell for last orders sounded, Tim waved to Mary and

held up his empty shot glass. He had managed to knock back four glasses since Janine had been there as well as three pints of ale.

From the dark tanned hue of his skin, Janine suspected that such revelling was a regular pursuit for him.

He certainly played the legendary part of the poet to perfection.

Mary brought over Tim's last drink and handed it to him. "Has this reprobate been annoying you all evening?" she asked, looking down at Janine.

Before she had a chance to answer, Tim piped up. "Which one of us are you referring to?"

Janine slapped him across his arm.

"Give him one for me while you're there," laughed Mary. "And I just want to say, your daughter has been a real treasure this evening, I'm not sure how we would have coped without her. She's a real natural."

Janine felt a swell of pride glowing inside her. "Thank you, you're very kind."

"Not at all, I speak as I find," Mary assured her.

Marie arrived back at the table a few minutes later.

She slumped down, releasing a huge sigh.

"Tough day at the office, honey?" Janine asked.

"You could say, but it was great fun," admitted Marie. "The customers here are much more laid back than at Sarah's restaurant. I should tell her to try for a job here, if her mother ever lets her out again."

Marie shoved her hand into her pocket and pulled out a wad of notes.

"Is that your wages?" asked Janine, shocked by a wad of notes.

"Yep," Marie nodded, proudly. "Mary said that, as it was such short notice, that she was giving me a bonus on top of my wages."

"I hoped you thanked her?" asked Janine.

Marie nodded. "Of course I did, your daughter knows her manners." She shoved the notes back in her pocket.

Just then, Marie's phone went off.

She glanced at the screen, then said. "Speak of the Devil… Hello there, how's life in Alcatraz suiting you?"

Janine presumed that it was Sarah on the other end.

She still felt sorry for the poor girl, taking the full force of her mother's blame for the party. She was glad that Marie and she were still in touch and perhaps, who knew, they might become firm friends for life. It was high time her daughter had at least one friend whom she actually looked forward to speaking to.

Marie turned to look at her mother. "Hang on, let me ask the boss," she covered her phone behind her hand to ensure that Sarah could not hear the next part of the conversation. "Is there any chance I could stay at Sarah's tonight? She can't sleep, and I'm still buzzing from tonight."

"What about taking Gypsy to the vets tomorrow?"

"Dammit," Marie bit her bottom lip. "I forgot to check local vets."

"Never mind, we can check tomorrow," Janine assured her.

"So, can I go?"

"May I go?" Janine reminded her.

"Mum!"

Janine smiled. "Yes, of course you can go. Come on, I'll drop you off."

Chapter Fifty

Colm Murphy staggered home through the park having spent the last three hours in his local.

Having dealt a just-deserved beating to both his wife and daughter upon his return from work that evening, he had hoped that a couple of civilised hours drinking might help to temper his anger.

In his eyes, he had always been a good husband and father, a fine provider who ensured that his family had a secure roof over their heads and food in the larder. Neither of them had ever wanted for clothes, shoes or even what he considered to be some of the more unnecessary luxuries which people bought into by watching too much television, such as perfume, makeup, more shoes than a body could possibly wear and umpteen visits to the hairdressers each year, even when their hair did not need cutting.

For all that, all he had ever demanded in return was respect and loyalty.

Enid had promised before God to love, honour and obey him, forsaking all others, and at the time she claimed to have taken her vows seriously. Yet over the last few years, it seemed that whenever Colm demanded she succumb to his conjugal rights, she had an excuse, whether it was a headache, or she was too tired and had to wake up early to clean the church, or because it was her time of the month. A time which seemed to stretch further and take longer with each passing year.

As for that ungrateful daughter of theirs, she had been spared too many beatings when she was younger, again because of her mother's intervention. Now that she was older, her true nature was coming through.

She was old enough to understand a man's needs once he was married. Enid had assured him that she had 'had the talk' with her ages ago, so what gave her the right to think that she could interfere when he was taking what was rightly his by God's law, he had no idea. But again, he put it down to his wife not explaining things to her properly.

She should know to make herself scarce when her parents were indulging in coitus.

Either that or stay in her room with the door closed out of respect.

But no, she misguidedly believed that she had the right to intervene and ruin his pleasure. Well, perhaps after her latest beating, she would think twice before she interfered in matters which did not concern her.

When he thought of how many men that he knew who regularly cheated on their wives, or left them and their kids with nothing while they swanned off with some bird half their age whom they had met online, he realised just how fortunate Enid and their daughter were.

So why did they not appreciate just how lucky they were to have him?

It was obvious to Colm that he had been far too lenient with the pair of them over the years, which doubtless had resulted in their insubordinate attitudes.

Well, enough was enough. From now on, he was no longer willing to spare the rod with either of them. If they deserved it, they were going to get it, and they only had themselves to blame.

Colm released a loud belch, the taste of strong ale permeating his mouth.

He stopped for a moment and leant up against the nearest tree to steady himself.

He realised that he should have eaten before venturing out that evening, but again, thanks to his wife and daughter, he had been so angry with the pair of them that he needed to leave the house and seek out some more congenial company down the pub.

He could have eaten there; the bar menu was pretty good. But he was still thinking about the steak and kidney back home in the oven. By now it was probably all cold and congealed, but a quick *zap* in the microwave with lashings of freshly made gravy and Enid could make the most inedible mush taste like restaurant quality.

He squinted at his wristwatch. The dial barely came into focus.

What difference did the time make? Enid would still be up waiting for him to return, or he would want to know the reason why.

She knew better from past experience not to leave him to his own devices when it came to his dinner, regardless of what time he arrived back at home. He had dragged her out of bed before, and he was not averse to doing it again, if need be, and she knew it.

His stomach started to growl.

Colm smacked his lips. Steak and kidney pudding with real mashed potato, peas and gravy, plus thick sliced bread and butter. Just what the doctor ordered.

His hunger spurred him on. Colm pushed himself away from

the tree he had used to support him and tried to maintain his balance unaided for the rest of the journey.

In hindsight, a cab from the pub might have been a better option. But no one could accuse Colm Murphy of wasting money needlessly.

There was a half-moon sitting high above the park, which cast a mystical glow over the trees and bushes which lined the pathway. The natural glow blended in with that created by the artificial street lamps, which were dotted few and far between along the way.

Colm stopped again.

His bladder was too full to continue any further without releasing its contents.

He had to admit, even if only to himself, that he was fast reaching an age where he could no longer hold it in indefinitely like he used to as a young man.

Colm glanced around. There was no one else in the park, at least no one he could see. People passing by on the street were too far away to be able to observe what he was about to do. The last thing he needed was some busybody taking snaps of him urinating in a public place with their smart-alec phones, then posting them on social media for all the world to see.

That would not do his credibility in the business world any good whatsoever.

Not to mention the fact that, if recognised, he could find himself up before a magistrate on the mainland.

Secure in the knowledge that he was sufficiently alone, Colm lurched over to the nearest tree and unzipped his trousers. He barely managed to release his member in time before the steady stream began to flow.

Colm breathed an audible sigh of deep relief as his bladder emptied.

He leant his forearm against the tree, resting his head on it and closing his eyes as the last few squirts left him.

Refastening his trousers, Colm checked once more that no one was about before continuing on his way.

As he reached the centre of the park, he heard it.

A high-pitched cry wafting over the park as if from miles away.

Colm stopped in his tracks and turned back. There was no evidence as to where the sound was emanating from, but it appeared to be all around him, rising in volume by the second.

Colm placed his index fingers in his ears and shook them in an effort to release any obstruction which might be responsible for the strange sound.

Removing his digits, he listened intently.

There it was again, only this time it was definitely louder and assailed his ears as if carried on the wind.

Colm spun around, convinced that there must be some young hooligans in the park playing a prank on him. They were probably hiding behind a bush using some sort of fancy military digital technology they had bought on the net from the States.

Little bastards, when he got his hands on them, he would give them what for.

Parents today were too soft on their kids.

He blamed the law. Stopping teachers from administering corporal punishment was the start of this slippery slope. Today, kids had no fear of retribution, so they just did as they pleased without a care.

Colm considered for a moment that if they had been watching him, they might well have videoed him urinating. If so, there was no chance that they would be willing to listen to reason and delete it before posting it. Even if he offered to bribe them. The little shits would doubtless take his money and still post it.

Now he felt real panic well up in his breast.

The shame and embarrassment of being hauled up before the beak for such an act would make it hard for him to lift his head in public. Nowadays, everyone had access to the internet, so the chance that no one in the town would see the film was remote at the very least.

The piercing shrillness of the cry assailed both his eardrums, making Colm feel as if someone had rammed a narrow metal rod through one ear and out the other.

"Come on now, kids," he called out. "A joke's a joke, but this isn't funny anymore."

There was no response. At least, none that he could hear above the cry reverberating through his brain.

They had to be somewhere nearby, he reasoned.

Colm began striding with weighty purpose towards the nearest set line bushes. If the kids were hiding behind there, he would give them the scare of their miserable lives.

"Gotcha!" he cried, leaning over the shrubbery.

But there was no one there.

Colm looked up.

The next nearest hiding place was too far away for anyone to be sending out the deafening sound. Or could their equipment really be that exceptional?

The bloody government should monitor what people could buy online these days.

Tomorrow, he was going to send a very strongly worded e-mail to whomever his local member of parliament was.

The sound increased in volume as if someone had just turned up the dial.

Colm slammed both palms against his ears in a vain attempt to block out the noise, but it still managed to penetrate through to his brain.

He turned around, first one way, then the other.

There was still no evidence as to where the sound was coming from.

Then, suddenly, in the distance, Colm could see what appeared to be a white cloud of vapour appear on the horizon. It was coming from the direction of the sea, but it sailed high above the trees and houses in its way, slowly heading in his direction.

Was he going insane?

Had he just had one pint too many?

Colm watched, fixated on the mist as it wafted over the horizon.

As he watched, transfixed, the mist began to develop into a more solid form.

The shape grew nearer, and as it did, it began to take on the substance of a white bedsheet with frayed edges.

Colm narrowed his eyes, trying desperately to see the wires or strings which held the shape aloft. Surely this had to be an elaborate prank that someone was playing on him.

Either that, or he had really lost his mind.

The shape drifted over the railings and made its way into the park.

It was now only a couple of hundred feet away from him, and Colm could make out a distinct outline which now appeared to have formed a head and two elongated arms which stretched out in his direction like some desperate lover in need of comfort.

The cry became a shriek.

Colm felt frozen to the spot. Desperate as he was to run away as fast as his drunken legs would carry him, he discovered, much to his horror, that his legs refused the command from his brain to do their duty.

The shape drifted closer.

The head now had a face. A twisted, contorted visage with eyes as black as pitch and a gaping maw for a mouth which grew in size the closer it came to him.

Now he could tell that the awful, high-pitched scream which he had been at the mercy of actually emanated from that expanding black hole which sat in the middle of that horrific countenance.

Colm grabbed his left arm with his other hand. He could feel his breathing starting to grow more laboured as the figure progressed towards him.

A sudden, excruciating pain shot through his chest, bringing him to his knees on the hard asphalt surface of the path.

The creature was almost upon him.

Colm opened his mouth to scream, but no sound came out.

The penetrating scream vibrated between his ears, but Colm no longer had the strength to try and block it out.

As the face of the Banshee came into focus, Colm felt a sudden rush of blood flood his eyes just before he slumped over, dead.

Chapter Fifty-One

JANINE AWOKE WITH AN IMMEDIATE SENSE OF *DÉJÀ VU*.

Her mobile beside her on the nightstand was vibrating into life, and as she opened her eyes and rubbed the sleep from them, she recognised her surroundings although they were not immediately familiar to her.

The movement from her right-hand side revealed the thick mop of hair which belonged to Tim.

Then she remembered. Having dropped Marie off at Sarah's, she noticed a saucy text from Tim asking if Marie's mum was allowed a sleepover now that her daughter was spending the night with her friend.

Janine's finger hovered over the keys of her phone while she decided what to do.

Finally, unable to make a decision, she continued on her way home. It was only when she reached the junction in the high street with right meaning home and left meaning Tim's place that she decided to turn left, and even then, right up until she rang his doorbell, Janine was not entirely convinced of her actions.

As it was, neither of them had much to say.

Tim opened a new bottle of single malt, they had a drink, then began kissing and exploring each other's naked bodies once more, before finally tumbling into bed.

Janine reached for her phone. Presuming it was Marie, she did not bother trying to focus on her screen. "Hello," she said, hoping that this early call did not signify that something was wrong.

"Jan? Hi, it's Sam, sorry for the ungodly hour, I take it you were asleep?"

Janine rubbed her eyes. "Yep, what time is it?"

"It's just after six, are you ready to rumble?"

Janine sat up in bed. She managed to catch the duvet before it dropped to her waist, and she held it up across her naked breasts with her free arm. It was an automatic response, although there was nothing left of her modesty to hide from Tim.

"What's happened?" she asked, stifling a yawn.

"Believe it or not, you've had another one," Sam revealed excitedly.

"Another what?" Janine asked, her mind still hazy from the previous evening.

"Another heart-attack victim," Sam revealed. "What's going on over there? Is there something dodgy in the water? I reckon the health and safety lobby will be taking a serious look at that island in the next couple of days. For such a small place, they certainly have more than their fair share of heart traumas."

Now Janine's mind cleared. "Who?" she asked, tentatively. Although she did not know that many people on the island, she still felt a creeping fear that it might be someone she had met. Her immediate fear was that it might be Father Boyle; after all, he was not a young man and he certainly seemed to carry the weight of the world on his shoulders where his parishioners were concerned.

"I've only managed to find out their first name," admitted

Sam. "It's a Colm someone, apparently, he's a businessman on the island, no idea yet if he has any family there, hence the reason I'm calling you. Do you think you could make some enquiries? It would make a great follow-up to your recent article. If we could get it in the can by tonight, we'd be laughing."

Janine sighed with relief. So at least it was not the old priest.

She did not remember meeting anyone named Colm.

Tim moaned in his sleep and pulled the duvet up over his shoulders.

Janine wondered if he might have any idea who the victim was. She could always ask him before she left, but that would mean having to wake him and, as before, she preferred to slip away without any awkward questions being asked.

That said, she hoped that he knew the score by now.

Then again, she did not have to sneak back into his bed last night. She had the option of driving home and spending the night alone, but she made a conscious decision to go to him.

"What d'you say?" urged Sam, her voice tinged with impatience.

"Okay, I'll see what I can find out this end, but I can't make any promises this early in the day," Janine admitted.

"That's my girl," Sam gushed. "And there's a bonus for an incentive if you manage to send me two thousand words minimum by cut-off time tonight. Just so you're aware."

"Bribery will get you everywhere," Janine replied, sarcastically.

"I'll let you know if I find anything else out at this end, happy hunting." With that, Sam disconnected the line.

Janine placed her mobile back on the table and ran her fingers through her hair.

She could really do with a shower before setting off on her latest venture, and she knew that Tim would not mind her using his facilities, but that would mean more chance of him waking up at the sound of the running water, which in turn might lead to an embarrassing conversation which Janine preferred not to have.

Slipping out of bed, Janine dressed hurriedly, crawling around on her hands and knees on the floor in an effort to locate her shoes without having to turn the lights on or draw open the curtains.

Having finally found everything, she glanced back at Tim's sleeping form, then crept out of the flat, closing the door as quietly as possible behind her.

Janine knew that her best option was Father Boyle, but as there was no way of her knowing if he had been informed of the victim yet, Janine decided that she would drive home and shower and change before attempting to contact him.

Once back at the cottage, she switched on the kettle and opened the back door to see if Gypsy was loitering anywhere in sight. Fortunately, Marie had fed her before they went to the pub, but knowing the little gannet's insatiable appetite, there was every chance that she would be ready for more.

By the time the kettle boiled, there was still no sign of the cat, so Janine put some food on a plate and placed it next to the cat's water bowl.

She took her coffee upstairs with her to drink straight after her shower.

As she passed Marie's room, she heard a cat meow.

Opening the door wide enough to enter, Janine walked in and found Gypsy curled up on the bed, with what looked like a fur muffler in front of her.

As Janine crept closer, she saw that the 'muffler' was, in fact, a litter of tiny kittens nestled inside their mother's warm embrace.

Janine was initially taken aback. Then she realised the reason why the cat had been so hungry recently. She was doubtless storing up calories in order to make enough milk to feed her babies.

Janine sighed. Now that Gypsy had kittens, she knew exactly what Marie's reaction would be. It was one thing to contemplate taking Gypsy home once they had ascertained that she had no owner, but a litter of new-born kittens as well, their house would be overrun within a couple of months.

For today at least, there was nothing to be done. Janine was no expert, but she knew that it might prove dangerous to try moving newborns, so she decided that for now they could stay on Marie's bed. She would call a vet later and ask for some advice.

Janine rushed back downstairs and brought up Gypsy's food and water and put them on the floor next to the bed.

Gypsy glanced up at her before licking her brood all over.

Janine took a picture. It was hard to focus with all the kittens and the mother being black, but she managed to determine that there were three little bodies huddled up next to their mother.

She sent the picture over to Marie with the words: 'Congrats, you're an aunty'.

After showering and changing, Janine dried her hair using Marie's hairdryer. Personally, she had always preferred towel-drying only, but as she was in a rush, she decided to make use of the technology available.

Her phone sprang into life beside her.

It was Marie. "Well, hello there, sleepy head. Sorry if I woke you so early, but I thought you might like to know that you've become an aunty overnight."

"Oh my God," Marie gushed, "I can't believe it, I wish I'd been there to see it, they're adorable."

In the background, Janine could hear Sarah shouting that she wanted one.

"Well, there's not much to see at the moment," Janine informed her. "For a start, they're all asleep with their mum. I'm pretty sure that kittens just sleep and eat and pooh for the first couple of weeks."

"I don't care," shrieked Marie, "I just wanna see them, can you come and get me?"

"Ah," Janine stopped to think. "Could it wait a while? I've just had a call from my editor, and believe it or not, there's been another heart-attack victim in the town, and she wants me to go and see if I can find any relatives to interview."

"Ohhh," Marie pleaded. "Would you really get anywhere disturbing the bereaved so early in the morning?"

She had a point. It was still before seven, and although she imagined Father Boyle may well be awake, there was still a chance that he had not been contacted about the incident.

Even so, Janine knew that she did not want to leave it too long before contacting him if she wanted in on the ground floor. He had been brilliant in organising interviews for her so far.

"Please, Mum," her tone was pitiful. Janine had not heard Marie use it since she was six and wanted Janine to take her to some boyband concert, which was miles away, and available tickets put them right at the back of a ten-thousand-seater venue.

She still remembered the abject look of disappointment on her daughter's face when she tried explaining the situation to her.

That was a look she still carried with her all these years later.

It was true that 'Mum guilt' stayed with you for life.

"Listen," Janine continued, "I'll leave some money on the hall table, you call a cab and you can pay him with it. I'm not sure when I'll be back, but we need to discuss matters concerning Gypsy and her brood. This makes the situation even more complicated; you do realise that?"

"It'll be fine, Mum, we'll work something out. I can look for a part-time job when we get home so I can help with the cat food and vet bills. Now that I'm a trained waitress, it can't be that difficult to find work."

Janine certainly could not deny her daughter's new-found

enthusiasm, and to be honest, she did not want to. This holiday had seen a positive change in Marie that Janine loved. She only hoped that it hung around after they returned home.

"Alright," she agreed, "we'll talk later, for now I need to get moving. You can bring Sarah with you so long as her mum doesn't object."

"Thanks, Mum, you're the greatest."

"Thank you," Sarah called from the distance.

"Yeah, well, we'll see how great I am after we take the brood to the vets to have the kitties checked over. And remember," she warned, "we still need to find out if she's chipped. There might be a young child somewhere still grieving for her return."

"Yeah, Mum, I know," Marie replied. "Love you."

Before Janine had the chance to respond in kind, Marie cut her off.

"Second time today," Janine mused, looking at her screen.

Chapter Fifty-Two

BEFORE LEAVING THE HOUSE, JANINE RUMMAGED about the house until she located an old cardboard box and a pile of newspapers in the cupboard under the stairs. She fashioned it into a make-shift litter tray, layering the newspaper to soak up whatever Gypsy might dispel.

She placed it on the other side of the bed away from the cat's food, making sure that she showed Gypsy what it was and where it was going. The cat merely looked up for a brief moment, then closed her eyes and went back to sleep.

Janine could not blame the new mother. Even after all these years, she could still remember how exhausting it was giving birth to Marie.

Leaving a ten-pound note under an ornament on the hall table as promised, Janine climbed into her car and checked her bag to ensure that she had all she might need for the day.

Once she was sure, she phoned Father Boyle.

"Hello," he answered, after several rings. His voice sounded a little hoarse as if he had not slept the night before. Janine could already feel her cheeks glowing at having to disturb him, but he had been immensely helpful to her thus far regarding her article, and beside that, who else could she turn to?

"Good morning, Father Boyle," Janine replied, cheerily. "I'm sorry for calling you so early."

"Oh, it's you. Good morning, Miss Carstairs. Do not concern yourself, I've always been an early riser. My day is almost halfway through already."

He seemed to brighten a little realising that it was Janine on the line, which she took as a good omen. "Father," she continued, steadily. "I'm afraid I'm calling with more bad news. I presume that you've heard that there's been another victim of heart-failure during the night. Apparently, his name was Colm, but as yet I don't have any more information."

The old priest sighed. "I'm afraid I do know about it," he admitted. "I take it you're enquiring after some details concerning his next of kin?"

Now Janine could feel the embarrassment sweep over her like a tidal wave.

She felt terrible that she only seemed to contact the priest when she needed something. But such was her situation on the island that as a reporter, she needed contacts, and he was by far the best one she had.

"I'm really sorry, Father," she continued, her tone belaying her awkwardness at having to approach him, again. "I know you've been extremely helpful to me since I've been here, and I've nothing to offer you as repayment for your kindness, but I've really no one else to turn to." She paused for a moment. She could hear the priest sighing as he moved around on the other end. There was the sound of a door closing. "Father, are you still there?"

"Yes, just give me a second, these old bones don't respond as quickly as they used to."

Janine listened. She heard another door opening and closing, and now there was the distant *hum* of traffic and the *cooing* of pigeons in the background.

"I've just come outside for some privacy," he admitted. "It would have been terribly indiscreet, not to mention upsetting, for the victim's loved ones to speak in front of them."

"Oh, I see, so you're with them now?"

"I am, I was notified during the wee small hours when a jogger came across the body. He contacted the police, naturally, and Constable Clark phoned me when he realised that the victim's family were members of my congregation. The constable had to remain at the scene while the forensics people were brought over from the mainland, so I volunteered to break the sad news to the victim's family. I felt it was better coming from me than some random officer from the mainland who had never even met them before."

"That must have been awful for you."

"Not the most pleasant of offices, but it isn't the first time I've been called upon for such a task. That said, it never gets any easier. Even the most devout member of my flock, I've discovered, are not interested in an old priest chundering on about their loved ones being in a better place, and no longer in pain, etc, etc."

Janine took in a deep breath. "I hate to ask, Father, but do you think it might be possible for me to have an interview with the deceased's loved ones? Obviously, I don't want to intrude on their grief, but this recent spate of heart-attack victims is turning into something of an epidemic on the island."

"I know what you mean," the priest confided. "I was speaking to Doctor Cleary about it only last evening. He assures me that the medical examiner on the mainland is satisfied that each of the victims died of natural causes and that there's no link that he can find to suggest anything untoward."

"Well, that's something, I suppose," Janine agreed. "But even so, it's still a mystery, especially as one of the victims was only a teenager and in the prime of good health."

"I know, that's what makes this latest incident so very tragic."

"How do you mean?" Janine asked, intrigued.

The priest waited a moment before replying. "I can trust your discretion, Miss Carstairs? I don't want to betray a trust only to turn up at the family's doorstep when they're too upset to give an interview."

Janine felt trapped.

She could still hear Sam's voice in her ear, dangling a bonus if she managed to extract the details of the incident from those in charge and to speak with the family to maintain a human angle interest in the story.

But by the same token, without Father Boyle, she knew that she would be on a hiding to nowhere, so she had to maintain his trust and accept his suggestion before destroying his faith in her.

"Father, if you'll trust me with whatever details you have, I promise not to make a move without checking with you first. How's that?"

"Good enough for me," he admitted, the relief evident in his voice. "The latest victim is one Colm Murphy. You met his daughter Erin yesterday; in fact, you took her out to lunch I believe."

"Oh no!" Janine's shock was sincere. That poor girl, having just lost her boyfriend, had now lost her father, all within a day of each other. Just how much misery could those narrow shoulders withstand?

"I'm afraid so," Father Boyle continued. "The doctor has only just left, he's had to sedate Mrs Murphy, she was close to hysterical when I first informed her of her husband's demise. Young Erin is only coping moderately better. She refused the offer of medical intervention, but I still don't think that she's ready to be interviewed."

"Of course not, I understand. The poor girl, and her poor mother. We met her yesterday too when we dropped Erin off, but we didn't actually manage to exchange any pleasantries."

"It sounds as if your daughter made quite an impression on her," the priest continued. "Erin has mentioned her twice so far since I've been here. Sounds as if she made a friend for life there."

Janine laughed. "My Marie has made more friends since we arrived than I've known her make in all her years at school. She's a very particular kind of girl, loves her own company. But both Erin and Sarah Byrne seemed to have ignited something new and exciting in her. She actually spent the night over at Sarah's last night."

"I know Sarah and her mother very well," Father Boyle gushed. "A lovely girl, little high-spirited at times, but to be honest, her mother, though extremely devout, can test the nature of her daughter on occasion."

"I'd have to agree," Janine laughed. "I've spoken to her over the phone. I suspect that we probably adhere to different approaches when it comes to parenting."

Now it was the priest's turn to laugh. "I can see what you mean," he agreed. "Now then, getting back to the situation at hand. I'm going to be here for a little while yet, but I am going to suggest that Erin join me later this afternoon at the presbytery, just to take her away from the stress of having to look after her mother for a while. I intend to speak to one of my ladies from the church to come over and sit with Enid so that she won't be alone. They're good friends, so I hope she won't think it intrusive of me for arranging it."

"I'm sure she'll appreciate it, Father," Janine said, approvingly.

"Thank you, I hope so too. Now what I'm suggesting is

that when Erin visits me that you come along to so that you can interview her. Perhaps you might bring young Marie along too, if you think it might help her to open up. What do you say?"

"That's a wonderful idea, Father, thank you so much."

"It's my pleasure," he replied. "But as for her mother, if you'll accept my advice, I don't think that she will be in any fit state for an interview for some time yet, certainly not today."

"Of course," Janine agreed. "I'll leave it to your discretion as and when you think that it's the right time." She paused a moment before continuing. "I hate to be an even bigger nuisance, but do you think that before we meet this afternoon, you might be able to dig up some background on Colm Murphy for me? When and where he was born, what he did for a living, his personality, that sort of thing."

"Ah, well, yes," he hesitated. Janine wondered if she had somehow hit a nerve. She waited for him to continue. "I suppose that could be arranged. I'm sure Erin can fill in any blanks. Let's discuss it this afternoon. I'll call you when Erin is on her way."

"Thanks again, Father, you really are a lifesaver."

"Oh well, I try, I suppose. You really are very kind."

They disconnected their call, and Janine sat behind the wheel wondering what her next course of action should be.

She had not asked where Colm's body was found, so she had no idea where to drive to so that she could possibly interview any bystanders who might have known him, or even the officers on duty.

That said, from what Father Boyle had told her, the body was found very early, so the chances of there still being anyone around to interview, save for some poor lone copper from the mainland guarding the site, were pretty slim.

She considered calling Constable Clark. She had saved his number from the other evening when he called her from the health suite. He may be willing to divulge something that Father Boyle was unaware of.

It was worth a try.

Janine let the phone ring until the officer's voicemail cut in.

She waited for it to end, then left a polite message, thanking him for alerting her to her daughter's condition the other night, then informing him that she was writing an article on the deceased and asking if he could call her back to answer some simple questions.

His machine cut out before she had a chance to finish, but she decided that he had enough information to decide whether to phone her or not.

Janine made a mental note to try him again later if she had still not heard from him.

Being free, Janine called Marie to offer her and Sarah a lift now that she had nowhere to rush off to. She heard Marie's voice message so left a reply informing her that if she still needed a lift that she should call her.

Just then, a car came around the corner and drove up to hers, parking in front.

Janine looked up and saw Marie and Sarah climb out from the back seat.

Janine exited and called out to them. "That was quick, I just called you."

Marie handed her card to the driver, who placed it in his machine. "We couldn't wait to rush home and see the kitties," she replied, excitedly.

Retrieving her card, the girls thanked the driver and came over to Janine.

"Morning," said Sarah, brightly.

"Morning, darling." Janine replied before turning to Marie. "I left you the money for that on the hall table," she reminded her.

"That's okay," her daughter replied, planting a kiss on her cheek. "Come on, let's go and see our new family."

"If she doesn't belong to anyone already," Janine reminded her. "Remember that before you get too carried away."

"I will," Marie promised. "Now come on, let's not waste any more time."

The two girls each took hold of Janine by the elbow and pulled her towards the front door.

Chapter Fifty-Three

ONCE JANINE HAD THE DOOR OPEN BOTH GIRLS charged up the stairs to see the new arrivals.

Janine listened to their excited shrieks from downstairs and smiled to herself. Secretly, she hoped that Gypsy did not have a registered owner because she could not imagine Marie's reaction if they had to give her up at this stage.

Janine sat at the kitchen table and scrolled through her phone, searching out some advice with regard to looking after newborn kittens and their mum.

The search offered her a vast array of scenarios and advice, which Janine suspected was probably all the same but geared towards individual websites.

Eventually, she located a local vet and gave them a call.

Having spoken to the vet, Janine raced upstairs where the two girls were sitting on either side of Gypsy, marvelling at the way her kittens were suckling from her.

"Look, Mum," announced Marie, excitedly, "they automatically seem to know how to feed, and their little eyes aren't even open yet. It must be pure instinct."

"They are just so gorgeous," Sarah chimed in. "I could just sit here and watch them forever."

"Well," Janine replied, "I'm afraid that's a luxury we can't afford right now."

Both girls looked up in distress. "Why? What's wrong?" Marie asked, a distinct edge of fear in her voice.

"I've just spoken to a local vet, and she has advised under the circumstances she thinks it necessary that she examine Gypsy and her brood to have them checked over."

Marie sat up. "Under what circumstances?" She looked to Janine as if she was about to burst into tears.

"Well, with Gypsy being a feral stray, the vet says that there's no way of knowing if she's ever been vaccinated or treated for worms or anything, so she wants to have a quick look over her and the kittens to check that there's no signs of anything untoward."

Marie relaxed. "You had me worried there for a moment. How are we going to take her in with her kittens? Do we just carry them in our arms?"

Janine shook her head. "No, the vet recommends that for transportation purposes we buy a carrycase that can comfortably fit them all in. She said that if we disturb Gypsy or she thinks we're trying to separate her from her litter then she might even kill them out of desperation, rather than let them go."

Both girls shot up from the bed. "Oh my God," exclaimed Sarah, "that's awful."

"So how do we ensure that Gypsy doesn't get the wrong message?" urged Marie, glancing back at the entwined balls of fur on her bed.

"Well, for a kick-off, hard as it might be, the vet says that we need to leave her alone with her kittens as much as possible for them to bond. The lovely vet has agreed that under the circumstances she will come here to check them over so as not to upset mum, plus which she can also check to see if Gypsy is microchipped at the same time."

Janine looked at her daughter. Marie's bottom lip began to protrude. It was an automatic reaction she had had since she was a girl and old enough to appreciate that she could not always have her own way, regardless of how much she played up.

"In the meantime," Janine continued, "I need you two to go shopping for some kitten food."

The girls exchanged a quizzical glance. "Aren't the kittens too young for solid food?" asked Marie, furrowing her brow.

"Yes, the food is for Gypsy," explained Janine. "Apparently, there's more protein in kitten food, and right now, as she is breastfeeding, she needs all the protein she can get, so hop to it, the pair of you, if you want to be back in time to see the vet when she arrives."

Both girls walked out together. Sarah gave Janine a quick salute as she went. "Leave this to us. Commander," she said, cheekily.

Janine gave Marie her bank card and asked her to take out some cash to pay for the food and to pay the vet, just in case she did not have a portable card machine with her.

She also told them to buy something for breakfast as none of them had eaten yet.

While they were gone, Janine began writing her article about the death of Colm Murphy. Although she had very few actual details, she was still able to create a framework for the piece, which she could fill in later when, hopefully, Father Boyle was able to arrange another interview with her.

The heart-attack victims' stories had definitely taken over from her original piece, which had been the whole reason for her journey over here, but Sam seemed more than pleased with her progress thus far, and she paid the bills, so Janine was not unduly concerned with her lack of progress on that story.

Once she had completed the formatting, Janine returned to the photos she had taken in the Calvert library. She plugged her mobile into her laptop and transferred the relevant pages over to the larger screen so that she could read them more intently.

Tim had been right, the details found in the pages concerning the legend of the Banshee and how to summon one were far more detailed than those he had managed to put together in his book.

That said, she wondered if such information should be made available to every Tom, Dick and Harry, considering the possible repercussions which might ensue from reciting the ancient spell.

Her research warned of the danger in summoning such a spirit, as to do so meant that the Banshee could not return without taking a soul with it, back to hell.

Janine remembered from Tim's talk that he hinted at the fact that if the intended victim was somehow already dead by the time the Banshee appeared, then it would take the soul of whomever had summoned it in the first place instead.

Definitely a warning to anyone considering meddling with such a practice.

Further on, Janine found another incantation which, according to the text, could even save an intended victim by sending the Banshee after the summoner instead.

The words, although written in an ancient text, were relatively simple to recite considering the potential power they were meant to exude, which made Janine wonder just how genuine the entire legend could be. Or was it simply an old wives' tale intended to frighten the dim-witted populace of days gone by, which had been handed down through the generations to eventually become embedded in modern folklore?

She wondered how many people living on the island who had grown up with the legend actually believed it.

After all, it was one thing to accept it as fact back in a time when people still believed in burning old women at the stake because they were convinced that they were in league with the Devil. But now in the twenty-first century, surely not.

Even so, Janine knew that cooperation was far easier to come by when you accepted other people's beliefs and traditions rather than mocking them for such attitudes, so for now, at least she intended to tread carefully if she found any other residents happy to be interviewed for her article on the Banshee Bride.

Aimlessly, Janine scribbled down the incantations for summoning the Banshee as well as the one for changing the focus of the intended victim.

She held the pad up in front of her.

The words appeared quite innocuous and without any obvious malice of evil intent.

Surely to recite them would have no effect.

Janine cleared her throat, then opened her mouth to begin the first incantation, but something stopped her from uttering a single word.

Had she managed to scare herself into believing the hidden power of the words?

Or, was she suddenly taken over by the idea that perhaps there was more to them than she was willing to admit?

Either way, she no longer wanted to carry on with such an experiment.

Janine closed her pad and placed it under her laptop.

She considered tearing out the pages she had just written on and destroying them, but she stopped herself from going to such an extreme.

She rationalised in her mind that no one could call forth a spirit merely by reciting a few words, no matter how much power they were meant to contain.

Then again, what was that film she had seen where if you watched a particular video the spirit of a dead girl climbed out through your television, and you died on the spot?

Janine shook her head. If she was going to start believing in everything that she had ever seen on the screen, then her life would become intolerable. Horror films were made specifically to scare people and often they did so by suggesting that strange things could happen merely by doing normal everyday things, such as having a shower.

Janine closed her laptop and went into the kitchen to make a coffee.

She hoped that the girls would return soon with some breakfast as her stomach was beginning to growl.

Her phone *buzzed*. Janine looked at the screen and saw that it was a text from Tim.

She opened it: *Woke up again without you next to me, this is becoming habit-forming.*

It was followed by two kisses.

Janine hit 'reply' and sent back a smiley face with the word 'sorry' after it.

As she sat down to drink her coffee, the doorbell sounded.

When she opened the door, there was a young woman, no more than mid-twenties in her opinion, standing on the mat with a black bag in one hand. She was dressed in jeans and a sweatshirt with the name of the veterinary practice emblazoned across the chest with a picture of a litter of kittens underneath.

"Hello," she said, brightly. "We spoke on the phone earlier."

Janine stepped back and ushered her in. "Yes, that's right, thank you so much for coming so soon, we are all very new to this."

Janine showed the vet upstairs to Marie's room.

The kittens were sound asleep, but Gypsy raised her head to inspect the newcomer with narrow eyes.

"Well now," said the vet, "aren't you just adorable?"

She made her way over to the bed and sat down gently beside Gypsy.

The cat was evidently not overjoyed by the new arrival and placed a cautionary paw across her brood.

"Now then, there's absolutely nothing for you to be afraid of," the vet continued, talking to the cat as if to a child. "I just want to check that you and your kittens are in fine fettle, then I'll leave you in peace to enjoy your well-deserved sleep. You must be exhausted from giving birth to these little ones."

The vet pulled a pair of thin plastic surgical gloves from her bag and slipped them on.

Steadily she moved one hand towards Gypsy.

Out of nowhere, Gypsy shot out her paw and managed to just miss the woman's extended hand. "Well now, you're a feisty one and no mistake," the vet said, keeping her hand in position so as to show the cat that she was not about to retreat.

"I'm really sorry about that," Janine said. "She's never snapped like that before."

"It's not surprising," the vet continued. "We're often seen as the enemy. It's like some people have white-coat syndrome. At least here in her own surroundings she should feel more at ease. Now let's try this again."

The vet slowly moved her hand towards Gypsy once more, this time the cat lowered her head as if cautious of the approaching fingers, but she did not strike out.

The vet gently stroked the cat's head. "There now, I said I wasn't going to hurt you. Now we can be friends, what d'you say?"

Over the next fifteen minutes Janine stood transfixed as the vet managed to check Gypsy's heartbeat with her stethoscope and pummelled her stomach gently with her fingers without the cat reacting in a negative manner. Even when she handled the kittens Gypsy only raised a weary head for a better look, but never actually *hissed* or *spat* as Janine was afraid that she might.

"Okay," said the vet, "time for the acid test."

She took out a handheld monitor from her bag and allowed it to hover very close to Gypsy's neck, before running it slowly down her back.

She turned to Janine. "No sign of a microchip, so I suspect you were right about her being feral."

Janine smiled, relieved. "My daughter's going to be over the moon about that, thank you."

The vet put away her instruments. "Ordinarily, when they have just given birth, we don't like to do anything that might interfere with the mummy cat's feeding of her young ones, but under the circumstances, I think it might be prudent to at least give her a roundworm shot. The vaccination will pass through her milk to help protect the little ones."

"Okay," Janine nodded. "Whatever you think is best."

From downstairs they heard the sound of the front door being opened, followed by Marie and Sarah running up the stairs.

"Here comes the earthquake," Janine explained, apologetically.

As the girls made their way along the corridor, Janine placed her index finger against her lips informing them to keep the noise down.

"We saw the vet's van outside, is he here yet?"

"No, but she is," replied the vet.

Marie looked in. "Oh, sorry, I didn't realise."

"Not to worry," the vet assured her.

Marie turned to Janine, a look of concern mixed with trepidation etched on her face.

Janine knew immediately what was foremost in her daughter's mind, so she smiled and nodded. "Yes, she isn't chipped," Janine assured her.

Marie hugged her, then turned to Sarah, and the two girls began high-fiving and squealing with delight.

"Whoa there," called the vet, lowering her hands in the air as if to calm the pair down.

"Young madam here needs peace and quiet," she informed

them. "Any noise or disturbance can cause her to panic and harm her kittens, so let's be careful."

The two girls apologised, sheepishly.

The vet took out a syringe and removed the plastic cap from the needle. She then inserted it into a small bottle and removed some of the liquid, squirting a little on the floor to remove any danger of trapped air.

Gypsy began to mewl as the vet brought the needle closer.

"Come on now, sweetie," she said, enticingly. "You know this is for your own good and that of your kitties. I won't hurt you; I promise."

Expertly she managed to grab some fur at the back of the cat's neck between her thumb and forefinger before inserting the needle and injecting the medication.

"There now," she said, brightly. "All done."

Having completed her checks, the vet followed Janine and the girls back downstairs.

"Now then," she began, "a few things you'll need to bear in mind. Unless the kittens or their mum show any signs that cause you concern, their best left in peace to bond and grow. Their mum will, I'm afraid, start feeling very horny within a short time, as little as two weeks, and if you let her out, she will find any old Tom to impregnate her again."

"That fast?" asked Marie, shocked by the information.

"Oh yes," assured the vet. "What's more, her kittens still need her for nourishment and warmth, so I'd heartily advise that you keep her inside until you can take her to a vet to be spayed, which vets won't do until four to five weeks after she's given birth."

"Okay," agreed Janine. "So, we just have to ensure that we keep her inside until then?"

"Yes, however, I warn you now, she will become desperate to break out and she'll probably spray all over the place to try and attract local Toms, so you'll no doubt have a cat's chorus outside your door offering their services."

"That's decent of them," offered Janine. "Is there anything we can do to dampen their ardour, so to speak?"

The vet smiled and shook her head. "Not really, I'm afraid. Some people throw water over the Toms, but as an animal lover, I cannot recommend it."

"I appreciate what you're saying, but Marie and I will be heading back to England in a couple of days, will it be okay to transport Gypsy and her kittens so soon?"

"It's not ideal, but so long as you make sure that you keep them all together in a suitable travel case it should be fine. Just make sure that you don't accidently let Gypsy escape. Her need for satisfaction will be greater than her mothering instincts."

"Right, we'll bear that in mind," agreed Janine.

"Now one other thing," continued the vet. "By law now, all cats must be chipped. That said, as she's just given birth, so long as you do not let her out before taking her to the vets to be spayed, you can ask them to do it then. They can vaccinate her then too."

"Boy, I didn't realise how much there would be to remember," said Marie. "I thought that looking after cats was easy."

"It's a huge responsibility," cautioned the vet. "An awful lot of potential cat owners don't realise, and pet insurance isn't cheap either. But you'll have plenty of time to start appreciating the glories of ownership soon enough. I'll leave you some information pamphlets to get you started."

The vet declined Janine's offer to stay for a late breakfast. She felt guilty that she had not even offered the woman a coffee upon her arrival, but the vet explained that she had already eaten and that she needed to make her way back to the surgery for her next appointment.

Janine paid her with some of the cash Marie had withdrawn,

and the three women settled down to a well-deserved brunch of croissants with melted cheese and bacon.

Chapter Fifty-Four

After brunch the women all sat around the kitchen table talking.

During their conversation, Sarah mentioned something about her mother being one of the gang of women who regularly helped out at the church for Father Boyle and how at times she and some of the other daughters were roped in to help prepare for one of the feast days, or a special mass.

This sparked an idea in Janine.

At first, she was reluctant to say anything because she felt that she owed the priest a certain confidence for all he had done for her so far.

But then she decided that Sarah was mature enough to know when to keep a secret, so she tentatively dropped her idea into the conversation. "So, do you know Erin Murphy?" she asked, casually.

Sarah's face immediately went dark. "Yes," she admitted, keeping her head down as if to avoid Janine's gaze.

"We met her yesterday," Marie added. "She seems lovely, although her mother gave us a very odd reception when we dropped Erin off after lunch."

Sarah nodded; her head still bent.

Both Janine and Marie exchanged confused glances.

"Is something wrong?" asked Janine, curiously.

Sarah looked up and attempted a smile. "Well, I'm sure if you were here long enough, you'd find out anyway. The local gossip has it that Erin's father beats his wife, and his daughter when the mood takes him. My mum says that Enid often has to miss her duties at the church because she's too embarrassed for the rest of the crew to see her bruises. He's a nasty piece of work that man from what I've heard, and no mistake."

"I knew it!" exclaimed Marie, excitedly. She turned to Janine. "You said yesterday that it was probably something of that nature, and you were right. Men like that make my blood boil. Why does she stay with him, for goodness' sake? There are plenty of places where she can take Erin that will provide her with safety and protection from men like him."

"I reckon it's because she feels that she must honour her sacred vow of marriage." Ventured Sarah. "If there's one thing about us Roman Catholics, we are petrified of not adhering to promises we make before God."

"But surely God would understand?" Marie interjected, her face starting to grow red with rage. "Considering the circumstances, who wouldn't?"

"I told you yesterday," Janine interrupted. "It's always easier to suggest things when you're on the outside, but none of us know what the real situation is, or why Erin's mum chooses to live her life with such a man."

"And he's not the only one on the island," Sarah admitted. "Depending on who you're willing to believe." She seemed to have opened up some more since Marie had chimed in with her opinion.

This gave Janine the courage to offer some further information.

"Now, if I tell you two girls something, do you promise me that you will not reveal it?"

The two girls glanced at each other before turning back to Janine and nodding enthusiastically.

"Are you sure?" urged Janine. "This is something I've been told this morning in confidence, so I'm trusting you both."

"Come on, Mum," Marie urged, impatiently. "You can't bait us and leave us hanging like this."

Janine took a deep breath. "Okay, Erin's father was found dead this morning. Father Boyle is over there with them now."

Both girls looked shocked.

Sarah sat up and made the sign of the cross. "Oh God, forgive me for speaking ill of the dead," she said.

"It wasn't your fault," offered Marie. "You didn't know he was dead when you spoke."

Sarah looked flushed. "Even so," she crossed herself again.

"What happened?" asked Marie. "Did his wife finally do for him?"

"You have a charming way with prose," Janine replied, unable to prevent a smile creasing up the sides of her mouth. "No, according to Father Boyle, he's just the latest victim to succumb to this spate of heart-attack victims."

"Huh, that was too good for him," Marie said, disgruntled. "Men like that should be named and shamed before being locked away forever."

"Oh, Marie," replied Sarah, clearly taken aback. "The poor man is dead now, we can cut him a little slack, surely."

Marie shrugged. "He's probably in a better place than he deserves," she remarked.

"Well, either way," Janine cut in, "Erin is obviously very distraught at her father's death, so she'll be in need of a little TLC."

"I can't see her getting much from her mum," Sarah offered, slapping her hand across her mouth as soon as she had spoken.

"Oh, I'm sorry, forgive me, that was out of line under the circumstances."

"What did you mean?" Janine prodded. "We're not going to judge you," she promised.

Sarah looked embarrassed, but she nodded solemnly. "Enid Murphy is not exactly what you might call the most... comforting of parents." She was obviously choosing her words carefully before speaking. "I don't know Erin that well, but I always had the feeling that her mother was more concerned with spiritual matters than she was in her own daughter's welfare."

"Give us an example," Marie pressed.

"I remember once when poor Erin had been off school for days with the flu. Her mother still insisted that she attend Sunday mass, even though the poor thing looked like death warmed over when she entered the church. All through the service, she was coughing and sneezing, and it was clear to anyone looking on that she should be tucked up in bed, but her mother made her stay for the entire service, then I heard her admonishing the poor kid for being so disruptive during the priest's eulogy."

"Oh wow," offered Marie. "I promise I'll never complain about you again," she said, looking at Janine.

"Thanks for nothing," Janine replied. "What have I ever done to cause you to complain?"

"Well, there are times when you act like a complete Karen, it's humiliating."

Janine sat back and spread out her arms. "Again, with this 'Karen' nonsense, what are you talking about? Please explain it to me because I really don't get it."

The two girls laughed, which helped to break any remaining tension in the air.

"Anyway, if all goes to plan, I'll be meeting up with Erin again this afternoon at the presbytery. Father Boyle feels confident that he can arrange it. I'd like to get an interview with Enid Murphy, but he reckons she's too distressed to talk right now, so he's arranging for one of his many helpers to go and be with her while she grieves."

"Do you want us to come down with you to see Erin?" Marie offered. "I mean, we got on really well yesterday, and Sarah already knows her. It might help to break the ice."

Janine thought for a moment, then shook her head. "No, but thank you for the offer. I just think that, under the circumstances, I might be able to achieve more on my own. The poor child only lost her boyfriend yesterday, now her father so soon after, not sure how I would be coping in her position. Besides, I need you two to go shopping for a suitable carrier to transport Gypsy and her kittens overseas. Not to mention a decent litter tray and some sort of odourless stuff to put in it."

Marie lit up. "I can't believe that we're able to keep her and the kittens, it's going to be so cute to watch them grow up. Sarah's going to beg her mum to let her keep one when they're old enough to be separated from their mum. It'll give us a good excuse for another holiday over here."

"True," Janine agreed. "Do you think that your mother will go for it?"

Sarah shrugged. "Perhaps if I promise to pay for all its food and vet bills, she might go for it. We did have a cat when I was little, but the poor thing died when I was about three, so my memories a quite hazy."

"Fingers crossed for you," Janine added. Secretly, she was hoping that they might be able to offload at least one, but preferably two of the kittens. Cute they may be, but expensive over time they most definitely would become.

Perhaps one of her friends back in England could be persuaded to take one; several of them had young children.

"Would it be alright if Sarah stayed the night?" Marie

announced, out of the blue. "We thought that we could have a pyjama party."

"Oh, really, and am I invited to the social event of the year?" asked Janine smiling.

"Naturally, so long as you don't do or say anything that might embarrass your favourite daughter," Marie added.

"Have you had a chance to ask your mum yet?" Janine enquired.

"No," Sarah admitted. "But as we'll be staying in, and you'll be here to chaperone us, I'm hoping that she'll relent on her threat to keep me grounded until Christmas."

"Speaking of which," Marie added. "Just in case Sarah's mum is still a little reluctant, I thought it might help if you spoke to her personally, just to set her mind at rest."

"Oh, you did, did you?"

"Come on, Mum, words are your power after all."

Janine pulled a face. "So, what's the plan for this night's festivities? I trust there's no shots on the menu?"

"Sarah and I thought maybe a pizza, plus a couple of decent films. Have you tried the DVD in the television yet to see if it works?"

Janine shook her head. "Nope, that can be another job for the pair of you to take care of while I'm at the presbytery. What sort of films did you have in mind, Rom-Coms?"

The girls exchanged quizzical glances. "Well, it turns out that Sarah here is quite a connoisseur when it comes to gory horror movies. A lady after my own heart in that respect."

"Charming," offered Janine. "Just not too gory, please, I need my beauty sleep. And speaking of which, with Gypsy taking possession of your bed, where are you two planning on sleeping tonight?"

The girls both laughed. "We hadn't given it much thought," Marie admitted. "We can crash on the sofa or the floor, or maybe one of us can sleep in the bath. Either way, we don't mind, we can make do in a good cause."

"Somehow, I get the feeling you two will be nicking my bed and leaving me with the sofa."

"As if we would do that," laughed Marie. "Hey, have you checked out the third bedroom yet? It might be the answer to all our prayers."

"I looked in when we arrived, it's in a bit of a mess, but now you mention it, I'm sure there was a bed of some description under the boxes of books and old magazines."

"We'll sort it," Marie promised. "I can't wait for tonight, it's going to be epic."

Chapter Fifty-Five

By the time Father Boyle called Janine to say that Erin was at the church and ready to speak to her, it was already late afternoon.

Janine had spent most of her time after brunch by filling in some of the details Sarah had given her about the Murphy family, and especially the behaviour of the father, Colm.

Whether she intended using the details largely depended on what information she received for Erin that afternoon. She certainly did not intend spilling the beans about the way Colm treated his wife and daughter unless at least one of them was comfortable with her using it in her piece.

But even so, it was handy to have it all written out in format to save time for when she completed her article.

While she was busy with her article, the girls stacked whatever they could find to block off the cat flap in the kitchen door, just in case Gypsy decided to try and make a run for it. They also hurried around the cottage, ensuring that all the windows were shut and bolted, just in case.

The sound of them laughing with each other as they went

about their task made Janine smile to herself. She could not remember the last time she saw Marie so engrossed in a project.

The prospect of travelling home with four cats in a basket did not exactly cause Janine to sing with joy, but Marie seemed intent on taking on as much responsibility as possible concerning the welfare of the cats, so that in itself was a good thing in Janine's book.

It would certainly be character-building for her daughter to appreciate the cost and energy involved in taking care of something which relied upon her for their very lives.

At least, if things went according to plan, they would be unloading one of the kittens onto Sarah in a couple of months or so. That was as long as she could persuade her mother to agree to the extra burden.

Janine was not so sure that the woman would allow it, although off the top of her head, she could not think of any reason why not. But then, her experience of Sarah's mother was not exactly favourable, so she kept her thoughts to herself and just hoped that Sarah's art of persuasion would do the trick.

On her drive to the church, Janine could not help but notice that the sky was looking overcast, and the low clouds had obliterated the sun from view.

She had not listened to the weather forecast for that day, but from the looks of things, it appeared as if they were heading for a downpour.

Janine had dropped the girls off in town on her way so that they could shop for some essentials for their girls' night in, as well as a proper litter tray for Gypsy.

She hoped that they made it home before the rain.

At the end of town, she stopped off at a corner shop and bought a bottle of single malt Irish whiskey. She desperately wanted to buy something for Father Boyle for all the help he had given her, and she had never heard of a priest who did not enjoy a drop of the hard stuff, so she hoped that it would be appreciated.

As she drove up the gravel path which led to the presbytery, the clouds overhead had taken on an even darker and more menacing hue. The spire on top of the church rose up towards the sky, almost looking for her angle as if it were attempting to pierce the cloud formation and let the sunlight through once more.

Janine parked and checked that she had everything she might need for her interview.

To her surprise, Jamie Wells opened the door when she knocked. His expression was one of irritation as if she had disrupted him in the middle of something important.

"Yes," he said, curtly.

"Hello," Janine replied as cheerfully as she could, desperate not to allow him to think that she was in any way intimidated by his discourteous manner. "I've come to see Father Boyle," she explained.

The curate remained blocking the entrance.

He kept the door up against the side of his torso as if afraid that Janine might try to slip past him without permission. "He's busy at the moment with one of his parishioners, you'll have to come back later."

Janine frowned. "He called me a little while ago and asked me to come down. He is expecting me."

"Well, I can't disturb him when he's giving confession," Jamie scowled, almost as if Janine had suggested it herself. "You'll have to wait for him in the church, you can use the main entrance round the front."

Before Janine had a chance to protest, or even ask him to inform the priest where she would be, the curate slammed the door shut.

Janine stood there for a moment, stunned by the man's behaviour.

He had never been the most friendly or inviting of individuals, and she knew that he was doubtless peeved by the fact that she had asked to intrude on his precious archive, but even so, there was no excuse for such rudeness.

She could feel her cheeks turning red with anger, but trying the door again seemed futile as the curate was probably either waiting behind the door to see if she dared, or at most only a few feet away.

Janine turned to head towards the main entrance.

She had only taken a few steps when the front door flew open, and Father Boyle's welcoming smile greeted her. "Hello, Mrs Carstairs, I thought I heard your voice from the living room. Please come on in. It looks as if we're in for a spot of rain."

Janine smiled back and entered the presbytery. "Thank you, your curate said that you were busy, so I was going to wait in the church." She decided not to go into detail concerning the younger man's behaviour as the poor priest had enough on his plate lately.

She handed him the plastic carrier bag with the whiskey in it.

"What's this?" he asked, evidently surprised.

"Just a little something from me for all your many kindnesses since I've been here," Janine explained. "I hope you like it; I didn't want to be too presumptuous."

Father Boyle looked inside.

His face lit up. "How did you know, my absolute favourite brand. I only finished my last bottle yesterday evening with Constable Clark." He glanced over his shoulder at the living room door, which he had left slightly ajar. Turning back to face her, he lowered his voice before continuing. "That was before we heard the terrible news about Colm Murphy," he explained as if feeling the need to justify his late-night drinking session.

Janine nodded. "Oh, I see, of course." She surmised from his actions that Erin was in the living room, so she too kept her tone low.

Father Boyle ushered her into the room where Erin was seated with her back to them.

When she heard the sound of their approach, she quickly wiped her eyes with a tissue and stood up to greet the new arrival.

Janine could see right away that the poor girl had been crying.

Although she had managed to wipe away her tears, her cheeks were still pink and her eyes remained puffy from the effort.

"Hello," said Janine, smiling. "Remember me?"

To her astonishment, Erin walked over and threw her arms around her, burying her face against Janine's shoulder.

Janine held her tightly and kissed the top of her head.

After a while, Janine said. "I was so sorry to hear about your father, you have my condolences."

Erin pulled back and wiped her nose with the crumpled tissue. "Miserable bastard, may he rot in hell for all I care."

Her words stunned Janine, but she did not respond.

"Erin, my child," countered Father Boyle. "You know you mustn't speak ill of the dead, he was your father after all."

She turned to look at him, fire in her eyes, her chest rising as if about to commence a tirade of abuse. But then she took a deep breath and seemed to calm down immediately.

She lowered her head. "I'm sorry, Father, forgive me, my words were ill-chosen."

"It's only God's forgiveness that's important," he reminded her, his tone assertive but more from concern than retribution. "He knows what's in your heart, my child, you can only earn his forgiveness if you truly mean it."

Erin nodded dejectedly.

"Come on now," the priest continued. "Please sit down, both of you, we have much to discuss."

Having heard the girl's outburst, Janine was confident that she would be able to use what she had already written for her report. Erin clearly felt that her father's untimely demise had released the stopper on the pressure cooker, allowing her to vent her anger and frustration, which had probably been building over several years.

Even so, Janine realised that the situation still called for tact and diplomacy, and she made a vow to herself that she would allow Erin to control the conversation without too much coercion from her.

They all took their seats. Janine sat next to Erin in front of the large wooden desk which Father Boyle sat behind.

He had barely relaxed when the priest suddenly shot up again and walked round past the two women before closing the door properly.

When he had retaken his seat, he said. "That's better, you never know who might be listening, even the house of God." He quickly looked up and made the sign of the cross. "Now then," he continued. "As you may have already surmised, I have spoken to Erin at great length this afternoon, and she feels strong enough to answer any questions you may have for her concerning her father's demise."

He glanced at Erin, who nodded.

Janine placed her recorder on the table in front of them and switched it on.

Janine tried as best she could to avoid any inflammatory questions concerning Colm's behaviour as a husband and father. But Erin insisted on revealing the truth in great detail.

At times, even Janine, with her hardened reporter instincts, felt uncomfortable as Erin relayed incident after incident of her father beating both her and her mother for no apparent reason, even detailing the implements he favoured when he embarked on such an endeavour.

"We never knew from one day to the next whether he would be satisfied with just coming home from work and having his dinner, or if he planned to lash out at either or both of us as soon as he entered the house," Erin explained.

Her tales of misery often caused a fresh stream of tears to come gushing forth, for which she always apologised despite both Father Boyle and Janine telling her that there was no need.

She revealed his actions from the previous night when he forced himself on Enid, hurting her as only a man could, and how his anger turned to unrelenting rage when Erin tried to step in and save her mother from the onslaught.

"I know you only ever saw him at mass when he was contrite and humble, Father," she explained. "But we saw what he was truly like when he was at home with the front door locked and bolted and the rest of the world oblivious to his actions. Only my mum and me know exactly what the man was like, and I know he was my father, but so far as I'm concerned, that was a title in name only. He certainly didn't deserve to be given it, nor husband either."

Father Boyle went to speak, then held himself back.

Although he knew that it was his calling to defend the virtues of the sanctity of marriage, he felt that, under the circumstances, his words would be unappreciated and possibly even misplaced.

It was clear from their many conversations in the past that Enid and her daughter had suffered horrendously at the hands of the man who should have rejoiced at being their provider and protector, for a more loyal wife and daughter would be hard to find.

The church taught that it was not the priest's place to inter-fere between a man and his wife, but there were times, such as this, when Father Boyle felt less allegiance to his calling and more towards those amongst his parish who needed genuine support.

In his opinion, the church should be allowed to open its doors to protect the vulnerable in society and assist them in seeking justice and, where necessary, rebuilding their lives.

But all he was allowed to do was dish out biblical platitudes, offering such people little hope and absolutely no practical and much-needed help.

Perhaps Canon Royce was right after all.

He had been in the role too long and should consider moving aside for a younger role model to take over.

But who would that be, he wondered? His curate, with his fire and brimstone attitudes and overall lack of empathy for anyone who was not in holy orders.

Was that really all he had left to offer his flock when he moved on?

How could he, in all good conscience, allow a man like that to run his church?

Of all the vows he had taken, humility still seemed to be the one to evade him. After all, who was he to sit in judgement and decide who might be better placed, or even, at least as good as him, to serve his flock?

"The father here has seen my poor mother attend church on many occasions with her face covered in bruises," continued Erin. "And that's not even to mention the ones that she keeps covered up under her clothes. Have you not seen her even in the midst of summer coming to church in a big winter coat, Father? Perspiring to the point of collapsing rather than revealing the shocking evidence of her latest beating."

Father Boyle could feel his heart sink.

In truth, he had no words of comfort fitting to the occasion.

He was already exhausted from hearing Erin's confession

earlier, and then their lengthy discussion concerning her unborn child.

He was glad, at least, that he had promised her that he would stand by her decision, regardless of whether or not it went against everything taught by the catholic church.

He promised to help arrange for a clinic on the mainland to carry out the procedure as surreptitiously as possible. He did have contacts over there, people he had met through conferences discussing the state of abortion and the church's outdated attitudes towards it.

Unlike many of his fellow brethren, he had managed to keep his temper in check and by doing so found himself being approached after the main forum by some of the nurses who helped run the small charitable clinics on the mainland.

He had listened to their arguments and had to admit that he could see their side.

But being a catholic priest, his hands were still somewhat tied.

One thing which had come out of their discussion that afternoon was that Erin was now prepared to inform her mother about her condition. She felt that she deserved to know, even if her supposed reaction would be one of screaming and wailing and re-doing the rosary over and over.

Father Boyle warned Erin that it might even result in her mother never wishing to speak to her again. But even so, he felt proud that she had made the decision that she had.

All he could do was pray for them to find a common thread to move forward.

Janine had hastily penned several notes, which Erin continued with her monstrous tale. She liked to keep a separate written account of the more salient points just in case she could not hear them when she played the tape back.

When she was finished, the poor girl looked completely drained.

She sat slumped in her chair, her cheeks stained with tears, her little torso hunched over as if she carried the world upon them.

Father Boyle had been quiet for a while, letting Erin get everything off her chest.

Now that she seemed spent, he asked. "Is there anything else you wish to say to Mrs Carstairs before we're done?"

Erin looked up and shook her head slowly.

"I have to ask Erin," Janine broke in. "As grateful as I am for your candour, how do you think your mother will react reading all this in print?"

Erin turned to her, a mischievous grin on her face. "She'll probably hate it, but it's all the truth, and it needs to come out. Maybe other women in the same situation may suddenly decide to fight back or up and leave their abusive husbands as a result of this. It can only do good."

Janine glanced over at Father Boyle.

He shrugged and sighed.

After a moment's silence, Erin stood up. "Well, I suppose I'd better get home to my mother, see how she's doing before we start our argument."

Father Boyle raised his hand. "Well now," he began, "just before Miss Carstairs here arrived, I made a call to Mrs Mathers. She's more than willing to stay with your mother, all night if necessary. They're old friends from church. When I called, she said that your mother was still sleeping off the sedative the doctor gave her, but that she would be there for her when she awoke."

"Oh, right," replied Erin, clearly not sure what to do next.

"It might be an idea if you left your intended conversation with your mother until tomorrow," the priest continued. "When, hopefully, she'll be feeling a little stronger."

"Okay then," Erin agreed.

"Tell you what," said Janine, tensing the girl's reluctance to go back home if it was not immediately necessary. "How do you fancy a girls' night in with Marie, her friend Sarah, and me? We're ordering pizza and we plan to watch a couple of movies and each junk. Oh, and you can come and see the kittens which Gypsy has just blessed us with." She leaned over and nudged the girl playfully. "What d'yer say?"

Chapter Fifty-Six

BY THE TIME JANINE AND ERIN LEFT THE PRESBYTERY, the sky had almost turned black.

The atmosphere was abnormally heavy for a summer's day, and it felt as if the clouds were about to unleash a month's worth of rain any minute.

Once they were inside the protective shell of the car, both women relaxed.

Janine turned to Erin. "I just want to check that you're cool with coming back to mine for pizza and a film?" she asked. "I felt a little as if I coerced you into the idea when we were with Father Boyle."

"No, not at all," Erin assured her. "To be honest, it'll be nice to get away from home for a couple of hours, and I'd like to see Marie again, she's really nice, just like you."

Janine smiled. "You're sweet," she noted. "Okay then, let the good times roll." She started the engine and drove down the path and out into the street.

By the time they reached the cottage, the rain had started to pelt down. Janine had switched the windscreen wipers on to full power while they were still in the town, but even with them, her visibility was extremely poor.

At one point, she slowed the car right down until she was barely able to move out of second gear, but fortunately, most of the other road users were of the same mind, so none was blaring their horns demanding that she speed up.

Janine made sure that her notes and recorder were zipped up in her bag so as not to be drenched on route to the front door. Her bag was not completely waterproof, but it still offered sufficient protection to keep her things dry. The last thing she wanted to risk was rain seeping into her machine or causing the ink to run on her notes.

Janine switched off the engine, and the windscreen immediately blurred from the onslaught.

"Shall we make a dash for it?" she suggested.

Erin nodded.

"One, two, three." They opened their doors together and raced for the front door.

Together they huddled under the arched frame above the door while Janine set the car alarm and took out her key to let them in.

Marie and Sarah were both in the living room, each wearing a pair of Marie's pyjamas. "You're back, great," announced Marie, we're starving." She suddenly noticed Erin standing behind her mum very much in shadow. "Hello again," she said, brightly. "Are you joining us for our movie night?"

Erin nodded shyly. "If that's okay," she answered, sheepishly.

"Of course it is," Marie assured her, coming over and giving the girl a welcome hug.

"The more the merrier," called Sarah from the couch. "We've met," she said, smiling.

"Oh yes, of course, your mother and mine help out at the church. We were drafted in a few times to assist them."

"Bullied, you mean," Sarah corrected her. "At least I was, I'm sure your mother is far more tactful than mine."

Erin laughed. The joke had definitely made her feel at ease, which Janine was very grateful for.

"I see you two have already managed to sort yourselves out," Janine noted. "Did you all manage to get back before the heavens opened?"

"Oh yeah," Marie assured her. "We came home ages ago."

"And is your mother okay with you staying the night?" Janine enquired.

"Yep," answered Sarah, grinning. "You may get a call from her later, though, just to check I'm not out injecting heroin in my eyeballs or something equally reprehensible."

"I was telling Erin about the kittens. Have you checked in on them?"

"We did," admitted Marie. "But after what the vet said, we didn't touch them or anything, we didn't want to spook Gypsy. We set up her litter tray and gave her some of the kitten food we bought earlier. I think she's all set."

"Excellent," said Janine. "Now, before the festivities start in earnest, I need about fifteen minutes to send in my article before the deadline. So, how about you offer our new guest a drink and then take her upstairs to see the brood? Then we can settle down for the evening."

Marie grabbed Erin's hand. "Come on, we've loads of drink and snacks," she led the girl to the kitchen, followed by Sarah. "Did Mum tell you we're ordering pizza? And we've got some terrific films to watch, I hope you like horror as much as we do?"

Janine smiled to herself. Marie was hardly giving the poor girl a chance to get a word in edgeways, but her approach had definitely worked wonders in making Erin feel more relaxed and at ease.

Janine sat down and took out her laptop. She put an earplug

in one ear so that she could listen to her interview with Erin from earlier. Meanwhile, she kept her notepad open in front of her so that she could access both options when filling in the blanks from her formatted notes, which she had written before leaving for the church.

In the background, she could hear the girls giggling and chattering in the background.

After a while, they emerged from the kitchen, and Marie announced that she and Sarah were taking Erin up to her bedroom to see the kittens.

By the time she was finished, Janine had written two articles.

One included everything that Erin had told her about her father, and the other omitted the more grizzly details and mainly focused on Colm as just another heart-attack victim.

She paused and re-read them both through once more.

Upstairs, she could hear the excited squeals from the girls as they lovingly watched over Gypsy and her brood.

The thought of sending in everything Erin had announced about her father's brutal behaviour towards her and her mother somehow seemed a little thoughtless at that moment.

Although Erin had given her full permission to use everything, at the back of Janine's mind, she could not help but wonder if tomorrow, in the cold light of day, Erin might regret what she had said.

It would be too late by then to do anything about it, as it would already be in print for all the world to read.

Therefore, Janine sent in the watered-down version with a note to Sam that she had arranged an interview with Colm's wife and daughter for the following day, and that she had heard a rumour that he had been very aggressive with them when he had had too much to drink.

She hoped that would hold for the night, then tomorrow she would discuss the matter again with Erin and perhaps her mother if she was up to it and decide then whether to submit the second article.

Once sent, Janine closed her laptop.

She could hear bickering coming from above her, so she went to the bottom of the stairs and called up. "What are you three arguing about?" she demanded. "You've only been on your own for a couple of minutes."

Marie appeared at the top of the stairs, smiling. "We're trying to convince Erin that she needs to stay the night so that she can help us take turns to watch the kittens, and make sure that Gypsy doesn't escape."

It was not such a bad idea at that, Janine thought to herself. A night away from her house with all the bad memories might be just what the doctor ordered for poor Erin.

That said, the decision would naturally have to be hers.

If she was feeling guilty about leaving her mum overnight, then Janine would have to overrule the girls and take her home as promised.

"Don't you go bullying her," Janine instructed, wagging her index finger at Marie.

"Oh, Mum, you're such a Karen sometimes," Marie retorted, disappearing out of sight before Janine had a chance to reply.

Janine took herself into the kitchen and opened the fridge.

There were three bottles of white wine lined up in the door shelf. Obviously, the girls had decided that they were going to somehow persuade Janine to allow them to become wasted that evening. Well, no such luck, she thought. Perhaps a glass or two each would suffice, and then only if they were already tucking into their pizzas to help soak it up.

She grabbed the nearest bottle and unscrewed the cap.

When she opened the cupboard above her to grab a glass, and avalanche of packets of snacks fell on her from above. They certainly had not stinted on preparing for their evening.

She could not help but laugh to herself.

When she thought of how disgruntled Marie had been at the beginning of the holiday, and how Janine herself had been filled with dread and trepidation that Marie would just sulk the entire time and make it impossible for her to complete her work, compared to how things had turned out, she felt a huge wave of relief wash over her.

Listening to her daughter upstairs laughing and joking with her new friends was possibly the best medicine she could have. That and the fact that Marie and Sarah were being so kind to Erin after all she had been through was certainly the icing on the cake.

Having restocked the shelves properly, Janine poured herself a glass of wine.

Even if she did have to drive Erin home later, one glass would not register, especially on top of pizza and crisps.

Janine walked back into the living room just as the three girls made it down the stairs.

Erin was dressed in a pair of her pyjama bottoms, looking slightly guilty that she had not asked for permission before doubtless being cajoled into changing.

"Oh, I see you've started without us, charming," exclaimed Marie, walking behind Erin.

"One more word from you, young lady, and you'll be on coke and orange squash for the rest of the evening," Janine warned her.

Ignoring the caution, Marie said. "Guess what, Erin has agreed to stay the night, isn't that great?"

Janine glanced at the shy girl who dropped her gaze as their eyes met.

"Agreed?" asked Janine. "Or bullied?"

"Nonsense," corrected Marie. "All she needed was a little subtle persuasion. We're going to have the best time ever. Erin loves horror films too, but her mum never lets her watch them, so tonight's the night."

Erin raised her head and smiled weakly.

"You are more than welcome to stay," Janine assured her. "But only if you want to, don't let these two force you into it."

Erin nodded. "To be honest, it would be lovely, so long as you're sure it's alright. I…" she paused a moment. "Borrowed one of your jams, I hope that's okay?"

"Of course it is," replied Janine, smiling. "But do you think you ought to check with your mum first, just in case?"

Erin nodded. "I'll call home now," she agreed, taking out her mobile and walking into the kitchen for some privacy.

"Right then you two," continued Janine. "What feasts from the silver screen have you in store for us?"

Marie excitedly ran to the hallway and retrieved a carrier bag she had left there earlier. "Ta-dah," she Announced, removing three DVDs from the bag and holding them up with one hand, splayed like a fan.

Janine craned her neck to read the titles. "Oh brother," she remarked. "I should have guessed."

Chapter Fifty-Seven

IN THE TWO AND A HALF HOURS SINCE JANINE AND Erin had left him, after a light supper, Father Boyle had busied himself by taking confession.

Despite the incredibly inclement weather, the faithful had flocked to church as always, ready to open their hearts and souls and declare their innermost thoughts and deeds in order to clear their consciences.

As usual, the vast majority of 'sins' he had to listen to were barely worth mentioning. Thoughts of jealousy at someone else's good fortune, impure thoughts concerning someone a penitent had always had a crush on, taking the lord's name in vain, using profanity, gossiping about someone's neighbour – always popular – the list went on.

Having served as parish priest for so many years, Father Boyle could usually guess which sins were about to be presented before him simply by recognising the voice of the penitent as they pleaded for forgiveness.

Even so, he knew how much comfort most of his flock took at knowing that God had forgiven them, some even relished the length of their penance, the longer the act the more they felt that their sin had been eradicated, and they could walk out into the world no longer weighed down by the incumbrance of their burden.

Regardless of the mundaneness of the practice, Father Boyle still rejoiced in the feeling of joy which always enveloped him as he emerged from the confessional. He knew that it was sheer pride, and he admonished himself for it, but he could not help but embrace the inner thought that, whilst conducting the ritual, he actually operated as a conduit to God.

The sheer comfort that his parishioners took in having their sins erased was in itself reward enough for him.

As he emerged from the confessional, Father Boyle gazed out over the bowed heads of those still reciting their devotions.

Outside, he could hear the sound of the rain crashing against the old church, and he shivered. In the distance, the first rumble of thunder echoed over the sea, and he wondered if they were due the accompaniment of lightning, the complete the trilogy.

The weather report for the day had mentioned the occasional shower, but this was proving to be far more torrential than had been forecast.

In such circumstances, Father Boyle kept the outer doors to the church closed. Not locked, he preferred to allow his parishioners access to the comfort of God's house whenever possible, despite what Canon Royce prescribed. He was always suspicious of looters, which Father Boyle appreciated were a modern consequence of life. But he always argued that the church should be a welcoming invitation to all who sought sanctuary, before being a barrier to those who with evil intent.

Even so, in such inclement weather, it was still important to ensure that the outer doors were kept close to help prevent the rain from crossing the threshold.

His volunteer cleaners had enough on their plates without

having to spend half the morning soaking up the deluge from the previous night.

Once he was convinced that the doors were fastened, Father Boyle retired to the kitchen and took a seat at the table.

At this time of the evening, he generally had a strong cup of tea to help ease himself into his night-time ritual of reading one of his favourite chapters from the bible.

He was about to put the kettle on when he suddenly remembered the kind gift that Janine had brought for him earlier.

The priest pondered his options for a moment. True, he had partaken of several glasses the previous evening in the company of the local constable, but today had been a trying one, what with the discovery of another heart-attack victim, and his private talk with Erin concerning her unborn child.

Their conversation had not gone the way he had hoped, but deep down he knew that he had been deceiving himself in thinking that he could somehow dissuade her from her course of action. Hard as it was to accept, there were times when circumstances dictated the actions of those who, under normal circumstances, would never do anything that did not conform to their religious teachings.

Here was such a case, and an extremely sad one at that.

Unable to convince Erin that someday she might regret aborting her unborn baby, he had finally relented and agreed to assist her in seeking out a suitable establishment to take care of her situation.

Regardless of his own teachings, he truly believed that he was doing the right thing, as guilty as it made him feel. He had already begged God for forgiveness, and he knew that he would continue to do so, possibly throughout the rest of his life.

Sighing deeply, Father Boyle switched off the kettle and took down his bottle of single malt from the cupboard.

He poured himself a large measure and held up his glass to the heavens before downing it in one swallow.

"Forgive me, Father," said a voice behind him. "I didn't mean to disturb you."

Father Boyle turned to see the gaunt figure of his curate framing the door.

"Oh, I'm sorry, Jamie, I didn't hear you come in," he said, apologetically. "Will you join me for a drop of God's nectar?" He held up his empty glass.

Jamie did not hide his disdain at the suggestion, tutting loudly and shaking his head in despair.

"You don't approve of such earthly pleasures, do you?" Father Boyle asked, resignedly.

"No, I don't," came the curt reply.

Now it was the old priest's turn to shake his head in despair. "Jamie, there's no joy in your life," he observed. "You never laugh, you never smile, you seem to be oblivious to the beauty that surrounds you in the flowers and the birdsong and the majestic sunsets we have the privilege of observing through the steeple window on a clear night. I've even seen you turn up your nose at some of the most delicious food offered to us by one of our volunteers in favour of plain bread and cheese. You don't even partake of wine, save for the communion wine during services. Why must you observe this archaic and almost draconian practice of closing yourself off from the wonders of God's miracles?"

The curate looked enraged at such a suggestion. "Whereas you subscribe to taking pleasure in earthly offerings in order to bring you closer to God!" he demanded. "My devotion remains unbroken; I will not have it weakened by alcohol or feigned laughter or ostentatious foodstuffs. I prefer the constant edge of hunger to a full belly."

"There is no sin in partaking of some of the more joyous indulgences that our Lord provides. It doesn't make us decadent or sinful. It actually helps to bring us closer to our parishioners by knocking down barriers, which hitherto might have come between us. If they see us as human, like them in every way, with our faults and temptations, it encourages them to embrace our teachings and follow a good Christian path."

"Such as murdering a poor babe in the womb?" the curate spat.

The remark took Father Boyle completely by surprise.

It hit him like a hard slap to the face.

"What... What are you talking about?" he demanded, weakly, unable to restore his former composure so soon after such a remark.

Father Wells crossed over to the table and stood on the opposing side, glaring down at his supposed mentor. "You know exactly what I mean," he insisted. "That foolish young girl you had here earlier who broke God's commandment and got herself pregnant."

Father Boyle could not hide his horror.

How on earth had his curate learned of such a thing?

He had been meticulous in ensuring that his conversations with Erin were all held in private.

"Instead of warning her of the condemnation of her soul," Jamie continued, "you openly encourage her to kill one of God's own creatures before it even has a chance to live. Sentencing it to spend eternity in purgatory just so that you might appear to be in touch with your softer side. What were you hoping for? That the young girl might someday show her gratitude to you in some physical or even sexual manner?"

Father Boyle pushed himself up from the table. "How dare you!" he shouted. "May God forgive you for daring to utter such a monstrous untruth."

"Is it?" replied the curate, his eyes narrowing. "I've heard you in confession, forgiving the most heinous sins with no more than a casual wave of the hand, and a couple of Hail Marys. Do you really think that God approves of such a cavalier attitude to his word? These sinners should be living in fear of fire and brimstone, not being mollycoddled into thinking that they can live such sinful lives only to have you expunge their guilt at will."

Father Boyle slumped back down in his chair. "How do you know what is said in the confessional?" he inquired. "The seal of the confessional is sacrosanct.

"Sacrosanct," the curate laughed, scornfully. "In a building as old as this, nothing could be further from the truth. Has it never occurred to you that the grates which form part of the structure allow sound to carry? Down in the archives, I can hear everything that is said in your confessional. Not to mention your private little talks here in the kitchen and in the living room. You don't even attempt to keep you voice down because you believe a closed door gives you privacy."

Father Boyle looked ashen.

His curate's words had cut him to the quick.

Such ingratitude after taking him in to try and teach and mentor him to become a fine priest who would dedicate his life to serving his parishioners.

Yet, behind his back, it was clear that Jamie did nothing but despise the old man for what he considered his weakness.

"Jamie," Father Boyle spoke, having taken in a calming breath. "I think that it's time that we sever this relationship. It's clear to me that you do not appreciate my approach when it comes to dealing with me flock, so perhaps I'd better approach Canon Royce and suggest a different diocese for you to continue your studies in."

"Too late," replied Jamie, scornfully. "I've already spoken to the canon, and he's coming down to see you tomorrow. I've told him all about your cosy chats and sinful ways, and he's very interested in intervening before you're allowed to completely destroy this parish."

"What do you mean? Please tell me you haven't mentioned

young Erin's plight to him, please, at least assure me of that?" The priest begged.

"And the rest," Jamie leaned on the table, a leather binder in one hand. "He knows all about your prostitutes and paedophiles, wife-beaters and fornicators. He'll put a stop to all the nonsense that has been going on around here, and you'll be retired off as you should have been years ago before you permeated this congregation with your modern-day wishy-washy teachings. Your parishioners will soon know the true meaning of paying for their sins, and that young whore, is next." With that, he held up his leather binder triumphantly. "I've been studying the ancient folklore of this island. I alone know the secret of its power. I alone have discovered the ritual that conjures up God's vengeance here on earth, and I alone have the Almighty's blessing to use it to dispose of those miserable creatures who deign to abuse his majesty with their wickedness."

Father Boyle could hardly believe what he was hearing.

It was clear to him now that Jamie needed psychiatric help and was evidently not in control of his faculties.

He tried to keep his tone calm to avoid causing his curate any further distress.

"Jamie, listen to me," he spoke gently. "You've obviously been under a great deal of stress lately, and I take full responsibility for giving you too much to do in such a short time. You must let me help you do or say something which cannot be retracted."

"It's already too late, don't you understand?" Jamie's eyes were wide, his voice hysterical. "I've conjured up God's power hear on earth, and tonight she's going to take his revenge on that little Jezebel you're trying to protect."

"I don't understand," the priest replied, quizzically. "What revenge? Who is this 'she' you're referring to?"

"The Banshee Bride!" Jamie almost screamed the words out through gritted teeth, saliva dripping down his chin. "I know the source of her power, God has shown me, and I have conjured her up to dispose of that unworthy creature tonight, before she has the chance to murder the child that sleeps in her belly. Just as I have on all those other miserable sinners whom you saw fit to absolve of their wrongdoings. She will die tonight, and may God have mercy on her soul!"

Chapter Fifty-Eight

JANINE HAD BEEN SOMEWHAT TENTATIVE ABOUT allowing the girls to watch Marie and Sarah's first choice of DVD. In hindsight, it did not surprise her that they chose *The Exorcist*, considering that Marie was reading the book and they had informed her earlier that they had intended looking for horror titles.

Her main concern was in allowing two girls who were under her charge for the evening to view an eighteen-certificate film, when they were both underage.

But much imploring from both her daughter and Sarah made it that much harder for Janine to refuse them. In the end, she turned to Erin and asked her how she felt about it, and the young girl admitted that she had always wanted to see it as it was considered such a classic in the horror genre.

Eventually, Janine gave in, considering that without too much make-up, all three girls could doubtless gain entrance at a cinema to watch any film they wanted, and the fact that they were all within a year of being the suitable age anyway. But she warned Sarah and Erin that if they ever grassed her up to their mums, she might be arrested and dragged before a magistrate.

Even Janine had forgotten how gory the film was.

During the film, the weather outside seemed to worsen. The rain continued to batter the window, and there was even the odd streak of lightning, closely followed by a rumble of thunder. Not the best conditions, in her opinion, for watching a horror film.

Much to her chagrin, she actually spent more time hiding behind her fingers than any of the girls, which resulted in much laughter and fun-poking from the three of them.

The combined laughter of her three charges did bring Janine a sense of fulfilment and warmth. Erin especially had been through an awful trauma over the last few days and seemed in desperate need of something to take her mind off it all.

Sara seemed just relieved to be allowed out of the house and not forced to spend the night with her mother at work.

She had even heard Marie discuss the option of Erin having one of the kittens which, if allowed by her mother, meant that Janine would only be left with Gypsy and one of her brood to take care of. Which, if she were being honest, was a great relief to Janine.

Once the film was over, they all agreed to have a short interval to refresh their drinks and lay out some snacks. The pizzas had arrived before the film began, and Janine had cautioned the girls that perhaps they should eat before watching the movie. But they all insisted that there was no need, and in the end, Janine was the only one who was unable to finish her share.

Having refilled their glasses-Janine had allowed each girl two small glasses of wine with their meals-and laid out some crisps and assorted salty snacks, the girls decided they wanted to check in on Gypsy before continuing with their evening's viewing.

Janine poured herself another large glass of wine. This would be her third, and due to the lack of food she had ingested, she was starting to feel the effects of the alcohol, so now that the film was over, she took advantage of the break and began nibbling on a slice of cold pizza.

Her phone rang just as she had taken a huge bite of the meaty treat.

She glanced at the screen, expecting to see either Tim or Sam's name come up, but she was taken by surprise to see that it was Father Boyle.

She chewed as quickly as she could, not wanting to sound rude by talking with her mouth full.

She presumed that he was checking in on Erin to make sure she was okay.

She swallowed half her mouthful. "Hello, Father, forgive me, I've just taken a massive bite of pizza," she explained.

"Miss Carstairs, is Erin still with you?" His voice sounded fraught; the tone carried an urgency which Janine had never heard from him before.

She hoped that it was not more bad news for the poor girl.

Surely there was nothing wrong with her mother now?

Perhaps she had woken up in a panic when she discovered that Erin was not at home.

"Yes," she assured him. "She's upstairs with the girls playing with the kittens. She phoned the lady you sent round to look after her mother to let her know she intended to spend the night with us." Janine felt that she needed to justify the situation before the priest grasped the wrong impression. "Is everything okay?"

"No," the answer was sharp. "I'm not sure how to tell you this, but my curate has just confessed to me that he is responsible for the recent spate of heart attacks."

His words took a moment to sink in. "What, how? I mean, how did he manage to cause someone to have a heart attack?" The concept sounded incredulous even as she spoke.

She heard the priest take in a deep breath on the other end.

"He claims that he has discovered a way of summoning a Banshee, and that she is the one who has caused the deaths."

"What? Seriously?"

"He seems to be in earnest," Father Boyle explained, his voice starting to tremble from the effort. "Ordinarily, I would not give such an idea credence, but he's just shown me the text he retrieved from our archive, which contains the spell for calling the Banshee forward. It's too horrendous for words."

Janine thought for a moment. "You know," she began, tentatively, "ordinarily neither would I, but it might explain how all the victims had that rictus grin on their faces when they were found, as if they'd been frightened to death."

"I know," he agreed. "I've been thinking the same thing."

"Is he there now?" Janine enquired. "Can he hear what you're telling me?" She suddenly felt fear for the old priest. If the curate, a much younger man, had somehow lost his mind, it was not inconceivable that he might attack Father Boyle for revealing his confession.

"No," the priest continued. "He's gone up to the steeple to watch the storm. He says he wants to see the Banshee approaching from the sea."

"He's called it again?" Janine felt a sudden shiver run down her spine.

The combination of the storm outside and the film she had just watched, combined with what she was being told by the good father made her glad that she was not home alone.

"That's just the thing," the priest replied, the fear rising in his voice. "He claims that he has summoned the Banshee to murder Erin!"

Janine froze.

That was the last thing she expected to hear.

Out of nowhere, a scream emanated from upstairs.

Reacting automatically, Janine dropped her phone and sprang up from her seat, taking the stairs two at a time.

The screaming continued, rising in volume and piercing her eardrums.

As she reached the landing, Marie backed out of her room, her expression betraying her inner shock and fear.

When she saw her mother approaching, she ran to her, grabbing her arms.

"What's the matter?" Janine asked, holding Marie's head between her hands and looking straight into her eyes. "Who screamed?"

"It's Erin," Marie replied. "She just grabbed hold of her head and started screaming."

Janine released her hold of her and swerved around her to gain entrance to the room where the other two girls were.

As she entered, Erin let out another earth-shattering shriek.

The girl was sitting on the floor at the foot of Marie's bed, holding both her palms flush up against her ears as if trying to prevent herself from hearing her own screams.

Sarah stood to one side, her face a mask of horror and disbelief.

She glanced over as Janine entered the room. "I don't know what happened," she uttered, her bottom lip trembling. "We were just watching the kittens, then she began saying that she could hear a whistling sound and that it was getting louder and louder. Neither of us could hear anything, and we told her. We thought she was joking. Next thing, she dropped to the floor holding her head and started screaming."

Janine fell to her knees beside Erin and tried to comfort her.

She gazed directly into her eyes and could tell that this was no joke.

Erin looked through her as if she was not even there.

The poor child had eyes as wide as saucers, as if she could see something truly monstrous in front of her.

Janine called out her name twice, but to no avail. Erin

continued to stare as if witnessing something horrific taking place before her eyes.

Janine turned to Marie, who had just re-entered the room. "Call an ambulance, quickly," she demanded.

Marie turned and ran back down the landing, almost slipping on the waxed wooden floor as she stopped to take the stairs.

"What's wrong with her?" Sarah asked, her hands covering her face as if she could no longer take in Erin's distress.

"I don't know," admitted Janine, still attempting to reach through to the stricken girl.

Janine gently tried to move Erin's hands away from her ears so that she could hear her, but Erin refused to allow it. Instead, she clamped her hands even harder in place and began rolling around on the floor, screaming as if she were in agony.

Janine moved in and did her best to hold the girl in an effort to give her some comfort that she was not alone, but Erin's involuntary movements almost turned violent in an effort to free herself.

Out of sheer desperation, Janine grabbed her wrists and managed to yank her hands free from her ears. The sudden movement caused Erin to snap out of her reverie as if she had been slapped around the face.

She stared directly into Janine's eyes, the startled expression of terror still evident.

"What's the matter, darling?" Janine asked, having to use all her strength to keep Erin's hands apart. "Tell me what's the matter, I'm here to help you."

Just then, Marie reappeared in the doorway. "They're on their way, Mum," she said, her focus glued on her distraught friend.

"Can't you hear her?" Erin suddenly screamed in Janine's face. "She's coming for me."

Janine pulled back slightly, taken aback by the girl's sudden reply.

She managed to keep her fingers clasped around Erin's wrists despite the girl thrashing about, desperately struggling to free herself.

Janine glanced over at Marie, then back towards Sarah as if for confirmation that they too could not hear anything.

From on top of the bed, Gypsy, who up until that moment had seemed oblivious to the goings on around her, raised her head and stared up at the ceiling.

The cat released a low mewl, followed by a hiss as if she were about to strike at something, although there was nothing in front of her.

She moved around and blocked her sleeping kittens with her body as if trying to protect them from some unseen force.

"SHE'S COMING!" Erin yelled, her face etched in terror.

Sarah ran over to Marie and the two girls held each other their gaze fixed on the tableau set out before them.

Father Boyle's words abruptly burst into Janine's subconscious.

'He has summoned the Banshee to murder Erin!'

Her mind raced.

Whether she believed in the phenomenon or not, the fact was that poor Erin was physically suffering and appeared as if she were about to die from fright.

Janine released her hold on the girl and ran out of the room, almost knocking the two girls huddled in the doorway over.

She needed to reach her phone, where she had the pictures of the pages which she photographed from the books in the library with the spell for reversing the summoning of the Banshee.

As she reached the bottom of the stairs, she flew at the armchair which she had been sitting in when the priest called. She remembered dropping the phone when she first heard Erin scream.

There was no sign of it. Plunging her hands down the insides of the arms, Janine desperately tried to locate her phone. With no success, she wrenched the cushion out and discarded it on the floor.

Outside the window, she saw another streak of lightning flash across the sky.

Concentrating on her search, Janine heard the thunder roar above her.

A thought struck her. What if Marie had used her phone to call the ambulance?

"Marie, where's my phone?" Janine shouted above the noise of the thunder.

"I've got it here," came the trembling reply.

Of course she has.

As Janine was about to race back up the stairs, another thought crashed into her brain.

She remembered writing down the information on her pad before she left for the presbytery. It would be far easier than scrolling through her mobile to find the information.

Janine grabbed her bag and plunged her hand inside, feeling her trusty pad at the bottom.

She grabbed it and ran for the stairs.

As she climbed them, she realised how ridiculous she would appear to her daughter and Sarah when she began reciting the ancient text, but there was no time to explain her reasons at that moment.

Poor Erin's need was greater, and if the spell did not work and there was some other medical reason for the girl's condition, then Janine would just have to admit that she had become overwhelmed in the heat of the moment.

As she reached the bedroom, Erin had her hands clamped firmly against the side of her head once more.

Marie and Sarah had moved to one side, allowing Janine to pass unhindered.

"Get downstairs now, the pair of you," she demanded. "Wait for the ambulance."

Both girls complied without question.

Janine waited until she heard the sound of their footsteps on the stairs.

Convinced that they were out of earshot, she stood in front of the tormented girl.

Back on the bed, Gypsy seemed almost beside herself, her gaze focused on the ceiling as before, her hackles raised, emitting a sharp *hiss* as she spread herself out in an attempt to cover her brood.

Without hesitation, Janine began to recite the words she had written down earlier for reversing the summoning of the Banshee.

As she recited the words from her pad, ensuring that each one was given its proper pronunciation so as to guarantee that they had their full effect, Janine concentrated on the ceiling above her, following Gypsy's lead.

The recital took no more than a couple of seconds.

The thunder outside seemed to applaud her commitment to the task.

Within seconds of completing the ritual, Erin stopped screaming and removed her hands from her ears.

She gazed about her as if only just realising that she was sitting on the floor with Janine standing over her.

Janine leaned over to help the bewildered girl to her feet.

On the bed, Gypsy had settled back down and was once again washing her kittens.

Chapter Fifty-Nine

FATHER BOYLE SAT DRUMMING HIS FINGERS ON THE table.

The abrupt end to his call with Janine had left him feeling somewhat unsettled. She did not appear to him to be the sort of person who would abandon a call halfway through and just leave a person hanging on the other end.

At the back of his mind, a seed began to take root. What if there was some truth in what Jamie had told him? What if he really had discovered the power to conjure up some vengeful spirit buried deep in folklore?

Everyone on the island knew the legend, it was common knowledge, but was it possible that there was actually some truth in the tale?

Could the wretched spirit of poor Molly McShane actually have transformed itself into a Banshee, ready at the will of anyone who recited the ritual to appear and claim the soul of an innocent victim?

According to Jamie, the souls in question were far from innocent, but that was just his opinion. Surely, the good Lord would not allow such a travesty to take place.

Father Boyle knew full well that God had given his children the power of freedom of choice. Therefore, many heinous crimes were committed, leaving victims of all ages, ethnicity, faith and sexual orientation behind in its wake. But surely God would not allow a spirit from the depths of Hell itself to wreak havoc here on his earth.

But then he remembered the many lectures and symposiums he had attended as a novice, listening to the tales of those amongst his calling who specialised in exorcising demons which had taken over the bodies and minds of innocent victims, including children.

So, if the Banshee was in itself a demon, it became extremely plausible that she could be summoned to take over another person's mind, body and soul.

The only difference seemed to be that when she was called, the poor victim was not given the chance to survive the visitation long enough to have her spirit exorcised.

If this were true, what hope was there for any of them?

Father Boyle clutched the crucifix around his neck and prayed for guidance.

Outside, the storm continued to rage.

He looked up at the ceiling and imagined his curate standing at the window of the steeple, gaining strength from his actions as he kept watch for his angel of death.

As his mentor, Father Boyle believed that he should have the authority to insist that Jamie put a stop to this evil activity and fall down on bended knees before God and pray for his forgiveness.

But deep down he feared that such a time had already passed.

Jamie had descended too far into the maelstrom of madness to be brought back now by anything Father Boyle could suggest, let alone insist on.

The poor man obviously needed psychiatric as well as spiritual help far beyond anything that he could administer. The problem was how to persuade him of that fact.

If there was indeed any truth in the fact that all the recent deaths on the island were caused by him evoking an evil spirit to murder at his will, then the chances of convincing him that he was wrong were at best pretty slim.

Father Boyle kissed his crucifix and poured himself another measure of single malt.

He gazed at his glass, the amber fluid reflecting off the etched crystal pattern resembling a cherished jewel, and he knew immediately that drink was not the answer.

The problem was he felt so unempowered to deal with this unique circumstance.

Jamie had informed him that Canon Royce was due to call the following day, perhaps he would know how best to proceed with his curate's obsession. But tomorrow might be too late if there was indeed any truth to what Jamie had told him.

Could poor Erin Murphy really be in danger?

If so, would Janine, her daughter and Sarah Byrne also be in the firing line just for being in her company?

Feeling compelled to do something, but not knowing exactly what, Father Boyle stood up from his chair and kissed his crucifix once more.

Before heading for the staircase which led to the steeple, he knocked back is drink, the burning warmth comforting him as well as affording him a modicum of courage.

He made his way to the bottom of the spiral stone staircase and gazed upwards.

There were very few working lights leading up to where his curate was stationed, but Father Boyle knew that such a situation could not be allowed to hinder his progress.

Grabbing hold of the thick rope handrail, he pulled himself up, taking each step tentatively. It had been an age since he had had cause to climb the crumbling steps to the upper tower, and now that he had started, he wished that he had the foresight to bring a torch with him.

"Nil desperandum," he muttered to himself, remembering his old Latin tutorials at seminary school. This was no time to be weak of heart or spirit. Regardless of whether Jamie really did have the power to summon a demon or not, Father Boyle had to do all in his power to ensure that no harm would come to Erin or the others.

As he climbed, his breath became more laboured. He had to accept that he was no longer a young man and such exertion would doubtless take its toll. Even so, there was no one else to complete the task for him, and besides that, he knew that it was his responsibility to try and negotiate a successful conclusion to this situation.

If only he could make Jamie see sense. Accept the error in his ways and abandon his quest, perhaps there was still a chance, with medical intervention, that he could one day become a valuable member of the church.

The climb seemed to go on for an eternity.

Father Boyle stopped to take in a few deep breaths. The arthritis in his knees did nothing to assist him in his climb, but he took comfort from the fact that his discomfort was nothing compared to Jesus' suffering on the cross and thus should not be used by him as an excuse to abandon his venture.

He took in another deep breath and continued on his way.

The small stained-glass windows, which were peppered throughout the staircase, did little to encourage his ascent. The storm still raged outside, and lightning streaked across the sky at random intervals, closely followed by the bellow of thunderclaps.

It was indeed, as his old mentor used to say, a night for the devils.

Crossing himself, Father Boyle gripped the rope line tighter just in case he misjudged a step. The higher he climbed, the more unsteady the ground beneath him became. The crumbling masonry almost seemed to flake away with every footstep.

In the shadowy darkness of the narrow passageway, Father Boyle could not ascertain where best to place his full weight before pushing himself up. Each step appeared to have a different weak spot to the one before.

It was too late now to go back for a torch, he knew that he needed to reach Jamie sooner rather than later.

He stopped once more, an acid taste in his throat made him regret his last glass of whiskey. It may have fortified him on the ground, but it certainly did nothing to assist his climb.

Pressing on, the priest could hear the sound of Jamie's voice echoing around the walls. He appeared to be reciting some sort of ritualistic prayer, though the words were unfamiliar to Father Boyle.

As he rounded the next corner, his curate came into sight.

Jamie was standing in front of the nearest window, his leather binder open in front of him, his concentration focused on its contents.

Father Boyle stopped and tried to catch his breath.

Once his breathing had steadied, he called out. "Jamie, please stop this, you don't mean anyone any harm, I know you well enough to understand that."

The curate spun round. His face contorted into a grimace of pure hatred.

He took a stride towards his mentor.

For a moment, Father Boyle feared that he was about to launch himself at him and send him flying head over heels back down the winding staircase.

The priest redoubled his grip on the rope banister.

His knuckles, now turned white, protruding due to the pressure.

"Jamie, please," he pleaded, hoping to appeal to what little sanity remained within his charge.

The curate stopped, hovering directly over his mentor. "How dare you attempt to interfere with my vocation," he spat the words through gritted teeth. "This is my destiny, to rid the world of all the scum who feed off the pity of weak men such as you. You who claim to be a servant of God regularly forgive them for their heinous crimes against him, then send them away with a couple of prayers to continue their evil ways."

"I perform my duty as I am called upon to do," Father Boyle protested. "No one can be expected to do more. We cannot seek retribution on his behalf. Vengeance is mine, sayeth the Lord, I will repay."

"Vengeance is mine!" Jamie screamed, indignantly. "The Lord has given me the power to exact his revenge here on earth," he held up his leather file. "This is all I need, I knew it the moment I came across it in the archives, the manner by which I, God's most humble servant, could carry out his wishes and bring those sinners, which you fawn over in your precious confessional to book."

"But can't you see, Jamie," Father Boyle explained. "God isn't the one asking you to perform this carnage. God rejoices in sinners who have repented. Why would he then instruct you to dispose of them?"

"I wouldn't expect an old, obsolete fossil like you to understand. This is way above your understanding. The Pope himself would struggle to appreciate the quest I am on. Only God knows the truth, and he speaks to me directly." Jamie advanced on Father Boyle, raising his free hand above his head as if about to strike. "Now get out of my sight, shaman, your time is over."

Father Boyle took an unsteady step backwards, missing his footing on the dilapidated stonework beneath him. He spiralled, losing his grip on the rope support beside him before tumbling down several steps, crying out as the sharp edges of the crumbling steps dug into his frail body.

He finally came to rest around the next bend, his head

against the wall and his legs splayed apart above him. He waited to allow his heartbeat to calm down, the shock of the fall having taken its toll.

He could no longer see Jamie from his position, but he could still hear him reciting words from his file, his shouts battling with the thunder for supremacy.

There was nothing left for him to do now but pray.

He closed his eyes and begged for God's assistance in helping Jamie to see the error of his ways. He was clearly insane and in need of God's protection regardless of his crimes.

Father Boyle tried to make himself as comfortable as his situation would allow.

He knew that he would be stuck in situ until some kindly parishioner came to his rescue. He had left his mobile downstairs on the table, so there was no chance of him calling for help until his cleaners arrived in the morning.

"No! No! Wait!"

He heard Jamie screaming above him. He craned his neck as far as it would allow, but he was still unable to see passed the next curve in the staircase.

"Not me, I sent you to seek out another, you have to do as I command."

The curate appeared to be having a conversation with someone, but Father Boyle knew that there was no one else up there with him.

Was he perhaps hallucinating?

Had the trauma from his exertions finally reached a pitch from which he could no longer maintain what little spark of sanity he still had control of?

Father Boyle tried once more to force himself up, desperate to reach his curate and administer whatever comfort he was able to try and reassure him that everything would be okay.

But he winced as he tried to put pressure on his twisted legs.

He feared his ankles might have been broken in the fall.

"No! Please, no, not me, you can't have me, you've been given your instructions you must obey me, I am your master, obey my command."

From above him, Jamie's voice rose to a crescendo of sheer terror.

He could not disguise the fear in his voice.

Whatever was happening to him, or at least, whatever he believed was happening was enough to scare the life out of him.

Just as Father Boyle was about to call up and suggest that Jamie come down to him, he heard a blood-curdling scream which vibrated all around him.

The scream continued for several seconds, drowning out any attempt by the priest to summon his charge.

Eventually, the screaming stopped.

Father Boyle waited.

There was no other sound save the storm raging outside.

He could no longer hear Jamie's voice.

"Jamie," he called up. "Are you alright, my son?"

But no answer filtered down to him.

Father Boyle attempted calling up several more times before eventually giving up.

His one hope was that his poor curate had merely passed out, overcome by the stress and strain of his fiery delusion.

For now, he would have to wait to find out.

Epilogue

ALTHOUGH HE WAS IN AGONY WITH WHAT WAS LATER diagnosed as a bad sprain, Father Boyle eventually managed to haul himself up and climb back to the landing where Jamie was.

To his horror, he found the body of his curate crumpled in a corner of the alcove, his face a terrifying mask of fear. Father Boyle tried to locate a pulse, but it was to no avail. Jamie had died in what appeared to be the same circumstances as all the other heart-attack victims.

Fortunately, the curate still had his mobile in his pocket, so Father Boyle was able to summon help. Before it arrived, he secreted the leather folder which Jamie had been reading from behind some loose paving. He felt it his duty to try and conceal any evidence that his charge had been responsible for the recent deaths.

In truth, he still could not believe that it was anything more than a coincidence himself. Jamie was clearly suffering from some mental disorder, which ultimately may have contributed to his demise, but it had nothing to do with demons or spirits.

That was the report he made to Canon Royce, who seemed

satisfied, although clearly shaken up by the loss of one so young with so much potential.

Janine came to visit him the morning after the ordeal with Erin.

She looked embarrassed when she spoke of the circumstances concerning the girl's fit and her subsequent reciting of the ritual to reverse the summoning of the Banshee, which led to Erin regaining her composure.

Father Boyle felt that he had no option but to take her in his confidence and pray that she accepted his reasoning for not revealing what they believed to anyone else.

The priest admitted that part of his reasoning was to protect the church from intrusive inquiries demanding to know how a curate had the power to summon a vengeful spirit to cause the death of innocent parishioners. Regardless of how misguided Jamie's actions were, Father Boyle conveyed his fears that he was suffering from some mental condition as yet undiagnosed.

He explained that the damage it might cause the church would be insurmountable and could set the catholic faith back centuries.

He had tears in his eyes when he spoke of his love for his church and the pride, which he felt from all the good that it achieved all over the world.

The reporter in her made Janine want to write a full exposé and tell the world of the ritual she performed back in the cottage in order to save Erin. But she was swayed by Father Boyle's pleas and the fact that the story would not be taken seriously enough to ever make it into print.

The Banshee Bride was a legend which deserved its own story, including what beliefs some of the residents of Manus held, but to try and justify it as fact without solid proof was a mountain she was not prepared to climb.

To convince the outside world that such phenomena existed, Janine would have to conjure up the Banshee herself in front of witnesses, and even if that were possible, she would have to name a sacrifice for the spirit to take back with it to the other side.

Her experience with Erin convinced her of that, at least.

Whatever else, these were practices beyond her comprehension, and she took comfort in knowing that Father Boyle had put his trust in her not to reveal what she knew to the outside world.

Erin's trauma was put down to stress caused by the recent loss of her boyfriend and father within a day of each other. Quite understandable under such circumstances, Doctor Cleary explained to her mother, and he prescribed some medication to help with her anxiety.

Jamie's death was deemed natural as a result of the post-mortem, and just another unexplained tragedy.

Father Boyle conducted his funeral mass and ensured that his eulogy only contained positive attributes concerning his young charge.

Janine destroyed her written notes detailing the ritual for summoning the Banshee.

In her article, she did not specify any actual words detailing the practice, and instead merely focused on the beliefs and suspicions of the locals who had been brought up on the tragic tale of Molly McShane. She insinuated that it was just as likely that the story was used by parents attempting to make their unruly children behave.

Do as you're told, or the Banshee Bride will steal you away in the night!

It made for good copy, and Sam was delighted with the finished product.

Janine contacted Tim one last time before she left the island. She felt guilty that she had unwittingly given him the actual words used in the ritual and was afraid that he might be tempted to try them out as a research tool for a future book.

Although unable to reveal to him exactly what she knew, she made him promise that if he were ever tempted to try the spell, he would speak to Father Boyle first.

She purposely kept her explanation evasive and insisted that they were dealing with things beyond their comprehension.

Before leaving the island, Janine, Marie, Sarah and Erin met for lunch.

By now, Erin had decided she was going to keep her baby, and she did not give a fig for what the gossips said about her behind her back.

Much to her astonishment, her mother accepted the news with great excitement at the prospect of becoming a grand-mother, and she too said that if anyone had anything negative to say about her daughter's condition that they could deal with her first.

Marie and Sarah were both excited at the prospect of becoming aunties.

As they all parted for the final time, there were hugs, tears and kisses galore to go round, and Janine promised that they would return with the kittens for Sarah and Erin just as soon as the vet said it was safe for Gypsy to be parted from them.

———

Once he was able to walk again unassisted, Father Boyle decided to take matters into his own hands. He had wrestled with his conscious ever since Jamie died and could not escape the thought that he should have done more to help understand what his charge was going through, and possibly, with his inter-vention, he might have saved the lives of several of his flock.

Having retrieved the file which Jamie had clung to prior to his demise, Father Boyle knelt one last time before the statue of Jesus, which stood majestically over the altar in his beloved church and prayed for both forgiveness and guidance.

Once he was done, the priest set off in the darkness of night towards Westside Cliff.

When he arrived, he first made sure that there was no one else around.

He needed solitude for his task and to eliminate the danger that his actions might cause to anyone who happened to be in the vicinity.

Although the stars were out in force and there was a full moon casting an eerie glow onto the beach, there was not enough light for the old priest to complete his task.

Therefore, reading by torchlight, Father Boyle uttered the words from the ritual, inserting his own name as the target for the Banshee.

He sat down on a large rock and waited, listening to the sound of the waves crashing against the rocks below.

He had always loved the sound of the sea and admonished himself for not making more time over the years to come out here and enjoy the splendour of one of God's precious gifts.

He closed his eyes and drank in the ambiance.

After a short while, he heard the cry echoing across from the sea, piercing his ears enough to make him wince in pain.

He opened his eyes.

There, far off in the distance, he could see the approaching apparition dancing on the wind like a bird in flight.

Father Boyle took in a deep breath and readied himself.

While he waited, he began reciting the Lord's prayer to himself, feeling the comfort from the words fortify him.

As the shadowy figure grew closer, Father Boyle stood up to face it.

The courage of his conviction began to waiver as he feared it might, so he leant against the rock he had been sitting on to steady himself.

As the Banshee grew closer, he could see it taking shape.

No longer just a fluttering fluid apparition, but now a fully formed figure of a woman with deep black holes where her eyes should be, and a yawning maw for a mouth where the pitiful cry of her soul emanated.

She hovered directly in front of him.

Father Boyle could feel a tightness in his chest starting to take hold.

He knew that his time was short.

"Molly McShane," he called out. "You have suffered torments that no one should ever be subject to. No one knows the full extent of your pain more than you, but you must believe me when I say that you need not continue to dwell in the wretched dark firmaments of Hell. God still loves you, and in spite of all the evil deeds that you have felt compelled to execute, he would still welcome you into his kingdom if only you would put your trust in him and turn your back on your evil master."

The figure continued to hover in place.

The ear-splitting sound that rang in the priest's ears seemed to take on a slightly lower tone, which made it easier for him to think.

Father Boyle gripped the crucifix around his neck in one hand. "God knows your heart, Molly McShane. He knows that in life you were cruelly treated and, overcome with grief, took your own life. But you can still leave all that behind you now."

He held up the crucifix towards the apparition.

For a moment, it actually seemed as if the stern features were beginning to soften.

The eyes, no longer just bottomless black pits, began to resemble the eyes of someone more sad than wicked.

There was a pleading quality to them which struck a strong chord in Father Boyle's heart. "You are not, and never have been evil," he continued. "Why continue to subject yourself to this eternity of misery and hatred? Embrace the Lord thy God and ask for his mercy. The repentant sinner is always welcome in his kingdom."

Now the figure before him resembled that of a woman far more so than just a shapeless apparition.

Father Boyle could make out specific features on the face, and there was a beauty in the eyes which he found rather captivating.

As he watched, the transformation took its full effect.

The Banshee was no longer a vision of hatred and malice, but a beautiful girl with long dark hair and an angelic face.

She smiled sweetly at the old man.

Father Boyle smiled back. "Trust me," he urged. "God will welcome you into his kingdom with open arms, and you need never suffer again. All your pain and sorrow will vanish forever, and you will dwell in his house for all eternity, just as you always should have done."

Molly McShane glanced up to heaven, then looked back at the priest.

She seemed to heave a great sigh, then smiled at him once again before shooting upwards and disappearing among the stars.

The End.

About the Author

 I have dreamt about being an author of horror fiction for as long as I can remember. Few other genres ever captured my interest enough to keep me engrossed and I have always been inspired by those whom I consider to be the greats in this field, the likes of Richard Laymon, Guy N. Smith and James Herbert to name a few. I have a law degree from the University of Westminster, and was a semi-pro wrestler until my body screamed NO MORE! I now work in the legal section for the Ministry of Justice and live in Kent (the garden of England), with my six adorable rescue cats.

———

To learn more about Mark L'Estrange and discover more Next Chapter authors, visit our website at www.nextchapter.pub.

Publisher contact information
Next Chapter
2-5-6 SANNO
SANNO BRIDGE
143-0023 Ota-Ku
Tokyo, Japan
https://nextchapter.pub

Printed in Dunstable, United Kingdom

64034144R00265